SPY SHADOWS

Also by Freddie P. Peters:

In the HENRY CROWNE PAYING THE PRICE series
INSURGENT
BREAKING POINT
NO TURNING BACK
HENRY CROWNE PAYING THE PRICE BOOKS 1-3
IMPOSTOR IN CHIEF
RED RENEGADE

In the NANCY WU CRIME THRILLER series
BLOOD DRAGON

Dear Reader,

I'm thrilled you've chosen SPY SHADOWS, Book 4 in the HENRY

CROWNE PAYING THE PRICE series.

Think about getting access for FREE to the exclusive Prequel to the

HENRY CROWNE PAYING THE PRICE series: INSURGENT.

Go to freddieppeters.com

SPY SHADOWS

FREDDIE P. PETERS

HENRY CROWNE PAYING THE PRICE BOOK 4

Spy Shadows
First published 2020 by Freddie P. Peters
www.freddieppeters.com

Text copyright © Freddie P. Peters 2020

The right of Freddie P. Peters to be identified as the author of this work has been asserted by her in accordance with the Copyright, Designs and Patents Act 1988.

Print ISBN: 978-1-8380760-1-6
eBook ISBN: 978-1-8380760-0-9

A CIP catalogue record for this book is available from the British Library.

Cover design by Jessica Bell.
Typesetting by Aimee Dewar.

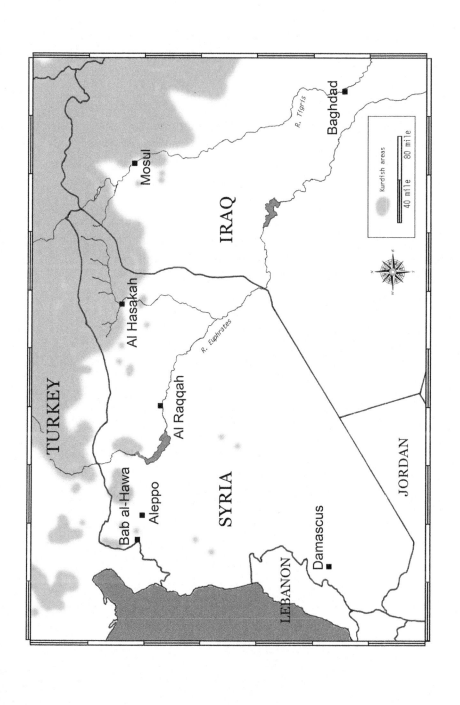

Glossary of Abbreviations

Term	Meaning
NGO	A non-profit organisation that operates independently of governments and addresses social or political issues.
TOR	A web browser designed for anonymous web surfing and protection against traffic analysis.
VPN	A virtual private network that enables users to send and receive data using public network (internet) through a virtual, private secure channel.

Other terms

Term	Meaning
Peshmerga	"Those who face death". It is a military force of the autonomous region of Kurdistan in Iraq, the only military force to include a female battalion known for its fierceness and feared in the region.

Glossary of Arabic Terms

Arabic Term	English Translation
Abaya	A loose overgarment, robe-like dress worn by women in the Middle East.
Allahu Akbar	God is most great. Used by Muslims in prayers, as a declaration of faith or thanks.
Kameez	A long tunic worn by many people in the Middle East and southern Asia.
Khoubz	A round flat shape bread with a slightly coarse texture eaten throughout the Middle East.
Marhabaan	Welcome, hello.
Niqab	A veil worn by Muslim women in public, covering all of the face apart from the eyes.
Qur'an surah	A chapter of the Qur'an.
Salaam alaikum… Alaikum as salaam	Greeting meaning "peace be upon you". The response being "and peace be upon you too".
Samovar	A greatly decorated tea urn.
Shemagh	A traditional Arabian scarf worn throughout the Middle East region, often in black and white or red and white.
Shura Council	A consultation council in Islamic law called Sharia law.
Taqiyah cap	A short, round skull cap.
Wahhabist	Someone who practises a strict and conservative interpretation of Islam's Sunni branch.

Chapter One

Wasim is lying on his belly, elbows stuck in the dusty soil, binoculars pushed against his eyes. The gunshots have refocused their attention. Henry crawls close to him and adjusts his own field glasses to follow the scene. Two people are running, desperately trying to reach the border between Syria and Turkey. Bab al-Hawa is a small place, a few houses, a compound that could be anything, a mosque... But it is the place where ISIL fighters cross to move between the two countries. Henry can't quite make out who is who in the distance. He has not used night vision glasses much before and his eyes still can't quite work out people and weapons.

The rapid discharge of a machine gun stops one of the men, but the other keeps going; in a few seconds he will soon enter Turkey and perhaps be safe. The same rattle of bullets shot in succession throws him to the ground. Still, he staggers up, holding his left arm.

"They are not jihadists... they're kafir," Wasim's low voice can't hide disquiet. Henry does not ask the question that burns his tongue. "Infidels? How do you know?"

"Should we hang around?" Henry asked instead.

"Not sure." Wasim half turns on his side, watching the other three young fighters that are with them. He had chosen them when they left the IS training camp to accompany Henry and himself across the border. Keen, inexperienced but stubborn as well, they want to fight the jihad. The heavy man who has been their driver for most of the journey is now on the phone. He knows one of the men who is in pursuit of the two fugitives... a cousin of a cousin. Henry can make out some of the words: *brother… help…* and the final one he has just learned in Arabic a few days ago… *hostage.*

Wasim shuffles back from his position to where the three men are bunched together, hidden behind a cluster of large boulders. He interrupts the conversation. There is no room for dissent in this forsaken place where so many political factions are at war.

Henry yet again fails to understand the whole of Wasim's sentences. His voice is low and harsh… *must deliver the banker… no time… Abu Bakr al-Baghdadi, the leader can't be made to wait.* The three men all start nodding at the name that inspires dread and awe. The phone rings again and the big man answers. These brothers really need our help with the hostages they were supposed to hand over. It would be a blow to their credibility. Wasim couldn't care less about their reputation. His task is to bring Henry Crowne, convicted IRA terrorist and former City banker to the leader of an emerging jihadi group called ISIL and the other fighters accompanying him had better remember it. The phone rings once more. The hostages and their captors are on their way, the rendezvous point half a mile from where Wasim and his group are heading.

Henry waits. He has learned not to address Wasim in English unless he has been spoken to first, only trying his Arabic when spoken to by the other men, much to their delight, a good way to ridicule him… He is still kafir after all. No matter what al-Baghdadi wants to do with him, they do not trust the English banker.

The air is damp, and the night sky of a brightness Henry has witnessed only since his arrival in ISIL's camps across the border in Turkey. There is no pollution in Bab al-Hawa… Just used cartridges from the rounds fired by machine guns, indicating the crossing point has been well used in recent months. The empty shells roll under Henry's heavy army boots as he crouches before standing up. He brings the white and blue shemagh around his face. Wasim and one of the other fighters run downhill towards the grimy 4x4 they have used to cross the border on rough terrain. Henry follows and climbs into the vehicle, squeezed between two of the men. The fetid smell of sweat and questionable hygiene has stopped bothering him.

Since he left the UK six months ago, he has travelled by every conceivable means of transportation, all of them far from the luxury he once knew... There were no five-star hotels and first-class lounges on his way to infiltrate a terror group in Syria. He has at least had some preparation in the letting go of unnecessary comfort. Four years spent in the High Security Unit of Belmarsh Prison in London has taught Henry a thing or two about minimal living and survival. Still, the road to Syria has been a harsh training ground, the way of the jihad is cruel beyond words and the newly formed army has no patience for the fighter who can't deliver on his promises.

The crossing from a small deserted beach on the shores of South Hole in the UK to Malta had been ridiculously smooth, taking less than four days. The flight from Malta to Turkey had been equally uneventful. He knows why, but he does not complain. Yet nothing has prepared him for the violence that hit him when he joined one of the boot camps near the border of Syria. He would not be allowed to join the inner circle of al-Baghdadi's commanders before he had proved himself.

The 4x4 engine revs as Wasim urges the vehicle to climb the steep slope, sliding sideways into the sludge left by recent rain. Such a blessing in this dry part of the world is nevertheless ill received by the small group – tracks left behind are easy to spot, not what they need when delivering their unusual cargo.

Henry spots the other vehicle coming their way. The mobile phone rings again. The rattle of the battered truck can now be heard echoing in the distance and drowning out the purr of the 4x4 engine. The big man, who is in contact with one of his relatives, replies. Wasim does not say anything when he hears one of the hostages in the truck needs assistance. At least that is what Henry has understood. Wasim parks the vehicle at the side of a surprisingly well-maintained road. They are now in Syrian territory and the plan had not been to stop for help, whatever the reason. The young fighter, Ali, who is squeezed in to the left of Henry, jumps out to move quickly towards the old truck. Henry can hear raised voices coming from the back of the vehicle. It now moves past the 4x4 and reverses, exposing its hold. Two fighters jump out, AK-47s slung over their shoulders. The full moon gives enough light for Henry to make out one form lying down and another crouching at the back of the pick-up.

Wasim stays put. The smell of recent gunfire is on the newcomers' skin. Henry can smell it from where he is sitting, his shoulder and head stuck out of the 4x4 window. The man lying down screams in pain as Ali climbs into the back of the truck. The scream shocks Henry but perhaps less than it would once have done.

"Who are they?" he whispers to Wasim.

"Hostages... journalists. This lot abducted them as they were crossing into Syria. They tried to run back towards the Turkish border. One of them is badly injured."

"Ransom?" Henry is keen to know. After all, he has been recruited by ISIL to consolidate the financial empire they are building to sustain their efforts in defeating the West. He might as well start learning right away the sources of income they intend to generate.

"Almost certainly."

"Why almost?"

Wasim has stopped speaking in English. One of the fighters comes back. Wasim eases his heavy body out of the 4x4. The situation won't get out of control. He will make sure of that. Henry has a point though, hostages are income and it might play in their favour. Henry shivers; the nights are cool despite the heat of the day. He is simply grateful that a childhood spent in Belfast, Northern Ireland has hardened him against harsh weather.

Wasim is bending over the journalist's body, opening up the jacket carefully. The man screams again. But this time Henry's body freezes – he has heard that kind of scream before, the agony of a wound that almost certainly cannot be treated... At least not here in the middle of this barren land. The fighters who are holding the journalists are now arguing. Wasim shakes his head. His own fighters have joined the fray.

Henry knows Wasim must be careful. He is a Muslim, but he is also British. He does not know Syria as well as these men do. He needs them to help deliver Henry to Raqqa. Not being able to speak freely to Wasim has been punishing. Henry's Arabic is coming along well. He has always learned fast, but he does not want people to know how fluent he has become. He can no longer show how brilliant he is. His stellar banking career is over. He does not regret it... it has taken time to come to this now obvious conclusion. Five years ago, he was accused of a crime he did not commit and yet it unveiled a crime perhaps greater, his involvement with the IRA and its finances. It has taken four years at HSU Belmarsh, amongst the worst of criminals, for Henry to decide what he must do next.

Wasim has now raised his voice; the Arabic language gives it a sharpness and command it does not always show in English. It is not a question of fluency, rather of intent. Henry understands more words… *responsibility, taking over*, but the other fighters are having none of it. Kidnapping has become a business and these young men want in on the action. Wasim comes back to the 4x4 and opens a small compartment below the wheel. He takes out the first aid kit and hands it over reluctantly.

"These bloody idiots are going to get us caught," he mutters in English.

"How bad is it?"

"He won't last the night," Wasim replies.

A drop of ice lodges itself into Henry's belly. "Where are they from?"

"One Brit, one Yank…" Wasim volunteers. "They want to find a doctor… he needs more than that."

"We can't let him die." Henry has spoken despite himself. He knows it is not his place to have an opinion about who lives and who dies in these ISIL-held territories, at least not yet. But he inevitably feels close to these two people who belong to his own culture.

Wasim darts him a cold look. "Yes, we can."

Henry is about to argue, gripped by anger; his back straightens and his fists tighten.

"Don't," Wasim cuts him short. Henry's jaw clenches. He trusts Wasim though. Henry is good at judging character and he has decided he can rely on him. He has known this since the moment MI6 presented him with their ISIL infiltration contact, who has become his minder. Wasim trained him after he helped Henry escape Belmarsh and he has followed him through the gruelling recruitment camps.

"How far are we from Raqqa?" Henry can't just drop the subject. Perhaps there is a compromise and something to gain from the situation.

"On the motorway, ten hours, but we are not going there the easy way, are we?"

"How long down the scenic route then?"

Wasim's features freeze into the mask that sets when he means to rebuke Henry. But Henry has seen the glimmer in his eyes. He has learned to appreciate Henry for who he is. A brilliant brain, an arrogant bastard and yet someone you cannot hate… a powerful combination.

"Eighteen hours, perhaps a little longer… We need to cross between Syria and Iraq at the right time of the day."

"If we saved this journalist guy, he might be worth a lot to ISIL… right?"

"Your point?" Henry can see Wasim has prepared his argument, but more raised voices interrupt them. One of the captors is shoving the young fighter Ali who has tried to help him use the medical kit. Wasim grabs the Sig Sauer pistol from underneath his seat and slides it into the waistband of his trousers. His entire body language has changed from alert to relaxed but ready for a fight. Henry moves back into the 4x4 and finds the Glock he has stashed away in his rucksack. Wasim approaches with raised hands to calm the situation down but the conversation has turned nasty. The captors want the 4x4 to deliver their hostages to the nearest hospital in Aleppo.

Henry has so far managed to avoid pulling the trigger on anyone who has got in his way. He has not yet been asked to show he can kill a man because everyone assumes he has. But soon, very soon, either to protect his life or to show that he truly belongs, he will have to. Wasim is trying to reason with the captors – he calls on verses of the Qur'an that invoke brotherhood. This seems a good move as the arguing suddenly stops. The fighters who accompany Henry and Wasim, and the captors they have just met, are young. Despite the beards that age them somewhat, they are in their early twenties at most. The moans of the injured man refocus everyone and the demands of the young captors are going to resume, more pressing this time, perhaps even violent. The older of the two, a gangly youth with a distinctive russet beard, moves towards Wasim, one hand clenched on his AK-47.

The gunshots roll like thunder over the low hills of Bab al-Hawa. Henry has reached for his Glock, his two hands secure on the piece, training it on the two captors. Four shots delivered in groups of two; the youth with the russet beard falls first, surprise etched on his face.

His companion does not fare much better. He has dropped his weapon as if on fire but to no avail.

Wasim still holds the gun at the ready. He has another 14 rounds to go. His own people can't believe it... Muslim on Muslim... he who has just spoken about brotherhood.

"...'Tis not brotherhood when a man seeks his own profit over that of his own tribe..." Wasim speaks slowly and with feeling. "You thought you knew them but perhaps not... why would they want to steal our transport... perhaps they sided with Bashar al-Assad after all..."

The big man who has insisted they should help has slunk away. The other two fighters look at him now with suspicion.

How easy it is to turn the minds of these young men. Henry slips his gun into the small of his back. He can see the blood splatters spread on the side of the pick-up truck. He tries not to look at the faces of the two dead fighters. Still, he moves forward and helps Wasim pull the bodies away from the road and into a shallow depression at its side. Wasim gives his instructions and this time no one argues.

Ali stays with them. The other two will take the pick-up, one driving, the other one looking after the hostages until they come to the next ISIL camp. Henry collapses into the back of the 4x4. He has not said a word. Silence is wise and yet trying his patience. The two vehicles turn off the main road and the dirt tracks immediately feel bumpy and uncomfortable. Henry can't stop thinking about the injured journalist. The shot of morphine he has been given will only go so far. He has seen much worse since his arrival in the Middle East.

They are running an obstacle course. They run it every day, several times a day. Crawling on their bellies, vaulting over makeshift barricades, darting around low walls, crouching as they try to avoid detection. Today, however, the blank munitions have been replaced by real ones and the fighters who use the guns have been told to aim half a metre over their targets... this is generous according to the trainer. On the battlefield the enemy will not be so thoughtful. One young man gets caught, collapses in agony. No one comes to his rescue. When the training is done, another two men limp out with injured limbs, but they've completed the course. They will recover. The youth who fell and did not get up is less fortunate. He has been caught in the gut. The training officer walks over to where he is still lying; he prods the moaning man with his boot. Henry can see the desperate attempt at getting up, his

feet trying to get a hold, scraping the ground, sliding and pushing the pain level up
again. His face desperately turns towards the standing man, begging. Henry turns
around before the officer draws out his gun. The shots are two clear slaps that send
the shrapnel of fear into everyone's belly.

Ali had jumped in next to Wasim. It was his idea the truck should go first… perhaps he too would rather not have two young men who have just witnessed a shooting they don't understand or agree with driving behind their car.

"This is complicating matters…" Wasim is speaking to Henry in English. "They need to guide us towards our crossing but also deal with the hostages."

"Only one of them is badly injured, right?"

"I gave him morphine… he may not wake up."

"What about the second one?" Henry changes position at the back of the car. Ali is listening intently. His English is not up to scratch, but he is keen to learn.

"Just a light injury. He hasn't said anything."

"Which is he, the Brit or the Yank?"

"Don't know… either way the Yanks certainly don't pay ransom and neither will the Brits… These idiots thought they were worth a lot of money."

"What happens if they won't pay?"

Wasim casts a sombre look at Henry from the rear-view mirror. Henry can hardly see it through the darkness, but he can feel its potency. Wasim won't answer the question.

Ali is thinking hard. Henry can just about make out his features, a face still smooth and fresh, a wispy beard he is trying to grow forms small clumps that he desperately tries to spread to make it look fuller.

"No pay… no life," he eventually says, turning back towards Henry with an almost childish grin.

"You mean… they might kill them?" Despite everything, Henry likes the young man. He must be in his late teens. He started to train as a doctor or similar. He has a good knowledge of how to treat wounds. Jihadis needed people like him and Henry surmised he was not given much choice when it came to recruitment.

"Enough," Wasim snaps in Arabic. If Wasim refuses to speak

about something it is not Ali's place to answer in his stead. Ali shrinks back into his seat. But Henry acknowledges him with a nod.

They have been driving for almost three hours non-stop. They are now nearing the crossing of the Euphrates, the large river that throws itself into Lake Assad, Syria's largest expanse of water, near Raqqa. Henry almost smiles at the thought of crossing this near mythical watercourse. There is something epic about coming in contact with the Euphrates, the basin of which gave shelter to early men 450,000 years ago. It has for all this time been shrouded in legends from Babylon to Hercules. It resonates with Henry's path, with what he is trying to achieve by crossing it to join ISIL, to infiltrate them as an MI6 agent. The river reaches back into ancient history… it is part of the land that witnessed the defeat of Darius III by Alexander the Great. Henry has drifted into his own past, the life he has left behind. Serving his 30-year sentence at HSU Belmarsh had never been an option… a man like him needs to prove himself. He had done wrong, so very wrong. Putting together an almost undetectable financing structure for the IRA, contributing to their finances… he knows why he did it. Still there are no excuses. How could he atone for what he had done by remaining in the confines of a prison cell?

He cut an almost impossible deal with the British intelligence service. He is glad of it… a life for a life. He has left everything behind… He had no time to say his goodbyes, but this too was part of the deal.

After his escape from Belmarsh, it has all been about training. Combat intelligence gathering – interrogation. Wasim is working under legend for MI6. The agency has spent years building a credible background so that he can navigate the world of terrorism unsuspected. His infiltration into ISIL has taken years and it has now given MI6 the opportunity to place someone else: Henry.

The sun is about to rise. The two vehicles are still bumping along the dirt tracks. The pick-up truck slows down. Ali's mobile rings. They should be very close to the camp they have been aiming for, but there is no sign of any encampment, just an arid landscape, bare and dusty. The two cars stop. Ali jumps out of the vehicle first without waiting for Wasim's order. He turns back then, hesitating, and Wasim nods. He goes to the back of the truck.

9

"What are you going to do?"

"Get rid of the other blokes... we have nearly reached the bridge and Ali knows the road after that. I don't trust them." Wasim slides away from the driver's seat. Henry grabs the Glock again. Ali is shaking his head. The wounded man needs assistance right away.

Henry can make out a few sentences.

He is doing better than I thought... need hospital soon... there is a dispensary in a town not very far if we can't find another camp...

The fighters have moved to the back of the truck too.

Henry pushes the gun into the back of his jeans making sure it is secure but ready.

"I want these hostages alive so that I can negotiate with their countries. I will remember what you have done when I meet with Abu Bakr al-Baghdadi, our leader."

They all turn around, stunned by Henry's almost fluent Arabic. Henry speaks in a guttural way that hisses at whoever he addresses. Wasim hesitates... but he gets it.

"I want the other hostage now so that we can negotiate immediately."

Henry moves past the group, grabs the frame of the truck and heaves himself into its back. In the dim light he can make out the small figure of the journalist who has also been taken. Henry stops. The silhouette rises, holding an arm. Lost in large army fatigues and an old army jacket, a woman staggers to stand up. She has dropped the scarf that was covering her head. Henry hesitates and fumbles to help.

"I'm fine." She replaces the scarf over her head. She winces as she jumps down from the vehicle.

Wasim shouts an order to Ali, who pushes the woman towards the 4x4. The truck is leaving and Wasim slows down. He speaks between gritted teeth. "You know you might have signed her death warrant, don't you?"

"Why?" Henry looks astonished. He fancies she has a better chance with them than with the beardos.

"She can't know you are here."

Chapter Two

Steve Harris entered RED HAWK Control Room for his daily check on his two operatives with feigned nonchalance. He hovered next to a screen on which two dots were advancing and popped yet another stick of gum into his mouth.

"They've moved away from the route they were supposed to take." Amina Brown kept focusing on the screen and did not bother to look up.

"Is it a worry?"

"Not sure… They are going in the right direction but making a detour, it seems."

"Any sign of hostile activity near Bab al-Hawa?"

"The satellite has picked up another car… a truck… They are both going in the same direction."

"Any contact with Wasim?"

"Not yet… It's complicated by the other three beardos who have been assigned to him to deliver Crowne."

"I'm glad Henry is not working undercover."

"Makes it easier, agreed… although perhaps a little light on his psy evaluation."

"We've been collecting information about him for long enough now. At least his profile is clear… what are you worried about? That he will join ISIL?"

"No, I worry we haven't tested his stress resilience enough and that he will be discovered quickly."

Amina shook her head. She had been Wasim's prime minder for over five years now. "It would be bad enough if Crowne were taken but I don't want to think about what they might do if they found out about Wasim."

Her voice had an edge Harris had rarely heard before. True, this operation, one of the most audacious they had put together so far, had not had nearly enough time to be prepared down to the smallest detail.

"I am aware," Harris said. Wasim mattered to him too.

Amina moved forward swiftly. She had been using a network of satellites to get a better sense of what was happening on the ground. Her fingers surfed the keyboard at speed. She pressed enter.

"Shit… Someone is down… no… two guys are down." She played back the recording of the live feed and slowed down the images. Dusk made it hard to always get a clear daytime image and infrared would not give her enough clarity yet. On the other screen she caught sight of a dot moving away from the scene of the shooting.

"What just happened?" Harris leaned forward over Amina's chair, his chest almost touching her head.

"Two people have just been shot…"

"Fuck… our guys?" Harris threw his over-chewed piece of gum in anger into a small bin.

"No, the dots are moving again…"

"Could it be the body of one of them being moved around?"

"Not sure yet…" Amina worked the satellite feeds again. "The cars are moving together now…"

"When will you know for sure?"

"That they are OK? Not until Wasim makes contact again."

Harris grunted. "He has to find a way to isolate himself from his escort first."

"He'll do that during prayer time… which is…" Amina looked at the clocks lined up on the wall showing both London and Middle Eastern times. "Nine hours' time."

Harris laid his head on the back of her chair. "Bugger… who is taking over tonight?"

"Bruce is… but I'll be on call."

"Fine… but any sign of complication…"

"We call you… yeah, yeah." Amina returned to the screens. "Anything else you need to know?"

12

"Nope…"

She nodded and prepared for the handover. She would be back long before the nine hours had elapsed.

* * *

Harris moved away from her desk. There was no point in hanging around. Amina would as usual get on with the job and he was reluctant to live up to his reputation. He did not mind being a pain in the butt but only for the right reasons. He walked out of the control room dedicated to Operation RED HAWK and moved along a long corridor. Control had been organised around several clusters to avoid breaches and non-critical ops having access to classified data. Harris glanced again at his watch. It was gone 7pm and yet he was not done by a long way. He had a last meeting that would require all his skills at recruitment. Harris took the lift, alighting three floors down. He left the Vauxhall Cross SIS building, hailing a cab for the short journey across the bridge to Pimlico. He would move to the AIRLOCK as he always did before a meeting with a potential recruit. Harris made himself comfortable in the back of the taxi. He closed his eyes and went through the file he had been reviewing all afternoon, ready to meet James Radlett at the Army and Navy Club, 36 Pall Mall.

As much as Harris enjoyed wrangling with some of his best assets, in particular the rather stuck-up and yet well-connected Brett Allner-Smith, Harris would be frank with James. He had read the file MI6 had compiled on him, asking for more research to be done on the man who was once Henry Crowne's number two in the successful team Henry headed at GL Investment Bank. His profile was not the usual business school/MBA graduate one would expect. James had started his career in the army. He had joined the Intelligence Corps after completing a degree in engineering at Imperial College London. James had been deployed alongside several regiments, always assisting with tactical intelligence on the ground. His last assignment in Kosovo with the 2nd Rifles had cost him dear. He had suffered multiple wounds when his military vehicle was hit by an RPG. He had been told he would never stand up again… But after two years in rehab he had walked out of the centre unaided. The wounds still occasionally caused him pain at the most unpredictable of moments. Harris admired his determination. Despite his promising career in the field being cut short, James had turned his life around by accessing a GL program for mature students and landing in one of the most prestigious financial engineering teams in the City, Henry's. And within a year of his joining, James had been promoted to the much-coveted position of Number 2 to his boss.

Harris walked down St James's Street and turned into Pall Mall. He never felt completely at ease in this upper-class part of London, with its imposing architecture and private clubs, but he recognised its influence. The glass façade of the Army and Navy Club was suitably intimidating for an institution of such reputation. A couple of young men, sporting the requisite Savile Row suits, were climbing the few steps that led through the entrance of the 'Rag', chatting purposefully. Their voices carried by the wind sounded poised yet excited. A middle-aged woman got out of a black cab, adjusting her suit by running both hands down its well-tailored front panel. She looked a little tense. Perhaps she too was coming for an interview.

Harris entered the Rag Club briskly, signing the guest book with his recruitment alias, Steve Jackson, and moved to the Smoking Room. He scanned the busy room for his contact. He had already arrived, engaged in conversation with James Radlett. Harris took his time to observe his target thoroughly… a solid frame, well built and of average height, brown hair still cut close to the skull, army style… once a soldier always a soldier? Radlett was focused on the conversation, nodding occasionally and taking notes.

Harris waited until he caught his contact's attention. They exchanged a quick look… time to engage. He walked purposefully towards a non-existent destination, until his contact stopped speaking to James, hesitated and half stood up… uncertainty showing on his face, a consummate piece of acting. Harris slowed down his pace, stopped, frowned and turned his head. Had he noticed someone he knew?

Yes, so pleased he seemed.

The men shook hands, all smiles at the unexpected pleasure of such a fortuitous encounter. James Radlett stood up as well. There was little sign the interruption had irritated him.

14

Good man, Harris thought, not fazed easily and able to enjoy positive human contact. Crowne had said as much.

"I wouldn't want to distract you from your business," Harris added after having been introduced. He had shaken James's hand, a firm, warm yet restrained grip. Harris's contact looked at James with a knowing smile. "Well, we were talking about military personnel transitioning into other careers... You've successfully done so, Steve. Perhaps you could join the conversation?" Steve's contact had already moved a chair he had appropriated from the cluster of seats next to theirs. "Unless of course, you'd rather carry on with me solely, James?" James smiled a welcoming smile. Harris sat down. It felt natural that they should talk.

"So, you're ex-army as well?" Harris raised his hand casually to place his drinks order. "How long ago was this?"

"Afghanistan, 2001." James leaned forward to take his whisky, his hand square yet attractive, holding the crystal tumbler carefully. He dipped his lips into his drink, no urgency. Harris could not detect anything that betrayed the severity of his injuries – broken legs, broken pelvis, a punctured lung and shrapnel across his body that still required him to carry a form from the military since he triggered every single metal detector he went through.

Harris simply nodded, giving time for James to decide how he wanted to play the meeting. How much he wanted to say about leaving the service and why.

"Bad injury, I decided I could no longer do the job the way I wanted to... there was a brief stint in Afghanistan, then I made my decision." James took another sip.

"I'm sorry to hear that." Harris had just been handed his own drink, choosing the same brand of whisky, and took a mouthful. He raised an appreciative eyebrow. "Did they treat you well?"

A flicker of irritation passed over James's eyes. "They did." The matter would be closed before it could even be opened, Harris registered.

"And why did you leave?" James's dark blue eyes ran over Harris. It was his turn to assess Harris's credibility.

"Afghanistan was not what I had anticipated it would be. I gave it two tours…" Harris let his voice hang. "I guess I didn't want to come back in a box like my best pal." Frank and almost abrupt, Harris did not avoid James's eyes. A soldier that could admit he was frightened of dying without sounding a coward always impressed.

"Were you with the territorial?"

"No, Para Regiment…"

"First Battalion?" James asked, slowing down his hand before the glass could reach his lips.

"If I had been, I couldn't disclose where my tours had taken me… as you well know…" Harris said with a lopsided smile. He liked James's ability to smell BS a mile off. "So, Second Battalion."

"Still, a first-class unit." James emptied his glass.

He knows my story might have a big hole in it… excellent. Harris chose another line of attack.

"After leaving the army what did you find yourself rolling towards?"

"Investment banking…" James had waved the waiter for another glass that Harris had accepted too. Harris's contact had by now faded away, retiring before the second round of drinks.

"Much better pay cheque." Harris nodded in acknowledgement. "And a different kind of warfare of course."

"But not entirely dissimilar," James added. "It's all about intelligence gathering."

Harris sat back in the large armchair… the word he was looking for had been spoken.

Intelligence.

"You were part of the Intelligence Corps?"

"Deployed alongside several regiments."

"Don't you miss it though?" Harris held his glass in mid-air, fingers propping the bottom.

James's body straightened. He locked eyes for an instant with Harris. "In what way?"

"Don't you miss the field? Data gathering, making sense of it… penetrating the mind of the enemy to anticipate their next move."

James replaced his untouched glass on the low table.

"Is it an offer?"

Harris nodded. "Let's find another place and time to discuss it further." He offered James a business card. James took it without hesitation. Harris had to owe it to Crowne... he knew the people of his former team remarkably well.

Harris could almost hear Crowne say... *I told you so.*

* * *

The 4x4 had stopped behind a barren mound in an almost lunar landscape. They were now only a few miles away from the Euphrates. They all needed a short rest before negotiating the crossing. The truck that was carrying the wounded journalist had finally taken a different route in search of another ISIL camp to offload their cargo, or perhaps the town Ali had mentioned. Henry hadn't spoken a word since they had bundled the British journalist into the back of their vehicle. He recollected her name, and her face was familiar, memorable features transformed by a deep scar etched over her left cheek. She held her wounded arm without asking for help, giving an occasional small yelp of pain when the vehicle hit a particularly bad patch of road. Ali had been trying to look threatening with his AK-47 held prone on his knees. She had hardly noticed him, and Henry was not sure whether she was in too much pain to care or had seen through the young man already.

Wasim jumped out of the car, Ali followed. They would be setting up camp for a few hours. Wasim moved slowly away. He stopped and looked around, getting his bearings. He resumed his walk and disappeared behind another small mound surrounded by heavy rocks. Henry had slid out of the car too, stretching his tall body; at least the front seat was less cramped than the back.

Setting up camp consisted only of throwing a few army sleeping bags on the gravelly ground and preparing some tea. Ali hesitated for a moment. The hostage had been left under his responsibility.

"I'll look after her." Henry used his Arabic again. He had never used it to give orders before but his intervention in Bab al-Hawa had subtly changed the balance of power. Ali's smooth face blushed slightly, his dark eyebrows forming a straight line.

"I won't let her escape... go on." Henry took the Glock out of his rucksack and Ali started unpacking the gear they had stashed away in the 4x4 boot. Henry would make sure Wasim had enough time to make his daily call to London… MOTHER had been waiting for her dutiful son to enquire about her health and relay the information he had gathered since their last call.

Henry walked to the side of the car and opened the door slowly, rejoining the journalist. They did not need a distraction so close to the crossing and he did not fancy having to shoot her down to stop her from fleeing.

"Thirsty?" Henry handed over a bottle of water. Her face had remained in the shadow of her makeshift scarf. She turned it towards him so that Henry could see her features more clearly. A tall forehead, deep-set eyes the colour of which he guessed was blue-green, her face a soft oval cut by strong expression lines around her mouth. He was about to repeat his question wondering whether she perhaps was scared into silence. He had not realised how badly sedated she had been when moved to the 4x4. Henry unscrewed the cap of the bottle and brought it to her lips. She held his hand as she started to drink. The roughness of her palms surprised him, her hands still stained with dry blood. Once Ali had finished setting up the camp, he needed to inspect her wound. Her hands tightened suddenly on his. "Where are we?"

"In Syria."

She did not reply and finished off the bottle, still unable to hold it on her own.

Henry looked towards the place where Wasim had disappeared. The hostage situation was not something London had planned for, but Henry relied on his ability to read a situation and make the most of it.

"What is your name?" He did not intend to initiate a chit-chat between two passengers. He just wanted the facts.

She pushed the scarf away from her face. If there was going to be an introduction, she would do it without hiding behind a veil, the way women had to in ISIL-held territory.

"Mattie Colmore, pleased to meet you."

No, she was not afraid to speak up.

"Who do you work for?"

"Freelance but currently the *Sunday Times*."

18

"When were you taken?" Henry's voice had turned blunt. He had always been good at giving his voice the edge it needed to cut into people. Years on the trading floor at GL Investment Banks had given him plenty of time to refine his technique.

"Yesterday morning... Aleppo." Mattie's voice had become a little clearer, the tranquilliser was wearing off and the water had helped. Her eyes roamed over Henry, not a full-blown investigation but moments of observation that gathered vital clues.

Skilful.

Someone had been observing them and Henry turned around.

"Have you finished?" he growled in Arabic. Ali nodded. The tea was ready and the sleeping bags spread over the ground.

Henry checked his watch... Wasim had been away for more than 15 minutes... a little too long for a simple comfort break.

* * *

The phone was ringing. Amina waited for the third ring before picking up.

"Wasim, my son... it is so good of you to call your ill mother. Praise Allah you are well." Amina's voice aged through a synthesiser sounded old and tired. The coded words had informed Wasim that she had detected a change in the route they were meant to take.

"Mother, I am so glad I can call you and we can speak." Wasim indicated he was able to speak freely on their secure line.

"What's happened in Bab al-Hawa?"

"The crossing went fine until the idiots who accompanied us made contact with other fighters who had been delivering two hostages to one of the factions in Syria."

Amina took stock. "Who died then?"

"Their captors... One of the hostages is badly wounded and I got the two cretins that had started the whole thing to take him to a doctor. He needs serious medical attention."

"The other?"

Wasim sighed. "With us."

"What? Whose bloody idea was that?"

"Hold your horses... It was Henry's idea but he may have a point..."

19

"What nationality?"

"British but…"

Amina butted in. "The Brits don't pay ransom. For fuck's sake, Henry is not asked to have ideas until he is in Raqqa and meets al-Baghdadi."

"That's the point… a hostage may be a good calling card."

Amina grunted. "Who are you left with then?"

"One other fighter, young but reliable."

"And what happens if you encounter other rebel groups… You're a bit on the light side."

"Trust me, these guys were bad news, too keen and too nosy."

"I still think this is too risky…"

"Everything is too risky here… This is Syria. We are in ISIL territory. I don't need a couple of bozos with me who I need to keep an eye on."

"Your call… you're on the ground." Amina relinquished a smidgen.

"I need some intel on movements between the territories at the east of the Euphrates and Raqqa. We are crossing into Iraq and I need to know where the best place is to make contact. The IS territory lines are shifting all the time. My contact in Raqqa will tell us who they are sending."

"No prob. Will redirect the satellites and see whether I can borrow one of the Reaper drones from RAF Akrotiri."

"Good stuff… you're the best."

"Yeah, yeah… How's Crowne coping apart from having brainwaves?"

"Better than I thought… still needs a bit of fine tuning and throws a curved ball when I least expect it, but…"

"Keep him on the straight and narrow."

Wasim laughed, shaking his head.

"Any other helpful advice?"

"Don't get yourself killed…"

Chapter Three

The dusty earth and rocks crumbled underneath his feet as he retraced his steps to the camp. The moon was almost full, giving the landscape a silvery glow and making its details clear. Wasim was on his way back to the place where he had left the 4x4. His solid frame appeared in the distance and Henry stepped away from the car to meet him. Ali was warming up the last of a mutton stew. They had stocked up on some khoubz, the typical round Arabic flat bread that Wasim could hardly get enough of. For all his efforts at finding a good source in London he could never find one that was as good as the one he found in the Middle East. Henry stopped to listen before moving forward. There was no sound apart from the crunching noise that Wasim's boots made as he approached the camp.

Henry moved a few more paces in his direction. They now had an English speaker which might complicate communication.

"Any news from MOTHER?"

"Grumpy and unimpressed…"

"What's new." Henry took it that his idea had not gone down very well but that it had not been rejected outright.

"Not compromising the op… we'll see what MOTHER decides."

The people at Vauxhall Cross had been clear with Henry… Operation RED HAWK was their only priority.

"Fine… Let her and Harris think about it… they'll come around." Hostages not only meant ransom, they meant publicity. Henry had studied the new ISIL group enough to have noticed that their communication skills were far superior to that of any other terrorist group MI6 had ever encountered. It also meant he might have a say on what happened to the woman journalist, but not something he would discuss with Wasim or MOTHER just yet.

They carried on together without another word. Ali had poured some tea into tin cups as he saw them coming. Mattie was sitting against one of the boulders, a blanket wrapped around her shoulders. Ali's face was relaxed, tending the bubbling pot, his features looking older than they usually did in the dancing light of the gas canister.

Henry had taken control of this small team in just the same way as he had done in the past. That felt an eternity ago and yet the skill of leadership had not died with his former banking career. He had made Ali at ease without pushing the young man too hard and he was gradually earning his respect. Even Mattie had joined the small group as if she fitted in.

Wasim sat down in silence. Ali handed him a tumbler full of hot tea. A coil of steam unfolded slowly and rose in the air. The temperature had dropped below what would have been seasonally comfortable and they all warmed their hands on their mugs. Everyone ate their food in silence, grateful they could finally feed themselves. Ali took the dishes, gave them a summary clean and restacked them in the boot of the truck. He wouldn't waste valuable water on the task.

"*Ahtaj ci'am 'atahadah 'iitayk.*" Wasim told Henry he needed a debrief after speaking to his ISIL contact in Raqqa. Ali wouldn't be part of the conversation and the young man did not expect anything else. Wasim and Henry moved out of earshot and sat on the ground with a fresh mug of tea.

"There is nothing new from London, but they are pretty pissed off about the journalist."

"Amina is so goddamn protective…"

"And that's what has kept us alive so far."

Henry shrugged. "Don't care what they say at The Cross. What did Raqqa say?"

Wasim rolled his eyes but gave a conciliatory smile. "They like it… a lot."

Henry hit Wasim's mug in a small 'cheers' gesture.

"What I said about her not finding out your name stands though.

If she does, Harris will put us under pressure not to…"

"Compromise the mission…" Henry cut him short. Yes, he did get it. "But at least she is alive and in damned sight better company with us… one day at a time. I am learning as I go in this environment."

"And you're learning pretty fast."

"I would drink to that if we could."

"We are drinking…"

"I'm missing the bubbles somewhat…"

Wasim shook his head. "Your sense of humour is going to get you into trouble in this country… there is zero tolerance for making fun of anything."

"I know… I'm just making the most of it while I still can."

"How about getting used to it right now."

"Nah… You'd get bored with me."

Wasim ran his solid hand over his face. "Sometimes I wonder whether you truly measure who it is we are going to meet."

Henry slapped Wasim's shoulder gently. "I get it Was… I don't want to get killed and more importantly I don't want to get you killed either."

Wasim's unconvinced face hesitated… Perhaps he believed Henry did get it…

Perhaps.

"The plan remains the same." Wasim changed the subject. "We are crossing the Euphrates at the M4 bridge, moving east inland, not following the river, therefore moving south towards Raqqa. It is ISIL territory. The route is not the most secure; the Syrian Army still roams around the area and the various militia factions opposed to Assad do too."

"So, we need to establish contacts with ISIL commander al-Haddawi asap."

"That's the plan."

"What are we going to do with Mattie?" Henry moved his head towards the place the others had already fallen asleep.

"You spoke to her?" Wasim's tone stiffened.

"Relax. I haven't become pally with her. I just needed to know a bit more."

"But you didn't need to, just don't take any bloody unnecessary risks."

Henry shrugged. "Her name is Mattie Colmore... *Sunday Times*, war correspondent. I couldn't place her to start with, but I remember now. I've read some of her articles, she's good."

"If you're trying to ascertain how big a ransom ISIL can get, forget it... The UK does not pay." The lines on Wasim's forehead had deepened.

"But her newspaper might... and don't worry. It's not because I want to understand what we can negotiate for her that I am going to become one of the beardos. The *Sunday Times* will move heaven and earth to get her back and this might just save her life."

"Or ISIL might use her for their propaganda." Wasim's eyes bored into Henry. "You don't know them well enough yet to anticipate how they think, at least not the way you used to in banking."

"Point taken." Henry raised his hands. "We'd better go back and grab a few hours' sleep."

"Agreed... we are crossing early morning before there's too much traffic and the Syrian army's on the move."

* * *

The distant buzz of his mobile phone dragged Steve Harris out of a dreamless sleep. He rolled onto his side, blinking to adjust to the brightness of the screen. Amina was calling him as soon as she'd heard, as agreed. It was not meant to be until the following morning though.

"I thought you'd gone for the day?"

"Bruce needed a bit of moral support... I spoke to Wasim."

Harris grunted and settled on his elbow. "I'm listening."

"The fight we spotted at Bab al-Hawa has brought complications. Wasim had to gun down a couple of beardos..."

"Part of the job down there." Harris turned on his back. "And..."

"And the reason why he had to do that is because they were involved in kidnapping hostages."

Harris sat up in one move. "What hostages?"

24

"Yep… two of them, although one is seriously wounded. Two journalists. Wasim has sent part of his escort away in search of a doctor to try and save him."

"Don't tell me they've kept one of the journalists with them?"

"How did you guess?"

"Why the fuck did they get involved?"

"Crowne's brainwave… hostage means money."

Harris refrained from launching into more expletives. "He wants to impress al-Baghdadi with an early offering."

"Are you for real?" Amina bit back. "We can't afford to have her identifying Crowne."

"It's a her… I'm impressed… in the middle of one of the worst war zones on the planet."

"Steve… I don't care whether you'd like to ask for her autograph… This is trouble."

"My brain might be slow at processing at 1am but give Crowne a chance. I too do not want to get Wasim killed. Who is she anyway?"

"Wasim did not know her name. I contacted GCHQ to get a list of all the known female journalists in the region… and one name stands out: Mattie Colmore, *Sunday Times*."

"Any recent contacts with her paper?"

"That's the point… nothing for the past three days."

"Mattie Colmore… very good articles. That's a high-profile catch."

"You bet. She is the daughter of Harold Colmore MP, Tory party and particularly vociferous when it comes to Al-Qaeda and terrorism."

"Now THAT really IS going to make life complicated." Harris stretched as he spoke. "I'll see you at The Cross early morning and not a word until we get more data on Colmore MP."

* * *

A small cry woke Henry. He sat up with a jerk, fully awake, eyes darting around to survey his surroundings for threats. Wasim was holding Mattie Colmore's arm and cautiously lifting the soiled bandages. They needed to be changed again or an infection might set in. Mattie had not said a word after her short conversation with Henry. He couldn't quite decide whether this was still the effect of the drugs she had been given or fear, perhaps a mixture of both? But he doubted she would be that easily unsettled... if he recalled correctly from her articles, she had covered Afghanistan, Iraq and now Syria. Wasim had settled her against the wheel of the 4x4, the last of their first aid kit open and items laid out ready for use. Mattie winced once more. Henry looked away and tried to locate Ali. The young man was nowhere to be seen. It was 5.07am and Henry expected Ali had retired to start with the first prayer of the day.

He rubbed his face with both hands to make himself fully awake. They would be on their way to the M4 bridge as the sun was rising. He pushed his army duvet away, rolled it up without a noise and stood up carefully. He looked around giving the landscape a thorough check and made his way towards the top of the small hill, crouching when he reached it. The glow of the sun on the horizon gave the air that was rising over the arid ground a golden shimmer. A few clouds had formed during the night, but the warm air would soon dissipate them.

The complete silence did not unsettle Henry. He had learned to enjoy it, a welcome moment in which he could imagine what it might be like to be at peace. The harshness of nature he had encountered in the desert had had some slow transformative effect... the shading of his skin. This snake-like comparison was perhaps apt. Many might have seen his IRA connection as treason and Henry could not blame them for feeling that way. He could have told them it was, rather, a misguided sense of brotherhood that had motivated him. But here, it no longer mattered. He had no time to revisit the reasons, the motivations. He had no time to indulge in remorse-fuelled reflection. He had a task to complete and that task was part of The Plan. Henry found a quiet spot to relieve himself and moved back to the camp. Ali was back and already producing a good pot of cardamom-scented coffee. Henry grabbed a mug and poured some of the freshly brewed liquid into it. He tore off a piece of khoubz and wolfed it down standing up. Everyone finished their drinks, throwing the dregs onto the ground. The 4x4 was packed and ready to go. Mattie had already taken her seat at the back, looking pale and tired.

"Is she going to be OK?" Henry asked before stepping in.

"She'll be fine. The wound is not deep, which lessens the risk of sepsis."

Henry inhaled, relieved.

"But I need to find something to cover her up for when we cross the bridge."

"You mean a proper abaya?"

"And a better scarf too."

"Where do you propose to find this in the middle of the desert?"

"Don't know yet but we need something that covers her body completely, otherwise we'll never cross that bridge."

"Any villages showing on the GPS?

"Why? Do you think we are going to find a shopping mall there?"

"No, but if we pay a good enough price, I'm sure some villagers might be very happy to sell us a piece of black cloth."

Wasim pulled a face. Not a bad idea.

Henry changed seats with Ali, who would now guide Wasim using their GPS.

Mattie had been given more sedative. Her head, loosely covered with a scarf, rolled softly with every movement the car made. Wasim drove the 4x4 away from the dirt track and onto the pebbled earth. He stopped the car at the top of the hill and Ali gave him directions. They were not very far from what looked like a cluster of farmhouses.

The drive took less than 15 minutes on the rocky ground. Wasim stopped and turned towards Henry.

"You stay here… I don't want anyone to lay eyes on you both."

"What happens if the farmhouses are held by hostiles?"

"We'll be fine."

Wasim left the car, placing his Sig Sauer in his waistband underneath his jacket. He and Ali took the two AK-47s that never left the front of the vehicle and disappeared behind the next hilltop. Henry brought the shemagh closer to his face. The Glock 17 that he had fished from his rucksack he placed in the small of his back ready for use. He would give them 20 minutes before he drove all the way to the farm. He stepped out and sat himself in the driver's seat, ready to make his escape.

Mattie's eyes fluttered open. For an instant fear crossed her face.

She had forgotten where she was. "Thirsty." Her croaky voice hardly audible.

Henry took a bottle from a supply he kept in his rucksack, unscrewed the cap and handed it to her. She almost dropped it. Henry bent over the front seat, helping her to hold the container to her lips. She started with small sips, firming up her grip on the bottle, then she took longer pulls. She gave him the bottle back.

"What's your name?"

Wrong question.

Mattie stared at him. Her light blue-green eyes were already searching for an explanation.

"I've got to call you something…"

Henry smiled. His full beard rose with the movement of his face.

"Abu Shabh…" Henry's chosen battle name.

"The Shadow… an interesting name for a jihadist from London." Mattie held her hand up, requesting the bottle back.

Henry held her gaze, hoping she would not detect his slight concern. He had been foolish to assume that Mattie was anything but fluent in Arabic.

"Many of us have made the journey."

"I know."

"Why did you cross into Syria?"

"To interview a rebel faction leader in Aleppo… I have been doing a lot of this since the beginning of the Arab Spring. The West needs to be aware of the horrendous crisis that's coming to Syria." Mattie flinched as she moved to find a more comfortable position.

Henry looked at his watch. Wasim had been gone about ten minutes.

Mattie was about to continue when her eyes shifted to the left of Henry. He heard the sound of pebbles shifting before he saw the little boy standing near the vehicle. A young lad perhaps no more than seven, clad in rags and herding three goats. He was near enough to see what was in the car, curious. Mattie drew the scarf around her head closely and pushed her body into the shadows of the 4x4 frame.

"He won't move unless you give him something," she whispered into her scarf.

28

"What if I talk to him?"

"He won't answer and he will almost certainly not understand you..."

Henry looked around. There was no one in sight. Wasim and Ali had been away for almost 15 minutes. He reached into the rucksack, looking for inspiration and took out a small battered sweet bag he had forgotten all about. He slowly secured the Glock in the back of his jeans, opening the door very carefully.

The young boy did not move but looked ready to make an escape. He stayed still though, fascinated and uncertain. His dark brown eyes darting from the vehicle to the six foot two, blue-eyed man who was sliding out of the large vehicle.

Henry smiled and extended his arm in slow motion, his fingers dangling the packet of sweets. The lad looked around, still hesitant. His grubby little hand snatched the goodies from Henry's grasp. Mumbling an almost inaudible '*Shukraan*', he stepped back carefully. The young shepherd suddenly took off, gathering the goats that had gone their separate ways. Henry watched him push them along, rushing to leave as quickly as he could.

Wasim and Ali had already been gone for far too long. Henry closed the door of the car and started the engine. The sound of a bell distracted him. He saw the young boy running back towards the vehicle chasing the most reluctant of his three goats. Before Henry could move away, he arrived at Mattie's level and looked inside the car. The woman sitting at the back was certainly not Muslim.

"Fuck." Henry followed the lad with his eyes as he ran away behind the hill. "Has he seen you?"

"You mean has he noticed I am a foreigner... yes."

"Shit... We need to get out of here." Henry released the clutch and started moving the 4x4 in the direction of the farm.

He was still deliberating whether he should move the vehicle closer or drive right up to the building when Wasim and Ali appeared in the distance, bearing under their arms a couple of bundles. Henry accelerated and skidded the car in front of them.

"Why did you not wait?" Wasim was already opening the passenger door.

"We had a visitor… a small boy… I gave him a few sweets to make him go away."

"That's good…" Wasim pushed a black length of material onto Mattie's lap.

"Except that one of his bloody goats wanted to join our party… He saw Mattie."

Wasim's jaw clenched.

"Drive."

* * *

Harris knew who Mattie Colmore was. Her father was a less well-known figure. Hard-core Tory party MP, supporter of David Cameron's view on terrorism. He had voted enthusiastically for the Iraq war, quipping he never thought he would support Labour policy. He was a zero-tolerance man… a phrase he liked and repeated to whoever spoke to him about the subject. Harris finished his cup of coffee, re-read the zero-tolerance paragraph of the GCHQ paper and wondered.

"What will you say when your own daughter is at stake?"

More urgent than speculating on the answer, Harris needed to compose an update for the man he reported to on operation RED HAWK. No intermediary for this high impact mission: it went straight to the top. Sir John Sawers, chief of British Intelligence was awaiting his paper. At least Sawers had seen from close up what the Syrian regime of al-Assad could do. He also knew the Middle East remarkably well. He would have an informed view and Harris hoped they would have this in common.

Harris called back on his monitor the images of what the satellites had recorded. The car had stopped again on its way to the M4 bridge.

More trouble?

One of his burner phones rang… one of his assets had been doing work for him on Syria. Time to gather some fresh intel before meeting The Chief.

"Brett… old chap… what have you got for me?"

Chapter Four

"We've got to ditch the car." Wasim's voice had lost its colour, almost speaking to himself as he looked ahead.

"Where?" Henry was holding the steering wheel firmly, fighting against the rough terrain.

"Ali, any town close by?"

"Manbij... very close." Ali gestured in the direction he wanted them to take. Wasim googled Manbij on his smartphone and scanned the short description of the 100,000-inhabitant city.

"Shit... I think it might still be in the hands of the Syrian Rebel Forces... too risky." Wasim sat back, weighing up options.

"Are the two other fighters who were taking care of the other journalist joining us for the crossing?" Henry glanced quickly at Wasim.

"That was their plan... although I did not encourage them. Why?" Wasim cast an eye towards Mattie. Henry read his hesitation. English was their usual language of choice for messages not meant for the ears of other passengers, but no longer.

The second lot of painkillers Wasim had given Mattie was starting to work through her system. She looked dozy and defocused.

"Call them back and make sure they join us..."

"Right." Wasim clenched and released his fist a few times and started dialling the number. Henry had a plan... He spoke in short abrupt sentences, redirecting the two men to another rendezvous point. They had lost time with the wounded journalist, finding an IS camp 20 km to the south. They were back on their way for the bridge crossing. Wasim gave them new coordinates. He killed the call and turned towards Mattie.

"You'd better put this on now before you fall asleep." Wasim pushed the bundle of black cloth towards her.

"You want me to put an abaya on."

"Just do it... It's clean, by the way, and the best we could find."

Mattie loosened the bundle. She took off her khaki jacket, wincing as she did so, and slowly manoeuvred the robe over her head. Her sore arm was complaining but she could not expect help from any of them. There was another piece of material that she finally unfolded, a large hood with a small opening for the face. She put it on and left the veil that came with it to the side.

"If I'm going to be compliant with the ISIL dress code, I need a pair of baggy slacks and gloves." Mattie's eyes had changed colour, locking them with Wasim's.

"That'll do for the time being." Wasim nodded.

"How far away are they?" Henry glanced at his watch.

"On this dirt track... an hour, maybe a little less."

"And on the M4?"

"That would be risky..." Wasim stopped in mid-sentence. Henry was a devious bastard. He smiled. Wasim called the two men again and told them the time frame had changed. There was a debate about using the main road but Wasim assured them that for such a short distance it would be safe. They would all soon be travelling on it after all.

"What's the new ETA?"

"Twenty minutes tops."

Henry nodded. He recalled what Wasim had said to him in the suburbs of Manchester as they were about to leave the UK forever.

"You're ready." Today he felt he was.

* * *

The doors of the lift opened on to a very different space and decor. From the functional and minimalist style of RED HAWK Control Room, Harris had travelled to the grand and yet cosy atmosphere of the management floor. Harris took a moment outside the lift to adapt to the transition. He ran his hand through his hair. He was glad he had it trimmed recently.

Sir John's PA was seated at her very large desk, barely noticing him it seemed. She lifted her head at the muffled sound of Harris's steps.

"He had to take an urgent call, I'm afraid." She removed her glasses with a swift and precise gesture. "He'll see you as soon as the call is over."

Steve Harris looked around to find a suitable chair. He had little choice. The chief of MI6 did not expect people to hang around his office. Harris chose the chair closest to the lift, stretching his hands across the iPad he had brought with him. Harris checked his shoes. He had given them a quick shine this morning, but the bright light of this immaculate office showed him what a bad job he had done.

Harris shuffled a little on his chair.

"He'll be with you shortly." Sir John's PA's voice expressed the patience you would give to a child.

He was not a kid, thank you, but he was entitled to feel nervous about meeting the boss of his boss's boss. And Harris hated waiting, although he was quite happy to keep some of his assets waiting when they met with him. A smile crept over his face. Brett Allner-Smith with whom he had spoken only yesterday was a favourite. The art dealer he had recruited a few years ago wore a habitual pinched expression of disapproval that amused Harris every time they met. The gentry did not like to be made to wait by the commoners... What fun. Still Brett had proven more than adept at his job. His connection with the shady world of art trafficking had been invaluable in creating a connection with The Sheik, the head of a newly formed terror cell in London.

The door of the anteroom opened and Sir John walked out, handing his PA a couple of sheets of paper. He gestured to Harris to come in, walked back through the entrance of his office without waiting.

Harris jumped to his feet. Sir John's PA raised an eyebrow. He grinned in return. He could never quite make out why The Chief, an easy to talk to man, had chosen such a stuck-up assistant. Harris had met him a few times before, when presenting Operation RED HAWK but always in the presence of his own boss. Today he was on his own.

Sir John was already sitting at his desk in the palatial room. The green-tinted windows, designed to safeguard against laser and radio frequency flooding techniques, gave the building its strange look, but they were even more noticeable from within.

Harris took his seat in front of Sir John's desk. He opened his iPad.

"Operation RED HAWK... you said you had urgent matters to discuss?" The Chief opened the file Harris had sent him.

"Yes, sir, a recent development is about to cause concern."

Sir John pushed his body further back into his armchair. "Shoot..."

Harris went through the events of Bab al-Hawa and was only interrupted when he mentioned Mattie Colmore's name.

"The *Sunday Times* war correspondent... daughter of Colmore MP?"

"A person of interest?" Harris puzzled.

"Not her... but I know her father well... in fact only too well. We have crossed swords in matters of government policy in the Middle East." Sir John moved forward towards his desk, forearms pressed against its top. "He barely speaks French although he thinks himself fluent, does not understand Arabic at all, knows little about the culture and complex issues facing the region, but has an opinion on Syria, Lebanon..." Sir John interrupted himself abruptly. "Apologies... I'm rambling."

"A demand for ransom is going to complicate matters."

"It most certainly will... You were right to come to me."

Sir John looked away for a moment. "How much terrain experience do you have?"

The question was unexpected. Surely The Chief would have received Harris's profile for the vetting of Operation RED HAWK.

"Not on paper, Harris... everybody tries to look good when an op is put together, even here at The Cross... proper terrain experience."

"You mean infiltration, working on the ground with the military, negotiating with terror groups and the warlords or tribal chiefs?"

"That sort of thing."

"I was deployed alongside the UK army during Afghanistan in 2001. I gathered information about Al-Qaeda and the Taliban from the locals, getting to know the local chiefs... I speak good Farsi and Pashto... some Arabic."

"Afghanistan… you must have been pretty young."

"Twenty-eight, sir… but I had a family of Afghani refugees living in my street in the East End. I became friends with one of the boys my age."

"Did they come from Kabul?"

"Yes, sir, ordinary people. The father was a tailor and the mother helped him with the sewing… They left when the communist regime came along."

"The East End is not very common for that community. I thought they congregated more towards Hounslow?"

"Now, yes, but the first wave of immigrants that arrived were not fussed as long as they had a roof over their heads."

Sir John nodded. "Back to my question then… how much did you achieve?"

"I recruited quite a few locals who helped with our intel gathering."

"And Iraq… what did you do there?"

"Same type of thing, but I also got inserted with the Yanks… I mean the Americans. The CIA was pretty keen on finding weapons of mass destruction then."

"What a lot of bull that was… by the way, 'Yanks' works for me." Sir John nodded, vivid blue eyes amused.

"No comment, sir." Harris grinned. "I've worked in the main cities there too, Baghdad, Basra, Mosul… I know Syria less well, although I've been to Damascus and Aleppo."

Sir John stood up abruptly and moved around his large mahogany desk. "Come with me."

Harris's short body sprang into action. Sir John walked out of his office, through the antechamber decorated with the portraits of some of the previous chiefs. He barely stopped in front of his PA.

"I'm going to Level -2, Emma… not to be disturbed."

"Certainly, Sir John." The woman smiled briefly and picked up the phone. The Chief was on the move.

"Sir, I'm sorry but I don't have clearance for Level -2." Harris hesitated outside the door.

"You have now." Sir John turned towards Emma. She nodded. Sir John summoned the lift.

The two men stepped inside together. The lift started moving down noiselessly. Harris wondered what it was in his background that had suddenly prompted this interest. RED HAWK was audacious, some might have even said foolhardy: the infiltration of ISIL not here in London but in its heartland, Raqqa. Henry Crowne had been the perfect, if unexpected candidate. His financial background, his extensive money laundering experience on behalf of the IRA, were attractive skills for a terror group rapidly building its financial base. Even more attractive was the fact that Henry had not been arrested for his illegal activities. Had one of his competitors not tried to pin a crime on him he had not committed, Crowne would never have been found out. His knowledge of fiscal paradises, opaque corporate structures and fund movements around the globe would serve anybody who aspired to keep their illicit money well hidden. Crowne was one of the best assets Harris had recruited in a long time. And working with Wasim, he was learning the skills of the trade fast.

The doors opened. Sir John went through a rigorous palm scan, retina scan and voice recognition sequence. The reinforced glass doors of Level -2 opened and they entered.

"Please register your name."

Harris moved to a screen display. He keyed in his name and authorisation credentials. A thumbprint pad appeared. He completed the task and turned towards The Chief. They moved alongside a long and narrow corridor.

"This is the way in," Sir John explained. "The adjacent corridor is for the way out... it minimises staff meeting each other."

They entered a small room. Sir John locked the door and moved towards a row of large monitors that he logged into from a central console.

"I am working on a plan involving Syria... it means direct intervention in the Syrian conflict. You have your team on the ground. I need to know what they have seen and heard... anything helps to build a detailed picture."

Sir John spoke as he waited for the information he sought to materialise on the screens. Maps appeared... Syria, Turkey, Iraq, Lebanon.

"I would not want to defocus them from their task." Harris ran his stocky hand through his light brown hair. "One of my assets still needs some coaching... he's learning fast but still learning and..."

Sir John lifted an appeasing hand. "I'm not asking them to be proactive and I fully appreciate how perilous their mission is, but... they may have come across, or have access to, information that could be helpful, information about the Rebel Syrian Army for example."

Harris nodded slowly. His eyes ran over the coloured maps that looked almost playful now that they were displayed on a floor-to-ceiling screen. It was extraordinarily detailed work, the exact positions of the various militia groups, some names he had hardly heard about, a completely up-to-date, in real time, map of the complicated geopolitical position of the Middle East.

"I like your honesty, by the way." Sir John was leaning against the small conference table at the side of the room, arms crossed over his chest, absorbed by the complex picture on the screen.

"Thank you, sir," Harris replied, reminded that his frankness had not always been that welcomed. "May I ask what it is that you are proposing... you mentioned direct action." He moved over to the conference table, leaning against it next to Sir John.

"First, let me make you part of the project team... unless you feel conflicted?"

Harris dropped his chin against his chest for a short moment. "I need to be realistic about how much I can contribute."

"Just intel, Steve... nothing else."

Harris hesitated.

"This project could be a decisive move in resolving the Syrian conflict and ending the civil war." Sir John stayed silent for a moment. Harris had to be free to decide without undue pressure.

"If I feel it becomes too much, I'll have to pull them back from intel gathering."

"Understood and agreed." Sir John gave an approving nod. He moved to the central console again, going through the sequence of passwords with rapid and precise gestures. Harris observed him, energetic, focused yet affable and, more to the point, open minded, a man who could definitely think outside the box.

"In summary..." Sir John was still finishing the job of adding Harris's name to his project team. "...extract, equip, train..." He turned towards Harris.

"You mean who... the Syrian Rebels, the people who oppose Bashar al-Assad's regime?"

"Precisely." Sir John moved away from the keyboard. "There are only two ways of stopping the Syrian conflict at this stage. Let al-Assad win or defeat him outright. There won't be a middle ground and he won't compromise."

"Especially as he's backed by the Russians." Harris shared his boss's view.

"It is not the way he saw his father rule and ultimately, despite all this so-called Western education or how modern he and his wife appear to be, it is not the way he will rule either."

"This is Shia Muslim against Sunni Muslim... in any case," Harris added.

"Perhaps a little more complex but not far off. The Russians back Iran, Syria and Yemen, all Shia Muslims."

"A proxy war against the US who back the Saudis and Iraq who have had Sunni leaders for a long time."

"As I said it's a lot more complex but not a bad summary for what we are trying to do... to stop this goddamn conflict that is going to help ISIL and Al-Qaeda recruit more fighters."

"I'll see what they can do. One of the team will be in contact again tonight."

"Excellent... Thank you." Sir John finally grabbed a chair at the conference table and Harris joined him. "But we haven't spoken about RED HAWK much."

Harris finished his update. Sir John interrupted a few times with pertinent questions:

Was Crowne up to the task? Yes.

Would Wasim's legend hold under scrutiny in Raqqa? Most definitely.

How did Crowne propose to become integrated into ISIL top circles? A few options had been explored.

"Crowne is on a mission. It's not only about doing the job and surviving. It's also about a personal crusade… if I dare say so." Harris waited to see the result of his aside before continuing.

"As long as we don't end up with a Lawrence of Arabia…" The Chief grinned.

Harris smiled in return. "You've read his file. It's all about making amends. He doesn't even hide the reason himself. He's prepared to put himself in danger… possibly a little too readily, though he knows he needs to come back here to deliver what he gathers out there, to complete the mission."

"What about endangering others' lives?"

"Good question. He was ruthless in banking so, if it fits the purpose, I'm sure he wouldn't hesitate. But strangely enough I don't think that would extend to the people in his team."

"You don't think he would try to double-cross us?"

"Not yet, in any case… He is still learning, and he needs our support for that."

"A reliable asset, you would say."

"For the time being… He will learn to become as proficient in the field of intelligence-gathering as he was in banking, of that I have no doubt."

"And later on…"

Harris pursed his lips. "Too early to tell. The psychometric testing and evaluation indicate that he likes taking sides and he sticks to that bond come what may. Part of his downfall as you know."

"The O'Connor brothers, IRA operatives…"

"Childhood friends, he felt he had a debt towards them… and of course he thinks his father was IRA himself."

"Hasn't he asked you about his father?"

"No. And I don't intend to give him much information even if asked."

"So, he is content with assumptions for the time being…" Sir John tapped his fingers on the surface of the conference table. "It will come one day though."

"Almost certainly, but we have some time before having to cross that bridge."

Sir John glanced at his watch. It was time to head back up. He had another battle to fight and Harris needed to prepare for a second interview he was very much looking forward to.

* * *

The 4x4 had stopped veering on the small rocks of the rough terrain they were traversing now they had found a better dirt track. The rendezvous point was close and Henry wanted to make sure they arrived before the truck did. Wasim told him to stop. They skidded to a halt. He opened his door, stood on the door frame of the car, scouring the landscape with his binoculars.

"I can't see them." Wasim sat back into the car. Henry moved the car towards a slight depression in the land that was hardly deep enough to hide the vehicle. The M4 motorway was now visible in the distance and the sun, although still low on the horizon, was giving enough light for their surroundings to become discernible.

Henry stopped the vehicle again. Wasim opened the door and resumed his binocular watch. He turned his head towards the M4.

Empty.

Wasim looked around again, not satisfied with their current location.

"Two o'clock… there are some shrubs that will give us better cover."

Henry started the engine again. "You need to call them."

"Not yet… I don't fancy them having been followed without noticing."

Henry parked the 4x4 now they had found a better hiding place. Wasim brought the binoculars up to his eyes again. "I see them."

Henry stepped out, moved to the boot and started taking out old rags. He threw one to Wasim. Ali walked out to join the activity whatever it was.

"Start cleaning…"

"Are you out of your mind? This is not London suburbia." Wasim looked annoyed.

"Couldn't agree more, old chap, but a clean motor looks so much more attractive and visible than a shitty looking one."

40

Wasim looked at the rag and shook his head, smiling.

"Boys will be boys... if you want to swap the car... get it looking good."

The three started vigorously rubbing the dirt and dust off the body of the vehicle. Within minutes it started to shine in the glow of the morning sun.

Wasim's mobile rang. The other two men had arrived at the meeting point yet couldn't see them. Wasim gave fresh instructions. They would be with them within moments.

Henry walked around the car, surveying their handywork and giving it a final rub.

"As good as new... ready for our friends."

Chapter Five

The rickety truck skidded to a halt when it reached the cluster of bushes where Henry and Wasim were waiting. The two young fighters jumped out of the vehicle and launched into their stories... how the hostage had survived, how the other mujahidin would make sure their leader knew they had done swell. Wasim indulged them for a moment. Henry stayed a pace behind, leaning against the as-good-as-new 4x4.

Wasim praised them... surely, they would be well recompensed, but he also reminded them that another important task remained... to ensure Abu Shabh reached Raqqa rapidly, today if possible. Their doubtful glance did not escape Henry. How could a kafir be allowed to carry such a grand battle name? He would not be a brother, a fighter, until he had embraced not only the Qur'an but also ISIL's interpretation of it. The question of conversion to Islam would come as soon as he had reached Raqqa. And yet, Henry had been given one of the best recommendations any infidel could have wished for from a man he had met at HSU Belmarsh. Abu Maeraka had been the mastermind of several successful terrorist attacks around the world before being caught in London. He was close to al-Baghdadi. ISIL had spent time and money bringing Henry over, based on that trust, and he would serve his purpose... inshallah...

Wasim slapped the two men on the shoulder, an acknowledgement that mattered. They had gained rank. He led them away from the Land Rover and explained their next move. They had to swap vehicles. The old truck was much better for transporting the woman hostage and the UK banker... Ali would be looking after them in the tarpaulin-clad back of the pick-up. Wasim would drive and they would take the 4x4 opening the way, making sure that all was clear in front of the small convoy.

The two men listened intently, glancing at the gleaming transport… they nodded, adding to the conversation with fresh suggestions, excited with the new arrangement, it seemed. Finally, Wasim simply walked to the 4x4 and opened Mattie's passenger door.

"We are changing vehicle."

Henry shrugged, looking disappointed, snatching up his rucksack in irritation. Ali opened the boot, started taking out some of the other bags and loaded the truck. The grinning young men did not find this odd.

Wasim handed the keys to them ceremoniously, giving a few pieces of advice about how to best engage the four-wheel drive. They jumped in, beaming.

It had been almost too easy.

The convoy started again. Less than 15 minutes later they were on the highway. A few clouds had gathered on the horizon, giving occasional respite from the morning sun. The oilcloth cover of the truck had been rolled down and secured tightly. Henry sat at the far end of the vehicle, next to the driver's cabin. The pane of glass that used to sit in the small opening between the cabin and the back had disappeared long since. Henry craned his neck a little. From where he sat, he could see the road ahead and speak to Wasim.

The truck slowed down as they started encountering some traffic. The 4x4 matched their slow progress; the two men were still paying attention. A large SUV approached at full speed. Wasim slowed down a little more and allowed it to squeeze between the truck and its escort. Other trucks and vehicles in various states of disrepair were now catching up with them. Wasim kept slowing down. This time the 4x4 did not match their speed… they were all going in the same direction, why not allow the engine a little free rein on the highway?

Tempting.

"How are we doing?" Henry stuck his face against the small opening.

"They haven't noticed we have two cars now between them and us."

"OK, good." Henry stood up, clinging to the frame of the truck to retain his balance. He reached the other end of the loading area, looking through a small opening in the tarp cover.

He moved back towards the seat where he had gathered both his and Wasim's rucksacks. He found the binoculars and returned to the tear in the fabric. He held the frame, stuck the glasses to his eyes, adjusting the vision with his thumb, and found what he was looking for. Several military vehicles were making their way towards them. He could see at least four. Henry rushed back to the small window, almost tripping.

"They're coming... four at least."

Wasim's hands opened and closed on the steering wheel in a mechanical gesture.

"How far away are they?"

"A mile, perhaps less."

"We need to get to the bridge before they stop the 4x4."

"How far is that?"

"We're nearly there, ten minutes at the most... I can see the structure already."

"Is the bridge guarded?"

"It will be... but they won't be stopping everyone."

"Shit... How about we wait it out?"

"Too risky, the others will notice we have stopped and if they stop too, we'll be done with them."

"How far are they?"

"They've slowed down again, only one car away now."

"Can you overtake them?"

"If I push this piece of junk hard enough, probably... why?"

"Just do it."

Henry grabbed his rucksack, and took out the Glock. He rummaged around the bottom of the bag and found what he was looking for. He fitted the silencer quickly to the muzzle of the gun.

Wasim had picked up speed – the engine complained in a racket of metal but the truck lurched forward. Henry took out his army knife, cutting a small opening in the material that covered the back of the pick-up. He sat on the bench, his shoulder wedged against the truck's frame and his boot squeezed underneath the bench leg for balance.

44

Wasim overtook the vehicle that separated them from the 4x4. They were coming now alongside their escort's vehicle.

"Do you want me to slow down?" Wasim shouted through the opening.

"I'll tell you when."

Henry trained his Glock low on the 4x4. "NOW."

A series of rounds hit the other vehicle, like corks popping, hardly audible over the roar of the truck's engine. One tyre exploded, sending the 4x4 swerving dangerously close to the truck. Wasim floored the accelerator and the truck lurched forward once more. They left behind the sound of skidding tyres and crushed metal. Henry removed the silencer, replaced it in his rucksack and stuck the Glock in the small of his back.

Ali woke up from his slumber, rocked by the truck's acceleration. He looked at Henry, puzzled. Henry ignored him and walked to the front of the loading bay, carefully creating an opening to survey the scene. The Land Rover had rolled on its side, barely avoided by other cars in a flurry of car horns. No one had bothered to stop. And in the distance the military convoy of five armoured vehicles was closing in.

* * *

Henry went back to where he had been sitting before, at the back of the truck near the driver's cabin. He placed his rucksack underneath the wooden bench that served as a chair. He leaned against the metal frame and met Mattie's eyes. They were feverish and somewhat out of focus but beyond the pain, Henry saw she had followed the scene and missed none of its significance. She said nothing but for the first time since they'd met, she was scrutinising him.

Who are you?

The force of her eyes startled him, an intense stare, uncompromising yet open minded. But the effort soon became too much. She closed her eyes and slid back into her drug-induced torpor.

"We are approaching the bridge… get ready." Wasim shouted in Arabic through the small opening.

Henry used one of the rugs they had taken with them to cover the two rucksacks. He sat on the part that was also covering the bench. Ali had straightened up since the accident and observed Henry without a word.

"What happened?" His voice was low and hesitant. He had moved to the place where the knife opening could still be seen.

"Why don't we stick to the plan?" Henry moved his head. The idea had been for Ali to sit on the ground next to Mattie, a son caring for his mother or an older relative. Mattie pulled the niqab over her face. The truck slowed down to a walking pace and then stopped altogether. They heard voices in the near distance.

Henry could not make out what they said. The tone of the conversation rose until shouting started. Car doors slammed open and shut. Henry fought the desire to stand up and check the cause of the commotion.

The guards at the Euphrates crossing were asking people to step out of their cars. Refusal was not an option.

A voice startled him. Someone was speaking to Wasim, asking for their final destination. Wasim mentioned Tell Abyad, a small city only a few miles away. The tarpaulin was wrenched open, a guard looked around, satisfied with the alarm evident on everyone's faces. He returned to Wasim. One of his colleagues joined him and cast a quick eye over the scene. A woman and a young boy huddled at the back in one corner, another man in tattered clothes sitting on an old blanket.

Nothing to report.

The radio of the man still in conversation with Wasim crackled. Henry could hear his voice receding as he answered. He suddenly called his colleague and they both ran towards their own vehicle parked at the side of the bridge entrance. Henry stood slowly to see their SUV leave at speed. He brought the thick material covering the truck down again. Wasim started the truck's engine, moving forward at a slow pace. No one was left to man the checkpoint. Wasim kept his nerve and drove unhurriedly over the bridge. On the other side he resisted the temptation to floor the accelerator. Other cars started overtaking them. Only when the structure was far in the distance did he finally let the truck pick up speed and escape.

Steve Harris reached his desk on the third floor of Vauxhall Cross. It was gone 6am and he has already gathered a day's worth of updated information. The small room did not enjoy the views that most of the SIS LEGOLAND building boasted but Harris liked it that way. It was ideally situated close to the Middle Eastern Operational Data Analyst team, DATA OP for short, which was devoted to evaluating information of importance, identifying trends, the movements of goods and people that might be of relevance to live operations. Operation RED HAWK Control Room was also close to the operational managers' Middle Eastern team. Their role was to gather information of any kind on the ground. Between these two resources, Harris was certain he would get what he needed at the pace he needed it; sometimes even raw data could be a game changer, giving him an edge. Harris had spent enough time on the ground to be helped in his decision making by what he gathered from the OMA team, decisions that could make a life-or-death difference to his assets on deployment.

Bruce had started preparing for the handover to Amina. Although he doubted she needed much of that, having called him through the night for updates. His inexhaustible patience impressed Harris. He plonked a cup of coffee in front of him. Bruce nodded his thanks and resumed his work. Harris moved over to his screens, drinking his own coffee still standing. He certainly needed the caffeine after his conversation with The Chief. He liked what he had seen though. His chunky hand loosened the tie he had knotted too tightly before the meeting. It came off with a sharp yank which almost toppled his coffee.

"Shit." Harris moved his hips sideways to dodge the hot liquid. He mopped it up with an old used paper towel and wiped his fingers. He glanced through the large window overlooking the grey building that rose at the side of Vauxhall Cross. It housed a collection of diverse organisations from Comic Relief to Macmillan Cancer support, its architectural simplicity contrasting with the skyline of the SIS building's contrived structure: LEGOLAND was an apt nickname. Harris sipped his coffee slowly... a very milky affair (skimmed to make the quantity he added less questionable) and a very sugary one (no excuse for this one). He finished his cup, replaced the lid and dumped the lot in the recycling bin... LEGOLAND was going green.

Harris moved his computer mouse a few times. The monitors came to life. Time to work on his next target for the day, James Radlett.

Henry had been eloquent about 'Jamie', his capabilities, the most reliable second in command he had ever had. A man he had without hesitation promoted within a year of his arrival, much to the consternation of other team members. Henry had been impressed by his lieutenant's sagacity and frankness. He had quizzed Henry when no one else had dared to and for good reason, never just to feed his ego.

James had been the only one who sensed Henry's dark side – he had had a hunch.

Harris kept re-reading James's clean, perhaps too clean, psych profile. Nothing he could lean on. There would be no bribery, no charm offensive and seduction to persuade the target fall into the trap.

Play it straight had been Henry's advice.

Don't tell me how to do my job had been Harris's first reply. But now that he had read the file, Harris had to admit it. Crowne might just have a point.

Play it straight he would.

Harris called up the email box of his recruitment alias, Steve Jackson. He composed an email to James.

Just happen to be working in your neck of the woods. Fancy lunch?

He pressed the send button and leaned back. He was curious to see whether his judgement had been right.

James Radlett wanted a change...

* * *

Mattie had started to come around, the heavy duty painkillers she had been given wearing off. She had asked for some water. The man whom she called Abu Shabh had given her a bottle. He had unscrewed the cap for her without thinking about it. She was almost certain she had caught the other man Wasim calling him Henry, though she wasn't sure. He looked at her in the eye when he gave her the drink. He was

48

no Muslim that much she could tell or perhaps a new convert, but she doubted it. She lifted the veil to drink from the bottle. But judging she would offend neither Ali nor Abu Shabh, she removed the face veil altogether to drain the bottle.

Despite the pain and the tiredness, she hadn't lost the sagacity that made her who she was, a powerful observer and interviewer. She caught Henry staring at her. He quickly lowered his gaze when she noticed.

He shuffled his tall body against the hard steel of the truck's frame and looked through the opening to the driver's cabin.

"How far are we?"

"Only a few miles before we enter ISIL territory."

Mattie had closed her eyes. The pain in her arm had returned, but she no longer wanted to ask for more painkillers. The road was better and she needed to gather as much information as she could about her new captors since they somehow did not quite fit the profile of the jihadists she had met previously. She let her head roll in a lull, hoping to catch through half closed eyelids more of their conversation.

Henry moved around a little. This time focusing his attention on Ali. He was following each exchange in English between Wasim and Henry more out of interest than suspicion it seemed to her. He had been half asleep during the shooting incident. Mattie hadn't.

The truck took a sudden turn to the left and its nose rose sharply. The shuddering started again, indicating Wasim had left the smooth asphalt of the main road. Everyone in the back grabbed part of the pick-up's frame. Mattie bit her lips, grateful the ride only took a few minutes. A short while later the vehicle came to an abrupt stop.

"We're stopping just for five minutes." Wasim's voice came through the small window. His door was opened and slammed shut. Henry stood up and reached the back of the truck before Wasim did. He unbuckled the straps of the cover, lifting one side of the material to jump out.

"Comfort break?"

Wasim answered in a low voice something Mattie could not make out and the oilcloth fell back again.

"Catch up break…"

Wasim's voice was grave and his lips formed a straight line. It was perhaps the last call he could make freely before they reached Raqqa.

Henry landed on the ground effortlessly, throwing a cloud of dust in the air in the process. He surveyed his surroundings. They had reached the top of a small hill, the landscape around it a flat and dry expanse with a just discernible splash of green in the far distance, thanks to the Euphrates' waters. Wasim had stopped the vehicle next to a deep enough ridge where a few bushes had managed to take hold to provide cover.

Ali pushed the tarpaulin all the way up over the truck's frame. He jumped out in one agile move. He spoke to Wasim briefly. He moved back to the vehicle, retrieved the AK-47 he had hidden in the flank of the car, took a pair of binoculars Wasim had left on his seat and started walking quickly towards the top of the hill.

"I've asked him to check whether we've been followed." Wasim was walking away from the vehicle.

"Do you think we have?"

"No… we would have been stopped a while ago if we had."

"What now?"

"I'll contact Raqqa again. I was given a new number yesterday. They'll tell me where to find our escort. We're less than half a day away."

"Sounds good." Henry was about to turn around.

"What did they see… Ali and Mattie?"

"When I shot the 4x4?"

Wasim jaw tensed quickly, his beard rising in a sharp move. "What else?"

"Ali was dozing. He didn't wake up fully till he heard the crash."

"And Mattie?"

"She was out of it on painkillers… not sure she registered anything at all until we stopped to cross the bridge."

Wasim's eyes bore into Henry. There was no margin for error and they both knew it.

Or did they?

Wasim kept silent.

"I understand infiltration is no small task, Was… I really do."

Henry looked frank. He did know.

Wasim waited for more.

"What do you want me to say… that I'm prepared to kill for the mission?"

"I won't be there to do it for you when we reach Raqqa."

"And I need to be ready for it… I understand that too."

Wasim said nothing as he walked away. He took out his smartphone and started dialling. Henry was left to his deliberations… could he go all the way?

Wasim stopped dead. "I need to make another call before Raqqa."

"Problem?"

"Don't know… need to call MOTHER."

* * *

The response came within the hour. Steve Harris was almost surprised at the speed of it. Or perhaps he should have expected it. Crowne had told him. "He'll call a spade a spade." Honest to a fault with the people he trusts, happy to take on anybody who tries to BS him. Harris could not expect to belong to category one yet and did want to ensure he did not fall into category two.

Harris re-read the short reply, which suggested a time and venue.

"You want to be in control of your meeting." Harris sent an email reply, amused at Radlett's attempt to take control.

Perfect… meeting in the City at Lamb Tavern in Leadenhall Market. 12.00pm.

Harris pondered on the choice of meeting place: good quality yet not ostentatious according to the Square Meal Good Food Guide. James Radlett was almost certain to meet friends and colleagues.

Good tactic, Harris smiled… Hiding in plain sight.

Chapter Six

Rumours about the fate of two journalists who had crossed into Syria and not been seen since were starting to filter through social media. Harris walked across to the Mid East OMA room. He swiped his card, entered his ID code, the door opened with a small sigh. He walked over to the desk of one of the analysts he had known and worked with for as long as he'd been at Vauxhall Cross.

"Any interesting chatter coming from Syria or Turkey?"

"What's in it for me?" Ahmed swirled his chair around to face Harris, arms crossed over his chest.

"Pint of beer or a bacon sandwich, mate… or even both if it's worth that much." Harris grinned. "And don't tell me I don't look after you… bad boy."

"Done." Ahmed started typing on his keyboard, calling up several chat surveillance screens he was monitoring. He pointed to a couple of them. "Just started last night… more speculations about the journalists. Nothing concrete yet."

"If it's a hostage situation the group that's taken them will keep things under wraps." Harris stood close to the screens and started reading.

"Normally, yes… but nothing's normal in Syria. Still, if the kidnappers want a ransom then the chatter will die pretty quickly, and then we'll know."

"Where does the chatter come from?"

"We picked up material from an Al-Qaeda source in Syria… We're still monitoring… may be ISIL too… bit of a newcomer so not so sure who we're picking up."

"I can't imagine those two working together." Harris would not give his own Op intel to Ahmed and Ahmed would not have expected him to. The data analysis had to come directly from Ahmed's group without any bias from the individual agents.

"You're right on that one. Since their recent split, no chance. I'll keep you posted as soon as something more concrete emerges."

Harris nodded his thanks and walked out. He hesitated. Asking DATA OP for their analysis of the situation might be premature. He had his own idea as to where the new jihadi group called ISIL was going. The question was whether it would inspire the devotion Al-Qaeda and Bin Laden had inspired in their followers. From what Harris had seen first-hand 18 months ago, he was convinced it would. Harris returned to RED HAWK Control Room. It was just gone 8.15am. He logged back into his machine, scrolled through his emails, switching between several mail accounts he held under different aliases. Another of his assets, Brett, was feeding in information he had received from the region. His art trafficking, a lucrative business that had become a key source of income for terrorists' groups like Al-Qaeda had provided Brett with the perfect cover. Brett had been lying low since his successful involvement in the dismantling of a new terror cell in London run by The Sheik. It was time for him to dig a little deeper into his knowledge of the market and refresh his links with his contacts.

* * *

Henry took his time to climb the slope that led to the top of the hill. He could feel the effect of the arid landscape that stretched to the East. They had left behind a zone where crops were cultivated to enter a drier part of Iraq.

Ali was crouching near a steep drop, eyes stuck to the binoculars he had brought with him, checking for unusual traffic on the road they had just left. Henry stood for a moment observing him. His slim fingers had turned almost white from clutching the field glasses. The Kalashnikov he had slung over his shoulder had slipped towards the ground. He must have felt Henry's gaze. He lowered the glasses, one hand now on the gun. He smiled when he saw Henry.

"All good." He pointed in the direction of the road and gave the thumbs up.

"Great stuff." Henry smiled back, returning the thumbs up.

He reached Ali and stretched out his hand. He was handed the binoculars, and began surveying the landscape below. The new track they were about to embark on to make contact with their ISIL escort and then reach Raqqa looked well established and easy to drive. Ali stood up, his lanky body wrapped in an oversized army jacket. Henry glanced at him sideways as he adjusted the binoculars to his eyes. He looked far too gentle to be a soldier let alone a jihadist, or perhaps not, perhaps the romantic idea of fighting for a cause had inspired him. Henry adjusted the field reach to long distance and turned towards the Euphrates. For a moment he enjoyed the spectacle, making out the dark blue colour of its waters and the sparkle of light on its surface. Henry checked his watch. He surveyed the contrasting landscape, that was almost lunar. There was nothing out of the ordinary.

"Must go back." Ali ventured, tapping his watch to make himself understood better.

"Not yet." Henry moved away from their initial position, walking to the other side of the hill top. The slope was much softer here. Vegetation hugged the hump of land as if seeking protection. Henry was surprised at how green the foliage looked. He spent a little less than ten minutes scouring the horizon for a yet-to-be-encountered enemy, moving the field glasses around methodically.

Ali was puzzled. Why wait? He sat on the ground, picking up a stick and drawing random shapes in the dust. Henry had almost given up when he spotted movement in the far distance. He closed his eyes for a few seconds and reopened them to make sure he was not mistaken. Something was on the move. He tried to adjust the reach of the binoculars again, but they were at their maximum extent. A flash of light told him it was metal he could see.

"Check this out?" Henry handed the glasses to Ali. The young man sprang up and adjusted them to his face.

"Cars." He moved around a little. "No... trucks... many..."

"Can you see who they are?"

Ali shook his head.

"Time to go."

Henry hurried down the path, sliding on the gravel and stones. Ali's agile steps were following him. Henry hoped he had given Wasim enough time to make his calls. But there was no question that they needed to move.

Wasim was still on a call when they turned the corner.

"People are coming…" Henry shouted, hoping he would give Wasim enough warning. "Trucks… lots of them."

Wasim put the call on hold.

"Who are they?"

"No idea… too far."

Ali explained in his quick Arabic what he had seen. Wasim moved his head towards the car. He ended the conversation abruptly.

Time to make a move.

Henry lifted the heavy tarp that covered the back of the truck to resume his place inside. He froze, one boot on the foot hold, ready to jump in.

"What is it?" Wasim's driver door was left half open.

"Mattie… she's not here."

* * *

She balanced a coffee cup on her iPad to get to the security pass stuck in her back pocket. There was no way she would wear it round her neck. She was not a cow… although some ill-intentioned colleagues may have argued otherwise. She could have clipped it to the lapel of a jacket, but Amina did not do jackets unless they were leather. The cup wobbled. She cursed but managed to avoid the disaster of dropping her drink. Vauxhall Cross's Control Command was buzzing, people changing shifts, relentless activity expressed in the hum of low voices greeting colleagues but never discussing "business" until huddled in the sound-proofed rooms arranged around its perimeter. The Cross inner sanctum oversaw all operations on the ground that required physical interventions, satellites, drones, eyes in the sky, eavesdropping of any shape and form.

Amina tapped Raj's shoulder. He ignored her for a second, then pushed his chair away from his desk to face her.

"They've got company… not sure who though."

"Can't be the Syrian army… they would be well out of their comfort zone."

"Al-Qaeda or ISIL?"

Amina pulled a face. "Al-Qaeda is retreating to the north east of Syria…"

"We are still pretty close to their old territory though." Raj opened the top drawer of his desk took out a packet of nuts. "All the satellite tracking is saved for you to take a look at as agreed," he said before throwing a handful of them in his mouth.

"Any chance of a surveillance drone being available to take a closer look?"

"I'll see what I can do."

Amina nodded her thanks. She left Control Command to return to RED HAWK Control Room. Harris had already called her about Sir John's request for intelligence to be gathered on the ground in Syria and Iraq. She had not bothered to protest. Wasim and Henry had already crossed the Euphrates, they would soon be reaching Raqqa. She had received by now a full account of the incident at the bridge. An excellent bit of information to keep The Chief happy. The Syrian army had been surprisingly fast at reacting to the tip off that a faction group vehicle was in the area. They had chased and promptly eliminated the threat. Through an MI6 eye in the sky Amina and Harris had seen how the two fighters in the 4x4 had been summarily executed. The Syrian army was not in the mood for taking prisoners.

The call with Wasim had yielded a little more information but it was now only a matter of time before Henry and Wasim made contact with the ISIL convoy that had been sent to accompany them to Raqqa. No matter what Raj said, Amina was certain Al-Qaeda would not dare venture into the territory now held by ISIL, the expanding terror group run by al-Baghdadi.

She sat back at her desk in RED HAWK Control Room, logged in and scrawled through the new data that was being sent to her using key name searches. A name popped out. "Shit." She clicked on it.

Mattie Colmore.

It was the draft of an announcement that would be released on Reuters, the news agency, within hours.

Speculation is mounting that Mattie Colmore, journalist and war correspondent for the Sunday Times, has been abducted in Syria. She was last seen in an internet café in Antakya, Turkey, the small town where journalists congregate before crossing into Syria. Rumours are circulating that a secret journalists' FB site has been hacked by spotters on the border between Turkey and Syria who sell information about reporters to Islamists and other rebel factions. Her cameraman has confirmed he has not seen her since they met in the café and her hotel has also confirmed she has not been seen for over 48 hours.

"Shit, shit, shit." Amina fitted her headphones over her head and speed dialled Harris's number.

He answered after the first ring. "What's up?"

"Reuters is about to release a news bulletin about Colmore."

"Shit, shit, shit."

"My take on the situation exactly."

"Who is the moron not understanding media information black out when it comes to abduction?"

"From what I can tell, whoever is writing this bulletin is still verifying the information." Amina went back to her screen. "But I'd say it will be ready for release in a couple of hours max."

"Leave it with me… I'll get on to Reuters. Where are our guys at the moment?"

"Back on the move but they've got company."

"Friendlies?"

"Well, if you can call the beardos friendly, I'd say almost certainly."

"But you're not sure?"

"I asked Raj whether we could use one of the surveillance drones to get a better look. He is pretty good at delivering. I should have access within minutes."

"OK… keep me posted."

"About Reuters… I'm wondering what the reaction is going to be. If we're too heavy handed, they'll know the story is true."

"You're worried there'll be a leak?"

"To another newspaper or news channel… maybe."

"Good point… I'll call The Chief too."

The phone went dead. Amina took no offence. There was seldom time for niceties when lives were at risk.

Amina returned to her monitors. A new request for a connection had come through. She clicked on it, tapped her fingers on her desk as she waited. The image was taking forever to materialise.

A convoy of trucks and armoured vehicles had stopped.

Henry and Wasim's old pick-up was not moving either. They were not close to one another, but there was no doubt in Amina's mind that the fighters had seen the truck and those in the car had seen the fighters.

She zoomed in as much as the lens of the drone allowed her to. She could make out four cars that looked like US Humvees, followed by a couple of desert patrol vehicles and three more trucks bursting with men seating on each side of the metal frame in the rear. She hesitated for an instant but there was no time to call Wasim. She was now certain these were ISIL fighters. Her hand was frozen on her mouse… powerless.

They were about to make contact.

She by-passed Raj, as agreed in an emergency, and dialled RAF Akrotiri UK Army base to speak to a sensor operator in the Reaper Drone Patrol.

"I am accessing images through Drone MQ-9/23. Any payload on this one? I have a situation."

"What's your access code Ma'am?" The young man was already accessing the information of her surveillance drone.

"TZR8HR" Amina read, one eye still on the scene on the ground in which no one had moved.

"Validation check." Amina could hear typing and the voice came back. "No Hellfire payload on this one Ma'am. Purely surveillance."

"How long from launch to target for a Hellfire strike?" Amina asked, but it would never come on time.

The line crackled with static. The young man's voice became intelligible again.

"Forty-two minutes."

"Nothing already airborne we could use?"

The line went dead for a short moment.

"Only one surveillance drone out at the moment, I'm afraid."

Amina held her breath.

The convoy was back on the move and so was the old pick-up.

* * *

The back of the truck was empty. The footsteps of the three men had receded, the grinding noise of heavy boots on gravel and dusty earth. She shuffled slowly along the bench that had been hastily welded to the side of the pick-up interior. The drugs she had been given had stopped working a short while ago, yet the pain had become bearable. Wasim's back was just visible, mostly hidden by the bend the track made around the rock. Ali and Abu Shabh had disappeared altogether. Abu Shabh presented a conundrum that Mattie would have very much liked to solve… if she lived long enough for that.

She gathered the heavy cloth of the abaya around her hips and jumped out of the truck. She winced as she landed on the ground. The sounds of her feet hitting the gravel were deafening. She froze for a moment. Wasim was still in deep conversation. The others had not returned. Mattie moved to the side of the vehicle and looked around to take her bearings. The land was dry and grey, the small hill typical of the desert landscape that characterised this part of Syria away from the Euphrates. In the distance she spotted cultivated fields. They were moving inland and if they were to re-join ISIL forces they would be going to Raqqa.

Mattie's attention moved to the track. She had no hope of climbing downhill without Wasim noticing. She turned towards the top of the hill and started moving noiselessly.

The track's steepness eased off after a few yards and it divided into two around the rock. She stopped, stooping cautiously to examine the ground. The dust of the left-hand path had been disturbed. She chose the other. The route was clear. She hesitated and shook her head with a smile, pulled her robes up again, her trousers down, and squatted. She relieved herself with a sigh.

So much material designed to hide her body and yet here she was peeing in full view of anyone who came along or looked up towards the hill.

She did not care. It was an excellent excuse should any of the men catch up with her. She was determined to test how far they were prepared to go, how much pain they were willing to inflict too.

She stood up, wriggled back into her trousers and abaya. Her watch had been taken from her. It was of little monetary value but deprived her of the ability to keep track of time and created confusion. It was not the first time she had found herself in a tight spot, robbed of her belongings or threatened by fighters, but it had never gone this far. She had tried to keep a mental record of what was happening but the medication she had been given had not helped. Still, she reckoned that no more than 48 hours had elapsed since her abduction. The sun had been creeping up over the horizon, it was 9, perhaps 10am, no later. The temperature had started to rise steadily, and it would soon be difficult to be out of the shade. Her chances of escaping in the middle of Syria, in ISIL territory, were next to nothing. A woman would be expected to travel accompanied. She had to stay put for the time being… but once in Raqqa perhaps? Her failed attempt at escaping near the Bab al-Hawa crossing might have worked. But here, close to the top of the hill, she was trapped. She waited a moment and heard hurried footsteps coming down the other path. Mattie turned away and instead of retracing her steps walked up to the top. The track came to an abrupt end. She walked to the edge of the rock face. It was not as sheer as she had expected. With proper shoes and a little equipment, she could have climbed down easily. The desire to escape or perhaps even the call of danger was almost irresistible. She inhaled deeply and closed her eyes.

She might have a story to tell if she survived the ordeal or even found out who Abu Shabh was and why a well-educated and intelligent man from London like him wanted to join the ranks of ISIL.

It was time to go back if she wanted to clinch that story.

She started retracing her steps and was almost at the fork where the two paths split when a figure stood in front of her. His face was thunder and he grabbed her by her uninjured arm.

"What are you doing out here on your own?"

"Did you know that a woman's bladder holds a third less water than a man's and that a women's period comes every 30 days?"

Henry's furious look and set jaw did not move... was she for real?

"If you needed a damn pee or a change of Tampax you should have asked."

A man who can talk about a woman's bodily functions without blushing... unusual.

"You guys had all disappeared." She shrugged and smiled.

"We have company... so you'd better get back inside the truck."

"Have you made contact with ISIL then?"

Henry could not hide his surprise. How did she know?

"Don't look so amazed... we're in Syria, who else could it be?"

She moved past Henry, accelerating the pace. Wasim was waiting inside the truck, his fists clenched on the wheel. He too looked furious but, like Henry's, his face lacked the cruelty that Mattie had seen on so many jihadists. Still, his eyes met hers asking a question.

How much trouble was Mattie Colmore going to be?

Quite a lot it seemed.

Chapter Seven

The truck started its slow descent towards the flat plains that extended in front of the small hill they had just left.

Ali had been tasked with making sure Mattie stuck to her place at the back of the vehicle duly covered and would not move again unless Wasim or Henry said so.

Henry sat in the passenger seat next to Wasim and rearranged his blue and white shemagh scarf over his head and round his neck. His dark beard and his tan had enhanced the blue of his eyes – distinctive, perceptive eyes that could show coolness and anger with a change in colour.

"How long before we make contact?"

"Twenty minutes tops." Wasim rolled his shoulders without noticing. He had already given Henry an ETA of 30 minutes for the ISIL welcome party ten minutes ago. He did not begrudge Henry's nervousness.

This was it… the contact with the people-traffickers who worked for ISIL. The camps, even the few fighters they had met, had been a pale introduction to what awaited them. Months of slow and persuasive infiltration had given them insight and credibility and yet in a few minutes' time these would be tested as never before.

Henry was about to find out whether Wasim's *You're ready*, back in Manchester's suburbs, still held good, and whether ISIL's leader was convinced by his story. Both Henry and Wasim knew that if he wasn't their end would not be swift but slow and painful.

"Can I say it?" Henry cleared his throat from the dust he had been breathing when he had run down the hill path.

"You may…"

"I am shitting myself."

"Don't tell me you need me to stop."

"I'm being metaphorical."

Wasim kept his eye firmly on the road. "If that's any consolation… so am I."

Henry half turned towards Wasim. "I was being flippant."

"Serves you right… You'd better remember… These people have zero sense of humour."

"Which is why I'm spending my very last minutes of relative freedom cracking a…"

Wasim's smartphone rang. He slowed down and picked up the call. Henry could hear a voice giving instructions in a tone that did not sound friendly.

"They're asking us to stop and wait for them."

Henry inhaled. His smooth and pleasant face took on a mask of harshness.

He was ready.

* * *

The Reaper drone had descended from its clean mission altitude of 50,000 feet to reach a more effective 40,000 feet. Amina was not in control of the drone the way she was of the satellites' imaging, but she could still zoom in and angle the camera carried by the drone to improve the pictures she was receiving.

The Humvees had increased their speed and the ISIL black flags were now visible at the back of the trucks that followed.

Henry and Wasim's pick-up had stopped, exposed in the middle of the valley that lead to the Euphrates. Amina sent another text to Harris.

Where the fuck are you?

If her texts were ever audited, she would end up filing data for the rest of her career… never mind. She chewed on her nails and pulled a face. A friend had convinced her to paint them with a terrible-tasting concoction.

You'll never find a man if you keep biting your nails as if you've not been given enough to eat.

But the only man who mattered now was Wasim and he was too far away to see what effect the mission was having on her hands.

The scene was unfolding without sound and it made it even more unnerving. She was accustomed to this by now but occasionally the silence of the action that unfolded in front of her made surveillance almost unbearable.

Henry and Wasim stepped out of the truck. There was no point in staying put – there was now no chance of escape.

The ISIL convoy stopped 300 yards away from them. There was no movement on either side for a couple of minutes. Three men stepped out of the second Humvee. Amina asked the operator to drop the drone to 30,000 feet. Every descent made the drone more visible and this would be the lowest it could go. Amina grumbled and drew her armchair even closer to the desk. She stretched her hand towards her now very cold coffee and mechanically took a sip.

Two of the three men started moving forward at a slow pace, each training their AK-47 on the truck and its passengers. Their uniform was recognisable, black trousers, black shirt, black scarf wrapped around their heads. These were not recycled army uniforms or the tribal outfits either Al-Qaeda or the Taliban wore. There was a strong desire to unify the fighters into one army, behind one flag, a potent image that told her much about the intention of its leader.

The two men had reached Henry and Wasim.

A request was made to Wasim. His body language told Amina he did not like what he had been asked to do.

Suddenly, Wasim was thrust against the truck. Amina could almost hear the thud of his body against the metal of the bonnet and feel the stab of pain from his arm being twisted behind his back. Henry had a rifle pointed at his chest. Amina stopped breathing. Her heart missed a beat when her mobile rang.

"Am I missing something?" Harris sounded less cocky than usual.

"Crowne and Wasim... it's not going well."

"They've made contact."

"Crowne has a gun to his chest and Wasim a gun to his head."

* * *

He stopped his car abruptly, almost causing the vehicle behind him to collide into his rear. The angry driver shouted insults and would have got out of his Mercedes to give Harris a piece of his mind and perhaps more. Harris moved his car around in an expert U-turn and floored the accelerator. He had stuck his mobile to the dashboard holder, listening to Amina's blow-by-blow description of what was happening in Syria.

Crowne has put his hands over his head, knees on the ground.

Wasim is leaning against the truck, arms stretched forward... one of the hostiles is frisking him.

They've found the side gun he keeps strapped to his left calf.

The other hostile is taking Mattie Colmore and a young guy out of the back of the truck... they are made to kneel down.

Amina's voice sounded constrained, gripped by fear.

They've taken the rucksacks out of the boot and are emptying the contents on the ground.

A sense of powerlessness almost overwhelmed Harris. If there was to be an execution in slow motion, it would be atrocious for the four of them.

They've grabbed the young guy and are walking him over to the man who has stayed behind.

Amina had resumed her running commentary.

He is asking him questions.

No... he is taking a gun out. He is moving towards the truck. The gun is back in his belt.

"Who is he?" Harris interrupted.

"Don't know, he's limping a little though, taking his time to get to them." Amina was moving something around.

"Oh my God," Amina almost shrieked. "Oh my God... it's Kasim al-Haddawi."

"One of al-Baghdadi's closest commanders?" Harris's voice rose. He was still far away from Vauxhall Cross, using his horn to move people along.

"Yes... I'm certain... the limp sustained in a fight with the US army during the Iraq war."

65

"What now?"

"He has almost reached them. Wasim is straightening up… speaking to him."

"How about Crowne?"

"Still on the ground. Haddawi is speaking to Crowne now. He's going around him… his gun's out…"

"Shit." Harris drove through a red light.

"He's fired the…"

Silence.

"Amina… Amina… What now?"

His phone had gone dead.

* * *

Lunch had been planned for noon. James glanced at the clocks on the wall of his office. The London one marked 10.17am. He had retired there a few minutes ago from his desk on the trading floor to think. This gave him a solid hour to consider what he was hoping to achieve from the meeting with Steve Jackson. He had searched for his name on the web but very little was available… intriguing. He could perhaps call some of his former pals still working for the British intelligence service within the armed forces. But it felt wrong to be soliciting favours when he had not troubled to keep in touch for a while. If it had been an emergency he might have got over his shyness, but he would rather keep his powder dry for a more worthy occasion.

James slid the engaged sign on, closed the door and the blinds over the glass wall that formed the trading floor-facing side of the office. No one would dare ignore his request for peace.

The room had not changed much since his former boss, Henry Crowne, had left… some of the old tombstones celebrating the closing of the large deals they'd worked on together were still lining the shelves. James smiled, remembering his confusion when Henry had asked him to choose the shape of the *tombstone* for the deal he had closed successfully. He had nodded, sensing it was an honour and enquired with Henry's PA. Morag had winked and given him a catalogue of glass slabs that were customised to commemorate the closing of significant business deals in investment banking. James ran his hand over the desk of solid wood: nothing too fancy. The armchair too was the same, a good ergonomic chair; two monitors for his PC; and the famous clocks that gave the time for Sydney, Tokyo, Hong Kong, Frankfurt, London and New York. James recalled Henry's silly mental gymnastics, moving from one city to another. It was in this same room that James and Henry had had their last face-to-face fractious conversation and the loaded word *murder* had been spoken.

The dark secret that Henry had been harbouring for years had not entirely surprised James. A former army intelligence officer working for an IRA operative… there was some bitter humour in this that he had not been allowed to ignore. He had been disappointed more than angry. James had been thoroughly questioned by the police and the Counter-Terrorist squad.

Had he not suspected?

No…

Or had he?

Had there not been any signs?

No.

But it was not quite the truth.

Was he not a former intelligence officer?

Yes.

And he still understood what this meant.

Should he have paid more attention to what Henry was up to, even in his private life?

Henry had a flawless record when it came to his banking deals… and James was not his mother.

Was he part of it?

James had almost clocked one to the little git who was enjoying asking the question. Still, in all fairness, he might have asked the same question had he been in his place.

Henry Crowne ran the most successful team at GL Investment Bank, possibly the most successful team in the City, London's financial district. And yet he had not been able or willing to shake off his association with his IRA friends from Belfast.

Had fame and prosperity not been enough? Was he not leading the dream life so many wanted? To Henry's former colleagues, his betrayal was not hurtful, it was beyond stupid… Henry Crowne was perhaps not so clever after all. And yet, in some strange way James understood. It was all about camaraderie, being authentic, being true to old friends. It was one of the reasons why James had enjoyed working for Henry.

The phone rang. It diverted to James's PA.

James sat back in his armchair and wondered why memories of Henry had come flooding back. Perhaps because he owed him his second chance at the lucrative career he had enjoyed for a while. Perhaps because having replaced Henry at the head of his old team he had realised it was not only about technical ability but about navigating the political minefield the bank had become. Henry had been a natural; James had to make the effort every day.

James wanted something new. He was not quite sure what.

Steve Jackson had an agenda. James did not care what it might be… he was going to explore this avenue. He knew what he was good at and what he was no longer prepared to accept. He had made the necessary changes, stabilised the platform, to borrow terms he did not like. The business was growing again after the financial crisis… job done.

* * *

The gun discharge rolled over the plain in a single burst of energy. It echoed against the hill they had just left. Henry had not flinched. He had held his breath but managed to keep his eyes open. He was still alive. He wanted to look around, to make sure the others were alive too.

The young man's body is limp and lifeless. The camp on the Turkish border has a reputation to maintain. This would-be jihadi has not done well in training, too slow and awkward. He has soon lost his eagerness for the cause. He doesn't say it, but he certainly does not shout loudly enough "death to all infidels" and "may the armies of Allah burn the West to a cinder." The few friends he had when he joined are now avoiding him. It is only a matter of time before he too becomes kafir. What he has not been told by the recruiter who has added his name to a long list of young recruits, is that ISIL does not only believe in the ultimate battle of Dabiq in which the Muslim armies will defeat the legions of Rome but that any Muslim who does not follow their strict Wahhabism will be declared an infidel and death will come knocking.

The shouting has started after the last exercise, a simulation of guerrilla warfare tactics in a city environment. The young man is being pushed by the training officer… the insults are raining down on him. The other young fighters first huddle in a group, one moves forward, bold and angry. He spits on the ground in disgust at the man whom he no longer considers his brother. The frenzy starts, more shouting, more spitting until the trainer takes his gun and shouts at the ground in front of the young man with a single instruction.

Run…

Anger has ripped through Henry like a wildfire. The screams inside the maze of streets are inhuman. Wasim grabs Henry's shoulder. There is nothing they can do.

Another hand fell on his shoulder, bringing him in a flash to the here and now.

"I am taking you to Raqqa… Abu Bakr al-Baghdadi wants to meet you."

* * *

Steve Harris burst into Vauxhall Cross. He swerved around his colleagues without apology. The lifts were full and he waited for one he could get into, fist clenched on the frame. He ran down the corridor and flung open the RED HAWK Control Room door.

"Are they…" He couldn't finish his sentence.

Amina waited to respond, turning away from her desk slowly. "No… they're on the move. They've separated them." Her face like thunder.

"What the fuck happened? Who took Henry?"

"The big man… al-Haddawi."

"Did he shoot anybody?"

"I would have said… no, just a bit of extra testosterone to burn. Intimidation… all that good beardo stuff."

The screen was showing satellite images. "I thought you had requested Reaper drone access?"

"I asked them to stop. Those can easily be spotted at 30,000 feet."

Amina had returned to her monitors.

"Are they going to Raqqa?"

"Looks like it."

"Anything else?"

"Get your bloody phone charged so I don't lose you in the middle of one of the most dangerous times in the op."

"Sorry… forgot my charger."

"That's so lame… you're working for bloody MI6 for Christ's sake." Amina suppressed a smile.

"Don't rub it in…" Harris rolled his eyes. "What's the other news?"

"More chatter about Mattie Colmore."

"Bugger… not my day."

"Doesn't look like it. You'd better charge your phone before you call the Reuters analyst."

Chapter Eight

The sun that had decided to make an appearance made the City streets much warmer. James removed his jacket and slung it over his left shoulder. City workers had not yet reached the street in droves around the Royal Exchange or the Bank of England.

James stopped at a set of traffic lights and waited for a moment, then changed his mind. He could walk up Threadneedle Street instead and cross at the top of the street, no need to wait for the green light. The City's heart, with its imposing buildings and narrow lanes, had taken time to feel like home. It looked too impregnable, too dense, the perfect place for a sniper to strike.

He shook his head to dispel the thought. Leadenhall Market was only a few minutes away. The old architecture, highly decorated and painted in bright red and gold felt solid and welcoming. James avoided the pavements and stepped onto the cobbled stones. He lifted his head. The sun coming through the spectacular square dome at the centre of the market almost blinded him. The history of the place had interested James when he first discovered it. Built in the 14th century, it had always been a market, eventually becoming the City granary. The famous fire of London in 1666 almost completely destroyed it. It was rebuilt as a market to house fishmongers and butchers. Today only one butcher remained in the central alley, all the other stalls turned into bistros, cafés and shops.

James arrived in front of the Lamb Tavern almost without noticing. He was one of the first customers. In less than 30 minutes' time the market would be teeming with people. A young woman in a sober black dress welcomed him. Had he made a reservation? Yes, he had. Would he like to go to the bar or the table? The table, please.

They climbed a flight of stairs, creaky and well worn. The odour of beer floated in the air as he ascended, replaced by the smell of cooking that made him want to check the menu for his favourite dish. The restaurant advertised *Great Seasonal British Food*.

If the meeting with Steve Jackson yielded no result at least he would enjoy a proper lunch of Angus steak and triple-cooked chips.

The head waitress pointed out a table for two, situated in the middle of the room. James stopped and looked around. He moved to another table, one that gave him the vantage point he was looking for, a good view of the market alleys, the staircase and its landing. Much could be gleaned from observing a man preparing to enter a meeting or walking into a room, unaware of being watched.

11.50am. James pulled out a chair noiselessly and waited for his guest to arrive. He took out his Blackberry, checking there was no last-minute crisis back at base. He stopped paying attention to it but kept holding it loosely in his hand, thinking it better to appear absorbed than expectant. James turned his attention to the market entrance.

* * *

The shop offered a variety of large, small, expensive or affordable pens. Steve Harris had been browsing through its selection when James Radlett arrived. The tall shelf holding stationery and other accessories provided an unexpected shelter. James would have had to look right into the shop to notice him.

He hadn't.

Harris smiled. James had arrived a good 15 minutes earlier, presumably choosing the right table, the best angle from which to observe his guest's entrance.

Once a spook…

Harris put down the pen he had been fingering for the past few minutes and bought a large pencil rubber in the shape of a London bus. The shopkeeper looked disappointed, hoping that the Montblanc Harris had been inspecting would take his fancy. Harris pocketed the item. He would give it to Amina on his return to base... something to fuel her fighting spirit... *Is that the best you could do?*

An enjoyable tease.

Harris walked through the door of the shop as James disappeared into the pub. He retraced his steps along the pavement, crossed the cobbled stone lane and moved to a spot a few yards away from the market entrance. If James had chosen a table at the window, he would see him arrive... as expected. At 11.57am Harris set foot into Leadenhall Market, again, and walked into the Lamb Tavern for a lunch he was eager to have. If the meeting with James did not go well at least he would enjoy a good lunch of Angus steak and triple-cooked chips.

* * *

The door of the Humvee had been left open. The tall man who had fired a gun just a foot away from him and then laughed, asked him to follow. He was now speaking to Henry in Arabic and Henry responded in short yet fluent sentences. Between the two front seats a raft of electronic equipment had been installed. Henry climbed into the back and waited. The rear of the Humvee was packed with jerrycans and two large boxes containing armament. He heard the man give instructions to one of the fighters who seemed to be the leader of the pack of trucks. Wasim had already joined the convoy with the pick-up. The tall man would deal with its occupants once they reached Raqqa.

He finally climbed inside the armoured vehicle. The two men who had advanced first joined them; one jumped into the driver's seat. He waited until the first Humvee had started its engine and followed. He tapped on one of the screens installed next to his seat and an image of the terrain materialised. A second screen was activated showing the best route to their destination. Henry failed to hide his surprise.

"We can tap into international satellites to give us our geo-position as well as ground imagery." His English was heavily accented yet fluent.

"Impressive." Henry nodded.

The convoy was on the move. The tall man handed Henry a bottle of water, opened one for himself and finished it in a few gulps.

"Abu Maeraka tells us you want to join our fight."

"I do." Henry's lowered his voice a few tones, his baritone reaching bass notes for effect, serious and focused. He had hoped his recent actions would make this clear: escaping from Belmarsh prison, the most secure in the UK, taking months to reach Iraq including time in ISIL's training camp, was, in his view, a good indication. He was not visiting the country on a tourist visa.

The man sat back and Henry waited. He racked his brain. Was he expecting Henry to recognise him? He was senior and feared. Henry had known it the second he had reached his men near the old truck, noticing the slight recoil under his gaze, the concern that they might not have carried out his orders to the letter.

The long face, the expected untrimmed beard, the smile that uncovered a perfect row of teeth and sharp incisors and, more noticeably, his eyes, often moving upwards to invoke the heavens, yet devoid of humanity... The name finally came to Henry.

"I am Commander Kasim al-Haddawi," he said turning towards Henry. "I have been sent by Abu Bakr al-Baghdadi."

"Abu Maeraka spoke about you a great deal." A small lie to stroke the man's ego might not go amiss... MI6 certainly had a lot to say about him though.

"Your Arabic is much better than I expected."

"Thank you." Henry dropped his head a little, an appreciative yet unassuming response.

"He also said you had managed to organise the finances of the IRA for many years without leaving any trace. I want to know how you did it... and what made it so successful."

Henry nodded. He had prepared for this moment for months. Time to live up to his reputation as the number one man in complex financial structures.

Henry did not need a flip chart or the usual 200-page PowerPoint presentation. He had been carrying the details of these intricate corporate structures in his mind for years. His description was factual, omitting unnecessary embellishments or boastfulness. He wanted to be clear and he was.

The multi-tier company and fund framework that protected the

74

cash the IRA received from generous donors in Ireland and Irish communities in the UK, the US and further afield had survived countless attempts at unravelling it.

Al-Haddawi smiled faintly… the great nations of the West could finance terrorism too.

Henry explained the level of protection he had used, including nominee accounts, companies registered in fiscal havens or countries that did not disclose vital corporate details such as share ownership… It flowed effortlessly. Whatever al-Haddawi had expected, Henry knew he would impress once he had the opportunity to describe the intricacies of his well-honed system. He had been, after all, one of the most successful financiers in the City of London and none of his schemes had ever failed.

The Commander asked pertinent questions. He had thought about it or discussed it with someone in the know. Still, his ability to grasp so quickly a raft of new, more detailed information, impressed Henry. He had a nimble intellect capable of integrating strategic and tactical aspects of a complex area of which he appeared to have no direct experience, dangerously focused.

Or, had they found someone just as clever as he was? The old Henry would have dismissed the idea immediately. He had after all been the best in his field. However, the past tense rattled him. Almost five years away from the front line of investment banking and innovation felt an eternity. Henry's throat had gone dry; he took a sip of water. In the back of this Humvee that was taking him to Raqqa, there was no space for doubt.

Al-Haddawi paused. His eyes had not left Henry since he had taken his seat next to him.

"So why were you caught?"

Henry closed the water bottle tight and dropped it into the side pocket of the vehicle door. Anything to gain a few moments before he spoke about a wound that might never heal.

"I was betrayed." Henry had not expected to be spared during his interrogation, but the words felt like dust in his mouth.

Betrayed by his oldest and best friend. He had understood why. Presented with the impossible choice between his brother's life and

Henry's future, Liam had chosen his brother. Henry had accepted Liam's decision. But it did not diminish the torment it had caused.

Henry finished his story in a few sentences. There was not much to say after that. He had not had to disguise his disappointment; on the contrary. He hoped this would be seen by the ISIL leader as a convincing motive to join.

"Forgiveness is sweet, but revenge is sweeter," the Commander smiled.

* * *

The choice of pub as old and reliable as the Lamb Tavern had worked well. James Radlett was making a conscious statement with this choice. It reflected the type of man he was – straightforward, reliable, no nonsense and yet appreciative of quality. Harris had composed himself as he climbed the stairs to create the impression he had wanted as he emerged onto the landing. Openness, a touch of eagerness, an air of confidence – the whole to be served with a dash of friendliness. That should set Harris on a good footing. James was scrolling through his emails, keeping an eye out for the man he was expecting. He stood up with a nod of the head… perfectly rehearsed and equally friendly. It seemed they had gone to the same school.

Good tactic, good choice of table and good attitude… James had forgotten none of his former training.

They shook hands, sat down, exchanged a few banalities about the weather and the beginning of the rugby season. Food was ordered.

Angus steak, triple-cooked fries, times two.

"We didn't have much time to speak about your current situation." Harris was tucking into his meat with appetite. "I gather you have a pretty senior position at GL?"

"It is an excellent team… although a lot of its success is based on the work of its previous boss."

Harris looked puzzled, convincingly so. He stopped himself from asking who it was. Then he recalled his own advice… no bullshit. "You mean Henry Crowne."

James squirmed a little. Perhaps he had not expected Harris to be so forthright, or to remember that Henry Crowne had once led his team at GL. "I did some digging around before I came. I hope you don't mind," Harris offered with a smile. "Tell me about Crowne. Why did you work for him?"

* * *

They had been journeying for over two hours. Al-Haddawi had listened to Henry, prodding him astutely when he felt Henry was being vague, and absorbing all the details of Henry's former life.

Al-Haddawi returned to the connection Henry had made with Abu Maeraka in Belmarsh. He could not quite believe Maeraka had approached Henry first. It rankled the commander. He came back at it, revisited the issue several times, asking the question differently and always receiving the same answer.

"He approached me in Belmarsh library... we started talking about books."

"How very educated... perhaps too educated." Al-Haddawi's eyes drilled into Henry.

"His *education* is what enables Abu Maeraka to recruit so many new followers in prison."

Al-Haddawi changed tack. He pushed Henry again on why he had joined the IRA, forcing him to speak about his father. Henry's father had joined the cause and died for it, young...

"Would your father be proud?" The question hit Henry in the gut. He had never considered it before. Al-Haddawi sat back a little. He had just scored a point and inflicted pain... a pleasant feeling.

"Who knows... he died when I was very young. I hardly knew him. But at least I honoured his memory." Henry locked eyes with al-Haddawi, challenging the side of him that refused to be cowed by anyone. He too could be dangerous. Al-Haddawi's nostrils flared a little. He had not expected such provocation.

Al-Haddawi abruptly stopped the conversation. He made a request for food and his aides handed over some khoubz and shanklish dried cheese, covered in Aleppo peppers. They would not be stopping until they had reached ISIL's headquarters. They ate in silence, al-Haddawi

scrolling though the messages he had received on his smartphone...
He was an important, busy man. Henry had not been allowed a device.
He certainly had none in Belmarsh and had accepted the embargo.

The convoy had picked up speed as the roads on which they were
now driving had improved. Henry was not ready for the sudden change
in the landscape when it came, lush green fields spread on each side of
the Humvee, a patchwork of different crops that grew enough to feed
people beyond the immediate area. In an arid country like Syria, Raqqa
and its surrounding land was priceless. It was no surprise that ISIL had
targeted the city and established its HQ there. The vehicles reached
another hill, beyond which nature's cornucopia retreated and the lush
green of plant life became sparse.

The Humvee gradually slowed down. They had come to the
first checkpoint indicating that Raqqa was now close. Henry noticed
the same outfit on the fighter who manned the post: either black
or camouflage trousers, but always a black shirt and a black scarf
wound around the head. There was no doubt in Henry's mind that
al-Baghdadi was not only building an army, he was building a new
brand of jihadists.

Some more trucks bearing the ISIL flag and a couple of armoured
vehicles appeared as they approached Raqqa. Henry's convoy slowed
down for the final checkpoint before they entered the city. On the
surface, Raqqa's streets felt surprisingly calm. White-painted buildings
of modern architecture, constructions that were only a few storeys
high, broad avenues planted with large evergreen trees providing much
needed shade. Henry had seen it much worse in Belfast. The cars on
the streets were driven by civilians, with numerous ISIL trucks joining
them. Perhaps al-Baghdadi's group had not yet dug its claws too deep
into the belly of the city. Few people were on the street, though at 2pm,
with the sun now high in the sky, they would have been foolish to be.
On the first junction they encountered, Henry noticed a large hoarding
had been covered in black paint and large Arabic letters painted over it
in white, erasing the former name of the street.

"We no longer tolerate names written in English," al-Haddawi
commented.

Their vehicle turned left into a smaller avenue, then left again.

78

Fifteen minutes later the Humvee drove into the driveway of a modern hotel. It could have been a Hilton or a Sheraton. Today, however, the words Islamic State of Iraq and the Levant had replaced the original name and Henry doubted the room service would be as impeccable as under the previous management.

"You will stay here for the time being." Al-Haddawi was already giving orders to his aides.

Henry nodded. He was about to leave the armoured vehicle but stopped. "What about the woman?"

"What about her?" Al-Haddawi looked puzzled. She was only a woman.

"She is a valuable asset, a journalist for the *Sunday Times* in London."

"The UK does not pay ransom for hostages." Al-Haddawi had turned his muscled body towards Henry.

"Perhaps not, but others might… for a price. I can perhaps be of help in finding the value of that price." Henry's voice was level… no emotions. This was business.

"Already keen to write a deal?" The other man grinned but his eyes were of steel.

Henry leaned back into his seat. He would not be pushed around so easily. "Is it not the idea… the reason why Abu Bakr al-Baghdadi wants me here?"

"Fine." Al-Haddawi clenched and released a fist. "I'll see she is treated as a valuable asset."

"Good." Henry left the car and walked to where Wasim and Ali were already waiting, beside the old battered truck.

Al-Haddawi gave more orders.

"Get into the hotel. I'll follow shortly." Henry waited a short moment and lifted the tarp away from the back of the truck. Mattie's dark shape had moved forward at the sound of his voice.

"What's happening?" Her voice muffled by the niqab.

"Can't give you the details but don't do anything stupid."

She was about to respond.

"Trust me," was all Henry had time to say before a man appeared at his elbow. "If anything happens to her, you'll regret it." Henry's Arabic delivered the message perfectly. His cold stare followed Mattie and her new guard until she resumed her position at the back the truck. The man looked back. Henry meant business and he understood it.

Henry grabbed his rucksack from the boot and slowly ascended the large steps that once had belonged to a five-star hotel.

* * *

James put down his knife and fork and wiped his mouth elegantly with the linen napkin. "Why is this so important?"

Steve cocked his head and gave James a sideways look. "Seriously? You were working for one of the most brilliant financiers in the City who turned out to be IRA... and you ask why I ask?"

James crossed his hands in front of his face, elbows on the table. He was torn. Torn between the desire to tell Steve to get lost... it was almost five years ago... and the desire to present his own side of the story... reiterating that he had *No God Damn Idea... officially.*

Steve read the situation.

"You can't expect never to be asked that question again, no matter how annoying it is for you." Steve's sounded conciliatory and he was. The Crowne story was too big to be ignored by anyone who would either offer or facilitate a new job – any interviewer worth their salt would broach the subject.

James straightened back in his chair, picked up his knife and fork, cut a piece of the excellent steak and savoured it.

"You're right of course... I can't expect people to simply remember what I said in court five years ago."

Steve nodded encouragingly. He salted his chips again, ate a couple, waiting for James to gather his thoughts.

"I was an unconventional choice for H... I mean Henry." James's face expressed disappointment. He had been close to his boss.

"Because of your retraining after you left the army."

"That's right."

"He gave you a chance."

"He did... a pretty big chance." James took a sip of water. "There were almost a dozen people applying for the job, better qualified, MBAs, top business schools."

80

"I can imagine."

"I'm not sure you can unless you know the environment well."

"I think I know enough." Not a defensive statement. Steve smiled. He did understand.

"It was a choice that few expected. His boss didn't like it, HR didn't like it and yet he stuck with it."

"He even promoted you after less than two years."

"Yes, he did… another battle with his boss and HR to do so…"

Steve simply nodded. "So, people inferred that you had turned a blind eye to his terrorist connections."

"They did, and I get it… but…"

"You knew nothing about it… I believe you," Steve interrupted.

"Just like that?" James's eyes crossed Steve's briefly.

"You're a former intelligence officer. You've been trained to detect people like Crowne… If you had had an inkling you would have protected yourself better for a start. I also doubt whether you would have joined in any case the very people you fought against in the army just because they offered you a job… It doesn't fit your profile."

"How do you know my…" James did not finish his sentence. The truth had just dawned on him. His jaw tensed. Before he could erupt at the thought of having been played, Harris lifted his hand. No bullshit.

"I'm going to be straight with you." Harris picked up another chip. James hesitated.

"I am offering you a chance to re-join the British intelligence service. I think you miss it, and you'll be good at the work in the same way you were before."

"Despite the fact that I didn't spot Henry?" James eyes narrowed, a faint smile on his face.

"No one spotted Henry… we had a file on him and yet zip, nada, nothing… my colleagues at MI5 are very sore about that."

"You had a file on Henry?"

"Yep… but one thing at a time."

James put his hands up.

"OK, sorry. I know the rules… but you must give me something. Why me and why now?"

"Very good questions of course."

"And…"

"You know how the recruitment works."

"I have been there before… but you've done a lot of due diligence already. Am I correct?" James tucked into his steak again; a couple of bites and it was finished. "You need me." He wiped his mouth.

Harris smiled a you-got-me smile.

"We do."

Chapter Nine

The truck moved slowly to start with. Whoever the driver was, he was fighting a losing battle with the gearbox. She could hear the grinding noise of the transmission rod being forced into action. Mattie slumped back against the metal frame of the vehicle. When Wasim had called Ali and lifted the heavy cover of the pick-up, she had hoped she could follow. A foolish hope, she knew. Wasim had slowly shaken his head. She could not quite read his expression, his face hidden by the shadow of the oilcloth and the shemagh around his face. Ali had stopped, looking at her without knowing what to say. She had shushed him away.

"Adhhab… go." She moved her head towards the opening that Wasim had created. He could not be seen to be reluctantly leaving her behind. She was kafir. She was a woman.

Henry words still swam in her head… *trust me*. He was different… that she could tell and his eyes looked… familiar. But why would he risk his life for her?

Mattie focused on keeping track of where they were heading. She had known Raqqa before the jihadists took over. An ancient city, that had emerged around 300BC if she recalled correctly. No doubt its Hellenistic and Byzantine past would not be relevant to a group like ISIL. Raqqa had once been a place where nomadic tribes and clans had settled, a diverse background that gave it its cultural richness. That mixed city was going to suffer terribly under its new ruler. Since the beginning of 2014, when ISIL captured Raqqa from the Syrian opposition forces, Mattie had received information from reliable sources that ISIL had started cleansing the city systematically. It had started by identifying and executing the quiet pro-Assad and Syrian opposition supporters alike, destroying at the same time all Shia mosques and Christian churches.

The truck picked up speed. She braced herself for another long journey. She touched her injured arm gingerly. The dressing Ali had changed when they were on their way to Raqqa would need to be refreshed tonight. But she doubted priority would be given to a foreign woman if medication and bandages were in short supply.

The vehicle veered abruptly, almost throwing her off the rickety bench where she sat. It jumped over a sharp ridge that made the whole structure shudder and come to a sudden stop. The brakes were pulled firmly, wincing with a screech. They had been driving for a little more than 15 minutes. She could almost certainly find her way back to the hotel.

The heavy cover was lifted and the small man who had driven the truck jerked his head, indicating that she should follow him. She made sure her face was properly covered and moved cautiously towards the opening. She gathered her heavy robe around her shins and managed to leave the truck without falling. The fighter was already impatiently waiting at the door of an apartment block.

She moved silently through the door. The smell of food and cleaning products welcomed her, a strange mix that Mattie could not quite make out. The man shrugged his head towards the stairs. They climbed to the second floor of what seemed a luxurious building. It was well maintained, with marble flooring and immaculate white-painted walls. They reached a spacious landing. The man removed his shoes, moved forwards towards one of the two main doors and knocked. The door opened after a few seconds. They had been expected. A slender woman in full niqab opened.

Mattie stepped into the type of environment she had not seen since she had left London a few weeks ago. Expensive marble had been used not only for the entrance but for the flooring of the apartment, the deep silk carpets spread over the ground looked expensive. Such opulence contrasted strangely with the emptiness of the built-in shelves around the room, and the sadness of their look. The place had no doubt been owned by a Christian or Shia family. Mattie simply hoped that they had had time to flee before ISIL came knocking at their door.

The rustling of fabric came from behind her. Another woman appeared from within the apartment. Mattie turned around to face her new jailors. The woman who had just arrived lowered her veil. Her face was plump and plain. No make-up and no smile either. She ran her eyes over Mattie. She was making a judgement, but Mattie did not understand of what, the coldness of her glance unsettling.

"Clean her up," was all she said. She kept looking at Mattie until she disappeared into the corridor, led by the woman who had opened the door. She too dropped her niqab to reveal a young, surprisingly beautiful face... no make-up needed there... large brown eyes, long lashes and perfectly shaped lips. A frightening thought dawned on Mattie. She hesitated but the young woman smiled and opened the door to an elegant bathroom. For now, Mattie needed to wash and have her wound dressed with proper bandages. The question of what came next could wait.

* * *

One of his burner phones had kept buzzing during the lunch. Harris had felt the repeated insect droning in his jacket inner pocket. He walked down Cornhill towards Bank Tube station and dialled the number back. His call was answered after the second ring...

Promising.

"News for me?" Harris was almost pleasant.

The man on the other side of the conversation wasn't. "If I call it means I have."

"I'll be back at The Cross in 30 minutes, will call you from there." Harris didn't care if Brett wasn't in the mood as long as his intel was worth it.

"I'm at the club." Brett softened a little.

"Tempting as it is, I need to be back at the ranch asap. Will call."

Harris pocketed his phone and took the stairs that led to the long corridors of Bank Station. Brett Allner-Smith was due to meet some of his Middle Eastern contacts who regularly sold him antiquities stolen from war-torn countries. Iraq had been a treasure trove. Syria seemed to be going the same way and Brett might provide Harris with a new way into ISIL.

As soon as he had cleared security at Vauxhall Cross, Harris found an empty room on the ground floor and called Brett.

"What's the latest from your Middle Eastern clients then?"

"They're not my clients... they're my suppliers." Brett sounded terribly proper.

"Beg your pardon, of course..." Harris could indulge Brett's punctiliousness.

"Do you want the intel I have or not?"

"Shoot." Harris had pulled out a chair and sat down.

"A number of high-quality artefacts are coming on the market... not from the usual providers."

"You mean Al-Qaeda?"

"That's right... These new people are rather amazing... pieces straight from the top sites in Iraq. Even after the level of extraction during the Iraq war they go where no one else has dared go. And now from Syria as well."

"I thought your Al-Qaeda contacts were pretty good at sourcing quality stuff?" This was not a trick question. Harris was genuinely intrigued.

"I do have the best contacts, true... but this new lot is on another level... nothing stops them."

"You're not trying to sell me a piece, are you?"

Brett grumbled some inaudible insult.

"What's so spectacular about these items then?"

"Some pieces come from Nimrud, Assyrian... King Ashurbanipal II, cuneiform tablets, manuscripts – I mean manuscripts of that era – and ancient gold jewellery of course."

Harris remained silent.

"You don't believe me?"

"To state the obvious, I only deal in current data, perhaps cold war stuff at a push, but certainly not manuscripts that predate our Lord JC."

"Still… this king was of immense importance, the last great king of Assyria… he built the first library ever known to man, a collection of over 30,000 clay tablets…"

"Brett, I don't need a lecture on ancient history… I'll take your word for it."

"What I'm trying to say is that this new terrorist group will make a lot of money when they sell these pieces on the black market."

"They are beefing up their war chest. How much do you think that stuff will fetch?"

A sigh of exasperation. "That stuff as you call it is extremely rare… tens of millions. The pieces are museum quality."

"Where are the buyers… your clients."

Brett coughed lightly. "Europe mainly… and before you tell me I shouldn't sell these, if it's not me…"

"It'll be someone else… I get that. The reason why you are not behind bars and working for HM's intelligence service instead."

"Always happy to help."

"Do these new guys trust you?"

"Why should they not? I deliver and I pay on time…"

"You sure?"

"Are you worried for me?"

"Always… wouldn't want to lose one of my best assets… bad for the profile and the reputation."

Brett's silence showed Harris he had scored as he wanted… nothing was more irresistible than being called best asset by MI6.

"What's next?"

"I have a call with their top negotiator tomorrow. I'll keep you posted."

"Will you be asked to go over there, do you think?"

"I think this time I'll rely on photographs to appraise the goods and if they want to meet in person it won't be in Syria or Iraq."

"Good call." At least for the moment. Harris might need Brett to become more involved but why make him aware of that now? A return ticket to Baghdad was no guarantee that the holder would ever be able to use it for the London leg back.

There were camp beds everywhere. The once luxurious entrance hall and comfortable waiting lounge had been transformed into a dormitory for young jihadists.

The rank smell of bodies in need of a proper wash combined with that of cooked food did not bother Henry as it once would have. Most of the camp beds were empty but the few fighters who were there did not bother to stop what they were doing when Henry, Wasim and Ali entered. Two men at the far end of the lounge near the large French windows that opened onto a wide terrace were sitting on their beds, prayer beads in hand. Their bandages looked new; two fighters freshly returned from combat.

A small man, thin and dishevelled, walked towards them. His eyes, deeply set in his skull, darted around the room. He expected to be jumped on at any moment. He told Wasim he had been instructed to show them to their room. His scruffy attire seemed to have once been a hotel uniform, but it had not been pressed for a while and it was hard to read the logo that might have revealed the hotel's name.

He handed Wasim and Henry a key. But when Ali tried to follow, he stopped him. "You're going somewhere else."

Henry was about to protest. Wasim cut him short. "Where are you putting him?"

"With the others, here downstairs." The man hesitated. Did he not understand the instruction correctly?

"We'll come and fetch you." Ali's face looked hopeful again.

Henry and Wasim reached their floor where everything changed. This floor must have been reserved for senior executives. The carpet was deep and clean. The wall bore no traces of grime. The small man showed them to their door and scuttled off. When the door closed Wasim signalled with his fingers closed together in a slicing throat move to keep silent. He pointed to the phone, the wall sockets, the ventilation and air conditioning vent.

Henry nodded. They were about to go through the room and do what all good spooks did... a bit of debugging. Henry doubted they would be spied on just yet, but he was after all still an infidel... a man who should never be trusted.

Both Henry and Wasim stood perfectly still… nothing… not the faintest noise.

They started moving through the room in opposite directions, methodically, stopping when they thought they heard something. Still no buzz or clicks that might betray the presence of surveillance equipment.

Henry opened the wardrobe carefully and moved his hand inside the frame, underneath the shelves.

Wasim had reached the far end of the room. Standing on a chair he took out his multipurpose pocket knife and unscrewed the bolts of the smoke detector, removing it from its base on the ceiling. He inspected it thoroughly, using the torch of his smartphone.

Still nothing…

Henry moved to the phone that lay on one of the bedside tables, giving it the same treatment Wasim had to the smoke alarm. Its innards revealed nothing suspicious.

Wasim moved to the lamps. Henry attacked the electrical sockets.

They finally moved once more around the room, looking for inconspicuous objects that might hide a camera. The room was bare, which would have been otherwise disappointing for a hotel of this standing, but welcome under the circumstances. It limited the number of objects that could be used to hide a camera… no cuddly teddy bear with a beady eye.

"Clear." Henry turned to Wasim.

"Clear." Wasim nodded.

They each moved to a bed and threw their rucksacks over the mattresses.

Wasim took his laptop out and booted it up. He checked the new hard drive he had installed a few days ago was still showing the right web history for the months he had been travelling. He switched to the hard drive he would soon destroy. It was time to connect one last time to the site he was using to message London.

Henry walked over to the large sliding doors, opening them slowly in a small controlled push. He stepped onto a large terrace, walked to the end and looked at the view below. The room was situated at the side of the building; trees had been planted around the hotel, providing some welcome shade in the hottest months. Beyond the trees, Henry saw the city sprawling in all directions, white buildings after white buildings, modern for the most part. The architecture was unmistakably Middle Eastern… flat roofs, flat façades, balconies on most floors. Satellites and air conditioning units everywhere.

Henry moved back towards the sliding doors and waited. The heat of the day was starting to subside; soon the terrace and its shade would be a perfect place to sit. The room had passed the test, but the terrace was a better option to discuss sensitive matters.

Wasim joined him in the open, closing the sliding doors behind him.

"I wish I could have a cigarette." His voice low and tired.

"Thought you'd given up when you started your new… assignment." Henry had moved a couple of chairs he had found on the terrace to where a small breeze had started to blow.

"Yep… but it doesn't mean I don't miss it sometimes."

Wasim did what Henry had just done … moved to the edge of the balustrade and surveyed their surroundings.

"Not bad for a quick escape." Henry sat down.

"To go where exactly? We're in the middle of Raqqa, in the middle of Syria and smack bang at the centre of ISIL's territory."

"You're such a pessimist."

Wasim did not answer.

"I'm surprised they didn't separate us," Henry carried on.

"You must have done fine at your *interview* with al-Haddawi. Otherwise we wouldn't be staying in this hotel but in one of their detention camps, undergoing some pretty nasty interrogation." Wasim crossed his arms over his heavy chest.

"Just as well I know how to handle a pretty difficult client." Henry grinned.

Wasim shook his head. "Keep your bloody sense of humour to yourself." But the tone was not there and Wasim grinned back.

"I think I did do well… Haddawi knows I can deliver on the financial side, but I'm not sure he…" Henry grew serious, "…likes it."

"Why?" Wasim frowned.

"Not sure… perhaps because whoever I'm going to work for is a rival, or because he had someone else in mind…"

"What makes you say that?"

"Because it was more than a competency interview... he wanted to get under my skin pretty quickly."

Wasim paused to consider Henry's take on his conversation with Haddawi.

"Perhaps Maeraka is no friend of his either... competition is fierce despite these people praising brotherhood."

"What now?" Henry stretched his long arms above his head. Tiredness had started to creep in, and he was ready for a decent shower and a good night's sleep.

"We wait... although I wouldn't be surprised if they didn't send for you again today."

"I thought I'd passed the *interview*?" Henry stressed the word with air quotes.

"Did you ever get one of your big jobs based on one interview alone? You're not rested yet, and you think the first contact has gone well... which it has... you are much more vulnerable now. And the man who's about to rely on you to put together ISIL's financial structure knows that. The Treasurer, as he is known, is an unforgiving man."

Wasim's phone rang. He answered in a burst of short sentences, his head beckoning Henry towards the room.

Henry walked in after him. "How does it feel to be right?"

"Scary."

* * *

Computer screens were stacked up, arranged in groups on each desk and the people in front of them paid attention to their content with the intensity Henry had seen only on the trading floor. If he had not been in Raqqa, Henry would have sworn he had entered the trading room of a large multinational corporation. The young men, all wearing white crocheted skull caps and white kameez, did not notice the arrival of the two men. Only a short plump fellow turned his head and stopped the discussion he was having with one of the young men. There was curiosity in his eyes, a fleeting moment of intense suspicion, but he radiated above all immense confidence. This was The Treasurer.

91

On the back wall of the room they had entered Henry noticed a large map of the region, spreading from floor to ceiling. He recognised the symbols for oil wells, shocked by the number against which the ISIL flag had been pinned.

"It's only the beginning." The Treasurer noted Henry's gaze. "We already have control of 300 wells in Iraq and 40% of the production in Syria." His Arabic was softly spoken, measured and clear.

Henry nodded approvingly.

Outstanding.

Henry came closer to the map, looked at the location of the wells. His fingers traced a route from these to the closest port… Turkey seemed the most obvious choice to ensure the oil reached its destination. This meant a large number of trucks needed to cross the border.

"You're smuggling into Turkey on a large scale, right?" Henry spoke slowly, in his heavily accented yet fluent Arabic.

The Treasurer's face dropped for an instant and then regained its amiable composure. "True, why ask the question?"

"It's all about logistics… You need to have a large border with the country into which you smuggle to spread the risk of being caught and you need a seaport to ship the goods. It's either Iran… not convenient from Syria and probably less amenable too… or Turkey."

The podgy man nodded. The kafir was quick.

"How many barrels do you sell a day?"

"Eight thousand at least." Pride shone in his eyes. "And we are increasing production."

"Excellent… If I recall correctly a barrel of crude is worth a little more than $85. You must make a bit over $0.6m a day." Henry grabbed a pencil and piece of paper that were lying on an empty table so he could take notes.

"What do you do with the cash? Are you using the same route to repatriate it into ISIL territories?"

The Treasurer looked at Wasim, then Henry… why not indulge the newcomers' interest?

"That's what I am here for." Henry's voice had the business tone he would have used with any good client, factual, keen to show his knowledge of the subject they were discussing yet accommodating.

"Yes, we do." The Treasurer had yielded to his curiosity.

"That might not be ideal... perhaps you might consider routing it to countries that would allow you to use it more productively."

The Treasurer had pulled out a chair from the next table, sitting down comfortably without inviting either Henry or Wasim to do so. He was here to be impressed... and he was waiting. Wasim retreated a little, taking in the scene and any other information he could glean.

"We have started looking into this."

"Have you made a decision?"

"Not yet."

"Good... I'd recommend the UAE, Qatar and Cyprus. You should use the legal structures available on your doorstep so you can keep in close touch with the people who help you set them up, and pay them a visit if needed."

"That should also increase our access to other clients or suppliers..."

"Exactly right." Henry nodded. "Do you need armament or medical supplies?"

"It's a war."

"I see the armament and vehicles around Raqqa." Henry stopped writing. "You must have captured a lot of supply from Iraq, both US and British. So, my question is, do you need more guns, munitions? Much more efficient and much easier to access the suppliers from abroad, hence my suggestion."

The podgy man, The Treasurer did not impress easily but he did not quite know how to take Henry's bluntness ... How did he know?

Henry smiled. "I was once an IRA terrorist... I know what it takes."

* * *

The mobile was threatening to go to voicemail. Harris looked at his watch. He had received the news about the impending Reuters publication of their article about Mattie Colmore almost two hours ago. He was cutting it fine, although he was certain The Chief's office had placed a call to the head of the news agency as soon as he had told Sir John of their intention to publish.

A voice that seemed distant replied just before the final ring...
Kerry Murdock.

Harris introduced himself and the voice focused immediately on their conversation. "No need to call twice... I've got it. Although I'm not convinced this is the right thing to do."

"You mean getting MI6's chief to call your boss or divulging information about a potential abduction?"

"I'd say both." The voice had turned belligerent and stubborn. "And please... let's drop the pretence... we all know what's happened to Mattie Colmore."

"Are you at your desk?"

"No... I'm in the middle of Trafalgar Square, shouting all I know about this kidnapping to whoever wants to hear..." There was a silence and Harris almost fell for it.

"Very amusing... you're at your desk... that is good. It will avoid me having to send some agents to physically gag you."

"A treat?"

"I wouldn't dare."

"I'll respect the media embargo for as long as there's no chatter about her... if this changes and I think it's important for people to know the truth, I'll think again."

Harris was about to make the point that this was not the way a media blackout was meant to work, but the line had gone dead. He looked at his mobile in disbelief. Ms Murdock needed to be met in person.

Chapter Ten

"They are in Raqqa." Amina had returned to her desk in Operation RED HAWK Control Room.

"How much imagery are we receiving from satellite surveillance?"

"They're good enough as long as we don't need to track them very closely."

Harris rolled his eyes... was that not the idea?

"It's not what you want to hear, but we can no longer rely on drone surveillance... it's too risky... I'd rather concentrate on the chatter Ahmed is following on social media."

"Whether they mention Henry's arrival?"

"Or mention the hostages." Amina pulled her chair out from underneath her desk and swirled it on its central axis so that it faced Harris's desk.

"What's on your mind?"

"We haven't heard anything more about Mattie Colmore... neither in the various chat rooms nor the messaging systems we monitor."

"Too early... they've just arrived. ISIL is deciding what they intend to do."

"Would they execute a female hostage?" A blunt but relevant question.

"Not that I know of, but now that ISIL has severed its links with Al-Qaeda, it's a young organisation going it alone and they need to show everyone they're the ultimate radicals."

"The Americans have said they have hostages of their own already and are making little progress." Amina had rolled her chair across the carpeted floor until she was almost sitting next to him.

"I'm not sure the Yanks are going to volunteer much anyway."

"They don't pay ransom either and they can't be seen to compromise on that…" Amina hesitated.

"C'mon, spit it out." Harris patted the back of her chair.

"Don't you have a contact at the CIA you could get info from… just so we know what to look out for, to anticipate…?"

"You mean Jack. I suppose I could ask, but kidnappings are also covered by the FBI."

"Because they involve American citizens?"

"Yup… and the two agencies are not known to work that well together."

"Unlike the UK of course, where everyone shares information no matter what." Amina raised her eyebrows and cocked her head.

"You're so cynical sometimes."

"I'm always cynical when it comes to high stakes like this one… and when we have assets on the ground."

"And patronising too… fine, I'll speak to Jack."

"Seriously, what happens to her when RED HAWK is over?"

"One step at a time… Henry has something in mind beyond bringing back a hostage to Raqqa."

"As long as she doesn't blow his cover."

"It's something to consider, I agree, but Henry's not stupid. He's going to try the ransom route first, then come up with another option. He needs to learn to read these people first before he can decide what to do."

"Let's hope Crowne's not going to bite off more than he can chew."

Harris shrugged. "Why? I think his reading of the situation so far is good. He may slightly overstretch himself but that was always going to be the case."

"The UK will do what the US does, they won't let anyone offer to pay either."

"But Mattie Colmore is a slightly different proposition, isn't she?"

"You mean because of her father Harold Colmore? Yes, he's an MP, but as Tory as Tory goes."

96

"Still, she is his daughter."

"Correction, estranged daughter." Amina stabbed her finger on her desk. "And I have the impression their relationship is not ready to thaw anytime soon."

"Let me find out what Jack knows... but I'm not calling on any favours from these guys just yet." Harris had moved his computer mouse to bring the screens to life again. "Reuters was hard enough to keep quiet. And I'm going to need to have a face-to-face conversation with one of their pig-headed journalists. I don't want to discuss Mattie with the CIA just yet. If I come up with the info too soon, they'll smell a rat and there's no way I want them to know or even suspect we have some assets in Raqqa."

"Don't you trust Jack?"

"I do but the fewer people know about our guys on the ground the better. You know that, I know that... and Jack would do the same thing in my shoes."

Amina rolled her chair back to her desk.

"You know I'm right, don't you?" Harris pushed himself away from his desk.

"Fine... but this hostage story has added a layer of complexity to the operation and we need to take stock."

"Agreed, let Henry and Wasim do the evaluation on the ground... I know you're MOTHER but give your boys a bit of free rope."

"If something goes wrong..."

"My arse will be on the line. I am fully aware of that."

"And you're used to it."

"Yep." Harris checked a couple of emails, did not find what he wanted and got up. Time to let Amina brew a little and to check for fresh intel with the DATA OP Mid East Team.

He was at the door when his phone rang. Amina picked up the call and immediately waved her hand in the air to stop him disappearing.

"Yes, sir... I will tell him... right away."

The Chief wanted a word.

* * *

The young woman who had helped clean her wounds did not leave the bathroom when Mattie started showering. Mattie removed her clothes and dumped them on the ground. She did not do shy, having shared many journalist digs, mostly with men.

She did her best to wash off the grime, careful not to wet the fresh bandages. She turned away from the woman and let the lukewarm water run over her body, savouring the soothing effect it was having on her tired muscles. She had almost forgotten she was not alone, but any desire to intimidate her would not work. The bathroom door opened, and the older woman entered with a fresh abaya. She took her time picking up Mattie's old clothes, handing over the fresh garment to her colleague. Mattie looked over her shoulder a few times and went about her business of getting clean, unperturbed. She grabbed the large towel that hung from a hook next to the shower and wrapped it round her body.

"Is that for me?" she asked in Arabic, pointing at the black dress.

Try to engage – Mattie's best chance of staying alive was to make people see she was a person, not some entity that did not practise their religion.

"Thank you. That's very kind." Mattie's Arabic seemed to intimidate the younger woman. Mattie felt empathy and made a note to get to know the woman better. The older woman left the bathroom, no doubt to report on progress.

Mattie dressed promptly. The large robe smelled of cheap soap but at least it was clean. She fitted her niqab around and over her head, the young woman watching her, curious that she knew how to put on Muslim female clothing. Mattie looked into the mirror at the results of her efforts: apart from the blue-green eyes that were such a distinctive feature of her face, there was nothing left for others to see.

"I am Mattie… What is your name?"

The young woman hesitated. She looked in the direction of the door. "Gulan," she whispered.

Mattie nodded. "Is she waiting for us?"

Gulan closed her eyes; yes, she was.

Mattie ventured one more question. "Is this her house?" Gulan shook her head.

Mattie opened the door slowly. It would not be a good idea to cause trouble for someone she was trying to befriend. Gulan tied her mask over her face whispering hurriedly. "We are slaves of Umm Sayyaf."

The old woman had prepared food. Her droopy cheeks, emphasised by her tightly bound scarf, made her resemble a large hamster. Mattie had moved into the main lounge and looked around to find a seat. The woman shooed her towards the far side where a few sofas had been arranged in a small square. There was already some khoubz, hummus and tea set out on a low table. Mattie thanked her and ate in silence, lifting her veil each time to take each mouthful or sip of her tea. She had not been told she could remove it and would play along for the time being. No need to upset anyone.

She was soon glad of her decision. The door of the apartment opened unexpectedly and the same man who had delivered her there entered. He looked around and seemed satisfied. Mattie noticed that the younger woman had made sure her veil was covering her face properly but the other hadn't. He had to be a close relative of hers... a son or brother. He made a sign, sharp and impatient, summoning Mattie to follow, a gesture that might as well have been directed to an animal. There were no words, no need either. She quickly finished her tea and moved towards him.

The young woman gave her a glance that told Mattie all she needed to know: sadness, concern and above all fear.

* * *

A tattered old Suzuki pick-up was waiting for them. The man took the front seat and Mattie sat at the back. They started the journey towards the north. Mattie turned her head towards the window, her field of vision greatly reduced by the cloth of the niqab. She wondered whether the rumours that had been circulating about what living under the new terror group was like in Raqqa were true. A few cars were on the road. The streets looked well maintained and bore no signs of fighting. White apartment blocks had not yet suffered from conflicts the way other cities in the Middle East had, no crumbling buildings, entire walls taken down by rockets and sharp incisions of shrapnel and bullets. A few men were walking along the pavements, all dressed in long white robes, a shemagh or taqiyah on their heads. Mattie did not expect to see any women on the street, even in groups, and there were none.

The car picked up speed and arrived at a large roundabout. The traffic was light but still there was some. Raqqa was starting to feel the pressure of a strict application of Islamic rule. She spotted a couple of cars on which the ISIL flag had been painted and the recognisable Arabic words that expressed its creed inscribed – *There is no god but Allah. Mohamed is the messenger of Allah.* The cars had stopped a motorcycle. Its driver was standing in the middle of a group of five men. He held his helmet in his hands in front of him, almost as protection. Mattie couldn't see his face, but his body spoke volumes, shoulders slumped, head bent forward. He was terrified. The fighters were shouting, laughing... pushing him around.

And then it started. One of the fighters took a stick out of one of the cars and hit the man with brutal force across the chest. It was the start of savage attack.

The man was now on the ground, curled up in a ball. Mattie turned around to see what happened next. The fighters were kicking him with their heavy boots. She couldn't help but let out a small cry.

"This is what happens to those who break Allah's law," the driver said to her, his voice sanctimonious and triumphant.

"What has he done?"

There was no reply. Mattie gritted her teeth. The most abhorrent of actions, abuse of power, would be rife in ISIL-dominated Raqqa.

The car slowed down after a few minutes. They had arrived, it seemed.

Mattie moved her body forward towards the door, her head cocked against the window. She recognised the place, not that she had ever visited it before. But the sports stadium looked like any other in the world: large, imposing, a tribute to men's achievement and ego. The white walls had suffered, unlike the place she had come from; fighting must have taken place there. At regular intervals, carved gates shaped in the typical pointed Arabic style had been positioned to provide multiple entrances. The car stopped and a couple of fighters, Kalashnikovs at the ready, moved towards them. A few words were exchanged, and they allowed the vehicle to enter. The driver parked the car, got out and, without waiting for her, set foot in a large entrance hall. It had been stripped bare of any features expected to be found there, no ticket booths or turnstiles, no logos or vending machines. These had been ripped from the ground roughly, leaving gaping holes in the floor.

Mattie followed the man towards a staircase that turned on itself, endlessly dropping downward.

She stopped at the top, her body rocking slowly at the edge of the first step. A fist tightened around her stomach and a small ripple of fear coursed down her spine. She turned around. Behind her she could still see the brightness of the air, the somewhat cloudy sky, through open doors. The desire to run gripped her.

The man had stopped, waiting. It would be so easy to catch her… Mattie ensconced in her abaya, he in his army fatigues. She might cover a short distance… and then give him a reason to hit her or worse. His calm surprised Mattie. For the first time since she had been abducted a sense of inevitability almost overwhelmed her.

She had been taken.

She would be used in whatever way they saw fit and there was nothing she could do.

Nothing.

The driver finally took a step towards her. If she delayed following him, she would pay for it. And if she was going to be beaten, it had to be for something worthwhile.

She gathered up her robes and made herself move cautiously, starting the descent into a world that would almost certainly resemble hell.

* * *

Harris had not anticipated being back into The Chief's office so soon. He was not certain he wanted all this attention from the top of the hierarchy. But here he was.

Sir John's frosty PA had been a little more welcoming than

yesterday and had offered him a cup of tea. He would have much preferred coffee but for once Harris decided not to be his awkward self… yes, he would very much like a cup of tea thank you.

He had been waiting for almost ten minutes when the door opened on a harassed Sir John. "Sorry for the delay."

Harris nodded a not-to-worry sign and they both entered Sir John's office.

"How much intelligence have you gathered on Mattie Colmore?" Sir John offered Harris a seat in front of his desk.

"We know she is in Raqqa…" Harris grunted.

Sir John stopped before sitting down himself. "The hostage situation is confirmed, I presume."

"It's not confirmed, sir…"

Sir John raised an eyebrow.

"By that I mean we haven't yet seen any demand linked to her."

"I have just had a conversation with her father the Rt Hon. Harold Colmore MP."

"Surprising… Has he received a request directly?"

"Not exactly, no. Let me show you a video I had someone pull for me."

Sir John moved away from his desk to a larger screen in the room. He switched on the monitor and started streaming the video.

Harold Colmore was addressing the House of Commons in Westminster. He was vociferous in defending US policy when it came to terrorists' requests.

"There can be no negotiations with evil." His voice carried across the Commons with the majesty and arrogance only a well-established MP could deliver. Did we not have a special relationship? Did we not think it an excellent idea to emulate the US in following their hostage response policy? The chamber roared in approval. There could be no payment of ransom, no exchange of prisoners… The UK would walk hand in hand with… Harris had stopped listening. His right arm was folded around his torso, supporting a left arm with fist stuck against his mouth.

Sir John froze the video. He too had no intention of viewing the performance till the end.

"I wonder what his take is going to be when he knows his daughter has been kidnapped."

"Estranged daughter... they haven't spoken in years. Apparently, he didn't approve of her becoming a journalist and giving voice to people she should have no time for... to quote the man himself." Harris moved away from the screen. "Why did he call?"

"I have the feeling his wife might have pushed him. Since she, on the other hand, is still in touch with his daughter."

Harris followed The Chief back to his desk.

"But he doesn't know his daughter has been taken."

"He doesn't, but she has gone missing and the rumours are still circulating. It is his version in any case."

"It can't come from us; of that I am sure."

"How about the Reuters journalist?"

Harris ran an angry hand through his hair. "I did have a very difficult conversation with Ms Murdock."

"You mean you read her the Riot Act?" Sir John nodded, approvingly.

"I think you beat me to it, sir."

"Is that so?" The Chief chuckled.

"I wish she had given me the time to give her a piece of my mind though..." Harris remained silent for a moment. "Could I offer an alternative explanation?"

He was invited to sit. "Please do."

"I may sound very Machiavellian."

Sir John moved his hand in the air in a so-what gesture.

"His thoughts on the matter of hostage-taking are clear... he doesn't know it for sure yet, but he knows there is at least a strong probability his daughter has been taken."

"Agreed."

"He is now in a very uncomfortable position... if he does nothing about Mattie." Harris hesitated. "We are not there yet, but he knows that kidnappings by terrorist groups rarely end up well... worst case scenario..." Harris again hesitated.

"Death." Sir John followed the thought through, completing the sentence Harris had hesitated to.

Harris nodded.

"He will be portrayed as a monster."

"Almost certainly. On the other hand, if he does advocate compromise, he'll be branded a hypocrite."

Sir John smiled. He appreciated the way Harris was tackling the problem and his no-nonsense approach.

"So, what do you think he will ask us to do?"

"He needs to receive information before everyone else so that he can anticipate what to do."

"He has asked for that already. But what is his endgame?" Sir John had turned his seat away from the desk, looking through the large, green-tinted windows. "There always is something else…"

Harris waited for a moment.

"Perhaps… what he is expecting is for MI6 to sort this out for him."

"In what way?" Sir John had not yet moved.

"A hostage rescue mission… risky but sometimes worthwhile."

"In particular as the British government will not pay ransom… and we will not be in a position to facilitate, even through an intermediary." A warning to Harris from The Chief – his assets on the ground had better be careful about what they imagined they could get.

Harris nodded. He knew what the policy was, but each policy had an exception when that exception brought a high enough reward.

"Do you deal with a lot of politicians? I didn't think you did." Sir John moved on.

"Not in the UK, but abroad… I have dealt with quite a few who were SIS assets."

Sir John made a short intake of breath. "I don't want this to interfere with Operation RED HAWK." Sir John moved his hands to his keyboard, calling up more data to come on screen.

A map of Turkey, Syria and Iraq materialised. "Since we're talking about it, let's have an update on the situation there."

Harris sat back in his chair. "They have arrived in Raqqa."

* * *

The Reuters news bulletin was not as damning as it could have been. It still referred to the disappearance of Mattie Colmore without giving any conclusions as to her whereabouts.

James read the news a couple of times. A media blackout would be imposed if Mattie Colmore had been abducted. He wondered whether his experience might have been of some help had he already joined the agency.

The day had been busy, but uneventful; his team was still engaged in client calls that would last until late into the evening. A few urgent emails still needed a reply. He could do this from his Blackberry. The information he required to do so was in his head – no need for the complex spreadsheets stored on his computer.

James read the news one more time. He needed a walk to clear his mind. The meeting with Steve Jackson, although he now doubted it was his real name, had unsettled him or perhaps given him hope that there was something out there he would enjoy doing more than what he was doing today. His ambition had never been to succeed Henry... an irony. He had been content to be his number two, to let Henry handle the politics, the schmoozing of egos, the tough negotiations about promotions, bonuses and budgets. But he had enjoyed standing by his beliefs during the takeover that had cost Henry so dearly. He was proud of the way he had handled himself.

Uncompromising.

For once the good guys had won the battle. After five years at the very top of management, James had to face the facts. He never was one of them and never would be.

He grabbed his jacket, warned his PA he was going out on an errand and disappeared.

It was still light and busy outside. He slung his jacket over his shoulder, not quite sure where he was going, but kept walking, taking a turn whenever the street ahead looked too crowded. He crossed a smaller street near St Paul's Tube station. Walking down Cheapside, he slowed down to take in more of the surrounding buildings he never usually bothered to look at properly.

The large shopping mall he had just left behind was still very new. He tried to remember which building had been savaged to make way for Boots, Hotel Chocolat and an array of other well-known brands. He hoped the little alleyways, tortuous passages and maze of small streets in the City would never be destroyed. They often made him queasy, bringing back memories of ambushes and return fires. But he liked the historical aspect, the fact that these places went back centuries, some of the street pattern having even survived the Great Fire of 1666. James found himself turning into another street and crossing a larger road, to end up in front of St Mary-le-Bow church. This was a piece of architecture after his own heart. Originally built in medieval times, 1080 to be exact, as the headquarters of the Archbishop of Canterbury. It had managed to survive for a few hundred years but was not spared by the Great Fire. It had been rebuilt by Wren, the architect of St Paul's, and damaged again during WWII; it had reopened in 1964. James liked its resilience, its ability to transform and inspire people to worship and visit.

James had rebuilt his life a few times too and might perhaps have to do so again. He hesitated, checked the time: 6.40pm. The church would be closing in 20 minutes. He could still steal a moment, sitting within the stillness of its walls. He pushed open the wooden door and entered.

Chapter Eleven

"I could murder a beer." Henry yawned as they were back on the terrace of their hotel room.

Wasim couldn't help but smile, the dimple in his cheeks barely showing through his thick beard. "You are incorrigible, Henry Crowne."

"Yup... but I'm pretty good too."

Wasim had been impressed – he had already said so – by Henry's capacity to grasp the financial workings of an organisation in a couple of hours.

A succession of well-targeted questions, the intelligence to look for solutions as soon as an issue presented itself and the ability to summon up an inexhaustible number of options... all this had taken aback the man ISIL people named The Treasurer. The podgy man would need more than just this to be completely won over but at least he wanted to hear more and had convened a second meeting.

Henry grew serious suddenly. "ISIL is sitting on an unimaginable amount of cash through the oil fields they have captured... I hadn't realised. If they keep expanding their territory, they'll keep increasing their wealth. It's going to be hard to fight a group that has so many resources."

"I didn't realise that either... I don't think anybody does. And, yes, money means good weaponry, good fighters that you pay well and good supplies."

"Their main issue is how to sell their oil without it being identified as ISIL oil... I spoke about Turkey and Mr Podgy Man was impressed but it can't be the only route they are using… the number of barrels a day is too great."

"Mr Podgy Man as you call him isn't going to tell you all his secrets in one go."

"And he will want to squeeze as much as possible out of me before he does… I get it."

Henry had bought coffee from a small street vendor who sold food and beverages (no alcohol of course). He had asked the man to fill his water bottle with the dark liquid. The man had looked puzzled but thought better than to query Henry, with his long beard and army fatigues… he must be one of them.

The cardamom coffee was delicious, the perfect balance of bitterness and velvety smoothness. He had poured the drink into two cups he had found in the room. Wasim had almost finished his. Henry was still sipping; such an enjoyable taste had to be savoured.

"How long do you think they are going to give me?" Henry had finished his coffee, putting the cup down on the floor.

"You mean before they ask you to prove you really are one of them?"

"There's only one way they'll ever trust me…"

"That's right… or at least it will be the beginning. You won't survive here otherwise." Wasim took a swig of the cold drink he had just opened and pulled a face. Henry shook his head at Wasim… it tasted the way it smelled… synthetic.

"I know… It's a bit too late to get cold feet now and so I won't. But I need to maximise the effect, find the right moment."

"As long as you don't leave it too late. Your understanding of the Qur'an is already pretty good."

"Surprisingly… I'm enjoying reading it."

"It all depends at what level and how you are reading the text, of course."

"Same with the Bible you know. You can believe that God created the earth and man in seven days, but you are going to be pushed hard the day you find out about Einstein and Darwin. On the other hand, if you see the text as a metaphor, an image that helps you live better within yourself and with others… that's a different matter."

108

Wasim smiled, his light brown eyes charged with kindness. His face turned serious and cautious again.

"The sort of theory that is going to get you killed in this place…"

"I thought Allah was merciful."

"He is… It depends what mercy means to the one wielding the sword."

Both men fell silent, returning to their respective drinks.

"Going back to your question about optimisation." Wasim stressed the last word. "You should do this before we meet al-Baghdadi."

"That I have gathered – the issue is where do I do it?"

"You need to swear allegiance in front of other Muslims… ones who will count."

"I still can't get over how easy it is to convert… I say the Shahada and then I'm in."

"That's the idea… to make it easy for people to join. As long as your heart is in it of course."

"And if it's not… I'm off the hook."

"No, you're a traitor…" Wasim handed Henry a can of the same fizzy drink he was having. "You need to behave like one of them once you have made that move."

"Otherwise they will come after me with vengeful Saifs… you told me."

Wasim did not reply. He simply waited.

"Sorry, I'm trying to make it sound easy, but I know I need to follow the five pillars of Islam if I'm going to survive here. Afterwards, well… I'll cross that bridge…" Henry cleared his throat and nodded, opening the can Wasim had given him. Even though he'd known the risks when he had agreed to join Operation RED HAWK, his chances of coming out of it alive were perhaps slimmer than he had anticipated.

"If you keep doing as well as you have, we have a chance."

Henry nodded. "I'll find the right audience at the right time."

Wasim stood up. He walked to the parapet, surveying their surroundings. A habit that had helped keep them alive so far.

"You must do what you have to do to combat these fanatics… I'm not offended at the way you're going about it… You're the one putting yourself in harm's way after all."

"My choice… a necessary one. But thanks anyway."

Wasim was about to reply, but he abruptly put a hand forward, silencing them both. There was someone at the door. He walked back into the room.

The air outside was finally cooling and Henry shivered. He stood up too; he was ready to go back inside. Wasim was at the door, craning his neck to speak to someone. Henry recognised Ali's voice, hesitant, and that of other men he did not know. Henry stood back, waiting.

Wasim closed the door. As he did the call to prayer reverberated through the city.

* * *

"I'm gobsmacked," Amina had pursed her lips into a mocking pout. "The Chief has called you twice in less than 24 hours…"

Harris fell into his chair. "Harold Colmore MP, father of Mattie Colmore journalist, has been in touch."

"Bummer, what does the big man want?"

"RED HAWK is already complicated enough as it is… I don't need a wretched politician getting involved."

"He and his daughter haven't seen each other for years. They've cut each other off and I'm not sure he is going to be that helpful to her."

"Precisely." Harris nodded. Amina always had the latest intel at her fingertips.

"He is the type who always covers their own arse… if it goes belly up, he doesn't want to be blamed."

"He may have a point." Amina rubbed her hands over her face. The late-night surveillance was starting to take its toll. "Why the fuck did Crowne have to get involved?"

"I think that's supposed to be my line… and the answer is… to save a life."

"I'm not saying we shouldn't save her life… incidentally, I think she's a bloody ballsy journalist. But Henry is in ISIL territory with zippo experience of infiltration."

110

"I'm sure he'll make it serve his plan."

"And the plan should be to get the intel we need and get out of there."

"Can't argue with that." Harris shrugged off his jacket, leaning backwards to let it slide down more easily. He fell into his seat. He did not need Amina to lose patience with Henry. She wouldn't, she was too professional for that. Still, he did not want to have to keep assessing whether his view was right.

"Look, it is what it is. Wasim let it happen too. And he, on the other hand, knows exactly what he is doing."

"Very true." Amina returned to her computer. She moved around screens that were splitting the monitored information into different sections. "There is a lot of activity on social media. From Syria and Iraq… and yet…" She moved a few more screens around. "We are hitting a blind spot on Raqqa."

Harris stood up to move over to her screens. "Do you think they've already imposed a ban, gone dark?"

"Sending an email to OMA – the guys can check that out for us. If it's the case, ISIL might have some key information they want to release and they will time it for the maximum impact."

"Can't be about Crowne, too early. They haven't tested him yet… It's more likely they are working on a new move they can't afford to leak."

"Whatever the reason, it won't prevent Wasim from contacting us. The Fire Chat he is using will work even if the internet or access to Wi-Fi is blocked."

"When are you expecting Wasim to make contact again?"

"Tomorrow, we'll see whether he's allowed to call his MOTHER. So far it has worked and, if it doesn't, we'll use the other route."

"Anything else?"

Amina stopped her hand in mid-air, before landing it back on her mouse. "How about this new bloke, James Radlett?"

"He is going to join… He's missing the action, and banking is not really his world…"

"Even if it means working with Crowne?"

"Especially because of that."

"What do you mean?"

"James is as straight as you can get… and I think he is the sort of guy who won't forget when someone has done him a big favour, even if he says the contrary."

"But we are talking Henry Crowne, right… disgraced financier, money launderer for the IRA…"

"It's got nothing to do with that. Of course he could not work *for* Henry, he'll be working *with* him. No, it's more about fairness. Given the opportunity, I think James Radlett will want to even things out. Henry employed him when no one else had any time for James. Henry promoted him to become his number two, despite the fact he was ex-British army… He too could have held a grudge. Henry could have used his influence to make James's life at work a misery; after all, the British boys haven't always been whiter than white in Belfast."

"Interesting." Amina stopped what she was doing, giving the idea consideration. "Your point is that James may want to give Crowne a chance too."

"I'll take a bet on that."

Amina sighed. "Steve, every time you take a bet, you know you're on a winner, you're not much fun."

"Don't be such a spoilsport." Harris scrunched up a piece of paper and threw it at her. It went wide of the mark.

"Thank God you're a better agent than a cricketer… otherwise…" Her sentence was interrupted by an alert on her screen. The OMA team wanted her attention – something material had been spotted in the chat rooms of the Middle East.

* * *

She had almost stumbled twice on the flowing material of her abaya as she descended the treacherous staircase. Her face was covered by the niqab so that only her eyes were visible. The veil kept sliding and obstructed her vision if she moved too quickly. They must have gone down at least three flights of stairs when they finally arrived at their destination in the basement. The concrete floor was dusty and grey. The walls were of the same ashen colour, marred with streaks of dirt, the origin of which she could not or perhaps did not want to identify. A stench she had not smelled for a while hit her unexpectedly, rancid, overpowering. It made her stomach heave. She had encountered it in other makeshift prisons... Iraq, Afghanistan.

A bunch of fighters were sitting at the entrance of a long corridor. There was no conversation going on, no smoking or drinking together. They stood, a heavy lurking presence. Mattie walked past the men. They did their best to ignore her, yet a few sly glances were cast in her direction. The fighter accompanying her stopped in front of a door that looked unmistakably like a prison door with its opening at face level and small flap. He did not say a word. He did not need to. When he opened the door, Mattie walked into a cell that stank of rot and human waste. The door shut behind her with a low creaking noise.

She was on her own.

Her feet were rooted to the floor. She closed her eyes and tried to control her fluttering heart. She was still alive... there was hope. What was it the English man called Henry had said to her? *Don't do anything stupid.* Not so much a warning but a piece of advice coming from someone who might help. She shrugged. Why would this perfect stranger help? And how could he?

The scarf around her head felt hot and she pulled it off. It might be risky to show her hair, but she was willing to appear unafraid. She took a couple of steps forward. The cell was dimly lit by a naked lightbulb. It had flickered a few times when the door had been closed. She advanced in the direction of the mattress that lay in the corner of the room. It looked stained and filthy. In the other corner there was a bucket – no need to check this one to know what it was for.

Mattie's eyes became accustomed to the faintness of the light. She spotted writing on the walls and moved closer, discovering names, dates and a few words or comments scratched into the stone.

Hussein killed 25/1/14, Abu Mana – 113 days, Abu Hussein Dwer (in Russian) had written a few words she could not understand, Abu Karan from France... She worked her way around the cell walls discovering more names and more of the same, days spent there and often, too often, a date of execution. ISIL had already started the cull... amongst its own people if they were felt wanting, amongst the people of Raqqa if they did not follow orders. The sorry end of those who would not embrace their blind fanaticism.

She had almost finished going round the room when she came across a strange manifesto written in English:

If you are reading this, there are 4 reasons:

You did the crime and were caught red-handed

Using twitter gps locations or leaving gps locations turned on the mobile phone (sic)

Uploading videos or photos from a WIFI internet source, i.e. you need your Amir's permission, which you didn't get

A suspect, off the street!

The police have a good reason to do this – Be Patience! Be Patience! Be Patience.

The enemy of the Muslims Satan will do every whispering while you stare at the wall or the floor.

Mattie read the few lines again. Already ISIL was looking at protecting the exchange of information, and its geographical position. The stadium, with its rooms dug deep underground, was the perfect building to house their operations. ISIL was already way ahead of its rival Al-Qaeda in so many ways. The few recruitment videos she had seen were slick, combining strong imagery, powerfully themed music and snappy one-liners that would inspire young Muslims, discontented with the West but also with their own countries around the world.

Voices were coming along the corridor. Mattie fought the panic at having perhaps removed the niqab too hastily. She controlled her movements, slowly, purposefully folding the piece of cloth into a triangle, adjusting it around her head, tucking the sides against her face and bringing the pieces of material across one another.

The voices were now clearly audible, arguing it seemed. The cloth almost fell out of her trembling hands. She swore, steeled herself; making the final knot and picking up the last piece from the floor, she hurriedly placed the veil across her face.

The door rattled. Her fingers were fighting to close the brooch that fastened the pieces together. The door of the adjacent cell opened. Voices raised turned into shouts; this time a third person had joined in. Protestations of innocence, it seemed to her. Mattie moved close to the cell's door; her face next to the window flap. The man's voice had turned shrill. The blows started raining down on the prisoner without stopping, oblivious to the shrieks and begging. Mattie walked to the far end of the small room. She collapsed on the makeshift bed, hands covering her ears, eyes screwed shut… the sound of her own heart beating in her palms. In her years as war reporter she had seen some beatings but the one happening a few feet away from her cell had a savagery she had never witnessed. It took some time for her to notice…

Silence.

Two voices spoke again after a moment and with them came the muffled sound of a body being dragged across the floor. She put a hand over her mouth and willed herself not to scream. The men disappeared down the corridor. She held back for as long as she could and let a muffled cry escape.

She would never walk out of here alive.

* * *

The Mattie Colmore kidnapping was preying on Harris's mind more than he had anticipated. Harris had run some difficult ops in the past but RED HAWK ranked at the top of his list. The chance of both his assets making it out alive was uncomfortably low. Both men were aware of the challenge and willing to take the risk. Harris owed it to them to do whatever he could at his end to tilt the probabilities in their favour.

Harris was queuing for a coffee. He did his best thinking when lining up with people, waiting to be served… He shuffled along and returned to the thorny issue of Mattie Colmore. The Chief was right, it would become a political matter. Her father's position both ideologically and in government was ideal for a group like ISIL. It might mean she would be kept alive for a while, but it could just as well sign an early death warrant. The Chief had also warned him… MI6 could not facilitate a ransom demand even if it were to be paid by a third party. European countries did… but not the British.

Harris ordered two coffees, one black no sugar, one white with plenty of the stuff… He found himself back at his desk almost without noticing. He unlocked one of the drawers and fetched out a new burner phone. It would take only a few minutes to charge with this latest high-performance, instant-charge battery. When the mobile was ready, he would place a call he had delayed making until now.

Time to speak to CIA Jack at Langley, Virginia.

* * *

The dampness of the mattress had started to seep through her clothes. In the absence of a watch, Mattie guessed she had been lying there for a couple of hours, perhaps a little more, trying to quieten her mind and calm her fears. Since the assault on the prisoner next door everything had been remarkably silent. She stood up wincing as the painkillers had now worn off completely.

Once more she surveyed the cell she had been placed in. The space had once been fitted with wall furniture, perhaps it had been used as a changing room. She could see the delineation of their structure. Perhaps some top player had readied himself here before the reign of ISIL had destroyed all forms of sporting event.

The sound of a door lock opening made her jump. Two guards entered, both clad in what she now knew was the ISIL uniform: black shirt, black baggy trousers and white trainers, black scarf worn on the head. The quality of their outfits was shabby, unlike the clothes she had seen on the man who had brought her here.

The younger man held a plate of what looked like food. He put it down in front of her and threw a water bottle on the mattress, retreating a couple of steps to fall in line with the older man.

No one moved.

Mattie's grumbling stomach was urging her to step forward and check the contents of the plate. Her mouth started to water uncontrollably.

She knew better.

The two men were looking at her with interest. Too much interest. The scarf had moved down without her noticing, uncovering a part of her face she should have kept hidden. Was it enough to provoke? The silence that grew between them swelled with possibilities.

Offence was perhaps the best form of defence.

"You must give me time to dress properly when you enter," Mattie said in perfect Arabic. Not what the two men had expected. The younger one recoiled at the words but the older one's surprise dissipated fast. He nodded towards the door and the other guard disappeared. He took one more step into the cell, eyes roving over Mattie's body. Despite the faintness of the light she sensed the intensity of his gaze.

Don't move, don't cry.

"I want to see Abu Shabh... he knows who I am."

Mattie's Arabic, spoken with confidence, the mention of someone who might be a high-ranking fighter, made the man hesitant. Was she worth it?

The older guard stepped backwards over the threshold of the cell. His eyes had one message for Mattie though.

Your time will come.

* * *

Raised voices came from the corridor, the bedroom door slammed open and three men walked in, a fourth one waiting outside. Henry stood at the sliding doors, his Glock stashed away in his rucksack at the other end of the room. Wasim followed the men, white in the face and arguing.

"What do you want?" Henry had entered the room. The men looked him over but kept moving around the space. They had a task to fulfil.

"They want the laptop and phone." Wasim stopped in the small entrance that led to the main room, assessing the situation.

"On whose authority?" Henry's Arabic was aimed at the man he thought was in charge. Athletic and muscled, he moved his head towards the devices that lay on Wasim's bed. One of the men grabbed them and slid them into a bag.

"Doesn't matter."

"I wonder what The Treasurer has to say about that?"

"Nothing." He laughed and the others followed.

Henry glanced towards Wasim for a clue. Wasim shook his head almost imperceptibly. There was no point in fighting now.

The men opened the wardrobe and the drawers of the bedside

117

tables. Neither Wasim nor Henry had very much by way of possessions and their clothes were old and tattered. The disgust on the men's faces was almost funny.

Henry's body tightened, ready for a fight. He was not yet prepared to give up but Wasim shook his head. Henry breathed in. The leader looked around the room, satisfied they had disturbed a place where there was so little to disturb in the first place. His eyes fell on the rucksack stashed away at the back of the wardrobe. He barked at one of the men who had not been thorough enough, and the rucksack's contents were poured over the floor. The thud of the Glock prompted the man to bend down and pick up the piece, handing it over to his leader. He grabbed the piece appreciatively, pulled back the slide and aimed at Henry's head in a swift, emphatic move.

Henry locked eyes with him.

"It's not going to do much damage without a clip in it."

The man's grin disappeared. Should he check Henry was right, or fire anyway but look foolish if he was? He crossed the distance between them in one long stride and crashed the Glock over his face with such force it threw Henry off balance, his tall body hitting the side of the sliding doors, almost dislodging them.

The man pocketed the gun, kicked one of the chairs, breaking its legs for the hell of it and moved out of the room.

Henry staggered up. Wasim crossed the room and dragged him to the nearest bed, checking his wound.

"Lesson 1... don't make these guys look stupid, it doesn't pay."

"Lesson 1... well understood," Henry mumbled.

Wasim raised his head towards the door. Someone was still there. Ali didn't know what to do. Wasim waved him in.

The young man darted in, apologising... He did not think they wanted to mug them... he did not understand... shocked and scared they might think he was with them.

Wasim shook his head in an appeasing movement. "We know it wasn't your fault."

Henry half turned towards Ali. "Did they say who their commander was?"

Ali nodded. "Commander al-Haddawi."

118

Chapter Twelve

The dawn call to prayer barely disturbed Henry. He had eventually managed to find a position in which his wound stopped pounding and had not moved since. Wasim got up, silently moved to the bathroom and then disappeared onto the terrace. It would be peaceful to pray there. Henry turned on his back, stretched and placed his hands under his head. In the room next to theirs, he heard someone going through the same ritual. The low chanting started, words of praise and prayer to Allah and his might.

Henry's mind drifted to the edge of sleep. He would soon be joining them, one more step in the direction he had chosen. When Wasim came back into the room and disappeared one more time into the bathroom, Henry got up for good, throwing the sheet away from his legs. He went to the sliding doors and leaned against them for a while. The morning was strangely peaceful. The smell of freshly used soap told him Wasim was ready.

"How is your head?"

"Swollen... nothing unusual about that, some might add." Henry turned around, gingerly touching his wound.

"Thanks to the beard and hair, the bruise won't show too much." Wasim got closer to inspect it.

"Are we seeing Mr Podgy Man today, d'you think?" Henry changed the subject. Henry had been an idiot to react... point taken.

Wasim grabbed two bottles of water from the fridge and sat on the sofa that occupied one of the bedroom's corners.

"We are... unless there's been a change of plan, but I don't think

The Treasurer will take any nonsense from al-Haddawi." Wasim threw one of the bottles to Henry. "Why?"

He caught it with one hand, unscrewed the cap and took a long pull.

"Because I need to befriend Mr Podgy Man so that we can get on with the plan... for that I need to be a regular feature in his diary."

"And what else?"

"Can't hide anything from you." Henry shook his head.

"That's my job."

"I'm thinking conversion..."

"With The Treasurer as witness?"

"Yup." Henry finished his water. "The more I delay, the more it costs us in credibility. And after last night the sooner I get on with it the better."

"I presume this is not the royal we."

"Nope... trying to show I too can be a team player."

Wasim nodded. For a fleeting moment Henry thought he saw relief in Wasim's eyes.

"I also need to know what's happening to Mattie." Henry was gathering his clothes, avoiding Wasim's eyes.

"What are you trying to achieve?" The coolness of the tone surprised Henry. All signs of relief had evaporated.

"That I can not only construct a financial structure no one will ever detect, but that I can deliver the source of income to go with it myself." Henry's bluntness was a match for Wasim's tone. "Kidnapping is one of the main sources of income for terrorist groups, so let me use her as a way of knowing how they proceed."

"The UK does not pay ransom."

"I'm aware of that, but her paper, *The Sunday Times*, might, it's worth a try."

"And if you fail... then what?"

"She had already been abducted when we came across her. If I don't do anything, she will..." Henry was stuck for words. The alternative to him not succeeding he could not contemplate.

Wasim leaned forward, elbows on knees, head bent. Henry waited for his verdict. He had no chance of pulling this off if Wasim said no and he had learned to trust his judgement too. This no longer was the trading floor at GL's offices in London.

"OK," he lifted his head, weary. "OK... but if I tell you to drop it because it threatens to scupper the mission, you drop it."

"You're the boss." Henry lifted his hands up in surrender. "As long as you convince me."

Wasim shot him a dark eye that Henry ignored. Wasim had worries of his own.

"I'm not entirely surprised about the laptop and mobile, but I need to find a way of replacing them."

"I presume the need to call your ailing MOTHER will go some way towards that."

"That was the idea when we set it up. Still my gear has ended up with al-Haddawi and The Treasurer doesn't know me yet."

"How about a good old fashioned phone call?" Henry jerked his head towards the phone that lay on one of the bedside tables, wincing as he did so.

"If it were only that simple... I fear I'll have to get an authorisation to make an international call... and I hope I don't need to ask al-Haddawi for it."

* * *

When they entered the room, the screens were flickering again with activity. Breaking news poured from well-known providers Bloomberg, Reuters, Al Jazeera, even CNN and Sky News. Others seemed to be plugged into sites Henry could not identify but knew enough of to recognise as part of the dark web.

Henry had not been given the official tour but twenty years in banking had taught him enough about the proper organisation of a treasury operation. And this operation was being run professionally...

Astonishing.

The treasury room was not only keenly following activity in the Middle East and in neighbouring countries but also the large international players that could affect the oil market, the US, Russia and their sworn enemy... Iran. A cluster of three men at the far end of the large room were actively discussing prices and trading the large volumes that ISIL was already extracting from the ground. There were another two or three groups that seemed to be tracking other activities. He was not yet sure what these were. He planned to find out what the rest of these young men were doing for ISIL. Perhaps they were managing the money collected from other sources of income: theft, kidnapping, the looting of assets… Henry was certain all this information would be flowing back to The Treasurer, filed and ready for inspection.

The Treasurer had appeared more interested in hearing what Henry had to say about the key subject on his mind… money laundering. It was important for the group to have at its disposal cash that looked clean. The purchase of armament was one, although it did not always require clean cash – but certainly the purchase of food, medical or IT supplies required a clean bank account and clean cash to go with it.

Henry smiled his best commercial smile. He would oblige The Treasurer with his top five tips for best results when it came to laundering money.

"First stage is placement." Henry and Wasim had been shown into The Treasurer's office. Henry had immediately walked to a whiteboard that hung on one of the walls, grabbed a couple of pens and started writing in large letters. Wasim started to translate from English into Arabic, keen to ensure that their interlocutor understood something more technical that perhaps Henry would not convey so well if he used Arabic. Henry and Wasim worked well together, Henry full of energy, Wasim providing the steadiness of well-expressed knowledge… two people giving the impression they had known each other for years.

A formidable team.

"Placement," Henry repeated, tapping on the board. "Many ways of disguising the origin of funds, but the best way is always the most complex way. Using derivative instruments and playing the market this will work."

"Not interest rates though." Wasim had butted in.

"Absolutely, not interest rates, only shares… If the transactions go one way, we make money, if they don't, we lose but we will in any case always recover something and that something will become clean cash… laundered through a bona fide bank."

The Treasurer had moved to the whiteboard too. A good indication that Henry had caught his imagination.

"I'll help you set up companies that are legitimate and that can justifiably enter into these transactions."

"The way we discussed yesterday?" The Treasurer had spoken in English, accented but fluent. Neither Henry nor Wasim showed surprise, a man moving in financial circles had to speak the language of business.

"Exactly, we use Qatar, the UAE and Cyprus."

The Treasurer hesitated and finally took a writing pad out of his desk and started taking some notes.

Encouraging.

"Next step after placement… layering." Henry was on a roll. His voice had taken a serene tone, purring like a well-oiled engine. He was doing what he had been so very good at doing all his career… making the complex world of finance comprehensible to whoever he was speaking to. His clients used to love him.

He drew the second word in another colour on the whiteboard.

"We make it more difficult for the money placed to then be detected…"

"And you suggest?" The Treasurer eyes glittered with the prospect of coming up with an international impregnable structure. All for the good and financial wealth of ISIL, of course.

"That's why the UAE is interesting… let's go for property purchase and sale. Again, we are not trying to make a lot of money, we are simply trying to buy and sell legitimately to produce clean cash that will reach ISIL's bank accounts."

Wasim was nodding reassuringly.

"Finally," Henry took another pen of a different colour, "integration." Henry wrote the word once more. "We use the cash we have *earned* from our property dealings."

Henry walked over to the water fountain, helped himself to a fresh glass of water and returned to his place next to the whiteboard. It was almost theatrical…

"We can do more property deals. We can buy our own oil, blend it with oil from other producers, and resell the blend on the market… Do this on a large scale."

The Treasurer ran his fat little fingers through his salt and pepper beard. "How do you…?"

"… know you already sell oil to other countries and that the buyers blend it?" Henry was not trying to make a point, rather he was helping a client articulate an important question.

The Treasurer waited.

"Because that's the only way oil can't be analysed and traced back to the wells that produced it in the first place."

Henry would certainly not mention he had done extensive research on the subject while preparing for his infiltration.

"How quickly can we implement?" The Treasurer had gone back to his desk and pushed his plump body back into his leather armchair. The lines of his face had become smooth. He could see a way of exploiting this new asset… called Henry Crowne.

"As soon as I have a desk in this room."

The Treasurer looked him up and down. "It'll be done by mid-afternoon today."

Henry nodded his thanks.

"But we are very full… you'll need to sit in another room."

"Of course…" Henry stayed relaxed… one step at a time.

There was nothing else to discuss. Henry replaced the pens where they belonged, in a small cradle off the whiteboard.

Wasim was already walking out of the door.

"I hear you had a visit last night." The Treasurer was back at his desk.

"We did." Wasim turned back. "Commander Haddawi doesn't seem to trust us." He shrugged. "I'd like to see my laptop back or at least my phone at some point. I call my mother who is unwell regularly."

The Treasurer nodded. "I'll speak to Commander al-Haddawi. He does not decide a move like this without telling me."

* * *

124

When they arrived back at their hotel Wasim and Henry were welcomed by the same dishevelled little man who had shown them their room the day before. He was fidgeting with a set of keys, oblivious to the movement of his hands.

Wasim checked that the keys were still in his pockets. He liked the feel of this good old-fashioned opening device.

"Problem?"

The receptionist shook his head. "The room next door has been made available."

Henry and Wasim exchanged a puzzled look. Arriving on their floor Wasim stood in front of the new room and hesitated. He opened the door. The room was indeed free and the bed had been freshly made up.

It seemed they had earned an upgrade, despite last night's mayhem... or perhaps The Treasurer was flexing his muscles.

This room's decoration had also been stripped, but the furniture that remained was comfortable. Apart from a stain next to the sliding doors, the room was identical to the one Henry and Wasim had shared. Henry entered too but neither man spoke.

They went meticulously through the room's electrical fixtures, looking for listening or videoing devices just the way they had done several times already with the first room. They finally stood in the centre of the place and nodded.

"Clear." Wasim let a long breath out.

"Clear," Henry agreed.

"I'll move in." Wasim handed Henry his set of keys.

"Well, it seems that the *integration phase* in our spy-laundering scheme is working." Henry chuckled.

"Perhaps..."

"What? You don't think it's a good sign."

"Nothing good ever comes from these people. And we don't have any means of contacting MOTHER... The Treasurer is in no hurry to kit me up. Why should he be?"

A rebuff that Henry did not mind. Vigilance was the key to staying alive in Raqqa, not only a job well done. Henry should have been more worried about Wasim's laptop and phone disappearing or his Glock being stolen. But he sensed that he was making progress with The Treasurer. If al-Haddawi had not been enthusiastic about Henry, The Treasurer was prepared to form his own opinion… he too had a political agenda.

Henry entered what was now his room and after Wasim had removed the couple of items which belonged to him, Henry went through the same debugging process again.

Vigilance… always.

* * *

The encrypted laptop had been re-booted almost an hour ago. Amina could not sleep. She had woken up at around 5.00am and spent 15 minutes pretending she might go back to sleep. She had then thrown off the bedcovers and gone over to her device, keen to find out what had landed in her inbox.

Amina yawned and walked from the kitchen table where she had placed the laptop to the coffee machine that was bubbling away. She poured herself another mug. The old machine had seen better days, but she liked to brew her coffee from freshly ground beans. Her husband had taken away the newly acquired Nespresso machine, good riddance on both counts. She glanced at the dishes left in the sink from the previous night. Her two daughters had been spending an evening with her, before her ex-husband had come to collect them for a two-week holiday. The pizza box was still on the counter, as were the Coca-Cola cans and the empty tub of double chocolate chip ice-cream. It had been the right call to have shared custody, but it still hurt her raw that she had had to make that choice.

Amina's mind drifted back to the mission she was supervising with Steve Harris, RED HAWK. She would get ready in a moment. Her fingers slid on the mouse to bring the screen to life one final time.

The words 'hostage' and 'execution' hit her square in the face. She scanned the email from OMA, holding her breath has she did.

The OMA team allocated to RED HAWK had been tracking coded messages for a few days now. On the face of it these men were exchanging mundane information… Where to buy a good quality

126

taqiyah or which mosque to visit for prayer in a foreign city, but hidden messages were embedded in the simple text. And the messages were clear: hostages were at risk.

Her cup of coffee wobbled in her hand, spilling drops across the wooden surface of the kitchen table. She hardly noticed. She left the half-drunk mug on the counter, ran to her bedroom, grabbed a clean shirt and her suit and dashed into the bathroom. Within 20 minutes she was collecting her laptop from the kitchen table, shoving it into her bag and running out of the door.

She called Harris. His mobile was engaged. He too must have seen the OMA email. She left her maisonette on Vauxhall Grove and started a breakneck walk towards the SIS building. She managed to make the journey in a record five minutes, catching the green lights at the Lambeth Road crossing, expertly negotiating the complex set of roads below Vauxhall train station.

It took her more time to clear security when entering the building than it had done to come from her home. The several checks to gain access to the floor on which she was working tested her patience. She tried Harris again… Still engaged. She finally alighted on the third floor, walked past the Control Room and went straight to OMA's office. She called Ahmed, no answer from his landline, his mobile going to voicemail.

Were they already huddled in an emergency response meeting? Surely Harris would have called her. Or perhaps there was no time. She typed her security credentials into the keypad and called the interphone.

"I am here for a meeting on RED HAWK," she chanced.

"You are?"

"Amina Brown… with Steve Harris."

The voice cut out and came back again.

"Room 5."

The door's latch released with a small sigh and Amina dashed in.

Steve Harris was in deep conversation with a young Asian man when she entered the room. She had knocked at the door and the young man had opened it without dropping the exchange with Harris.

"We've just started to go through the data in detail." Harris had not bothered to greet her and she did not care.

"Is it legit?"

"Almost certainly... information obtained from sources in Raqqa."

"I thought Raqqa had gone dark?"

"This is very recent chatter... never picked up before." The young man nodded.

"Is it a negotiation stance or have they decided already?"

Amina sat next to a set of laptops that had been connected for the meeting.

"Difficult to say... But from what we can tell, ISIL has abducted a good number of hostages, Americans and Europeans."

Amina slid a look at Harris. He nodded almost imperceptibly; Jack, his Langley contact, must have confirmed the American side of things.

"We are aware of four men, all British, who are building a reputation for themselves amongst the ranks of ISIL."

"Reputation for what?" Amina glanced at the laptops that were still churning data.

"Savagery with the kafir." The young man did not hesitate. To him there was no doubt the situation had become critical. "What we don't know yet is whether this has been approved."

"You mean... by al-Baghdadi?"

"Correct."

"How close are these four guys to him?"

"We don't know."

Harris and Amina fell silent. Beyond the dreadful news for Mattie Colmore and all the other hostages lay the worrying question about Henry and Wasim. How exposed were they now?

They had not had news from them since yesterday... an eternity in the volatile environment that was Raqqa.

Chapter Thirteen

It had been less than 24 hours since Henry had seen Mattie, but perhaps already too long. The more time it took for him to claim her, the more likely other jihadists would decide her fate.

His mind drifted from the room to the day of the crossing at Bab-al-Hawa. She had tried to escape, a brave though foolish move that Henry somewhat admired. He moved back inside, walked to the corner of the room where an electrical ring had been installed. He lined up the ingredients necessary to make a cup of spiced tea, the only enjoyable thing he had learned from the camps. It soothed him to go through a ritual that was simple and brought pleasure when done.

The tea, spices, milk and sugar were now simmering… It would take another few minutes.

A silhouette materialised in front of the sliding doors. Henry turned around, surprised. Wasim knocked at the glass but did not enter. Ali was in his shadow.

Wasim's knitted eyebrows and ashen face told him a lot.

"That bad?"

"Ali has been talking to some of the other fighters he shares a room with. There are rumours of a hostage execution."

"Where?"

"In Raqqa." Ali had found his voice again.

"Mattie?"

"No one knows… But there are other hostages around the city."

"What about the other journalist?"

"No idea what happened to him but according to the others he's not here."

"Are you sure?" Henry had moved his attention to the young man and his searching blue eyes made him recoil.

"Yes… Good intel." Ali nodded.

"OK…" Henry ran his hand over his cheek and slid it down his neck. "We need to go back to The Treasurer today."

Ali did not quite understand what was happening. He simply looked eager to help.

"Not a good idea."

"We can't let her die."

"Henry, we don't know it's her." Wasim's thunderous face told Henry to hold back. He turned towards Ali and gave him swift instructions. The young man disappeared into Wasim's bedroom. They heard the sliding door close behind him. Wasim waited for a short moment, checked Ali had left his room and came back to Henry.

"What the fuck do you think you're doing?" Wasim's use of foul language sobered Henry up.

"But we can't…"

"Of course, we can't let her die… and I wish we could prevent any of them dying." Wasim's voice was shaking. "But Ali's not part of the plan. He may look innocent, but he has chosen the jihad, nonetheless. Don't bloody well put us in more danger than we need to be."

"Understood." Henry felt his cheeks burn a little, grateful for the beard that was covering them.

Wasim walked to the balustrade of the terrace, looked over it, then passed up and down its length a few times.

"We do need, as you say, to talk to The Treasurer, but we also need to know who we are facing."

"You mean someone has taken Mattie and already claimed her…" Henry's voice wobbled a little.

"That's probably right… If it is one of al-Baghdadi's lieutenants, then we'd better know how high he is in the food chain… and if it is al-Baghdadi himself… don't even think about going there… she's lost."

The unexpected lump in his throat surprised Henry. He had not anticipated al-Baghdadi might be involved. Or might be as irrational as not trying for a ransom first…

"Hang on… You might be right. The big man might be involved

himself but from what I've seen of his operation he won't pass up the chance of making money."

Wasim was about to protest but Henry held his hands up.

"Hear me out." Henry walked back inside his room and returned with two glasses of spiced tea, carrying the financial report under his arm. "I have been through this in detail." He let the financial report drop to the floor. "It's incredible, I mean it, there's a real desire to make ISIL look, well… legitimate, organised… with the financial rectitude a well-run organisation should have."

Henry offered a glass of tea to Wasim and flicked through the report he had picked up.

"Pages upon pages of information, showing how well financed they are and how strict they are with their money."

"And so…" Wasim's face had relaxed a little. The message had hit home.

"I really don't think The Treasurer would want to let an opportunity to make money go without exploring it in the first place. He's the one supervising the way money is managed and I'll wager that al-Baghdadi will listen to him."

"You want to tell The Treasurer you could get a ransom for Mattie?"

"I certainly want to tell him it's worth trying before anything happens to her…"

"And if you fail?"

"I can't fail…"

"He will know the UK doesn't pay ransom."

"The UK doesn't, but the *Sunday Times* might, as I said before. Mattie Colmore is a well-known journalist. They won't want to let her down."

"It's not as simple as that. The UK won't let even an organisation like that make a deal with jihadists."

"Then I'll have to find a way they can make the payment without it being identified as ransom. I should be good at that."

Wasim remained silent for a moment.

"Fine, let me find out who's holding her."

"Know thy enemy." Henry nodded.

The website had hundreds of posts. It specialised in military-grade weapons made available to the public. Particularly popular and generating much comment was an article about Winchester now making ammo, developed for the army's Modular Handgun System, available to consumers. The enthusiasm was palpable. Amina ignored the noise and went to a place on the website where transactions were taking place… the buying and selling of weapons which should never have reached the public.

She looked for a specific request and still couldn't find a reply.

Her mouth went dry. They had not spoken for 24 hours since Henry and Wasim had made contact with ISIL. Amina tried another website and yet again her message had not been answered. She cleared her throat. Once in Raqqa it would be more difficult to communicate. She had not expected it to become an issue so soon but perhaps she should have. Both men would have to prove themselves before they could be trusted. Amina placed a call with the Crypto team. Could they please check for any unusual activity on Wasim's laptop or phone?

"Anything in particular… I'll do the normal sweep, but if you're expecting something specific…?" Rachel asked.

"I need to know whether the laptop is controlled by someone else."

"OK, I'll make it a priority… I'll call you back in a couple of hours."

"Thanks, Rach…" Amina bit her nails and pulled a face.

Harris had remained a little longer with the OMA team. He reappeared in their office just as Amina was sending the last of her messages. He pulled his office chair out and rolled it over to her desk.

"So?"

"Still no news…"

"Which may not be good news…" Harris shook his head. "Have you…"

"Called Crypto… Rach is on the case."

"How long?"

"Couple of hours… Anything worse reported on your side?" Amina didn't give him time to speculate further.

"I was going to come to that." Harris slapped the arms of his chair.

"The Chief or the CIA?"

"Don't steal his thunder from a bloke... That puts him in the wrong frame of mind."

"Don't care... we're nowhere near evaluation time... c'mon, what is it?"

"CIA." Harris grinned. No one could hide from Amina Brown and he liked it that way.

"Something big and ugly to share?"

"Mosul is about to be attacked by ISIL... and, yes, ISIL are actively discussing hostages with other countries around the world, France, Italy and Japan, apart from the US."

"Mosul." Amina grimaced. "That's a big city with a lot of American-type weaponry and a very rich place too."

"I checked this morning with the DATA OP team. The Iraqi army has been kitted out with the latest US armament and munitions, vehicles, helicopters... and the Iraqis have moved two divisions there."

"Who says ISIL is close?"

"Kurdish intelligence has sounded the alert. Now the ex-Ba'athists, who used to support Bashar al-Assad and formed the rebel groups in Syria, are also seeing movements of troops."

"Shit... this could be a turning point... what are the Yanks doing on the ground?"

"So far nothing, neither are the Brits for that matter... the Iraqi prime minister seems to want to go solo on that one."

"If ISIL captures Mosul..." Amina let it hang.

"They're not there yet." Harris had not decided on where the balance of power lay.

"I need to let them know. This could change things for them in Raqqa." Amina's forehead creased. "On the face of it, they might not capture the city, but if they do..."

"It's a game-changer for everyone... including our guys on the ground."

Amina's fingers were running over her keyboard. "Let me do some more digging about the city, but I'm certain it's a prize."

"On the other hand, it also means that the big chiefs around al-Baghdadi will go into battle, fighting for the privilege of becoming a martyr and meeting in paradise with their full quota of virgins, milk and honey."

"Which might give our guys a break."

"Let's get more intel before we tell the boys."

They both avoided the question of comms… it was still business as usual. Wasim would find a way to contact them.

"Why?" Amina was already pulling data from GCHQ files.

"I want them to focus on The Treasurer." Harris raised his hand before Amina could protest. "And before you tell me this is crap, I know Wasim can take it but Henry might get a bit too carried away."

* * *

He was on time, one minute early to be exact. James Radlett walked through the reception area of Vauxhall Cross, went through the extensive security checks… mobile and all metals in a separate tray, to be returned upon exiting the building, body scan, body search, walk through a second metal detector… cumbersome.

The receptionist directed him towards the meeting area, where another security guard took over from her and led him to a meeting room. No visitor was allowed to walk alone at The Cross. Steve Jackson was already waiting, James noted; courtesy or keenness… he would have to see.

Harris had been remarkably straightforward and to the point with him. It had surprised James. Had Harris been tipped off by someone who knew him well? He had wondered who that person could be without coming up with any name. He would keep playing his own hand straight. This is who he was and he made no apology for it.

Their handshake was amicable. Harris offered tea and coffee. They both chose the latter.

"I'm not going to give you the usual spiel about joining MI6. You know your way around the service already even if most of your time was spent with the army." Harris sat down and indicated James should join him.

"And I'm not going to pretend I'm not interested."

Harris smiled, nodded, drank a little coffee.

"Would you go back to the field? Local presence if need be?"

"Do you mean infiltration or support?"

"For the time being local support… with possible intervention on the ground."

It was James's turn to drink some coffee. "I should be fine with that. My wounds won't allow me to be part of an active op team, but I can do support."

Harris registered the immediate mention of what had cost James his career. A warning… never use this to treat me like an underdog.

"Middle East OK? You have learned Arabic and Pashto… right."

"Middle East is the place to be… I would go back there without hesitation. Although things have moved greatly since I was last there."

Harris refreshed both their coffees.

"Tell me more about what you are looking for. What are you missing?"

"I've enjoyed being at the cutting edge of high finance in the city… Some of it has been challenging as I explained yesterday, but worth it. I have learned a lot from an industry that finances everything… armaments, research, cyber but it is also very… abstract."

"You want to be back in the field, having a direct impact on what you see, the conflicts, terrorism…"

"That's a good way of putting it… and I also need a new challenge. My job has become predictable. True financial innovation is rare and the political shenanigans, the tension within teams or with competition have remained the same… People, or at least bankers, never seem to learn."

"Would you work around people you find questionable, or that you have been disappointed with?" Harris nodded, bringing his cup to his lips slowly.

"You mean people who were considered hostile and who have changed camp?"

"Something like that…"

"That's part of the game... Convince people they can change camp and that you will look after them." James had finished his coffee and replaced the cup on its saucer. "Is there someone you have in mind?"

Harris's face was smooth and his eyes calm.

"Henry Crowne."

Chapter Fourteen

"You're certain?"

"One hundred percent." Ali gave Henry two thumbs up. It was hard to imagine him as a hard-core jihadist. Why had he joined the fight? To make his mother proud? To avenge the death of a brother? Or perhaps because he was lost and needed to belong, caught in the ideals of the fight?

Henry gave Ali two thumbs up in return. He beamed a smile and his face looked even younger. Wasim shook his head but he too could not quite figure out what drove Ali.

"Kasim al-Haddawi..." Henry detached each word. "The man who interviewed me for *The Job,* wants a bite of the action. Blast, this guy is everywhere."

Ali frowned and Henry slapped his shoulder. "You did good."

"I find more information." Ali grew serious.

"You sure?"

"Yes, sure." Ali stood up from his squatting position and disappeared from the secluded gardens at the back their hotel.

"Why is he helping?" Henry hoped Wasim might have an answer.

"It's a good question... And I hope the answer is that his heart is not in the jihad."

"If not?"

"Then he has been sent to observe us... giving us information to make us trust him."

"Ali?" Henry pulled a questioning face.

Wasim did not answer... Trust no one, Henry had been told.

"I s'pose you're right. I used to be a pretty good judge of character, until I was betrayed by my best friend, that is."

They both fell silent for a moment.

"We need to see The Treasurer…"

"We do." Wasim nodded. "And don't tell me you were right in the first place."

"Never."

They both walked back into the hotel and jumped into the old truck that had been parked in the hotel's driveway. Wasim had not bothered to take the key out of the ignition, half hoping the vehicle would disappear. But there had been no takers and he crunched the gearbox, moving the truck slowly onto the road.

"How much do you know about al-Haddawi?"

"He is part of al-Baghdadi's close circle of lieutenants. He has recently been made Emir of Deir ez-Zor, the Eastern Syrian Province. Yet, he is only a medium-ranking officer. He has a bit more to prove to al-Baghdadi."

"Do you think he sees this hostage-taking situation as a way to promote himself?"

"Very probably… What we need to find out is his relationship to The Treasurer."

"Ah… A bit of run-of-the-mill corporate infighting and competition."

"The more I think about it the more it seems likely." Wasim's eyes were on the road, making sure he did not attract attention to the truck and its occupants. Perhaps an old battered vehicle was a good thing after all.

"The Treasurer is part of al-Baghdadi's inner circle, right?"

"Right."

Henry fell silent. Mattie's face kept creeping into his mind since he had heard the news about hostage execution. The large blue-green eyes, the dark lashes that created a shadow over them. The tall forehead that creased and smoothed when she spoke. Her determination had been captured in these lines, waves expressing her opinion without fear of being contradicted.

The truck slowed down and turned into a gated entrance.

138

Two armed men dressed in the usual black ISIL uniform walked towards them. Their brand new M249 light machine guns glimmered in the sun.

One of the guards leaned forward to inspect the occupants of the humble vehicle. Wasim gave their names and asked him to contact The Treasurer. The walkie-talkie crackled. There seemed to be some hesitation at the other end. Wasim was about to insist, but the gate opened with a smooth sound.

The Treasurer was waiting at his desk. He looked more puzzled than displeased, his large round face and bushy eyebrows twitching a little in anticipation.

Henry did not bother to sit down when offered. He launched immediately into Arabic.

"I fear one of our assets might be misused."

The Treasurer grinned. The new recruit was showing promising keenness. His face became serious again and he asked Henry to please explain.

"Hostage execution..."

The silence that followed reassured Henry. If it had been decided, he would have known and looked less surprised.

"The group derives revenue, large sums from ransom money... It would be ill advised to execute a hostage outright." Henry's fluency was improving, the slightly guttural sound of Arabic rolling out of his throat easily.

"Are you certain your information is correct?"

"We don't have the network to check it out, but we're concerned there is enough truth in it."

Wasim stepped in. "We would not want it to be the English journalist we brought with us."

"The British do not pay ransom." The Treasurer was expecting a fresh argument as to the value of this new asset.

"But a well-known newspaper like the *Sunday Times* might well pay. At least we should try it."

The Treasurer half-closed his eyes. He pulled a face that seemed to indicate he had bought the idea and moved his hand slowly towards his phone.

Both Henry and Wasim took the hint. He needed to make a few calls to find out who had decided on this action without informing him.

Out of the room, Henry walked towards the bank of desks he had spotted during his first visit. One of the young men was having an animated conversation with a buyer. He spoke fast so that Henry could not follow the whole conversation. He gathered though that the argument concerned the value of a barrel of ISIL oil. The price was heavily discounted, but was it discounted enough? Wasim joined Henry's eavesdropping. The young man slammed the phone down. There would be no further discount given by ISIL. The group needed every dollar they made to fight the jihad.

"Ask him where his buyer is located." Henry thought better than to approach him directly.

The young man turned around to speak to Wasim. "Border between Iraq and Syria."

Henry walked to the map of oil wells that stretched over the far wall. Most of the young men ignored him but a few started staring. Henry could feel the burn of their glares on the back of his neck. He stood calmly, tracing the border between the two countries with a finger, following the various pipelines that coursed towards the sea irrespective of frontiers. Henry turned around, walked back to Wasim's side with a slow and measured step.

"Ask him whether the Kirkuk-Ceyhan pipeline has entrance points in ISIL territory."

Wasim translated.

The young man nodded. "Several," he said in English.

"Then tell your dealer he can mix the oil you're selling him in the Kirkuk pipeline and that it will be impossible to establish the origin of the oil arriving at the other end when it reaches Ceyhan in Turkey… No need for a second discount."

The younger man nodded and called back. The deal was back on.

Henry walked to a place in the large room where a fridge had been installed. He opened it and took out a bottle of water. He had grown out of Fanta and Coca-Cola many years ago.

The Treasurer opened the door of his office and called both men in. His placid face had turned a dangerous shade of red. They needed to have a conversation urgently.

Henry and Wasim walked into the room, closing the door behind them.

The Treasurer was running his fingers through the prayer beads that never left his side with a twitchy rhythm.

"Kasim al-Haddawi is on his way."

Wasim shot a sideways look at Henry.

"That's fine." Henry pointed to the chair in front of The Treasurer's desk. "May I?"

The other man nodded.

"I don't understand why he can't wait until we know whether the *Sunday Times* is prepared to pay or not."

The Treasurer tapped his fat fingers a few times on the desk. Politics was involved and this newcomer did not understand how the game was played.

"Does he have a plan to use the hostage-taking to promote ISIL?" Wasim asked whilst sitting down.

"Al-Haddawi is the brother-in-law of a member of the Saddam al-Jawal family. Al-Jawal has risen through the ranks pretty quickly and he has discussed the programme of hard-hitting videos with Abu Bakr al-Baghdadi."

Reality hit Henry square in the chest. He found it hard to control the revulsion and anger. Wasim had clenched his fists and released them almost immediately.

The Treasurer exhaled deeply, sitting back in his leather armchair. He was observing them carefully.

"Do you mean they will be… graphic?"

"Yes…" The Treasurer stopped playing with his prayer beads.

Henry fought the desire to stand up and savage the man in front of him, to inflict as much pain as ISIL were inflicting.

"It would be a shame to sacrifice a lucrative deal for a video shoot…" Wasim had spoken, breaking the heavy silence and easing off the tension that had risen in the room.

"That is exactly the point I made, but al-Haddawi wants to discuss it with me."

Henry felt a tremor run down his spine, anger still coursing through his body like a wild animal. "Who will decide if a course of action cannot be agreed?"

The Treasurer's gaze ran coolly over him. "Only one person can decide."

The sound of loud voices and movement stopped Henry in his tracks. Al-Haddawi was making his way to The Treasurer's office, accentuating his limp a little too much but greeted like a rock star by the young men in the room… A warrior and a hero. The Treasurer's face darkened. These were his men and he did not like his authority to be overshadowed.

There was no knock at the door. It simply opened and al-Haddawi walked through its frame. One of his men pulled out a chair, al-Haddawi sat heavily into it, placing his dirty boots on The Treasurer's desk.

"So, Treasurer, you want to save the life of a kafir, for the sake of money." The words had been spoken in English, distinctly, emphatically.

The dark shirt, the dark army slacks, the black turban with extra cloth draped around his left shoulder gave al-Haddawi a theatrical air. He was on show, wielding power mercilessly.

The Treasurer had stood up at the commotion created by al-Haddawi. He sat down again, taking his time to draw his chair closer to his desk, elbows on its armrests, fingertips touching. "So, Commander, you want to spoil the life of a kafir for the sake of a video… When the money we could make out of it would serve the cause better."

"The British do not pay ransom." Al-Haddawi pushed his boots further on top of the desk.

"The British government may not… But others may."

"Who? The family? Her father, the well-known English politician who would rather let his own people die than pay."

The words stunned the other three men. Al-Haddawi had been doing his homework since Mattie had been brought to Raqqa.

The Treasurer stalled for a moment, casting a quick look towards Henry and Wasim.

"But the newspaper she works for, *The Sunday Times*, might." Henry leaned his body forward, turning it to face al-Haddawi. It

142

was hard to believe the same man had somehow given Henry the OK or perhaps he had looked upon Henry as someone to be exploited until no longer needed and then…

Al-Haddawi spat on the floor. "You listen to another kafir, who has come to us under the pretence that he believes in the jihad but who is no brother and never will be."

Henry bent forward towards the backpack he had dropped at the bottom of his chair. Out of it came his Qur'an, a small book, bound in green leather and by the looks of it well thumbed.

"There is no god but Allah, and Muhammad is the messenger of Allah."

"*La ilaha illallah muhammadur rasulullah.*" Henry repeated in perfect Arabic.

The Treasurer sat back in his seat, content about the sudden commitment to the faith of this latest recruit. Abu Maeraka was right… he would be an asset, at least for a while. Wasim's eyes widened for an instant and he held his breath for what was coming next.

"You think that because you speak the words, you are a Muslim… but is your heart in it I wonder?" Al-Haddawi's jaw clenched so hard, muscles in his neck shot out, twitching. His hand moved closer to his handgun.

"If my heart was not in it, I would not have come to Raqqa." Henry sat still. He could see from the corner of his eyes Wasim's hand moving to his own handgun hidden in the small of his back.

Al-Haddawi grabbed Henry's Qur'an from his hands and stood face to face with him.

"I wonder how much of the holy book you know… How many verses you can recite?"

Henry smiled, amused.

He closed his eyes and recited, without hesitation the Al-Fatiha Surah, the opening prayer of the Qur'an, one of the most important of the entire book.

The Treasurer could not suppress a grin. There was no doubt in his mind that Henry had memorised most of the Surahs by heart. There was no need to test him in that respect.

Al-Haddawi recoiled in anger.

143

When Henry opened his eyes, he was already through the door. The limp in his leg, this time almost absent, did not slow him down. His men had followed him in silence.

Not losing a moment, The Treasurer placed a call to Raqqa Stadium. Mattie Colmore was to be taken out of jail this instant and brought to another location. He placed another call to one of his own lieutenants and issued the same order. He then invited Henry and Wasim to sit down again.

"How do you propose we contact the *Sunday Times*?"

Henry replaced his Qur'an in his rucksack, took out a bottle of water and gulped down the last few mouthfuls.

"There's a journalist at the *Sunday Times* I know well. I'll make contact."

The Treasurer had started slowly fingering his prayer beads again, his round face replete with the satisfaction of victory.

Chapter Fifteen

The previous night's meal had been hard to swallow. She suspected these were leftovers from what the fighters had been served but she was too hungry to give it further thought. She had wondered whether there would be only one meal a day, until a guard, this time on his own, had thrown another bottle of water into her cell without looking at her. The plate of food she was hoping for never came.

She was losing track of time, caught between moments of slumber, fear and despair. She had only heard silence when she had last ventured to the door and tried to listen, keeping motionless, leaning against its frame. Unlike some of the prisons she had seen in Eastern Europe where the guards made a lot of raucous noise, the sinister calm of this jail somehow made it less humane.

Mattie moved to the door once more. She wondered whether perhaps she was on her own. Her hearing had grown much sharper, tuning into sounds she would have otherwise ignored. A small but persistent tapping noise at the right of her cell attracted her attention. She moved closer to the wall and stuck her ear to it. The noise had stopped. She was disappointed.

She returned to reading again the messages some of the past prisoners had left behind. A chilling reminder that so few had left the basement of Raqqa Stadium alive.

The rattle of keys took her by surprise and she again forgot to cover her face when the door opened. She had not expected a visit so soon.

This could not be good.

The older guard who had ogled her for far too long entered. Mattie hurriedly brought the veil to her face, whilst a trickle of ice dropped into her stomach... it could not be happening... She looked around for something she could use to defend herself.

Another man entered.

The lightbulb seemed to gain in intensity, controlled from outside the cell. Its brightness blinded her. She brought a protective hand over her eyes. The man who had just come in waited until she was able to see again. He surveyed her with interest.

"You are being moved." He had spoken in Arabic, knowing he would be understood.

Mattie hesitated. "Why?"

"You'll see." The swift move of a hood over her head muffled her cry. Two hands grabbed her arms and she was dragged out of the cell. She stumbled, almost falling, but the hands did not let go.

They drove a short distance.

One of the guards abruptly removed the hood from over her head. The neighbourhood they had arrived in looked unexpectedly peaceful. The only indication perhaps that a war was going on was the number of American Humvees parked in the streets.

The gates of a large villa were opened. Someone Mattie recognised was waiting for her on the porch of the luxury house when her car arrived. Henry walked down the few steps that led him to the driveway. Mattie opened the car door and forced herself to take her time. Wasim appeared from within the property, waiting at the door.

"We'll take it from here." Henry extended a hand towards Mattie. The guards did not bother to reply. The car simply turned around and left.

Mattie followed Henry into the wealthy looking house, still wary of what his intentions were. They entered a room which was well-furnished and comfortable. Mattie bit her lip to suppress a sob. She doubted it was the end of her ordeal in Raqqa but at least for a moment she could feel safe.

No one spoke. Henry sat down on the large sofa that curved round the room, extending a hand towards the seat as if to soften his landing. Mattie's eyes roved around the room before deciding to join

146

them. Wasim had disappeared and after a few minutes he came back with three glasses and a small samovar of tea on an ornate brass tray.

"How did you manage this?" Mattie's hand was shaking as she extended it to take the tea that had been offered to her. She closed her fingers around the glass to make the tremors stop.

"I'm afraid it's all about money." Henry was sipping his tea.

Mattie moved her slender hand over her face, letting the scarf slide from her hair. "You mean ransom?"

"That's right."

"Then I'm in deep bloody trouble... The UK does not pay ransom and even if it did my father would certainly refuse as a matter of principle." Mattie inhaled deeply. "He is a Tory MP and..."

Henry lifted a hand, refilled his glass and offered to refill hers. "We know."

His blue eyes narrowed as he drank the burning liquid. "I'm not relying on the UK government at all..."

"I don't think you understand how determined my father is and I don't mind telling you. He won't move one finger to help, or perhaps worse." Mattie sipped her tea with a sigh.

"There is sometimes a difference between sounding tough and acting tough." Henry was searching her face. Was it really possible that Harold Colmore MP would let his own daughter... die?

"He would." Mattie nodded. "I know you think I'm being perhaps too harsh, but he has no empathy for anyone, absolutely none..."

"Understood." Henry bent forward and refilled her glass. "But we're not relying on the UK government."

"I've no money of my own if that's what you are thinking..." Mattie's voice tilted down as she finished her sentence. It was a silly thing to say, Henry had done his research and there was only one other possibility...

"*The Sunday Times*, I'm sure, would very much like to have you back."

"Is my name already out there?"

"You mean in the media?"

"Well yes, where else?" Mattie's eyes drilled into Henry for a second. She could not quite figure out why this man who knew so little about the Middle East was so self-assured. Was it pure façade?

Henry grinned. He was enjoying her pluckiness. And it seemed she was quite prepared to give him more of it.

"I need a name or names from you. Someone I can contact and who will listen."

Mattie drank some more tea. Her hands had stopped shaking. *Would the Sunday Times pay? Did she want them to pay?*

"This is the only way you can make it out of Raqqa alive." Wasim had spoken in his slow and considerate voice.

"Why are you helping?" Mattie moved her eyes from Henry to Wasim and back to Henry again. Both men pulled back from the edge of their seats.

A no-go area.

"Ted Parker is the international editor and a good friend. If anyone is going to fight for me, it's him."

"Is there anyone else who could help?"

"I'm not sure... I've had my... moments with the Director..." Mattie's head dipped a little. Better not to mention her latest blistering row with him about her going to Aleppo... If she ever got out of this mess alive, he would greet her return with a typical *I told you so...* and this time he would be right.

"You mean you disagreed with him about reporting from Syria?" Henry's eyes became animated again, in amusement.

Mattie pursed her lips, but she too could see the dark humour in this. How the hell did he know?

"Your reputation precedes you."

"Glad the niqab hasn't dented any of it."

Wasim stood up abruptly and they both fell silent. He walked to the door and opened it suddenly. A dark shadow made off to get away. Wasim closed the door behind him, leaving Henry and Mattie on their own.

"Why?" Mattie asked again, her voice now pressing. She needed to know whether she could trust him. Henry gave her a quick smile. "Trust me."

"How can I trust you if I don't understand..."

Henry stood up and came to sit down next to her. "I can't tell you any more than just that... for your own safety."

148

Mattie grabbed his hands with surprising strength. "Please… give me something."

Henry pressed his fingers into hers. "I will get you out." Their eyes had locked into each other. He meant it.

The handle of the door turned, sending Henry swiftly back to his original seat.

"Who was it?" he asked Wasim as he entered the room.

"One of the women who prepared the tea. She doesn't seem to speak English and I gave her a good fright. Still, we need to be more careful."

"I've got what I need in any case." Henry was about to stand up.

"Are you sending me back to the stadium?"

"No." Wasim shook his head. "We have another plan for you in mind."

* * *

The composure James Radlett displayed when he was told about Henry had surprised Harris. He had expected an explosion of protest or worse. He had even imagined James walking out of Vauxhall Cross after having slammed the door in his face. But he had not anticipated James's response. His light blue eyes had become cold and distant. He was a professional assessing a serious proposition.

First class.

"Who came up with the idea?" James crossed his legs and settled into the back of his chair.

"Does it make a difference?"

"Just tell me."

"Crowne himself." Steve stopped himself from moving towards his table – no indication of his keenness, please. Keep it calm and cool.

James pulled a knowing face. "I'm only half surprised."

"How so?"

"If he can convince me, through you… and he knows it's a pretty big if, but if he can, he knows how I operate. He knows how I think. He knows I will understand what support he needs in the field because I know how he in turn operates. And if you are using him because of his understanding of finance then I will be the natural bridge between

149

understanding the technicalities of what he uncovers and knowing how to operate at SIS."

Harris remained silent for a moment. James had got to the point impressively fast. Still one question remained. "You don't think he's worried about your seeking revenge for who he was, for his IRA involvement?"

"That's your job, Steve," James gave the beginning of a smile. "That's your job to ascertain whether I'm the sort who can put his former life aside and work with the likes of Henry." James moved forward, picked up the cup of coffee and leaned back against his chair. "And he knows that too."

"So… James, can you work with Crowne?" Steve had been told by Henry… no BS, go straight to the centre of the issue.

"I used to think I owed him…"

"But that's not the question."

"It's part of the question… If I go ahead with this, I can't be doing it simply because Crowne gave me a chance when I was looking for another job after my injury."

"Don't care about why, James… the question for me is… can you deliver?"

"If I say yes, I will… you know that, otherwise I wouldn't be here."

"So, what's it gonna be?" Steve leaned across the table. Time to get off the fence and find out whether James wanted back in.

"Where is Crowne?"

"Afraid I can't give you that information… you of all people know the drill, you need to be vetted with the right clearance level."

"OK, so a pretty hot place somewhere around the globe then…"

Harris's face remained eager but unflinching. He was good at this game too.

James drained his coffee cup, unfolded his legs and grabbed the visitor pass he had been given at reception.

"You'll have my answer in 24 hours… I want to make sure I won't be tempted to slaughter the bastard when I set eyes on him."

He walked out of the room, without waiting for Harris to call for the standard escort to show him out of the SIS building.

* * *

150

"How did it go?" Amina didn't move from her screens when Harris entered.

"He's hooked… don't know yet when he's going to agree, but he wants to work again with Crowne. I am surprised he gave me this spill about I don't owe him. But perhaps he does mean it."

"Bad boys always appeal… so much more intriguing." Amina's head moved to and for between the different displays on her monitors.

"What's so interesting?" Harris stood over the back of her chair, peering over her shoulder.

"Your intel was right… I've requested a Reaper drone flight over Mosul… ISIL is on the warpath again… they're approaching it from different directions."

Harris followed the convoys of vehicles on her screens, trucks carrying six to ten fighters, AK-47s stuck on their hips, flying the ISIL flag.

"How many of them?"

"Not that many but the beardos are determined…"

"News from our boys on the ground…?"

"Nothing…" Amina turned towards Harris. Her dark brown eyes rested on him for a moment. "And nothing for Encryption yet."

"It's too late in any case to tell them about the attack… and it's not their problem." Harris shook his head.

"Disagree." Amina moved her lower lip over the upper one. "Disagree totally… That's exactly why they are there… The Chief wanted information on the Syrian forces and now he might well want to know which way the next major battle is going to go."

"They are not on the front… they're not with the fighters. If they start asking too many questions, they'll blow their cover…"

"Not necessarily…" Amina called up another page. "I've just asked the Mid East DATA OP Analysts to give me as much intel as they can on Mosul… and its financial assets."

Harris stopped frowning and broke into grin. "You're devious… I love it…"

"Yes, yes… and I can tell you there's a hell of a lot to loot, gold from some of the largest banks in the country, cash in the form of dollar reserves…"

"OK, change of plan… as soon as you can, give them the info… it looks like a decent cover for questions."

"Decent… you mean bloody good!"

Harris sigh. "Granted… bloody good it is."

Amina brought up the website on which she was posting updates to Wasim, encoded her message and pressed send. "What are you still doing here?" She stopped typing. "The Chief would be pleased to know what you're up to." She waved him off.

"Aren't I supposed to be the boss?"

"You are." Amina returned to her work, ignoring Harris's last comment. She was sending yet another message to Encryption.

* * *

Within 15 minutes of the conversation he had had with Amina, Harris had been summoned to Vauxhall Cross's fifth floor. Sir John wanted to see him urgently. Harold Colmore MP was becoming restless. It would not do to have one's daughter, even estranged, causing havoc for the British government.

Harris did not have to wait this time. Sir John's PA was almost pleasant, ushering him into The Chief's office.

Sir John was at his desk, just finishing to read a document when Harris entered. He waved him in without looking up, made a note in the margin of one of the pages with some bland-looking biro and closed his file.

"What have you got for me?"

"There has been no message received from the team, so we should assume they are all still alive."

"When did you last have contact?"

"Twenty-four hours ago… We're checking whether the devices are still in their possession."

"Colmore has called… again. I told him we had no evidence his daughter was the subject of the chatter we've picked up…"

"I'll let you know as soon as we hear anything. Whatever has happened they'll find a way to communicate with us."

"Good, I don't want Colmore trying to pull some stunt or getting involved in some way in order to boost his political career… If we're going to try to save her life, I'd rather do this our own way."

"Agreed, sir…" Harris hesitated.

"Something else for me?"

"Perhaps an opportunity to glean more information on a developing situation."

Sir John moved away from his desk and invited Harris to the corner of his office where large screens were permanently ready for use, relaying the latest data that he had chosen to invoke on the day.

"ISIL is about to launch an attack on Mosul…"

"Did you get this from the locals?"

"CIA but confirmed through their contact in the Kurdish army. We've re-routed a Reaper drone from Akrotiri in Cyprus… ISIL is on the move. We don't know yet how large their manpower will be."

"Have you checked on our Kurdish contacts?"

"Not yet… Amina… I mean Ms Brown is making contact."

"I'm not questioning, I'm suggesting." Sir John gave Harris a friendly smile that reached his eyes. "But you have something else in mind?"

"We can get some intelligence about the progress of ISIL from the team in Raqqa."

"How so?" Sir John's eyes lit up; the more data, the better.

"Ms Brown has established that there are large financial resources in Mosul. These would require a strong financial market strategy to be exploited properly."

"Ah, and you think the team on the ground could try to find out whether these assets might be available for… investment…"

"That's right… Crowne could become even more relevant for them if this is the case."

Sir John fell silent. He pressed enter on one of the keyboards and the screens lit up. His fingers ran over the keys and a digital map of the Middle East appeared on the wall in front of them.

"Their advance has been phenomenal… In terms of fighters, they're outnumbered every time, but their guerrilla strategy and determination have made them successful… They are facing an even greater force in Mosul. By rights, they shouldn't win this battle and yet… It would be foolish to rule out the possibility."

"If we could give the Iraqi army a little help it might change the outcome."

"I'd like to be as optimistic as you are, Steve… But I'm not. They just don't have the strategists I'm afraid. And they need to ask us for the help you suggest… anyway, get as much good intel as you can, and I'll contact my opposite number in Iraq."

"As regards Mattie Colmore… the media is observing the news blackout. The Reuters journalist has gone quiet… for now. Although the piece Kerry Murdock wrote did mention Mattie's name. I am keeping a close eye on her."

"In terms of the rumours about execution… I hope they remain just that."

"I hope you're right… It gives us time to think about options when it comes to the hostages."

Chapter Sixteen

Mattie recognised the building straight away. She had expected to have another hood put on her head but the pressure she had been put under had eased off. She had visited Raqqa many years ago, but her recollection of the city's layout was intact. A sense of nostalgia and sorrow crept over her, memories of the people she had met kept returning. Faces she recognised immediately, although the names had faded away with time. She was good at summoning vivid images to mind. It helped her when writing her articles, even though some of the pictures of places and people she had seen in war-torn countries often proved terrifying. She had told herself she could live with them, compelled by her desire to make the tragedies that unfolded in front of her eyes true and alive for her readers.

She entered the block of flats she had visited once before when she had been first taken away from Henry and Wasim. The guard moved his head, indicating she should follow him. She arrived in front of the same door and the same older women opened it. The young woman who was at her side was different from the beauty who had taken care of her previously and helped her with her wounds.

The matron did not ask Mattie to come in. Instead she moved down the corridor towards another set of doors, the sound of her large abaya the only sound she made. Mattie noticed a slight limp, something she had not observed the last time she had been here. Mattie followed. There was nothing much she could do, at least not for the time being. She walked slowly, creating an increasing distance between her and her new jailor. The woman arrived at the door of another apartment, taking hold of a set of keys that she was keeping on a chain around her neck, hidden by her long head cloth. She called a name – Nabiha – and finally looked in Mattie's direction. The slow pace at which Mattie was walking towards her new prison neither irritated nor moved the old woman. There was certainty in her eyes that Mattie would not be going anywhere other than where she was intended to be. Raqqa was not a place in which a single woman of foreign origin would want to be alone if she valued her life. There was nowhere else for Mattie to go and she knew it.

Nabiha arrived on the threshold and eyed the new arrival with curiosity. Her silence was perhaps less hostile, yet it was clear that she did not intend to befriend Mattie.

She moved aside to let Mattie through the door. The lounge was as sparse furnished as the one she had visited a couple of days ago, bare of the ornaments or knick-knacks that make a home a home. The deep leather sofa and armchair looked incongruously comfortable in this spartan decoration. The rugs were lush and the only sign of colour to be found in the room, a deep crimson red that Mattie recognised to be of expensive Persian quality.

Whoever had owned this property had been wealthy but had had no time to take with them these cumbersome possessions.

Nabiha moved across the lounge towards a passageway that led to more rooms. The place smelled of food being cooked, a mix of meat and spices. Mattie's mouth watered; her stomach rumbled. She quickly placed her arm across it to muffle the sound. The young woman took a key from the long chain that she too kept around her neck underneath her head cloth and opened the first door they came to. She looked into the room, making sure she was moving Mattie to the right one.

"I speak Arabic." Mattie's voice sounded thick and dry.

"I've been told." Nabiha moved away from the door to let Mattie in, and as she entered, she simply closed the door behind her, locking it. Mattie stepped into a large bedroom. Two women stood up hesitantly. Like her they were westerners and Mattie understood why she had been moved here.

* * *

156

"We have two sources confirmed." Henry was sitting in The Treasurer's office, the can of lemonade he had been offered in one hand... He was making slow progress... one can at a time. Wasim had perched on a table that stood near one of the windows, a little further away. His body was half turned towards the open door, a casual but effective way of surveying from a distance the young men and the location ISIL operated from.

"I have some good contacts at Al Jazeera. I'll ask them to validate the names you suggested. When the times comes, we can use them to release the news about the woman hostage."

"Perfect. I'm going to need means of communication though..."

Henry did not push it. So far, he had had to do without a computer and mobile of his own. He was now grateful that five years at HMP Belmarsh had not only weaned him off mobile binges but made him more resourceful.

The Treasurer moved the prayer beads around his fingers a little faster. Henry turned towards Wasim. "I could have used Wasim's mobile and laptop, but they have not resurfaced."

The Treasurer nodded and stood up. His long white dishdasha flowed over his slack trousers. Henry noticed the expensive Rolex Cosmograph Daytona watch on his wrist; much like some the Middle Eastern clients Henry had dealt with in his past banking career, The Treasurer seemed to appreciated a good timepiece. The Treasurer moved to the window of his office, hands behind his back, prayer beads still running through his fingers.

Malahi Avenue was busier than it had been the day before. Wasim had moved his attention to the street below. Henry had noticed his interest was pricked by something. The Treasurer had clearly noticed too and moved to take a look as well.

"May I ask when you will contact Al Jazeera...?" Henry's voice almost startled the two men. He stood up to join them at the window.

"Today... It will shortly be prayer time... but afterwards I'll make the call." The Treasurer did not move from his observation post. "Will you join us for prayer? We have a prayer room within the building... unless you would rather go to Al-Qadim?"

"I'll welcome the opportunity to pray with my brothers." Henry gave him a grave smile that seemed to please.

The call to Zuhr rolled over the city from its minarets. The team of young men that always looked so busy and purposeful rose in unison, leaving the main trading room. Wasim and Henry followed, taking their time to note who had or had not logged out of their computers. The Treasurer had locked his office shut and a young man wearing the traditional taqiyah and white robes shut the door behind them. Other people, all men, had appeared along the corridors. Henry followed Wasim's lead. He had been told time and time again of the ritual preceding prayer, but he felt self-conscious, making gestures and saying words that did not ring true or make real sense to him. Still, needs must. He had assured Steve Harris back in London that he would deliver and deliver he would. Henry could not falter now and be caught, not just yet... and then there was Wasim. If Henry failed, he would drag down Wasim with him. And he had no intention of letting him down. Wasim, the patient bull who had taught him all he needed to survive not only in the extreme world of the jihad but also as a spy. Wasim had trusted him... he would repay that trust... handsomely.

Henry took off his shoes and waited at the back for more people to enter the prayer room. No one noticed him or at least no one showed they had seen the new convert.

The room filled within minutes and when it was full one of the men at the front, an older man, turned around to check all had settled. He raised his two hands at the level of his chest, crossed them over it, and uttered the first words of prayer.

Allahu Akbar.

All followed and the chanting commenced. Henry mouthed the words, stumbling to let the sound come out of his throat.

At the end, one word, Amen, transports him back to the place of his birth... Belfast.

The others carry on, but Henry no longer listens. He follows Wasim's motion. Body forward, head on the ground.

The intensity of the memory shocks Henry and he starts shivering.

The coffin has been laid in the church and Henry is sitting in the front row. He so would like to squeeze his mother's hand, but she is holding a handkerchief to her face with one hand and a flower in the other. Henry is barely eight years of age. He has been told his dad has died but he does not yet understand what that truly means.

158

Henry is looking into the bowels of his father's grave. It is the committal, the moment the coffin is lowered into the earth. There is a small group of friends, hardly any family, and people he does not know... Later in life he will imagine these people have been members of the IRA, who had come to pay their respects to a fallen brother. His mother has stopped crying. Perhaps she has cried all the tears she will ever cry. The priest comes to the edge of the deep hole in the ground, sprinkles in some holy water and speaks the words that Henry will remember forever.

Earth to earth,

Ashes to ashes,

Dust to dust.

A chill enters little Henry's heart and he knows he will never feel the warmth of his father's arms around him again. His body goes limp and almost falls forward. Someone pulls him back, two solid hands on his shoulders. He does not know to this day the identity of man who saved him from the fall.

Wasim's voice startled him. He was looking at him, speaking to him, from his kneeling position.

Salaam alaikum... he repeated to Henry. Henry mumbled the words too. It had been hard to snap back.

Everyone stood up and the shuffling of feet soon replaced the sanctity of prayer. Henry waited until everyone had left. He still felt the lump in his throat and the moisture that had welled up in his eyes.

Wasim squeezed his shoulder... Someone else to save him from the abyss.

* * *

When Henry returned to The Treasurer's office, he was already on the phone. The door of his office was closed and he was having an animated conversation with his interlocutor.

Wasim was engaged in a friendly conversation with one of the young men in the office. He was asking for the best place to get a coffee or tea, and some food to eat. Henry noticed his features were relaxed, warm... someone one wanted to help. He nodded appreciatively at the answer he had been given, stood up from his leaning position... "I'm going out for a tea," he simply said. No one seemed to notice. Henry stayed behind, an opportunity to engage with some of the young men who looked so eager. He had not yet been shown his desk in the separate The Treasurer had spoken about. Henry could hang around now that he had a good reason.

The young man whom he had spoken to the day before about oil prices was not at his desk. Henry surveyed the room more keenly than he had done before. The office contrasted with what they had seen on the streets of Raqqa. The loose robes, the baggy trousers and the taqiyah, all in white. It felt strangely peaceful and almost ordinary. Yet nothing was normal about the actions of this 20-strong team.

Henry had already identified who was doing what, but he could not expect to be given information about the assets they were managing until The Treasurer had indicated his trust. The young man he wanted to see had returned, making a detour to drop a small box in front of Henry.

"Abu Shabh." Henry took the parcel in one hand, rotating it with interest. "Abu Hamia, The Treasurer, would like you to have this."

Henry shook off the cover and opened the box. A brand-new iPhone was waiting to be activated. He nodded to the young man by way of thanks.

"What's your name?"

"Hamza." He bent forward a little when speaking his name, his voice smooth and pleasant. The shift was palpable in the room. The Treasurer had given him a mobile... note was taken.

Henry took the device out and started to set it up. He worked fast and wondered whether he could use it to communicate with London. The phone had an international range... trust or temptation?

Wasim reappeared just as Henry was about to test his mobile by calling him. "We need to speak." His face was calm but his tone insistent.

The Treasurer's door opened, waving them in. Wasim dropped his voice. "Ask about new assets requiring your expertise... from new territories."

The Treasurer looked satisfied with his conversation. "My contact has validated the name you want to approach at the *Sunday Times*... It has also been approved by our leader, Abu Bakr al-Baghdadi." His eyes spoke of something else that Henry had not yet witnessed... greed and cruelty.

160

"I am glad our leader thinks it is worth pursuing." Henry's voice was smooth, content and yet measured.

"You are free to contact the *Sunday Times* journalists, although I would recommend you use an intermediary."

"Intermediary...?" Henry's voice trailed.

"We know of reliable people we can use. They are not part of our organisation, but we have dealt with them in the past for more..." The Treasurer thought it through for a short moment, "...complex transactions."

Henry cursed himself. He should have thought about this too. Why would he want to expose himself to a direct contact with London... unless... he had a hidden agenda.

A first mistake.

"Very good..." Henry gave an approving nod and hoped it was convincing.

"I'll communicate the name to you shortly." The Treasurer did not seem to have thought he would want to do this any other way.

"And I'll be using this?" Henry waved the iPhone.

"You will, but you will have to disconnect on a regular basis. We do not permit mobile phones to be used and switched on all the time."

"Understood..."

"You will receive instructions on your phone telling you when you need to switch off... then you must obey."

The Treasurer looked at the two men, waiting for them to leave.

"I am not yet sure how I can best help consolidate your operation around a difficult-to-detect corporate structure. But perhaps if we could speak about the range of assets being used it would help."

The Treasurer fiddled with his pen. It was tempting... Henry knew what he was talking about. "Let's focus on the ransom idea first."

He was about to return to his task, dismissing Henry and Wasim, but an argument made him raise his head again. Hamza was calling a client to say he was not happy about the outcome of his conversation. Hamza slammed the phone down. The entire room had come to a standstill. The Treasurer stood up. His placid face hardened. A problem with the sale of oil was not what he needed and Henry noticed a fleeting moment of concern pass over his eyes.

Hamza was still sitting at his desk. The Treasurer waited. Henry walked straight to the young man. Wasim had drifted out, ready to be of use without wanting to interfere.

"Distribution problems again?"

Hamza lifted his head. He hesitated, looking towards The Treasurer's office. Should he reveal the problem? The Treasurer had appeared at the door of his office and nodded.

"The Turkish contact is still insisting on a discount and he agrees that the oil mixing alongside the Kirkuk pipeline works, but he says the Turkish authorities are becoming very inquisitive…"

"He is lying." Henry had moved closer to Hamza's desk. He took a piece of paper and wrote a name and number on it. "This is a contact who will make a call to your dealer. Mention Liam O'Connor of Belfast and his father Pat O'Connor."

Henry stepped back. "Let me know when you've done that."

Hamza nodded. He had nothing to lose.

"Is the other desk ready?" Henry turned towards The Treasurer who clicked his fingers at another of his men. He stood up and led the way to a small room adjacent to the Treasury Office. It had a desk, a chair. Another couple of seats of shabby quality were stacked against the wall. Even as a trainee in banking, Henry had had a better place to work.

Wasim entered after Henry. He grabbed one of the spare chairs and sat himself down in front of what was now Henry's desk. "What did you mean out there… Liam O'Connor and his father?"

"The IRA sourced some of its weaponry from Libya. Did you know that?"

"I've never got into the IRA background, so no… but what's the link with Turkey?"

"Transit… it was too hot to import armament directly from Libya when it was run by Qaddafi. Some well-connected people in Turkey facilitated and the structure I put in place was used to make payments even after the IRA was decommissioned."

"How high is he? Government?"

"Senior officials… exactly."

"And he doesn't want their names mentioned…"

162

"That's the idea... he may also like to get a bit of the action in oil trafficking, if he hasn't already, that is."

Wasim stretched. "That's a good move... let's see what Hamza manages to agree."

"How about your tea break?" Henry sat in the armchair of the diminutive office he had been allocated and rolled it towards the desk.

Wasim smiled. "I found a tearoom that serves ISIL fighters exclusively... and guess what?"

"Tell me... the suspense is killing me."

"As long as it's only the suspense... I'll tell you a little later." Wasim circled his head round in a strange sweeping fashion and Henry understood it would have to wait until they were in a more secure place.

The door of the office opened without a knock and Hamza walked through it. He looked relieved, but perhaps less content than Henry had expected. "Abu Hamia wants to see you."

Henry stood up slowly. No need to show keenness. "Do you mind?" Wasim nodded. It was Henry's moment to shine on his own.

"Who is this contact?" The Treasurer was sitting at his desk, hands outstretched over it.

Henry gave the same explanation he had given to Wasim. "I ran the IRA fund structure for a very long time... this has given me access to senior people in the world of arms trafficking." He let this take effect...

"Why did Qaddafi help the IRA? Muslim... Catholics... Why?"

"Because he saw the IRA as sharing his own anti-imperialist views of England... a way to destabilise the establishment that represented colonial exploitation."

The Treasurer pondered for a short moment.

He opened a drawer in his desk kept locked with a key he had on a keyring. He took out a document that looked official and placed it into Henry's hands.

"We believe in a fanatical spending discipline." He was most serious in making the statement. "This is our annual financial report, dated 2012."

Henry took the document with precaution.

"You can read it in your office and bring it back when you have finished... today."

Henry nodded, already flicking through the report's pages.

If Henry had not spotted the AK-47 that lay against the side of his desk, he would have sworn he had just met a most thorough corporate CFO.

* * *

Someone was standing in front of the table where he had chosen to have his lunch... Alone.

Harris raised his head from his book.

"Ahmed... What can I do for you?" Harris smiled. He would have respectfully told anybody else to get lost but not the head of the Middle East OMA team at The Cross.

Ahmed dropped his tray on the table with a clunk. Harris surveyed the contents of his plate and tutted, shaking his head.

"Mate, this stuff will kill you... sausages, bacon... A full English breakfast at 1pm."

"No, my mother will kill me if she ever finds out I've been eating pork on the sly..."

"As long as Nilay doesn't mind."

Ahmed grinned but did not reply. Harris put his book away, still shaking his head in mock reprobation.

"I've got intel for you, mate..." Ahmed sliced decisively into his sausage and took a mouthful. His face said it all... Heaven.

"'bout Raqqa?"

"Nope... about Mosul. ... Amina told us we need to concentrate on this new target."

"You used a drone?"

"And directed it on the Kurdish outpost near Dubok to the north of Mosul. The ISIL army is on the move... from a number of directions."

"How about the Iraqis?"

"They have about two divisions gathered in the city, 30,000 men plus the latest US equipment."

164

Harris toyed with some of the food he had left on his plate. What did it mean for RED HAWK?

"Will that deter ISIL?"

"Deter?... Not a chance... The Kurdish intel I have is pretty reliable. ISIL needs another big win to reach the credibility they aspire to. Raqqa's fall rattled everyone, and it enabled ISIL to establish a strong base, but they need something bigger if they're to dislodge Al-Qaeda in the region." Ahmed scooped up the yolk of an egg with a piece of his toast. "More territory means many things, but most importantly the ability to persuade more people to join."

"Because they have some wealth and land to distribute?"

"Exactly, houses, women, money for the fighters..."

"I suspect we've not seen the worst yet..."

"Ethnic minorities are already being rounded up and people are disappearing in Raqqa, never to be seen again."

"Rape and pillage to instil fear... an old tactic that works every time."

Ahmed put his fork down. His face had turned unusually serious.

"We're facing something much more potent than Al-Qaeda ever was... I can't quite get you the intel about it yet... but we'd better be ready to strike at the bastards as soon as we can..."

"You don't need to convince me.... the Americans are in withdrawal mode though..."

"And so are the Brits..."

"And so are the Brits... What can I say? Iraq... disaster, no strategy for after Saddam, Libya... disaster, no strategy for after Qaddafi... Afghanistan... still a war zone." Harris stopped himself... ranting would not solve anything. "How many people do you reckon ISIL has on the ground?"

"Maybe 2,000, perhaps a few more."

"Got to be more... surely." Harris arched his mouth in disbelief.

"Don't think so..."

"Are you telling me they're going to mount an offensive outnumbered 15 to 1?"

"I am... or rather..." Ahmed had started attacking his bacon. "The Kurds do. I've been following these guys for a while... I believe Kurdish intel... They'll give the assault."

"And win?" Harris had forgotten about his food.

Ahmed became thoughtful and put his cutlery down again. He nodded. "They might... no, I'll get off the fence..." He nodded convincingly.

"They will."

* * *

It had taken him a little over an hour. Wasim had disappeared again.

"I have finished reading the financial report you just gave me." Henry had settled in the chair in front of The Treasurer's desk; the latter raised an intrigued eyebrow and looked at his watch. He had much to do but Henry's skills at doing business were proving too important to ignore.

"Strong performance, but still... You need to consolidate your assets." Henry ignored the sudden disquiet that had descended into the room.

"How so?"

"You need easier access to your cash, for example, enough to make large transfers quickly and smoothly in case of urgent need."

"Oil brings us $0.6 million a day..."

"Very true but you need to lay your hands on that money effectively..." Henry scratched his beard. "You can't do account-to-account transfers..."

"What do you suggest?"

"Cash readily available, here in Raqqa... perhaps gold."

The Treasurer drummed his fingers on the desk. His eyes were half closed behind his thick glasses. His chubby hand pulled the glasses off and started cleaning them on a small piece of soft cloth he took out of a desk drawer.

"You might have your wish."

"New assets?" Henry's question came naturally, a financier keen to work with new money.

"That's right." The. Treasurer's words came out slowly.

"Anything to do with the activity we saw on the street earlier on?"

The Treasurer fiddled with a pen. Henry could hear Wasim's advice...

166

Don't push too hard…

"I couldn't help noticing. In any case the only way to increase wealth is to acquire new territory." Henry said, matter of fact. "But you're busy… I'll let you know as soon as I've contacted the *Sunday Times*."

The Treasurer nodded, relieved he hadn't had to discuss the imminent attack on a target.

Henry stood up. He walked out unnoticed by the young men, working hard at managing ISIL's money.

Only Hamza lifted his head.

Chapter Seventeen

Their battered truck was going against the traffic. Other large vehicles of much better quality and sturdiness, SUVs and Humvees, were driving past them carrying fighters equipped with assault rifles as well as the expected Kalashnikovs. The darkness of their uniforms, the black flags proclaiming ISIL's motto flying over the convoys, made their chants and shouts powerful and sinister. It was not a fight, more an execution.

"Where are they going?" Henry craned his neck to follow the third convoy they had passed within the space of five minutes.

"Mosul." Wasim slowed down to let another convoy drive past before he could take the turn into the street leading them back to their hotel.

"Confirmed from…?"

"MOTHER."

"You managed to make contact?" Henry turned in his seat to half face Wasim.

"Told you… if I found a tearoom with internet."

"And they let you use the computer?"

"I had to do a bit of arguing. Raqqa is on limited web access at the moment, but ISIL must have decided not to piss off their fighters too much. As long as you don't use an email account or other social media account… you're good."

"And you only wanted to check a website…"

"With lots of guns on it… what else?"

"So… an assault on Mosul you said."

"And they want us to find out more."

"Is this why you wanted me to ask about new assets?"

Wasim gave a grunt.

"This could be a good way of delving deeper into IS operations."

"But I don't want to think about what's going to happen to the poor buggers who are going to be at the receiving end of their assault."

"I haven't said I want them to win." Henry waved a correcting finger. "I said it's an opportunity... as long as The Treasurer and Baghdadi's war council are convinced they're going to win. I can gather intel on their next move."

"That's the idea." Wasim nodded.

"I'm starting to understand how these people think... as always in finance... Greed Is Good... And I've been made to read their financial report..."

"What?" Wasim moved his face towards Henry for a brief moment.

"Eyes on the road, Was. Yup... a financial report... Very well put together I may add. I'll tell you more about it over a cool drink of soapy lemonade later on."

Wasim parked the truck almost in front of the hotel's main door and they both jumped out. They had not seen Ali since the morning. Wasim walked towards the hotel gardens... Time for him to exploit what he knew the ISIL fighters who remained in Raqqa loved doing... gossip about those who had gone to Mosul. Henry followed him at a distance. He spotted Ali in the middle of a group of young men dressed in the expected black uniform, some sporting black bandanas, white Arabic letters scrawled over them... a chilling example of what a suicide squad might look like.

Henry walked towards them and stopped halfway. He was not sure he should interrupt the banter, young men talking up their stories of fights and trying to ascertain whether Ali was one of them.

Ali must have noticed him. He walked away from the group and came straight over to Henry. Would he too volunteer to join the next big attack, the push to extend ISIL's advance in the region, Ali asked, speaking half in English, half in Arabic. Henry kept nodding, the way an attentive parent might listen to his eager child. The young man's face had lit up with such enthusiasm.

"The Jihad, The Faith, Allah's greatness, the final fight of Dabiq…"

Henry had heard the same banal rhetoric before, spoken perhaps with a little more reserve by his Irish friends. He too had believed in the IRA cause. Ali's chattering had soon become a background noise.

The small booth in the Belfast pub feels cosy and safe. Henry is speaking to Liam, his best friend. The smell of beer and roasted meat floats around the place. It makes it more homely, more welcoming. They have been debating for months how to support the cause, even at this late hour, even if a peace process and the decommissioning of armaments that follows go through. Henry is about to leave for London, the Big City where he hopes to make money. No. He knows he will make money… a lot of it. What else can he do to help but contribute his hard-earned cash to the IRA slush fund and perhaps better, since his plan is to become a lawyer, find out how the law can help him in beating the system that has crushed Ireland for too many centuries.

The chatter had stopped. Ali was no longer talking, wondering whether Henry did not approve. It could not be he did not support the fight, otherwise he would not be here, but perhaps he doubted Ali's determination and strength. Distress was etched on Ali's face. Henry shook off the slumber of memories and slapped Ali on the shoulder.

"Well done." What else could he say? He could not admit that perhaps Ali was right. That Henry did not think this young man, who had barely lived, was ready for what awaited him. The training camps were gruesome, but they were nothing in comparison to what Ali was about to face in the field.

Ali beamed a large smile at Henry. The group of young lads, for that is what they were, was calling him back. They had not drunk alcohol, yet they sounded just as intoxicated by the beliefs they professed.

Henry walked back inside, overtaken by an immense sadness. He knew how this would finish. He wished he could do something to save Ali from the abomination that the Mosul attack would prove to be.

His mobile was buzzing in his pocket. Such a strange feeling after so long.

"Hello." He could no longer say Henry but 'Abu Shabh' sounded fake.

"Where are you?" Wasim's voice shifted Henry's mood.

"Back in a minute."

170

"So… Fancy a can of fizz on the balcony?" Henry laughed – for one second he thought Wasim was about to offer him a can of smuggled beer.

"Lemonade or Fanta?" Wasim was holding the cans one in each hand and presenting them with fake excitement.

"Go on… I'll try the lemonade." Henry grabbed the drink, cracked open the can and took a few long pulls. "News from MOTHER?"

"Have you swept your room for devices?" Wasim was sitting on one of the lounge chairs that had recently been added to the furniture on the terrace.

Henry rolled his eyes. "What do you take me for? Ain't a newbie any more… I left the phone in the bedroom, too… I'll check it later."

"MOTHER would be impressed…"

"Has SHE asked you to make doubly sure?"

"No, she's much more concerned about Mosul's attack…"

Henry had sat down too. He bent his body forwards, elbows on knees. "Does MOTHER confirm it has a large asset base?"

"She made that point exactly… and how do you know, may I ask?" Wasim swirled the liquid around in his can.

"Because I gathered as much information as I could about Syria and Iraq before I left the UK. If I'm going to pretend I'm helping them with money laundering, I have to understand where the assets are… Mosul is a really good quarry."

"And staked up with the latest US weaponry supplies…"

"As long as they can pull off the attack…"

Both men remained silent for a short while.

"Could we have done something more?" Henry eventually asked. He was certain Wasim was thinking about the same thing.

"I wish we could, but we have already progressed a lot in less than 48 hours…" Wasim finished his can of lemonade and crushed it in his fist. "How about this financial report…? I'm more than intrigued."

The financial report was comprehensive and strangely accurate. ISIL did not have the intention to hide the sources of its income. They had presented their finances the way a good corporate would. Expenses were equally captured with diligence. The report bragged about the strengths of ISIL's fanatical spending discipline.

Everything seemed to be accounted for, armament from large to small, transport, food, accommodation, payment of their army.

Henry had read the report twice in the hour he had given himself back in The Treasurer's office. He now knew with certainty what constituted the undisputed strength of this terror group... a ruthless capacity to exploit all avenues to create and safeguard income.

He had suspected oil would be high on the list, but since his conversation with The Treasurer he had measured the magnitude of its impact. He also knew about the looting of antiquities and other artefacts from historical sites in Iraq and he suspected Syria would be next. Henry had known about the trafficking of ancient pieces first hand. He had been tempted, when the large bonuses of investment banking were rolling into his pocket, to buy a unique piece from his then art dealer Brett Allner-Smith. Henry loathed the man; still, he had an uncanny flair for knowing what his clients wanted most. Henry had come back to his senses, withdrawing from a substantial purchase at the last minute. He had landed Brett in a tight spot, owing terrorists $0.5 million was a little tricky. Somehow Brett seemed to have survived.

Henry ran his long hand through his hair. It felt coarse and unkempt, after so many months on the road. He forced his focus away from a past that had started to feel so very distant.

"The document is incredibly thorough. A good corporation could not have done better. I would be impressed even if we were not talking ISIL."

"What else apart from oil and antiquities theft?"

"Taxation... It took me less than ten seconds to decide this was a rather disingenuous way of portraying extortion and protection money."

"I'll remember that next time I fill in my tax return..." Wasim shook his head.

"The final item managed to surprise me." Henry had been punched in the gut at reading the heading. In black and white the word kidnapping had been recorded as another income stream. Countries and individuals were paying to free their citizens or loved ones. "Kidnapping has become an absolute money machine."

He squeezed his can a little harder; the metal complained under his grip. Anger had been a constant companion in his life but not always a good adviser. He had learned to be wary of it.

"You need to tell MOTHER about the oil production."

"Yes, I've started mapping the tearooms in Raqqa that have internet access. We are also moving websites, more secure... as soon as this is ready I'll start uploading the information onto our new comms portal. I need a couple of days before I can upload all the data regarding the oil fields under ISIL's control."

"I'll speak again with Hamza tomorrow. I want to know how much of an impact my name-dropping bombshell has had on the price he will be able to negotiate. The Kirkuk mixing idea should also make it easier to achieve a good outcome."

"How can we use it to our advantage?"

"We know how much is produced in the area and how much ISIL controls, so it's a matter of percentages."

"You mean if the production is 10% of the total, that 10% of the oil arriving in Turkey from the pipe is ISIL's oil?"

"Yup... perhaps you could convert to the City once you're done with this." Henry bumped his fist against Wasim's muscular shoulder.

"And wear a tailor-made suit, drive an expensive car, rather than slumming it in a black shirt, military fatigues at the wheel of a derelict truck... Never." Wasim smiled and the two dimples in his cheeks deepened.

"You don't know what you're missing... war of a different kind."

"You mean subtle assassination through gossip and lies."

"Good way of putting it..." Henry stood up, disappeared into his bedroom and came back with two more drinks. "Let's get really smashed on more lemonade." He handed one to Wasim. "Next step is for me to understand where else and through whom they export the oil. Turkey has got to be their biggest target. Turkey sends oil from a number of its ports. It has a large border with Syria and Iraq... ideal. But they can't be the only country ISIL deal with."

"And there is plenty of suspicious activity already around armament supplies, so I agree, Turkey's a prime candidate. Otherwise... I'm not sure... Lebanon, Jordan perhaps."

"I don't think Lebanon is organised enough... but Jordan... a very good suggestion." Henry pulled the ring out of the can's top. "The next interesting question is going to be how high does this trafficking go?"

"What do you mean?"

"We're not talking about a few barrels of oil... we're talking massive volumes and that will attract the attention of people who want to make serious money by facilitating, keeping the border open, finding clients..."

"You're thinking names in places of power."

"I'm thinking exactly that..."

"Political contacts?"

The call that came on his mobile phone surprised Henry. He almost hesitated... then he got up and fetched the phone from his bedroom, sliding his thumb on the screen after a couple of rings as he came back.

"The name of the intermediary is on a text I sent you." The Treasurer's voice was all business. "Call him this evening."

Wasim raised his eyebrows. Henry read the text. "The intermediary is from Qatar... senior post in a Middle Eastern NGO."

"Then... place the call."

* * *

Harris's iPhone buzzed. DATA OP was calling him. Amina's computer screen had lit up with a newsflash.

"Mattie Colmore disappearance confirmed."

"Shit... This is not on..." Harris was following up on a new lead from his other asset, Brett, the art dealer. He had no time to lose on some wannabe journalist trying to make a name for herself by writing a scoop on Mattie Colmore.

Harris was reading through the Reuters article. It was short and said very little. But it was a good way of keeping the Mattie Colmore story alive until the big story came... clever yet reckless.

"Colmore is going to use this." Amina shook her head.

"You're right, he will." Harris stood up and moved to the window of RED HAWK Control Room. "We can't have him trying to organise a response in parallel or, worse, finding out we have assets on the ground."

174

"I can't see The Chief lying if the Rt Hon. Harold Colmore MP asks MI6 to help save his daughter." Amina pulled a face.

"Load the website with the information you have... Wasim may find a way to get to the intel."

"This is not the way it's supposed to work, Steve. You know that... I put intel up at the last minute and take it down so that we minimise intrusion."

"I understand, but they need to be aware. What if someone tries to pin that leak on them?"

Amina sighed. "I'll see how far I can stretch it."

"In the meantime, I'm going to have a little chit chat with Ms Murdock..." Harris had grabbed his jacket from the back of his seat. "... in person."

Amina was keeping an eye on her emails... nothing yet from the Crypto team. She barely noticed a message popping up on the alternative website Wasim might be using if he needed to communicate on the web.

She held her breath for a short moment. A message was flashing. Her fingers flew over the keys as she called up the webpage on full screen and started to read the text. The website was selling army-decommissioned but still functioning armament.

She copied the message on to a new page and started decoding his words, words Wasim had learned by heart before leaving for the Middle East in order to communicate with his MI6 minder.

Laptop and mobile confiscated.

Henry established credible contact with Treasurer.

Obtaining details of ISIL's operation.

Need to use alternative website.

Proceeding as agreed.

Amina had to pull her code equivalents out to make sure she had not misunderstood. She too had learned the words by heart, but today she did not trust herself. The loss of comms had to be expected... still Wasim had to find at least a mobile in case the emergency protocol had to be activated.

The second part of the message that she found in the response to another ad was giving more positive news about Mattie Colmore.

She had been taken away from them though and they had not seen her for a day.

Amina checked the timestamp of the posted messages. Less than an hour ago. She breathed a sigh of relief. If there was chatter on the web about hostages, it was not about her team.

It was her turn to reply and pass on information that both men would find helpful.

She opted for a short communication confirming they were aware of Mattie's predicament. For the time being, however, newspapers and other media had respected the blackout convention on kidnapping. This could nevertheless change swiftly. She also shared the information she had about Mosul. This made Crowne more relevant… She thought it through again. It was in their favour. Surely… There was nothing else to say apart from the few words she couldn't write.

Be so bloody careful…

* * *

He walked back to the City on foot, defeated only on the last mile by a bout of heavy rain that would have drenched him had he not spotted a black cab near Blackfriars Bridge. James Radlett needed the walk. He had lived in the shadow of Henry Crowne for over five years. The man who had given him a chance, elevated him to the envied position of number two in his hugely successful team. The man who had never lied to him when it came to work matters, sharing his doubts about team management strategies and anxieties about the proposed merger between their bank and their greatest competitor during the 2008 financial crisis. The man who, nevertheless, had laundered money for the IRA for years. It was ironic that what had brought Henry down had been someone else's rather twisted case of greed and revenge rather than his Irish connection.

People had been whispering about Henry's potential then… CEO material… Born leader… Inspirational thinker… What a load of bullshit.

James had forced himself to feel betrayed by Henry, to speak the language of the disappointed and the disaffected. But when he gave himself the time to reflect on what he truly felt about Henry's treachery, every time he let honesty prevail, he could not quite bring himself to feel the hatred and the spite he thought he ought to feel.

Henry had never pretended he was an angel. He kept his private life private. He had never lied to James in that respect... The critical part of James, of course, laughed about the argument. It was unlikely Henry would have walked into his office and confessed he was an IRA operative. And the response to the mocking voice that taunted James into thinking he was a fool was always the same.

Henry had been faithful to his friends and to his cause.

James walked into the spacious atrium of GL's investment bank. He shook the rain off his coat in a wet dog motion and walked to the turnstiles. A security guard approached him with a smile. He nodded, stopped and turned back. The office did not feel the right place to reflect on what MI6 was offering. He might say yes without thinking, just for the chance of avoiding yet another management meeting. The complications of the merger between GL and HXBK were still rumbling four years on. He might say no because, walking into Henry's office, the mocking voice would remind him he had been made a fool of, he, the former British intelligence officer.

James moved to the far end of the atrium, towards another entrance reserved for staff. He flashed his ID pass at the electronic eye and walked back into the street. He turned left towards Smithfield Market, crossed the road and spotted in the distance the distinct green tiles of Beppe's Café. The heavy rain had not deterred a couple of clients from sitting outside, sheltered by the green awning. James walked in and the familiar smell of brewing coffee and toasted sandwiches lifted James's mood.

The young woman who had started her waitress job a few months ago recognised him. "The usual?" she shouted with a smile. He nodded, looked around for a cosy place and saw he was in luck, a table had become free in the window. The coffee appeared faster that he had expected, accompanied by a chunky sausage and bacon roll.

James pulled his iPhone out and checked his messages. His team was updating him on the deals they were working on. Another management meeting had been squeezed into his already overburdened

177

schedule. A client was asking for another set of simulations on his latest large and complex transaction... routine. James replaced the iPhone in his jacket pocket and started on his sandwich... Nothing better than hearty comfort food to help a man think straight. The café was still full. He drank some of Beppe's craft coffee and let his eyes rove over the crowd. Two women were huddled over the table in front of him, exchanging confidences and giggling like two schoolgirls. It was good to see people having fun, able to enjoy a meal and leave work behind. One of the women glanced at her watch. Her eyes opened wide. She told her friend the time. Both donned their raincoats, zipped up their bags and hurried off.

James sat back at the table he had been lucky to get. The green fabric of the double seat had seen better days, but was faded rather than dirty. The café was starting to empty; in a few minutes he would have it to himself.

The young woman behind the counter waved at him; *Another coffee?* she mouthed. He smiled *Yes, please.* When the coffee arrived, he took his private phone from his jacket pocket. Paused. And brought up his contacts list. Time to call a few acquaintances in the field.

Chapter Eighteen

The two women who were sitting in the room stood up slowly. They too were dressed in black abayas but in the seclusion of their bedroom they had been allowed to remove their veils. Mattie stood still, her heart pounding, her mouth dry… She inhaled deeply and wondered whether she should make the first move. The young woman who had light brown hair pulled back in a bun walked the few paces that separated them and extended a friendly hand.

"I'm Jean." The soft American accent took Mattie unawares, a gentle yet powerful shock. Fighting back tears, she extended her hand. "Mattie."

The other woman stood up slowly. "Gretta."

A third bed beneath the window was empty. "Shall I…" Mattie stopped, her legs buckling underneath her. She felt two pairs of hands grabbing her, holding her until she reached the nearest bed. She crumpled onto it, bringing her knees to her chin, tears streaming down her face. Jean moved to the head of the bed and sat down next to Mattie, stroking her back gently. There was no need for words. The simple motion of a gentle hand over her aching muscles wrenched Mattie's heart. Such unexpected kindness in such a desperate and cruel place.

Gretta fetched a glass of water. She was kneeling next to where Mattie had collapsed. Her sobs gradually died away. She pushed herself up onto one arm. Gretta handed her the glass with a soft smile. Mattie took a sip, worried her throat would be too tight to take in anything. But the water soothed her. She took a little more.

"Thank you."

Jean kept her hand on her shoulder as she sat next to Mattie.

"Take this bed." Jean squeezed her shoulder and moved slowly to the bed that had been added to the room.

"No." Mattie's hoarse voice felt loud in a place where only whispers were spoken. "You don't need to move."

Jean smiled. "You need some proper rest... Don't say a word... just sleep. Then we can talk..."

Mattie felt too weary to protest any further. She grabbed the thin blanket that covered the bed on which she lay and fell asleep as her head touched the pillow.

* * *

Canary Wharf was gradually emptying, bankers and other businessmen, few women, were returning to their desks as Harris arrived. He didn't like the place... artificial, efficient, expensive. The second financial centre in London would always be that for him... second choice. He entered the large glass and steel building and walked straight to reception.

"Kerry Murdock... please."

The receptionist asked for a name. "Steve Jackson." Harris almost added MI6 but it might not sound credible.

"Ms Murdock is in a meeting."

"Tell whoever you have on the phone to get her out of her meeting now or I'll be speaking to the head of Reuters UK instead."

The young man at reception remained stoical. It was not the first time he had dealt with a demanding pain in the arse. Harris was asked to take the lift to the top floor where he was greeted by a fuming blonde fury.

"Follow me," was the only thing she said, and they turned into a small meeting room off the top floor reception area. Ms Murdock did not scare easily.

"What the fuck did you have to get me out of my daily midday brief for?"

"Because you don't seem to fucking well understand the meaning of the fucking words *media blackout*." If she wanted expletives, Harris was her man.

"I'm only speaking the truth…" She crossed her arms over her chest as a petulant child would.

"Are you for real? What do you think ISIL will do if they know the press is talking kidnapping?"

"It IS kidnapping then?"

"I never said it was… I'm asking you to think about what ISIL will do if YOU talk about it."

"Maybe it will help."

Harris cocked his head. He had not been expecting this.

"Yes, perhaps the public will put pressure on the government to act… I'm not an idiot. I know the UK government doesn't pay ransom."

Harris sighed. "Kerry… this is not the way it works." Harris took a moment to consider Ms Murdock… young, very young… after a story for sure, but perhaps eager to make a difference. "I have been in this job for a long time… you will not do her any favours if you keep pushing."

Ms Murdock in turn was not expecting this conciliatory tone. "I'll back off…" She pouted. "…on one condition…"

"What?"

"If you need to let the news out you come to me first."

Harris raised an eyebrow and the beginning of an idea popped into his mind. "If I need the press… you'll be it."

Ms Murdock gave him the biggest of smiles.

* * *

Movement around her woke her with a jolt. Two women in full niqab were speaking to Gretta. Mattie could not quite make out what they were saying until she realised they were speaking Arabic.

"Get ready… quickly."

Gretta was frozen with fear. One of the Arab women threw the veil to her face. Still Gretta did not move. Her round cheeks had turned red, her pale blue eyes opened wide with dread. She shook her head

181

and the women who had thrown the cloth slapped her hard across the face. Gretta's skull hit the wall behind her with a dull thud. Mattie threw aside her blanket and stood up. It was three against two.

The stick that hit her across the back seemed to come from nowhere. She tried to hold back a cry without success. She looked around for a makeshift weapon. Jean threw herself between Mattie and her assailant. "She'll be fine."

Gretta rubbed her skull and slowly picked up the cloth from the floor, adjusting it over her face. Jean stretched her arms sideways, her hands lifted in a protective yet forbidding manner.

Don't fight a fight you cannot win…

Gretta did not look back at the two women as she walked out of the door. When the door was locked, Jean turned towards Mattie, tears in her eyes.

"This is not the time," she whispered.

"Where are they taking her?" Mattie's voice trembled, rage and powerlessness coursing inside her. Jean sat down on her bed, head in hands.

"Al-Baghdadi…"

"You mean…?" Mattie's hand folded around her throat. It was unthinkable and yet she had written about it so many times… rape… the fate of so many women in many war-torn countries. Jean nodded and raised her head. Mattie stopped herself from asking the next question. If Jean knew about Gretta's fate it was because she had endured the same. Mattie turned around towards the small wash basin squeezed in the corner of the room and barely made it. She threw up the little water that was left in her stomach.

* * *

The multi-tool screwdriver was turning in his hand, buzzing in a rhythmic way. Henry had already removed three screws from the wall plug, part of his daily ritual… Nothing showing so far. He was almost disappointed. He went to the bedside table and opened the drawer. Within it he had arranged a few items, a pair of shoelaces, a pen and a small writing pad, a couple of sweets he would never eat. He had arranged the same items on the top of the bedside table, in a same specific order, small clusters that did not need to be moved to clean the room.

Henry smiled; someone had indeed displaced his items to get to the contents of a file he had placed in the same drawer. Would The Treasurer need to add a further layer of surveillance when he was already keeping an eye on him? He was glad he had spotted the intrusion. But he would keep an open mind as to its origins. Henry sat back on his bed and looked around. He had finished his routine. There was perhaps one item he had not yet checked.

Henry switched on the TV and turned the volume full on. He cautiously lifted his iPhone from his bed and opened up its back. The battery was protruding more than usual. Henry moved the battery a little without it losing contact. There was a small device nestled underneath it… a tiny recording device. Henry replaced the back with caution. He was ready to give The Treasurer or whoever was eavesdropping on him a run for their money. He dropped the phone on the bed, yawned loudly and walked to the sliding doors that led to the terrace. He opened them slowly, the soft sound barely noticeable over the racket of the TV programme he was not watching. He slid the doors shut and reached the side of the terrace, vaulted over the low wall partition and landed on Wasim's side. He knocked at the glass doors. Wasim stepped onto the terrace and closed the glass doors.

"Had some visitors?"

"Yup… I think they're getting a lot more interested in me now I'm about to earn them some money."

"Me too… Anything else?"

"iPhone has a recording device under the battery case."

"Not surprised."

"No, but I'd like to know who's listening…"

"Doesn't matter… You can now feed these people as much disinformation as you can."

"Still, I might want to say different things depending on my audience."

"You don't think it's The Treasurer."

Henry shrugged. He had no evidence. It was only a gut feeling and that was not good enough.

"Do you think you'll get a laptop?" Wasim asked.

"I don't want access to a laptop and even if they gave me one it would have more bugs than a rotten apple."

"You're right… Let's see what new comms package MOTHER comes up with now I have a way of making contact."

"Another website? How much browsing can you do without arousing suspicion though?"

"That's the point. She'll find a way. I can then ask for more data on the fixer."

"Would be good to know more about this Qatari guy."

"When will you be back in contact with him?"

"Early morning. He's finding out the best route to contact the *Sunday Times*." Henry leaned back on the chair. "Do you think al-Haddawi will be part of the Mosul campaign?"

"Not sure he is part of it, from what I gathered… Some other senior commander is leading the attack."

"That's not good… He's going to stay on our backs, feeling frustrated he's not showing off at the front."

"Have you discussed details with the fixer?"

"Not quite, I have given an indication about amount and timetable… It's a long shot. You and I know this, but I am thinking about an alternative…"

"A Plan B?" Wasim raised a quizzical eyebrow.

"I've been thinking a lot about all the permutations and there's one idea we might want to explore…" Henry fell silent, measuring once more the viability of the plan.

"Are you going to let me in on the idea then?"

"I'm thinking about a hostage exchange."

Wasim sat up. "Do you have someone in mind?"

"I think I do…" Henry met Wasim's eyes. They had both known the terror cell that had eventually managed to extract Henry from HMP Belmarsh. They had both dealt with the two leaders until the cell was destroyed in a special ops raid. And yet one man was still alive, still active in recruiting young men from his prison cell.

184

"You don't mean…?"

"Why not? And that would give us maximum credibility too."

* * *

"Any news?" Harris walked back from his meeting with Ms Murdock, looking much happier than he had when he left.

"Yup… made contact."

Harris stopped halfway to his desk and span around with a frown. "You mean?"

"I didn't want to interrupt your conversation with Reuters or use your mobile… just in case it wasn't fully charged."

"Bloody hell Amina… will you ever let me forget I… once… failed to remember to charge my phone?"

"Nope…" Amina turned around from her screens to face Harris. "Wasim's phone and laptop were taken away. He's found a couple of places that have internet connections and computers."

"And…" Harris waved his hand to speed up the delivery of news.

"Progress…" Amina told Harris about Wasim's message and confirmed she had in turn given him details about Mosul's imminent attack.

"What's the plan as far as comms is concerned?"

"We moved to the alternative website for the time being but I'm looking for other ways of exchanging information. Rach has confirmed someone has gone into Wasim's laptop. So she has cleaned it up to leave no traces of activity."

"What's the next window to exchange information?"

"Wasim is looking for the best time to contact me again… when the tearooms are not too busy. Some places are stricter than others when it comes to using the internet."

Harris nodded and glanced at his watch. He had just enough time to catch OMA before Ahmed left for the day.

When he returned, Amina was on the phone to her comms specialists' team. She had given up on using yet another website to increase the exchange she was hoping to have with Wasim. She had recently learned about a new method she'd never used before – map overlay. Any type of map would do. Railway maps (used by the French DGSE to communicate with a defecting officer in Algeria in the 60s), city maps, land maps. She was hoping to introduce the same idea. Wasim was entitled to survey the terrain around Syria and Iraq. Nothing obviously questionable there. They would agree on the map, then the next time agree on the codes to be embedded into it. Then they would create a single download, the riskiest part of the operation, either on a new device if Wasim managed to get one or in a newly created email account… not the preferred route.

"Heard from them?" Harris asked as soon as she came off the phone.

"Too soon…"

"Just one quick message to say Crowne is about to call the fixer. Before I posted… so no response on the Colmore message yet."

"What did comms say about your map idea?"

"Old school but can work. They're choosing the best map and they'll confirm codes and keys by the end of the day."

Harris nodded. Could they really pull it off? RED HAWK was slowly becoming a monster, springing new heads every day… Mattie Colmore's kidnapping, Mosul's attack…

"Sorry. My optimistic self is starting to have doubts… aren't we stretching our guys too far?"

"Which is what I said to you only this morning." Amina's voice did not carry the habitual *I told you so* chime.

"I know." Harris pulled his chair closer to Amina's desk.

"But we need the intel, don't we?"

"It's usually me who insists on collecting data come what may."

"I've been thinking a lot about that." Amina ignored Harris's banter. "We'll get quality intel from them both. Crowne is getting good at it and Wasim has always been one of our best operatives."

"There is a 'but' I am not going to like." Harris crossed his arm over his chest.

"We need to be prepared to extract them sooner than we'd hoped."

"They've just arrived." Harris's tone lacked the edge it normally had when he didn't like a new idea.

"And they'll be of zero use to us dead."

"Even if we agree to extract them... if... there is no way it can be done out of Raqqa. No one's going to authorise that, not the Brits and certainly not the Yanks."

Amina's phone rang. She gave it an annoyed look. The comms team had results.

"We're not talking extraction," Harris returned to his desk, "... yet."

Chapter Nineteen

Harris left his office with an old burner phone. He would allow James Radlett a couple of days if he needed the extra time to make up his mind. Patience was the daughter of time... time he may not have.

And time to call his other asset in London. Brett had been taking it easy for the past 18 months since Crowne had joined MI6. The art dealer had proven a surprisingly valuable man. If Mosul were to fall, Brett would know what stolen artefacts would come to market and would establish contact with the sellers. He had a tested route. He had connections all over the Middle East and he had been unusually resourceful at exploiting these. Harris had taken a lot of flak for giving Brett too much rope but it had allowed Brett to become an even more credible contact for extremists in London. Perhaps Brett would like to help a little further? Harris smiled at the thought.

How soon can you be at the club? Harris sent his text.

I am at the club... Where else?

Perfect. Be with you in half an hour.

Why?

Harris did not bother to reply. Brett would wait. Despite telling him otherwise 18 months ago, Harris was not done with Brett Allner-Smith... not by a long way.

Harris had changed into his Savile Row suit before he crossed the threshold of The St James's Club. He had made the necessary stop in Pimlico at a block of flats, a few of which were used by MI6. A couple of apartments known as the 'airlock' enabled staff to change and adapt to the requirements of their meetings. Harris gave a coy smile at the reflection in the mirror that decorated the Club's entrance. The doorman greeted him with the usual distant courtesy. Harris walked confidently through the first few rooms, heading to the smoking room, Brett's favourite. The man was there, comfortably seated in a deep leather armchair, a glass of excellent whisky awaiting his attention on the small table beside his seat. Harris noticed the glass was still full.

Wise. Brett would need a pick-me-up for what Harris had in mind.

Harris plonked himself int the chair to the right of Brett, who did not bother to lower his newspaper.

"You look relaxed." Harris grinned, signalling to the steward. "The same for me, please."

Brett turned a page.

"Of course I do. I have not been involved with you for over a year."

"Nah. You miss the action… admit it."

"You mean dealing with a terror group whose leader threatened to slit my throat if I didn't do his bidding…"

"The Sheik liked you."

"No. The Sheik didn't have time to make up his mind about me before the Counter-Terrorist Squad put a few bullets into him."

"See. I always look after you."

Brett folded his paper neatly and threw it onto the table.

"What do you want?"

"What do you know about Mosul's museum?"

Harris's drink arrived. Brett took a sip of his whisky, smiling with satisfaction, before responding.

"The second largest museum in Iraq after Baghdad. It was looted in the 2003 Iraq war."

"Damn, you've already sold everything that was worth selling there then?"

Brett raised an eyebrow but ignored Harris's banter. "But…" He took another sip. "It has been rebuilt and is about to re-open. There are still some very valuable contents that makes it a place worth visiting."

Harris took a sip of whisky in turn. Brett could not help himself. Mention antiquities and he would come running, mention looting and he would be unstoppable.

"Is MI6 finally paying you enough that you can afford some of these treasures?" Brett raised his glass to Harris.

"My antiques come from Camden Market, mate." Harris tapped his nose and took another slug. "What would it take for you to bring some of them across to Europe?"

Brett's lanky face grew still. His faint blue eyes squinted. Was Harris serious?

"I do have contacts, but the goods need to come on the market... I can't arrange a..."

"Say the goods come on the market as you say," Harris interrupted, his voice's serious edge changing the atmosphere between the two men in an instant.

"I have received offers from Nimrud, as I said over the phone. So yes, if the museum was looted I would be in a position to import goods either to Europe or the UK."

"How quickly?"

Brett was holding the elegant tumbler with the tips of his fingers. He balanced it on the large arm of the chair, considering. "What are you not telling me?"

"You've been in the game long enough, Brett."

"Need-to-know basis crap again. Really?"

"Yup, just give me an idea."

"If you're talking large artefacts, probably a week."

Harris shook his head, a little disappointed; not as quick as he might have hoped.

"But," Brett took a couple of sips, "if you have something else in mind, something smaller, like tablets or scrolls... it could be quicker."

"And what if we are talking about something else?"

Brett's face changed colour and a tinge of pink made the roots of his hair look even lighter. "You're not serious?"

"Might be... Give me an idea."

Brett considered his almost empty glass. He made a small move of the hand, calling the steward... he most definitely needed a refill.

* * *

Harris checked his MI6 mobile, no news from Amina or Sir John. He was walking along St James's and soon turned into Piccadilly. Crowne would make contact to ask for a ransom, but Harris wondered whether Crowne had another plan. He increased the pace of his walk. Too much had happened too soon, and he needed to put RED HAWK into perspective. A gust of unseasonably cold wind blew into Harris. He lurched forward, lifting the collar of the jacket up. His stocky body had seen so much worse and yet he wondered how much he could now endure.

The Baghdad skyline is highlighted by a burst of lights against the darkness of the night, reds and oranges. Harris has been sitting at the window of a flat near the city centre for hours. The coalition forces are making the final assault and he has infiltrated Baghdad with other CIA agents. As soon as they can they need to lay their hands on the intelligence that lies in Saddam Hussein's palace. Where are the weapons of mass destruction? Harris is smoking a cigarette, the last one he shares with his CIA contact, Jack O'Brian.

The flat they occupy has been vacant for days, left behind by a fleeing family. April in Baghdad can be cold and dreary. Harris has poured another cup of coffee from the flask he prepared earlier on. Jack is following the progress of a US infantry brigade. They are close to one of Saddam's palaces and the fighting is fierce. US Marines are faced with heavy shelling from Iraqi artillery. The palace needs to be taken even if it means casualties. Harris brings the binoculars up to his eyes. They are not far from the bridge the coalition forces must cross to reach the place they intend to take. Harris knows the city well. Despite his fair skin and light brown hair, he has managed to move around Baghdad in times of peace without attracting much attention, sometimes as journalist or businessman. Harris's nondescript physique helps him to become unremarkable.

The building rocks again. The fighting has intensified for the final push. Harris is only mildly concerned. The Iraqi forces are too engaged in the battle with the US Marines to divert their attention anywhere else. Jack is commenting on progress. Another large explosion, some plaster, dislodged from the ceiling, falls next to Harris. Jack has stopped talking and from the corner of his eyes Harris sees Jack putting down his binos, his hand slowly creeping towards the walkie-talkie. Harris then knows that when he is going to turn back, someone with a gun will be aiming at his head.

The traffic light at the crossing turned red, stopping Harris in his tracks. The images of what followed in Baghdad had pressed themselves into his mind. He knew the outcome, no need to recall events. But the feeling stayed with him to this day… he had shot a man dead and that man had been his first killing.

Harris reached the 'airlock' in Pimlico and changed back into his usual work clothes. Memories of Baghdad had unsettled him more than he liked to admit. Perhaps he didn't need to convince James Radlett so quickly. Perhaps he should ask his team in Raqqa to step back. But intel must be gathered, and they had come too far to simply turn back.

Harris checked his phone mechanically… Amina had called. Sir John's PA had called. Before leaving the Pimlico flat, Harris moved to the bathroom, splashed his face with cold water and rested his body against the basin for a short moment… washing away the memories of Baghdad.

* * *

The fixer's English was remarkably good. A man educated in America, used to talking the language of business. This fixer knew exactly what to do. It both impressed and repelled Henry at the same time, giving him an insight into a world Henry barely suspected existed… kidnapping for ransom was a lucrative business.

"Once we agree on the price, I receive 75% of what I charge you up front." The educated voice was pleasant, professional.

"ISIL has been generous… 10% is a lot; 75% of 10% is a lot."

"Perhaps, but what if something goes wrong?"

"Then you'll be out of pocket."

Silence at the other end of the line. Henry waited.

"What do you offer?"

"40% when we agree on the deal, the rest when we receive the money."

"65, 35."

"45, 55… my last offer." Henry wouldn't budge. He would simply go back to The Treasurer to complain about the fixer.

"Done." The voice had lost its affable tone. This was just another deal even if the fixer was dealing with ISIL. Henry argued the details of how and when the fixer would contact the journalists and management at the *Sunday Times*. The fixer assured him he knew what to do. Henry did not care. Mattie was the daughter of Harold Colmore MP. IS wanted to avoid any interference from the British government.

Wasim knocked at Henry's door, as they had agreed earlier on. As soon as he entered they started their scripted conversation. Henry placed his mobile so that each word they spoke could be heard distinctly. Wasim smiled; it was enjoyable to beat ISIL at its own game of disinformation.

"The fixer will contact the head of international affairs first." Henry handed Wasim a can of lemonade from the fridge.

"I presume he won't go direct?"

"Didn't ask and doesn't care. We can assume the *Sunday Times* won't contact the UK government if they're serious about negotiating with us."

"Very good… we just wait and see." Wasim took a swig of lemonade.

"We'll give the *Sunday Times* 48 hours and then… we move to Plan B."

"Does the fixer know?"

"He doesn't but he is not stupid. He will hang around even if the first deal doesn't go through."

"Anybody else involved?"

"My guess is that he'll contact some local NGOs. It's good to have them on side when the deal goes through."

Wasim nodded. "Great job." He moved away from the subject of ransom to that of oil. Yet again another scripted conversation that he and Henry had rehearsed.

"I hope Hamza takes my suggestions seriously now he has a senior contact in Turkey who'll make sure he can sell at a decent price."

"Which is?"

"Use the Kirkuk oil pipeline to feed in ISIL's oil at several entry points. It will be almost impossible to detect where the oil comes from as so many production units feed into this oleoduct. We simply need to agree with other intermediaries how much we feed in to receive payment. But the oil itself will not be traceable."

"Kirkuk ends up in Turkey, right?"

"Right."

"Do you think your contact will play ball?"

"He will… the last thing he needs is his name being mentioned in association with armament trafficking involving Qaddafi and the IRA."

"But he can't be helping us on his own… Do you think the Turks will let it go if they discover what's going on?"

"They can't do so openly, but there's far too much money to be made not to attract the serious attention of other senior figures."

"Do you have any idea about who to contact?"

"Certainly. I've done business in Turkey before… as a banker that is… and I'm pretty sure that we'll find men in the PM's entourage amenable to the deal."

"Are you serious?" Wasim's voice hit the right amazed tone.

"I am more than serious. I will find someone, and we will be paid handsomely for the oil we export… in size. I think The Treasurer has realised that… but I'm not giving him my contacts access until he's a bit more forthcoming. I think he knows that too."

"Do you have an estimate?"

"Rough calculation from the product figures Hamza gave me. We'll reach $1m a day."

"Through Kirkuk alone?"

"No, you're right, that wouldn't be enough. We need to increase our smuggling through Jordan but that's very doable. We need to be a bit more generous with the border guards and the intermediaries… The Far East is thirsty for oil and a good number of countries will not be asking too many questions."

"A clever strategy." Wasim's face broadened into a smile.

"I said I would help, and I shall. There's so much I can do with the assets ISIL has already amassed." Henry gave the thumbs up to Wasim. Excellent piece of *Henry Crowne: The Expert Financier*.

Wasim's job was done… there was little he could add. He left quickly. There was still time to visit one of the tearooms he had spotted near the hotel. He could perhaps reach MOTHER again today, after all, he was only browsing a website… Henry picked up his mobile, turned it over a few times in his hand and made a wager. If his little charade had worked, he should have a call from The Treasurer or one of his people quite soon. If he didn't... well. He would have to think about another strategy to bolster his credibility. Or perhaps it would mean something entirely different... perhaps it was not The Treasurer eavesdropping on him.

He stretched his arms over his head and decided on a shower. At least a luxury he was enjoying to the full before it was taken from him again. He discarded his clothes and entered the bathroom, welcomed by the scent of fresh soap that reminded him of his apartment in London. As he was about to turn the water on, his mobile phone started ringing.

* * *

A message was waiting for him at reception after he had gone through Vauxhall Cross's multi-tier security checks. Sir John was requiring his presence soonest. Harris took the elevator to the fifth floor. Sir John's PA was waiting for him as the door opened. She greeted him with a smile, ushered him into Sir John's office without announcing him. He was expected.

"Mosul's attack has started." Sir John did not bother to greet Harris. He had become a daily presence in The Chief's timetable, no need for common courtesies. Harris joined him in the part of his office fitted with a row of monitors. A large digital map of the area showing terrain, roads and cities in Iraq and Syria as well as the allocation of territory to various factions was projected onto the back wall. Harris noticed the sheer complexity of the colour coding. He had experienced how fractious and divided the region was, during his own time there, but things had got much worse. Since the Arab Spring, the Middle East had become an even more complex region to navigate. The most alarming development visible on the map was the growing presence of ISIL, capturing territories in both Iraq and Syria, unchallenged. The screens were relaying live pictures from Reaper drones deployed from the UK Cyprus base in Akrotiri. The convoys of ISIL fighters, easily recognisable by the black flags they were flying, were moving at speed.

195

Caterpillars of trucks, SUVs and Humvees were approaching the city from several directions. The monitors relaying these images split into four screens, showing the effort ISIL was putting in attacking its target. The first screen showed the city itself. Another screen showed the two divisions of Iraqi fighters, each division counting 15,000 men. The third screen had zeroed in on Mosul's airport and its armament. The final screen showed a summary of the forces confronting in battle and their commanders: Lieutenant General Mahdi Al-Gharrawi on the Iraqi side, Abu Abdulrahman al-Bilawi for ISIL. A military HQ could not have drawn a more complete picture.

"Any news from your people on the ground?"

"They're making progress in understanding ISIL's structure."

Sir John turned towards Harris. "At last, some good news."

"Crowne has made contact with one of the fixers ISIL works with."

"Mosul?"

"Nothing yet, I'm afraid. Henry and Wasim are confident they'll hear about the attack soon… the question is in how much detail."

"I've had Sir Mortimer on the phone. The MoD is hoping our Iraqi friends will listen to our intel and act upon it."

Harris nodded. He pulled a chair, helped himself to coffee and started scrutinising the maps.

"Who is manning the drones, sir?"

"British pilots in Cyprus. Why?"

"UK drones?"

"I can ask them to redirect them somewhere else if you think it's important."

"Do we know how many ISIL fighters are on the ground?"

"It's only an estimate, but so far 100,000."

"Against 30,000 Iraqi soldiers?"

"That's right. I am expecting they will pause and regroup… assess their position. Perhaps wait for other fighters to arrive. They are outnumbered 30 to 1."

"That's precisely what ISIL would want us to think. Death doesn't matter to them. They're seeking to be martyred to their cause… the most noble of deaths." Harris balled a fist… Even in Muslim countries, the sheer dedication or perhaps fanaticism of ISIL followers was underestimated.

Sir John eyed Harris with interest. "You know the area better than anyone. You think they will attack?"

"If their commander is on the move and has galvanised his troops, he will. We can also expect some locals to join ISIL to save their skins."

Harris drank his coffee in small sips, almost oblivious to the motion of his head towards his cup. "The Iraqis need to strike hard now if they have a chance of stopping them."

"Do you know this ISIL commander?" Sir John turned towards the screen and read the name out loud. "Abu Abdulrahman al-Bilawi."

"He has a reputation of always being the first to join a fight. If he's leading his men, at the forefront. The other convoys have not even reached Mosul… then there is a chance. He may launch the attack before consolidating his troops."

"Would he really be that careless?"

"Yet again, sir. It's not carelessness… it's a show of strength."

"I'll relay this to Sir Mortimer. Anything else?"

"No… but I'll go back to Amina, I mean Ms Brown, and check our latest intel."

"Excellent. Keep me updated at all times. Mosul must not fall."

Harris nodded. He would not be holding his breath. ISIL was on a roll, deadly and, he feared, unstoppable.

Chapter Twenty

Henry emerged from the bathroom and ran to the phone. He held back for the fourth ring to go through and answered just before it went to voicemail.

"Marhabaan."

"A car will pick you up after early prayer, come on your own." The Treasurer replied in Arabic.

"Of course, I'll wait to be picked up." The phone went dead.

Henry wondered why Wasim had not been invited. A test? He had expected it might happen but perhaps not so soon. He left the phone on the bedside table. He fought the urge to walk out to the balcony and speak to Wasim. Instead he moved back to the bathroom and started to shower. He had left the door open. If they wanted to spy on his every move, they would have to put up with some pretty boring stuff too.

The call to prayer would be reverberating around Raqqa in half an hour. He walked out of the bathroom and inspected a pile of fresh clothes that had been left for him. Khaki fatigues, black shirts, army boots and a large black scarf. He put on his new uniform quickly and walked out onto the terrace of his room. Wasim was stretched out on the lounger. He had returned from his tearoom expedition unsuccessful, too many people were asking too many questions.

"Hey, no time to explain but The Treasurer is sending a car."

Wasim stopped reading the ISIL magazine he had picked up in the lobby. "That's it … they need to test you on your own…"

"Another job interview, nothing to worry about… right?"

Wasim shook his head with a broad smile. "Remember what I said… You're ready."

Henry shook his head in return. "And if I'm not you'd better get the hell out of here as soon as you can."

* * *

The fighters had left in the afternoon, jumping into trucks old and new… the jihad awaited. Ali was one of them and Henry could not shake off the feeling of sadness at knowing he might never see the young man again. His phone buzzed. He took it out from his army fatigues pocket expecting a text telling him that the car was approaching.

All mobile and other devices are to be switched off now or remain open in aeroplane mode. No exception will be tolerated.

Not the text he was expecting.

"And so it begins…" Henry thought about turning back to speak to Wasim, but there was no point. He would not attempt to return to the tearoom today.

A brand new Hummer pulled into the driveway. The mark of the American flag had been removed, but it was otherwise impossible to detect which army faction was using it. Together with the use of Red Cross vehicles and humanitarian food trucks, these provided an excellent way of getting around undetected.

Henry stepped into it. He was alone in the armed vehicle. The driver did not acknowledge him. Henry looked around the inside of the car. It was organised not for warfare but transport.

The drive took less than 30 minutes. The men who belonged to al-Baghdadi's inner circle had moved into the luxury quarter of Raqqa. It was wise to live at a distance from the stadium, which might quickly become the target of airstrikes.

The car slowed down, stopping in front of a large gate; heavy metal sheeting had been added to the cast iron frame. The guards barely looked inside the vehicle as the driver lowered the window. The gate opened and it took another few minutes to reach a large mansion. The sun had almost disappeared, and the fading light made the white structure look almost ghostly. There was a light on the ground floor, but the rest of the house was plunged into darkness.

Henry stepped out of the vehicle as soon as it stopped. Two guards waited for him to arrive at the door. They radioed in on their walkie talkie, speaking to someone inside the house. The Finance Council was waiting for him. He was frisked by another guard inside the property. Whoever Henry was meeting, it was not meant to be a pleasant experience.

The room he entered must have been a glorious display of luxury once upon a time. Today only deep woollen rugs sank underfoot, and large leather sofas overburdened with cushions provided seating. The low table at their centre was laden with food. Henry felt his mouth water. The Treasurer was sitting on one of the sofas, at his right al-Haddawi had chosen a comfortable armchair. Two other men sat on the remaining couches. Henry understood the pecking order... al-Haddawi was no longer the main man. Another armchair had been left empty on the left of The Treasurer.

There were no introductions. The other two men eyed Henry up and down, doubt in their eyes. The Treasurer had adopted the formal black robe that ISIL seemed to promote for its most senior members. His black turban with a long piece of cloth dropping at the back made him look more like some fifth-century sultan than a modern statesman. But this was precisely the idea... to go back to the time when men thought the earth was flat.

Al-Haddawi was the only man still sporting a pair of camouflage trousers. A statement of his status as a Commander of God's army? Al-Qaeda were mere lambs in comparison to them.

"It has started." The Treasurer said to Henry when he sat down in the seat designated to him. The exchange of opinion on strategy that followed eluded Henry. Arabic was being spoken at speed. He was not meant to understand, it seemed, and Henry wondered why he had been asked to come in the first place.

The smaller of the two unknown men stopped running his prayer beads through his fingers. "You have ideas about how to use Mosul's assets."

"Certainly, it will depend what your strategy is around the purchase of weapons and other goods. Cash and gold can be laundered easily. A number of countries such as the UAE, Qatar, Malta or Cyprus, I know how to use well."

"You've done this before, I understand."

"For the IRA, yes I have. Different locations, same principles and I was operating from locations that looked a lot more suspicious such as Panama."

Henry was interrupted by a call that al-Haddawi took. He had not yet said a word, but his nostrils had flared. He was ready to unleash the hatred he carried in his eyes and destroy Henry without mercy. Al-Haddawi stood up suddenly and walked briskly to the other end of the large room. The council member who had not yet spoken assessed his reaction. It was a welcome response. He turned towards Henry and asked him to explain once more what he had in mind.

Al-Haddawi spent ten minutes on the phone. The others started to help themselves to food. Two women in full niqab and gloves came in with tea. Henry hesitated but finally decided it was time to join the men. No need to be shy. He too was a man of value...

The mobile flew across the room, crashing against the floor. "The dogs have killed our brother." The Treasurer put his plate down and glanced at Henry. It was not the result he had expected. "Explain..."

Al-Haddawi re-joined the group. If he had not been in the presence of two elders who would report to al-Baghdadi, he would have sent food flying or taken revenge on the women who had served the tea. More importantly he would have taken revenge on Henry.

"Our army was pushing towards Mosul, when one of the Iraqi security forces battalions caught our fighters. Abu Abdulrahman did not look for safety. He led his men into the battle outnumbered 20 to 1. He fell with the fighters... martyred to our cause."

"Then let Mosul's capture become Bilawi's vengeance," the man who had spoken first said calmly. He speed-dialled a number on his phone and spoke a few words. It was clear he was speaking to al-Baghdadi. When he had finished, he turned to al-Haddawi. "And you, my brother, are to be the instrument of their fall."

The smile on al-Haddawi's face chilled Henry to the bone, a mix of glee, hatred and savagery.

* * *

201

"They've gone dark." Amina had called Harris as he was about to leave The Chief's office.

"When?" Harris broke into a jog as he exited the lift.

"Ten minutes ago. Not only Crowne's."

"Shit… anything else?"

"OMA has confirmed the blackout covers the entire Raqqa area."

"Can we still communicate with them?" Harris opened the door of the office.

"Only if we activate the emergency protocol on Crowne's phone… far too risky. Wasim won't be able to communicate even through the website. He won't be allowed access."

"Mosul has started. Fuck." Harris threw the mobile on his desk. "We need their intel more than ever."

"I can activate the emergency comms on my side but I'm not risking blowing his cover… as I said, it's too risky."

"I'm not suggesting you blow their cover… but we need to know what ISIL's plan for Mosul is."

"Wasim or Crowne are doing well but I can't imagine either of them being granted access to ISIL's war room."

"It's their job to find out and transmit intel… Mosul can't fall."

"That's ridiculous. I've put in place a second web access. Wasim can use this when Raqqa is back on the grid."

"Unless you use the emergency protocol," Harris insisted.

"Steve. That's bollocks and you know it. If there's something Wasim or Crowne need to tell us they'll find a way."

"And if it's too late?"

"No matter how much you'd like to think they can gather that type of intel… they're not going to get the intel you want until it's too late, as you say."

"Why?"

"Because they are not on the battlefield. They can't ask the sort of questions that would help you or the Iraqis."

"I'm not asking for the details of the attack… but simply knowing whether ISIL is regrouping or launching an assault outnumbered 30 to 1… might make a difference."

"How do you propose they get the intel?"

202

Harris fished a fresh packet of gums from his desk. Amina held out a hand and Harris dropped a couple into it. She could have done with her old stress ball, a shame her daughter's dog had shown a keen interest in it during his last visit. Harris's mobile rang. He cast a wary eye towards it.

"Harris." The dry reply was designed to put the caller off.

"Hello, sir… Yes." Harris mouthed Sir John to Amina.

"You haven't but…" Harris squeezed his eyes shut and opened them wide again.

"I'll be with you right away."

"What now?" Amina frowned.

"Colmore has just called The Chief… he would like to discuss options."

* * *

It was almost dark outside when Mattie woke up again. She had willed herself to sleep, not wanting to think about what might be happening to her soon. She needed the rest to function, to remain calm and plan how best to survive. In her disturbed sleep she had been dreaming of Henry. The room in which they had met had disappeared. They were both standing on top of a steep sand dune, alone and yet she could hear voices, a ring of gunshots that made her look around, frightened.

"You'll be fine… We'll be fine…" Henry was repeating time and time again, and for some unknown reason she would quieten down at the sound of his soothing voice. Mattie rolled on her back. She turned her head sideways and started inspecting the room. The beds were small and spartan. The place was stripped of comfort. The blanket she had nestled under felt inadequate against the cold, even though it was an immense improvement compared with the squalid cell she had been thrown in at Raqqa Stadium.

Jean had moved to the bed that had been squeezed underneath the largest window in the bedroom. Mattie would offer to swap back with her tonight but for the moment she indulged in the relative shelter of the bed she occupied.

"Are you awake?" Jean's voice was only a whisper. Mattie sat up.

She could make out her roommate's shape in the dim light of dusk.

"Yes." Mattie slid from underneath the blanket, moving to where Jean was lying.

"How long have you been here?"

"Over a year. Abducted in Aleppo."

"Why did you cross into Syria?"

"I work for an NGO, providing help to refugees in war zones. With my Syrian boyfriend. We wanted to help."

"Is he...?" Mattie's voice tailed off.

"You mean dead? No, I was told they let him go and I believe they did."

"How many of us are there?"

"Other journalists, like you, one photographer, and a couple of people who are also humanitarian workers."

"All Americans?"

"No, two British people. And Gretta who is dual nationality American and Swedish. Some Europeans too although I have not heard from them since before I was transferred here."

"Were you at the stadium?"

"To start with, then we were transferred here a few days ago. I mean the women were... I'm not sure what happened to the men."

"Do you know where we are?"

"Close to where al-Baghdadi lives. As far as I can tell he moves around quite a lot, never staying in the same place for long, so that he can't be traced."

Mattie heard the anxiety in Jean's voice as she spoke their captor's name. She had wanted to ask her a question but she now knew the answer to it. Whether she was practising or not, she was a Christian, she was kafir, and men would do with her what they pleased. Mattie sat on the floor next to Jean's bed. Despite Jean's ordeal, a quiet resolve emanated from her and it moved Mattie... whatever she would be put through, Jean would not yield.

"Has anyone tried to escape?"

"We've all been thinking about it... but so far none of us has found a way."

"We're in the centre of Raqqa, right?"

"Right." Jean swung her legs over the edge of her bed and bent forward towards Mattie, whispering even more quietly. "It's very difficult for women, even in groups, to move around Raqqa and impossible alone. We need to be escorted by a man wherever we go."

"But in a car, Raqqa is close to Aleppo... four hours tops."

"How many checkpoints are there between the two cities though?"

"And at night there is also a curfew."

"Exactly."

Mattie brought her knees to her chin. "There must be a way."

Jean squeezed Mattie's shoulder gently. "We must keep faith that our government and families will do what they can to help us."

Mattie let her head fall back against the frame of the bed. "I'm not sure my father will do very much and even less sure about the British government."

"You'd be surprised what people are prepared to do when they are faced with the prospect of losing their loved ones."

Mattie squeezed Jean's hand in return. "Thank you for trying to give me hope but I can assure you my father is a lost cause... love is not in his vocabulary."

Mattie moved away from the subject before Jean asked her about her mother. "Who are the women looking after us?"

"The two women who brought you in are the wives of Abu Sayyaf. He belongs to al-Baghdadi's inner circle."

"I met a girl called Gulan when I was first brought in?"

"Yes, she brings us food. She is one of the Yazidi women who have been... enslaved."

Mattie turned her head towards Jean.

"I know it's a terrible word... but I can't describe it better than that."

"Why? Because they are not Sunni Muslims?"

"Yes... they have their own set of beliefs that set them apart from mainstream Islam, but ISIL has gone further... unless you follow their extreme interpretation of Islam, you are an infidel. One of the hostages I met had converted and he practised every day... but they still don't recognise him as Muslim."

Mattie thought about what this would mean for the thousands

of people living in ISIL-conquered territories… a reign of terror and death on an unprecedented scale even by Middle Eastern standards.

"Why do you want to know?"

"I'm trying to figure out whether those women could be on our side."

Jean rolled closer to Mattie.

"You mean help us to escape?"

"That's the idea."

"We can only do that if we have a man who is willing to help us though…"

Mattie's voice hesitated. "I may know someone who can."

Voices coming from the corridor silenced both women. Mattie went back to her bed and Jean lay down again. The door opened and light streamed into the room. The two women who had brought Mattie into the room walked in, alone. They dragged Jean out of bed, hardly giving her time to move from under the blanket. She slid her abaya on and wrapped the niqab around her face. Mattie sprang out of bed and moved towards the door, blocking it.

"Where are you taking her?"

The two women stopped, taken aback by Mattie's rebelliousness.

"Don't!" Jean said. "Not now…"

The slap in the face almost toppled Mattie and the taste of blood filled her mouth. The door closed before Mattie could summon her strength again… she was alone.

Chapter Twenty-One

It was late when Henry came back to his hotel room. The meeting with al-Baghdadi's Finance Council had been almost surreal, a cross between business acumen and zealotry. He had been questioned and quizzed in Arabic. By all accounts he felt he had done well. The Treasurer had looked relaxed and the two other men who questioned him had failed to find issues with the implementation of his plan. When it came to money laundering Henry knew what he was doing, and he did not need to fake it. His conversion to Islam had been well received, but with caution.

"I have been looking for a true belief and I have never been satisfied with what the Catholic faith gave to me." Henry's voice had deepened a little, the voice of an honest if perhaps blunt conversation. "Christianity puts too many intermediaries between God and the believer, too many ways of buying a favourable intercession without testing the strength of one's faith... I've had enough of such weakness." God bless Wasim who had made him rehearse his arguments for converting until they sounded credible even to Henry himself.

"Do you read the Qur'an repeatedly?"

"It is the Third Pillar of Islam. I do. And I did before I converted too."

"But you knew you would never survive amongst us if you did not." The man who had spoken to al-Haddawi, sending him to Mosul to avenge his brother's death, had not yet spoken to Henry. Henry would not have expected anything else from him. After all, it was the question that was on everybody's mind.

"But would I have come to you here, in Raqqa, if I had not felt I wanted to…? I could have offered to help you set up the funds you needed from another location and yet here I am."

The Treasurer nodded. The other two men remained more circumspect.

"You will soon see the results of my dedication, the only true way I can convince you of my genuine conversion." Henry this time had Harris to thank for putting him through the mill when it came to interrogation.

The door of the cell opens and four men wearing hoods come in. He has been sitting on the chair for hours. The white noise that fills the room has not stopped even since he has been dragged into it. He knows it is an exercise, yet his mind is starting to play tricks on him. He thinks he hears words in the random sounds that bounce off the walls. It becomes a strange presence that prevents him from relaxing. Its mix of grating, banging, audio tuning in and out of frequency, crawls into his mind after a while. His head has rolled to one side. His eyes feel gritty and tired. The ice cold water that hits his face makes him gasp.

"Not the cloth…" Henry does not know whether he has spoken aloud or not. Someone shines a light in his face.

"Why should I believe you? Convince me."

Henry snapped out of the memory. Everybody had gone quiet at his reply. They were helping themselves to more food. The women who served them tea had reappeared with fresh beverages.

"That is true," the man who had challenged him finally said. It wasn't yet a pass but for the time being it would have to do.

"Tell us about your meeting with Abu Maeraka in London." The Treasurer had finished his plate of baba ganoush and lamb koftas. He had wiped his mouth with a cloth napkin and placed it on his plate. In other circumstances Henry might have liked to do business with him.

"Abu Maeraka moved to the High Security Unit of HMP Belmarsh in London a few months after me."

"We know."

"He approached me after we had spoken in the library. I was one of the librarians there, sharing the role with other inmates. His brother worked in the City too."

208

Henry did not have to make it up either. Abu Maeraka had been convicted for masterminding a terror attack on Paddington station. The police van that was transporting Henry for interrogation at Paddington Counter-Terrorism Squad HQ had been caught in the blast. Henry had been spared by the explosion; one of the police officers accompanying him had not been so lucky.

"The fact that he approached me surprised me." Henry forced himself to eat some of the food on his plate, measuring what his words should be. He cleared his throat. "To be frank… I was reluctant to start with. I did not want to be involved with anything, take any side."

Abu Maeraka had not been deterred by the reputation of HSU Belmarsh. He could fight the fight in any place, converting inmates around him. His restrained manners combined with an unbreakable determination and a strong understanding of human motivations made him a powerful leader. He did not need to use force, it was all in the way he conducted himself, the way he knew what to say, when and to whom. Even the prison officers could not fault him, and HSU Belmarsh officers had received training over and above what could be expected from the most uncompromising prison training programme.

That Abu Maeraka had thought fit to help Henry escape HSU spoke volumes. No one had ever managed to break out before. His brother had lost his life in the process. Henry had been smuggled out of the UK after lying low for a while. The story as they saw it looked credible, a story confirmed by the sleeper cells that had been activated to protect him whilst still on British soil.

"Explain." The Treasurer raised a quizzical eyebrow.

"I believed in defeating the English, making them pay for their colonialist ways in Ireland. ISIL believes in defeating governments that seek to impose their ways against Islam's interests… it is another imperialist intrusion." He had debated some of that rhetoric with Liam in his student days and he had believed in it enough to join the IRA. That belief he did not need to fake.

Silence descended on the room again. The man who had spoken to him first also put his plate down. They were nearing the end of the interview.

"It is easy to convert, but not so easy to lead the life of a true Muslim."

Henry's voice deepened, humble. "I felt I had to convert in the presence of people who could help me hold firm to the promise I made."

"But as you say, it is the life, the devotion to the five pillars of Islam that matters," the other man added.

"That is the reason I tried to understand Islam as much as I could before I answered the call." Henry shuffled in the seat: a little unease for good measure.

The Treasurer sat back, sold on Henry's performance.

The man who had stayed silent all along seemed to now follow The Treasurer's lead. The round head on his equally round torso nodded slowly. The third man was still holding out. Henry could never convince him, but if he could keep him neutral for the time being, that was all he needed.

* * *

A soft knock at the bay window startled Henry. He placed his mobile on the bedside table the furthest away from the terrace and opened the sliding doors slowly. Wasim was already settled in one of the chairs, waiting for Henry to join him.

"Do I need to pack my bags and run?"

"No, but it was tough… they're nasty bastards."

"What did you expect?"

"I know, but I'm used to being top dog when it comes to interviews."

"You may be back to dealing with finance but, to state the obvious, it no longer is 'The City'."

Henry smiled. "Could have fooled me, though… the way The Treasurer is running his operation."

"You won't have any trouble from him. He's sold on your ideas."

"Yes. I think you're right."

"However…" Wasim bent forward, lowering his voice a fraction.

"Two more beardos questioned me. Actually, one beardo

questioned me, the other one listened and then seemed to follow The Treasurer."

"But the other one?"

"I think for the time being..." Henry hesitated, "neutral..."

"Do you have his name?"

"Sorry mate, we didn't exchange business cards."

Incorrigible Henry; Wasim lifted a disappointed eyebrow.

"Yes, I know, very unpro of me. Small guy, long grey beard, reminded me of Osama bin Laden."

"Any other distinctive features?"

"I don't know. He didn't get up from his seat, but I could have sworn moving around was difficult for him."

"I don't think I have any intel on him. That's worrying... We should have mapped all of al-Baghdadi's inner circle by now."

"I'll get the name from The Treasurer. MOTHER can add him to the list."

"I'm sure you've been told that Raqqa has gone dark, so no contact is possible at the moment."

"What about the emergency protocol?"

Wasim frowned. "Why? It would have to be activated from your phone."

"We need to know what they are planning to do in London as soon as the *Sunday Times* responds to the ransom demand."

"We shall do what we've agreed to do. Implement Plan A first, then discuss Plan B with London if A doesn't work."

"It may not be as simple as that." Henry moved his chair round so he could sit closer to Wasim. "The ISIL commander who led the assault on Mosul has been killed."

"Don't tell me that..."

"Yes, exactly... al-Haddawi has replaced him."

Henry ran his long hand through his thick mane of hair. "That's not good for us."

"An understatement. I have been speaking to quite a few of the men here before they left for Mosul. Al-Haddawi is liked by his fighters and they will martyr themselves for him without hesitation."

"Shit. Let's hope he leads by example." Henry wasn't joking.

"Because if he comes back victorious, I can tell you he'll revisit the hostage situation… with a vengeance. That guy is a nutter."

"But at least Mattie is out of his reach as long as the ransom negotiations go ahead."

"Not so sure." Henry stood up, walked to the end of the terrace and leaned back against the balustrade, facing Wasim. There was no sound in the city, but absolute silence.

"There's nothing more we can do for now. If we push too hard it will backfire on us."

"I know." The scent of Mattie's freshly washed hair floated around him. Henry felt her fingers pressing around his. He closed his own hand on an empty space.

"Let's get some sleep." Henry nodded and wished he could have spoken about Mattie more. He trusted Wasim but perhaps not to that extent.

* * *

The distant buzz of an insect made him turn over. It was persistent and Harris moved his hand around his head to chase the intruder. He opened his eyes in the dark. The buzz of the mobile returned, reminding him he was at home. He checked the time on his phone, 4.30am. He pushed the recall button. Amina sounded as sleepy as he was. OMA had called her 30 minutes earlier with an update. ISIL pick-up trucks had entered Mosul, storming through every checkpoint that was manned by too few Iraqi soldiers. At the same time sleeper cells in the city had been activated, suicide bomb cars had exploded at key targets, assassinating most of Mosul's leaders. The city was left without a government. Soldiers were being captured, hanged, burned or even crucified. ISIL was in the process of capturing security forces. And they too were executed summarily. Only one battalion was left to defend the city. The rest had run away or joined ISIL.

"Where is ISIL at the moment?"

"Fighting for the international airport."

"Valuable assets there?"

212

"It's the hub of the US military in the region."

"Complete with helicopters and various high-end weaponry, I presume."

"Correct."

"Fuck."

"Mosul is going to fall." Harris's voice was focused, all vestiges of sleep had evaporated.

"It's a matter of hours now."

"Is Raqqa still dark?"

"No change there, but OMA is picking up the beginning of some activity."

"The bastards can't help themselves... got to brag about a good massacre..." Harris's voice trembled. He did not want to imagine what the city would look like in a few hours' time.

"And when you look at the number of Iraqi troops versus the number of ISIL fighters... It's going to be the best propaganda ever for the group."

Harris threw the blanket away from him. "I'm coming in. I can't stay in bed while that's going on."

"Is Sarah not around?"

"No, she's gone to visit her mother and she's taken the dog with her."

"I'll join you." Amina yawned.

"Sarah wouldn't like it."

"Harris. I could get you done for a remark like that," Amina piped up.

"I know but that bloody well woke you up, didn't it?" Harris hung up without waiting for a reply.

It was now 4.50am. Perhaps not the best time to have a chat with The Chief. Harris would give him another hour in bed. More time to go through what OMA had gathered. Harris was certain that by 6am The Chief would be already up, readying himself for another day at the helm of MI6.

* * *

213

"You look like I feel." Harris put down a cup of coffee in front of Ahmed.

"Always so nice to work with you." Ahmed rolled his head around a few times, picked up the cup and drank a mouthful. "At this rate I'm going to need caffeine intravenously."

"Been up all night?"

"Yup. This stuff is really keeping me awake."

"Very bad then?"

Ahmed shook his head. "The poor bastards in the city haven't been able to flee and whoever is caught... well." Ahmed took another sip and cleared his throat. "Amina knows already what they've done with whoever they've caught but it's the scale of it that is horrendous."

Harris remained silent. He pulled up a chair to Ahmed's desk. "How about the airport?"

Ahmed was about to answer. More chatter and data were flowing in. He put his cup down and read aloud. "The Iraqis have just given the order to retreat."

Harris slumped back in the chair. "That means they're writing off the US base in that part of the country."

"And it means ISIL will take control of the aircraft and the munitions there too."

"I have to speak to The Chief..."

Ahmed stopped Harris. "I know you can't tell me, and I don't want to know the details, but if you've got some guys there... get them out." He did not wait for Harris's reply and turned back to read the rest of the data stream.

* * *

"I'm in." Sir John had perhaps not spent the night at his desk, but he had certainly made it in long before a lot of his staff. Harris took the now familiar lift ride. Sir John was waiting for him at the door of his office.

"Mosul has just fallen." Harris stepped in.

"Colmore is demanding information about his daughter."

Both men fell silent, absorbed in assessing each other's information.

214

"There is nothing we can do about Mosul now." Harris went first.

"But there is plenty we can do about Colmore."

"Raqqa has remained dark, still we have spotted some activity. ISIL will flood the media, and all their other comms channels as soon as the fall is confirmed to Baghdadi."

"Unfortunately," The Chief agreed.

"Al-Qaeda was good at using the media, but ISIL has raised the bar. Their videos for recruitment are much more polished… they have accounts on Instagram, WhatsApp, YouTube… they're reaching out to young Muslims around the world."

Sir John looked sceptical. "You think they're becoming more dangerous than Al-Qaeda. Is that what you're telling me?"

"Yes, sir, I think I am." Harris stressed each word, weighing what the impact of his conclusion might be.

"But they're not organised as a state. Assad needs rooting out now otherwise he'll survive the uprising with the help of the Russians and the Iranians."

"I know, sir, but I don't think we should underestimate what a problem ISIL has become."

"Just the way we underestimated Al-Qaeda, I get it."

Harris pulled a face. He did not have the proof yet, but ISIL was in a different league. "What about Colmore though?"

"I'll play the delaying tactic for as long as I can. Until you tell me what the *Sunday Times* reaction has been."

"I'm starting to wonder whether he might be tempted to take the matter into his own hands," Harris said.

"You mean… speak to someone else… like the Americans?"

"He must have contacts in Washington."

"That's a very good point," Sir John mused. "I could ask, of course, but that would be too visible. What about your CIA contact… could you try him perhaps?"

"I can speak to Jack again… If he knows something, he'll tell me and if he doesn't, he can find out."

Sir John's PA knocked on the door. "Your conference call is scheduled in 15 minutes, Sir John."

"Many thanks, Martha."

Harris did not stand up immediately. Sir John stayed where he was.

"I'll let you know as soon as I have news from Langley."

"And I'll let you know as soon as I have spoken to Colmore and the Iraqis."

Harris left for the third floor. It was barely 6.30am.

* * *

The door had creaked open in the early hours of the morning. Mattie had not moved, ready to fight with all she had if one of the women in black came for her. She heard the door of the bathroom open and shut quietly and a ray of light told her that someone was in there. The shower came on, a soft sound that lasted for a while. Tears had gathered underneath her closed eyes, brought by a mixture of fear and anger.

Whoever had come back needed to let the water run on their skin, cleansing, removing, hoping to wipe out the stench and remains of abuse.

Mattie kept her eyes shut when the light went out in the bathroom. Gretta's bed creaked. Mattie turned her face towards it, eyes still shut; perhaps Gretta could see her face turned towards her and talk if she wanted.

The room became still again, and Mattie rolled back her head after a moment. The pressure in her chest squeezed her lungs, clamped her throat. She could not cry, not if the women next to her managed not to.

Jean arrived a few minutes later. She went across to Gretta's bed and pulled the blanket over her shoulders. She came to Mattie's bed and sat next to her.

"Nothing happened," she whispered. Mattie brought her hand to her mouth and muffled a small cry of relief. An explanation would come later.

Mattie watched Jean's shadow remove her niqab and abaya and slide into bed. Tomorrow Mattie would swap with her; at least they could take it in turns to sleep on the least comfortable mattress in the room.

Mattie stretched underneath the sheet and recalled a face.

"Trust me." Henry had sounded certain. She grappled to remember

216

the tone of his voice, deep, urgent. He knew what to do to free her from this nightmare. Mattie rolled towards the wall. She couldn't wait for him to contact her. Calling him, calling Henry or Abu Shabh as he was known, had to be her next move or perhaps she needed to wait a little longer... She wondered how much more she would be able to endure. She wrapped her arms around her body, brought her knees to her chest. It was time to get some rest if she could. Tomorrow she would find a way out.

Chapter Twenty-Two

Beppe's Café on West Smithfield was slowly filling up. He had been their first customer today. Nothing unusual about that. James Radlett liked to start his day early. He had chosen a seat at the far end of the row of tables, next to the window in one of the comfortable green two-seaters. James had placed the call at 6.05am, exactly as agreed. It had not taken long for his contact to confirm what he had suspected. Henry Crowne had literally disappeared. There was no trace of him to be found anywhere in the UK, nor in Europe.

A shadow.

The young waitress who had taken a shine to him came to refill his cup. She smiled but said nothing. Her English was sometimes a little difficult to understand with her strong Eastern European accent that became stronger the harder she tried, but her beaming face made up for her mistakes. James returned her smile and nodded a thank you. He would have normally tried to have a conversation with her, even if only a few words, but today he was absorbed by a question he found difficult to answer.

Why? Why had Crowne disappeared... completely?

One answer was that Crowne wanted his freedom back, but James had seen a broken man in the dock during his trial. Some may not have believed in Crowne's act of atonement. He had fooled everyone in the City for years, but James's gut did not go with that. Yet, how could Henry Crowne have stayed continuously under the radar for so long? Even by MI6 standards, making a man completely disappear required planning and training in the survival skills intended for deep infiltration.

James shifted on his seat. More people were pouring in, ordering juicy sandwiches they might keep for their lunch or have for breakfast. The tables were filling up and soon someone would ask permission to sit at the same table as James to enjoy the succulent fry-up Beppe was renowned for. The glass sugar dispenser looked almost as old as the premises. James liked the worn furniture of this quirky place. He scooped a generous helping and let it drop into his coffee, stirring the liquid methodically until the granulated sugar had dissolved fully.

James smiled at his fussiness and picked up his trail of thoughts. There was no reason why MI6 might want to whisk him to one of their black sites for interrogation. Henry and his two friends had given MI6 the information it wanted, or at least so his contact said.

James drained his cup. Should he indulge in a third? Why not. He raised his hand and Laita came promptly to serve him. The same smile. The same shyness. A burly man who did not look the City type asked whether he could share James's booth. His voice was surprisingly amiable. James nodded a friendly *of course*. He did not mind him sitting opposite him so long as he did not have to put up with the pompous banter of another investment banker.

James resumed his methodical analysis. He could not quite fathom out what working with Henry Crowne might entail. Harris needed to give him a better idea of what would be involved. Sitting in a room as part of the Operational Data Analyst team alongside Henry did not inspire him. What else could Henry offer but his in-depth knowledge of finance? James shook his head. Harris should have been more forthcoming. Still, he had not agreed anything with Harris and he certainly would not be played. Perhaps his days in the City were not over just yet.

* * *

"Do you ever sleep?" Harris had popped his first gum of the day into his mouth.

"You should take up smoking again, you know." Ahmed had called him, and had Amina sent him a text.

"And yes, I just have a sleeping bag rolled up underneath my desk."

Ahmed was not joking. "Raqqa's chatting... a lot. The ban on comms has clearly been lifted."

"What are they saying?"

"It's all about the victory, beating the infidels... all of that good beardo stuff."

"How bad is it in Mosul?"

Ahmed shook his head and pulled away from the screen. "It's a bloodbath. I am trying not to go through the videos if can help it... I've seen a lot in my time, but this is a real massacre."

"Any reaction from the Yanks yet?"

"Zip. It's as if losing one of the main airports they operate from has not happened."

"Together with what was in it of course."

"That's probably why they haven't said anything yet... assessing the damage."

Amina had joined them silently, her eyes roaming over Ahmed's screens of scrolling data.

"There... There," she pointed out.

Ahmed promptly selected the words and captured the Arabic text on another screen.

"Our leader, Abu Bakr al-Baghdadi, enters victorious Mosul. He will clear our land of all infidels with Allah's protection and blessing. He will address us today."

"What do you think that means?"

"I don't know, but we'd better keep track of what Baghdadi has to say for himself. He never addresses his followers in person... Always through social media."

"I'm going back to my desk." Amina was telling Harris she was expecting contact with Wasim.

"And I'll keep you updated as soon as Baghdadi makes his announcement."

Harris walked out of OMA's maze of offices. A permanent frown had not left his forehead since he had seen the volume of data flooding cyberspace.

"What's on your mind?"

"I need to speak to my CIA contact again."

"Fat good it did last time you told them what we knew."

"It's got nothing to do with Jack. He did pick up the intel too… but he can't action things all on his own."

"I'm not saying Jack ignored you, but I agree that his bosses are crap. They always assume they know more than we do."

"Fair point, but bearing in mind the cock-up in Iraq and the loss of Mosul, they might listen this time."

Amina logged into her computer. She forgot about Harris for a moment, checking the chatline of the website for a message.

Nothing.

"I'll speak to Radlett tomorrow if there's still no news from them. We are going to need him sooner than expected."

* * *

Morning prayer had just finished. Henry had unfolded the rug he had found in his room the day before, a beautiful Hereke piece of geometrical forms in soft silk. The first token of The Treasurer's generosity. He had laid his forehead on the ground and prayed the way Wasim had taught him. The rhythm of the words started to feel familiar, almost comforting. He sat back on his legs and rested for a moment. It was a strange moment of peace it afforded but based on a creed he did not want to believe in.

The sudden burst of car horns irritated him. The roar of vehicles driving past the hotel and the shouting that came with it could announce only one thing. Henry stood up in one jump, opened the bay window and went to the edge of the terrace. The road at the bottom of the building was teaming with pick-up trucks, Humvees, SUVs and men on foot waving the black flag with one word on their lips.

Victory.

Henry clutched the banister. His head sank to his chest. Mosul had fallen and al-Haddawi was returning to Raqqa.

"Fucking idiots." Henry gritted his teeth.

Wasim was outside his room as well. He jumped over the low wall that separated their terraces and stood next to Henry, arms crossed over his chest.

"Mosul?"

"Of course, what else?"

"The ban on comms will be lifted."

"You bet, it's time to gloat about their victory."

"And we'd better look happy about it too."

"Don't worry. I'll be putting on my happy face when I meet The Treasurer today."

"It's good for business but not so good for his little power battle with al-Haddawi."

"Or for the hostages."

Henry held his breath for a short moment. "I need to speed up the process, make a deal that will be difficult to unwind."

Wasim nodded. "If you can, but remember anything can happen in this place."

Henry turned around to face Wasim. "Mattie won't be safe until she gets out of here. I get it."

Henry returned to his room and looked around for a few moments. He stilled himself. This was no longer the trading floor of GL Investment Bank. For all the money he had made in the past, the stakes today were infinitely higher. Henry snapped out of it. He switched the mobile back on. A message was waiting for him. Henry could not help smiling. The Treasurer was asking him to come to his office, as soon as possible. News of Mosul's victory must have reached him in the early hours of the morning. Another more subtle battle had started, and The Treasurer needed his help to win it. Henry responded that he was on his way.

But before making his move, a call to his Qatari fixer was overdue.

* * *

"You're coming with me." Harris had barely started his day when the summons came.

"You mean…?" Harris looked at the faded jeans, with a hole that had started to appear at the knee, not a fashionable newly created designer hole, but a hole that was there because his jeans were old and he was comfortable in them.

"Yes… Colmore is starting to be a pain and I need back-up."

"Sir, are you sure…" Harris raised his eyebrows and The Chief waved his hand.

"We're not meeting in Westminster. We'll meet Colmore in one of our dedicated London sites and you're coming as you are."

"What did he suggest?"

"A high-grade military extraction." Sir John grunted.

"In the middle of Raqqa?"

Sir John did not answer and walked into the lift. Both fell silent during the ride to the car park. Sir John's car was waiting for them as they walked out of the underground space. The BMW was sitting a little low on its tyres, a testament to the extra work that had been carried out on the body of the vehicle, fitting armour plating and reworking its suspension. Sir John did not wait for his driver to open the door and took his seat at the back of the car. Harris followed.

"Have you spoken to your contact at Langley?"

"I have."

Sir John nodded. It was all he needed to know and there would be no rehearsing of the interaction with Colmore in his car. The strategy as far as Sir John was concerned was clear. Lay off and let us do our jobs.

The underground car park had not been used for a while. Colmore's silver Bentley was already there. Sir John's car slipped slowly alongside Colmore's. Sir John opened his window waiting for a short moment before Colmore realised he was meant to do the same. The purr of the window gliding down felt almost soothing. Colmore's equine face appeared as the glass slid down, grey hair, unexpectedly unkempt, bushy eyebrows, dark rings under his eyes and a sagging mouth showing spite and sadness.

"If you do not mind, Harold, you need to change car."

"This is ridiculous, John, you know that."

"You know I wouldn't ask unless it was necessary – but it is."

"We could have met at The Cross."

"Harold, please, we're losing valuable time."

Colmore pushed himself back into his car to grab something he had placed on the back seat alongside him. Sir John's car moved so as to give him space to open his door. Harris had already stepped out of the car and climbed into the front seat. Colmore's driver came to hold open the car door and he finally took his seat next to Sir John.

"I expect we won't be talking about what's at stake in the car either."

"That's right."

Colmore grumbled some inaudible complaint.

Sir John moved his body sideways to better face Colmore. "But I can at least make some introductions. Please meet one of my best agents, Steve Harris."

Harris turned around and extended his hand between the two front seats. "How do you do?"

Colmore's face looked in horror at one of MI6's best agents, jeans that he thought would have looked bad even on a tramp, an open-necked shirt that had seen better days and still the faint accent of an East End boy. Colmore extended a reluctant hand.

* * *

The old pick-up truck groaned as Henry shifted the gearbox into reverse. He moved the truck carefully along the entrance of the hotel and accelerated to slot into the heavy traffic on Malahi Avenue. Cars, trucks and armoured vehicles were speeding up and down the dual track road like crazy insects in search of fresh food. Henry used his horn to join in the celebration, certain that no one would spot the 'Rule Britannia' rhythm of his tune. It was the best he could think of.

He arrived at the Treasury office on Fardos Street 20 minutes later. The guards opened the gates without question. Henry slung his rucksack over his shoulder and stepped into the large building. On the Treasury floor, the atmosphere was more controlled. Hamza was at his screens, nodding to Henry when he came in.

"Salaam alaikum." Henry dropped his rucksack onto the desk next to Hamza's.

"Alaikum as salaam." Hamza straightened up in the chair. "There's been a small spike in the oil price. I've released some of our own along the Kirkuk pipes and asked for the price to reflect the reduced risk."

"Very well done, brother."

Henry had kept an eye on The Treasurer's door. It was shut. Through the glass, the pudgy little man could be seen moving one arm in the air; it was not a move of victory.

Oh, to be a fly on the wall... Henry's attention came back to Hamza who had been speaking about being more proactive on the Jordanian border.

"Sure, let's talk about it."

The door finally opened, and Henry walked into The Treasurer's office without knocking.

"What took you so long?"

"It's mayhem out there."

The Treasurer shut the door behind Henry.

"Mosul is good for business." Henry's face was all smiles, with clenched fists.

The Treasurer slumped into his chair and eyed Henry. There was no need to bullshit him. He knew it would increase the asset base of the group dramatically. He also knew who had made it happen and that the result was not good for his own business.

"Al-Haddawi is going to make demands."

"Unless I can agree something before he does."

The Treasurer stopped the movement of his prayer beads. "Why are you so confident?"

"Because I know how these people think. I made another call to our fixer... *The Sunday Times* are willing to talk."

"The UK may still interfere with their plan to organise payment of the ransom... The use of an NGO is clever but perhaps the *Sunday Times* can't take the risk." The Treasurer pouted, not hiding he was in fact pleased.

"Then we come to my Plan B."

The Treasurer's heavy eyebrows twitched a little. A man who could think about a number of alternative options and anticipate the need for them, was a man very much after his own heart.

"What would that be?"

Henry sat in the chair in front of his desk. "The UK government does not pay cash ransom, that's true but… cash is not the only asset available."

"Go on." The Treasurer leaned forward, arms on the desk, fingertips touching. He had forgotten about the prayer beads.

"An exchange could be a good thing."

The Treasurer's round face lit up.

"And… I know who we could ask for." Henry engineered a grin. "Abu Maeraka."

The Treasurer slapped both hands on the desk and roared with laughter. "Genius."

"But we need to keep Mattie Colmore safe."

"There are many more hostages hidden in Raqqa. Al-Haddawi can have them all."

"Except Mattie."

"That would be the deal."

"I'll speak to the fixer again in the afternoon."

"Don't let me down." The bonhomie of The Treasurer disappeared in an instant. Henry knew that look, cold and heartless. He had seen it in the eyes of many men with whom he had done business in the past. Whereas he might have got away with a bad reputation in London, there was no doubt in his mind that The Treasurer would hold a knife to his throat and slit it open without hesitation.

Chapter Twenty-Three

"This moron is going to get my team killed." Harris could not hold back. He did not care whether he was still in the car that was taking them back to Vauxhall Cross. Sir John did not rebuke him. He looked glad Harris had said aloud what he was himself thinking quietly.

"I'm not going to let it happen." Sir John's clear eyes briefly dug into Steve's. He meant every word he said. He would use the full breadth of MI6 capability to stick to his word. Both men fell silent. The conversation would be continued in the secrecy of Sir John's office.

Harris picked up his iPhone, rotating it in his hand mechanically. They had passed Lambeth Palace, and the car was making good progress through light traffic. They would be able to continue their conversation at the Cross in a few moments. Harris's iPhone buzzed angrily in his hand. Amina's name displayed on the screen. Harris fought the desire to respond and endured the ride in the elevator to Sir John's office in silence until they reached the fifth floor.

"I'm sorry if I don't share your confidence, sir, but..." Harris hesitated. "Two MI6 assets infiltrating ISIL and operating in the middle of Raqqa. No one has ever succeeded to go that far into a terror group. It will cost them dear if we make the slightest mistake and we can't extract them the way we may have planned with other missions." Harris felt breathless. "And before you ask, sir, yes, I have lost some of my operatives in the past, but I don't make a habit of it."

Sir John nodded. "Then I think we are on the same page." His voice had a comfortable warmth that still failed to convince Harris.

He had been at the sharp end. He knew what would happen if he floundered and did not want to contemplate the consequences.

"There is a long way between Colmore's demand for military intervention and our acting upon it."

"What if he starts negotiations at another level?"

"What do you mean?"

"I'm not sure yet... But he has set his mind on this idea... To him nothing else is worth considering and he won't stop until he gets what he wants..."

"Have you spoken to your team?"

"Good point..." Harris pressed redial. Amina picked up immediately. Harris's face grew pale. He squeezed the phone tightly in his hand.

"Are you sure?" Amina repeated what she had said. "I'm putting you on loudspeaker." Her voice bounced around in the office. "There is talk of a caliphate."

"What do you mean?" Harris's mind felt at a loss for a reference. The word sounded almost obsolete.

"It means that al-Baghdadi is creating a new country... ruled under Sharia law as interpreted by ISIL... A caliphate."

The news had left both men silent...

"Are you still there... where are you?"

Sir John joined in on the call. "We have just got back to my office... we're coming down."

A few minutes later, both men burst into RED HAWK Control Room on the third floor. Amina did not quite lose her usual grumpiness at the sight of Sir John.

"Social media is full of the news and it won't be long before they pull one of their video stunts." Amina's words tumbled out, fast, fiery. She could sense the impact of what had just happened before her mind could begin to analyse the outcome.

"I'm sorry if I appear a little rusty here... Could you both remind me how a caliphate works?" Sir John's admission of ignorance calmed Amina down. She needed to help him make sense of what had just happened, to make people unfamiliar with Wahhabism understand the full impact of the declaration.

"You're right, sir. It's a term that hasn't been used since the Middle Ages. What ISIL's leader seems to be saying is that ISIL is more than a geopolitical state. A caliphate claims religious, political and military authority over all Muslims worldwide. By calling itself this, it claims its global statehood and encourages all 'true' Muslims to join it." Amina's throat had run dry. She reached for her bottle of water and took a sip from it. "It's challenging the entire Middle East, not only the West." Amina's eyes darted from Harris to Sir John. Did they understand the full extent of what she meant?

"How large is the territory al-Baghdadi is claiming?"

She swirled on her chair and enlarged a map on her screen. "With the latest conquest... A third of Iraq, half of Syria, without forgetting its other provinces."

"You mean Afghanistan, Pakistan, Yemen, etc."

"That's right." Amina kept typing on her keyboard for more data to appear. "It covers land inhabited by 12 million people in Iraq and Syria alone."

Sir John ran his hand through his light brown hair and held it there for a moment to help him think. "So much for Barack Obama's disengagement."

"Did you manage to get hold of Wasim?"

"It's proving more difficult without his laptop and mobile. He's hoping for a mobile so we can resume daily briefings to MOTHER. But we can't yet predict when he might be able to contact us."

"But what's the best time?" Sir John had moved closer to Amina's screens to check the data.

"Just before Zuhr... I mean..."

"I know, early afternoon prayer. I'm not completely ignorant about the Muslim world." His smile was amused, interrupted by the buzz of his phone. "Got to go to my next meeting. Keep me posted. I'll make some calls in the UK."

"I'll see what the CIA has got to say for themselves too."

"Obviously very little it seems." Sir John shot back, leaving hurriedly.

Harris and Amina felt a load had been lifted from their shoulders.

"Wow. Much more approachable than I had anticipated."

"Even with your grumpy self too."

"Yup. Don't care whether I deal with The Chief or the PM, I'm at my best that way."

"It's the fighter in you. Not being able to deal with these bastards on the ground."

"You're right. I should join the Peshmerga so I can go and finish them all off."

Harris shuddered. "Scary…"

A call indicator started to flash on Amina's screen. It was Wasim and it was too early for him to be using the tearooms of Raqqa.

* * *

The fixer was on the line and he was not happy.

"I know we agreed I would give the UK another 24 hours, but things have changed substantially."

"You need to think about your other plan carefully."

"Prisoner exchange?"

Silence. Henry wondered whether he was still on the phone.

"If it's about your share of the ransom, the deal still stands." Henry's voice was calm and level. "A deal is a deal."

"I'll see what I can do."

"Call me in a couple of hours." Henry killed the call. It was 10am in Raqqa. Al-Haddawi would soon be on his way back to Raqqa from Mosul. Thankfully he almost certainly would need to give a full account of his prowess to al-Baghdadi as well as the military chief and the head of the Shura Council… the price of becoming a jihadi superstar. Wasim had spent time explaining to Henry how a traditional Sunni Muslim state would work. It was cumbersome and rigid… al-Haddawi would have to follow the rules.

Henry checked his watch again. He had a few hours to wait and nothing else to do. Wasim was contacting MOTHER. Hamza had started to let him in on how the IS oil trade was doing, but Henry was not in the mood. It was perhaps time to check on one of their most precious assets, Mattie Colmore.

He scrolled through the notes he had started to capture on a small pad he carried with him at all times. He found what he was looking for, the address Mattie had been taken to after their conversation. Henry walked back to the large office, grabbed his rucksack and disappeared. Hamza lifted his head in expectation and his eyes followed Henry with interest when he left.

The pick-up truck joined the flow of traffic and turned left at Fardos Street into another large boulevard. It felt palatial and spacious. Trees afforded the road welcome shade against the summer sun; the area felt unmistakably Middle Eastern and yet the houses were almost European in style. Henry parked the car opposite a block of luxury apartments. He spotted two guards at the entrance of the building. This had to be the place. Henry walked slowly towards them, fingering in his pocket a letter carrying the IS seal and signed by The Treasurer. It was the latest move by The Treasurer to enable him to circulate more freely and go about on ISIL business, notably checking on Mattie Colmore's whereabouts. She had become the victim of a power struggle between al-Haddawi and The Treasurer. Henry would make good use of it.

The guards looked up. Henry presented the letter. He needed to see the hostages immediately. There was a conversation between the two men that Henry could not understand. Perhaps it was a different dialect? Their body language expressed irritation, hesitation but also fear of displeasing one of the most powerful men within ISIL's command structure, The Treasurer.

"It is urgent… The Treasurer can't be kept waiting."

The shorter of the two men moved aside and let Henry through the entrance. He felt the eye of the guard on his back until he disappeared inside the property. Henry climbed the marble stairwell two at a time and found himself on the first floor. There were only two apartments on this floor. He turned to the first front door and stopped. The building was unusually quiet. No voices or sound of activity in the apartment he was about to enter. Everyday life seemed to have ground to a halt around Raqqa.

The solid wooden door, the marble floors, the white walls, felt suddenly cold and lifeless. Henry shuddered. The almost imperceptible sound of cloth moving around surprised him. A woman clad in full niqab and gloves appeared at the top of the steps. Her eyes were barely visible, underneath the heavy black cloth that covered her face. Still, she looked neither scared nor surprised.

"Salaam alaikum." Henry avoided looking at her directly.

"Alaikum as salaam." She had not moved, deciding whether she wanted to cry for help.

"I came to see Mattie Colmore. The Treasurer wishes me to speak to her." Henry sounded demanding. "Come on. I don't have all day. Shall I return to him not having spoken to her?"

The woman took a set of keys from underneath her face cloth. The metallic jingle of the keys took him by surprise. Her keyring was laden, making her more jailor than housekeeper. Henry stepped in as soon as the door was opened. Another woman appeared from a room further down the corridor. She brought her veil around her face when she caught sight of Henry. Henry's stomach clenched. The place felt sombre and threatening.

"Where is Mattie Colmore?" The urgency to check on Mattie became overwhelming. Henry struggled to stay calm, reminding himself that raising a hand against any of these women would compromise all he had achieved so far. The woman who had opened the door disappeared down the corridor, but the second woman stayed put.

Henry walked into the lounge. The spacious room overlooked large gardens. Henry opened the French doors that led onto a shaded balcony. He would find a space speak to Mattie alone. A dark shape moved into the lounge captured in the reflection of the French doors as he closed them. He did not recognise her until he heard her voice.

"Salaam alaikum, Abu Shabh."

Henry hesitated. He turned around abruptly in a mix of rage and relief. Mattie had changed her clothes and the dark blue abaya intensified the blue of her eyes. She dropped the veil around her face. She looked tired and the marks of resilience on her face he liked so much had died a little. She had opened the French doors and stood on their threshold, the two Arab women standing behind her.

"Leave us." Henry's voice had taken the sharp edge of a serrated knife. The two women hesitated once more. "I will not ask again." The threat might be empty – what could he really do? Still, he was a man in a world in which women were given little importance; it did the trick.

Mattie moved slowly past him onto the balcony. Henry brought a finger to his lips indicating they were not yet free to speak. Mattie nodded. He pointed towards the far end of the balcony.

The gardens below were empty. Mattie leaned against the wall and inhaled deeply.

"How have you been?"

Mattie closed her eyes. "I'm… alive." Her voice faltered.

Henry turned around. His hands grasped the thick stone balustrade. He could not look her in the face. He heard Mattie's light step come closer. She rested her head against his back and closed her arms around his chest. Henry moved one hand and wrapped it around one of her arms. "I promise you. I will get you out of this." Mattie nodded. Henry felt the movement through his shirt, and it took all his will not to move around, take Mattie by the hand and walk out of this godforsaken place. He breathed in slowly and her arms tightened further around his chest, pressing against it. Henry loosened her arms gently and slowly turned around. Mattie drew back with a slight inclination of her head. She managed a faint smile.

"Am I allowed to call you Henry… again, Mr Cro…" Henry placed his fingers quickly on her lips before she could speak his name.

He looked at her for a moment in silence. She had finally recognised him. Perhaps the memories of their encounter at an art charity dinner, years ago, was still etched in her mind as it was in his.

"I don't think that's a good idea."

"Of course not." They both looked around for somewhere to sit, but had to sit on the floor or the balcony, sheltered by the balustrade.

"I can't stay long. Tell me everything you think I need to know." Henry held her gloved hands in his.

"There are at least two other women staying in the same room as me. Two US girls. As far as I can tell, we are not alone here. There are others."

"What nationality?"

"Yazidis, Christians… Europeans… according to the girls I'm with."

"How long have they been here?"

"Not long, each of them has spent time at Raqqa Stadium, before being moved to this place."

"Who are the women who look after you?"

"The women at the door, they are relatives of a very senior ISIL figure, Umm Sayyaf... his sister and daughter, and the others are... slaves."

"Slaves?" Henry face whitened.

"Yes, one of the worst forms of Wahhabist ISIL's practices, it allows them to enslave people, non-Muslims and Muslims who do not share their interpretation of Islam alike."

"What else?" Henry moved his hands around hers.

Mattie's eyes shifted away from Henry's face.

"What is it?" Henry squeezed her hands gently in is. "Tell me."

Mattie squeezed back. "This is irrelevant."

"Have you been hurt?" He clenched his jaw so hard he could feel his teeth grating. "How bad..."

Mattie put a finger over his lips "I am fine. You must trust me in turn to manage what's happening here."

"Why have they moved you all here?" The thought that flooded his mind was unbearable. It could not be the case and yet he had been told it happened all the time.

"Nothing has happened to me." Mattie read his mind. "Nothing."

"You mean not yet." Henry closed his eyes. "If you think you are in danger, ask these women to call me. Tell them... you are under my protection. I'll speak to The Treasurer."

Mattie gave him a kind smile. He was no longer in London... This was ISIL Raqqa.

"Don't... we are all here at al-Baghdadi's request."

* * *

The drive back to the hotel was as slow as the journey to visit Mattie had been. Henry's jaw had been clenched all this time and it ached. The memories of their meeting at the art charity dinner came to mind. They had been sitting next to one another and the conversation had moved in every direction, from art to politics, from economics to philosophy...

234

Mattie had shone in the depth of her knowledge but also in her ability to take risks for what she believed in… a lot of risks. For the space of an evening Henry had felt he had perhaps found a kindred spirit. They had exchanged phone numbers, but he never heard from her and for some reason he did not call either. Henry Crowne did not get close to anyone… ever. And it seemed neither did Mattie Colmore.

Henry left his truck in front of the hotel, aiming a glare at a couple of men who seemed to question his parking there. He rode in the elevator to the fifth floor and entered his room, yanking the door open. He threw his rucksack with rage onto the bed and shoved the terrace doors open.

Wasim was already out there, waiting.

"Where have you been?"

"We need to talk."

"I know…"

Henry looked confused. How could he know? He could not… surely.

"You go first." Wasim picked up on his confusion.

"I went to see Mattie." Henry ignored Wasim's frown. "I have a pass from The Treasurer. There are women in the same flat as she is, American, European." Henry's story felt disjointed. "I'm sure they are abusing them. They are…" The word stuck in Henry's throat.

"Raping them?" Wasim moved his hand over the back of his neck.

"How do you… know?"

"This is a war zone, Henry. What do you expect?"

The fist came out of nowhere and Wasim avoided it by a fraction of an inch. The missed blow threw Henry off balance. Wasim dug his elbow into Henry's ribs and stopped him with an arm lock. Not a word had been spoken. Henry remained silent. He let his body relax. Wasim was right, having a go at him in that fashion was the most stupid thing he could have done.

"Sorry."

Wasim let go of the arm lock. "I was wondering when that would come…" he said with a nod.

"Am I that predictable?"

"No, but you've never been in a war zone before. Even the training camps don't prepare you for all this and for what you're going to see."

"I've seen nothing yet." Henry slumped onto one of the chairs, head lowered. "I don't want to let people down. I can't let people down."

"I told you… you were ready when we left Manchester and I still stand by that."

"This did not feel that ready to me." Henry massaged his sore arm.

"As long as you still trust me, everything's under control."

Henry nodded. "The only thing Mattie knew is that it was al-Baghdadi who ordered those women to be kept where they are."

"Shit, that really complicates matters." Wasim slumped back in his chair.

"That's really got to be bad, Wasim. I'd never heard you swear before and you've just done this twice in less than 24 hours."

"I spoke to MOTHER and things are not going smoothly in London either." Wasim changed tack.

"The UK government's sticking its nose into our deal?"

"Colmore has spoken to The Chief."

Henry's eyes widened. "What… Why? He couldn't care less about his daughter from what I've gathered."

"I don't know why but I know the how… and that involved a combined SAS and SEAL operation."

"You mean, extraction?"

"That's the sum of it."

"This fucking idiot is going to get everybody killed."

"That's what MOTHER is afraid of. So, she's asking for an alternative course of action."

"Good, because I've got one."

"Why am I not surprised?" Wasim cocked his head. "Will I have to say sorry before you tell me what you've got in mind?"

"Nope." Henry grinned. "We're going to ask for an exchange. Abu Maeraka in return for Mattie Colmore."

236

Chapter Twenty-Four

The burner phone with the Union Jack cover had not rung since James Radlett had confirmed their lunch appointment. Harris could wait no longer. He picked up the second burner phone that lay on his desk, black casing in fake leather, complete with a few spiky studs. He always suspected Brett had a kinky personality... why pretend, he knew he did. Brett had not called either, but Harris's request would take a little time for him to process. Irritating on both counts.

Harris shrugged on his old leather jacket. He left Vauxhall Cross, turned right at Albert Embankment. The roar of the traffic had died down at the junction with Vauxhall Station. He headed for the station itself and took another turn toward Vauxhall Arcade. The rumble of trains departing from and arriving at the platforms overhead made him miss a call. Harris cursed himself for having left his office... no point in going back though. Vauxhall Dirty Burger would be empty. He could do with a cup of their surprisingly good coffee whilst returning the call. Harris walked in, chose a table at the back of the café and ordered. The owner was not the chatty type which was fine by Harris. He pressed the recall button, tapping the top of the table with the tips of his fingers.

Radlett picked up the phone as it was about to switch to voicemail.

"Hello Steve." Harris could hear Radlett walking at a pace, making his way out of earshot.

"Hello James. Can you talk?" Harris looked around, not that he was expecting any company, but he still had to make sure.

"Now, I can." A door closed. "The story about Henry doesn't

quite make sense to me after reflection. I'm not sure I can help you as much as I thought I could."

Harris took a breath and held it. Not the answer he was expecting.

"What makes you say that?"

"I thought I could read him, but I can't walk away from the fact that he managed to con me into thinking he was a decent bloke."

"Fair enough, but didn't you question his involvement in the Albert murder? You must have been close to suspecting something then?"

"How did you..." The details of Henry and James's stormy conversation had never been divulged to anyone.

"Know...? That's my job." Harris took a sip of coffee and smiled... good coffee and good point. "Look. I can't, for obvious reasons, disclose much about Crowne." Henry had said it to Harris and he, now more than ever, needed to heed the advice. *Be straight with him.*

"Still, I need more information before I make up my mind."

Harris almost cursed. But he had nothing on James that would enable him to *convince him* the way he had Brett or Henry. Dealing with a squeaky-clean prospect was such a bore.

"I'll see what else I can give you but I'm not promising anything."

"That's fine. I'm in no hurry."

Harris and Radlett exchanged civil goodbyes.

"I have a fucking emergency in Syria. What about that?" Harris growled at the dark screen that lay on the table. He finished his cup, turned his attention to his second mobile, still pondering on his conversation. How could he convince James Radlett to play ball? If Radlett could not be coerced, he had to be convinced.

Duty. Harris smiled a wicked smile. Oh yes, duty it would be.

His second mobile phone rang. Brett must have done his homework. Surprising... Brett enjoyed being bullied into action, perhaps the remnants of a public school education.

"Yup." Harris answered the call.

"I have the information you asked for."

"Good man."

"Nothing is going to come out of Mosul for the foreseeable future."

"You mean, even stolen bits of art?"

"These are not bits of art, these are... never mind." Brett's irritated voice did not quite have the bite it usually had. "Something important is happening there. The city is in lockdown. Even smugglers won't get near it."

"Have you been penny-pinching... not paying these guys enough?"

"Harris... I'm not goddamn penny-pinching as you say. There is a real reluctance." Brett's voice trailed. "Perhaps even fear."

"What if we get the parcel out of Iraq, over the frontier into Turkey or even Aleppo?"

Brett was thinking. "Look if the parcel as you call it is only *a parcel* then I'll try Turkey, but if the parcel is something else..."

"What makes you say that?"

"Having to traffic people into the UK for a bunch of terrorists that the Counter-Terrorist Squad subsequently reduced to pulp and all at your request has given me a view on how you operate." Brett blurted out. "I could have been there..."

"You couldn't have been because I wouldn't have let you... Don't be such a drama queen."

"Extremely unfair of you. You didn't have to see the pictures of a certain former acquaintance with his throat..." Brett's voice stuck in his own throat. It had been horrendous.

"Point taken, Brett. But you know I look after my assets... always."

"So you say," Brett grumbled.

"Try the Turkish route and let me know." Harris killed the call.

* * *

"That could work."

Wasim had said nothing to start with, going back into his room. Henry had wondered whether he had walked out, in the direction one of the tearooms to contact MOTHER and relay that Henry had gone mad or even worse gone rogue.

Wasim came back and handed him a can of fizzy drink. Henry had stopped moaning about no longer being a kid.

"I've been giving it a lot of thought... It will take time which we don't have, for Mattie's newspaper to gather the money we are asking for." Henry pulled the metallic ring of the can and a little foam bubbled out. "And at the end the UK government might interfere with the payment, her father might interfere with the payment… but a straightforward exchange…"

"The UK government might even welcome getting rid of someone who has managed to radicalise thousands of inmates… at least when he is back in Syria they can order a drone strike."

"That's a bloody good point, Was."

Wasim raised his can and they toasted. "Shame it's not beer."

"Stop complaining, it's got bubbles. What's the plan?"

"The Treasurer is convinced… The fixer wasn't happy, but he knows he will be paid so now he doesn't care who or what we ask for in exchange for Mattie. We need MOTHER to play ball… That might be the tricky part."

"Always happy to have a good old argument with Mom."

Henry moved to the edge of the balcony and cast a watchful eye towards the far end of the building. The racket of traffic had died down somewhat. Still he could see more trucks arriving, disgorging the jubilant fighters who had earned the right to stay in the most luxurious hotel in town. Henry had noticed that the beds that had been crammed into the hotel lobby when they arrived had been removed to give way to more comfortable surroundings of armchairs and leather sofas.

"Any news from Ali?" Henry focused a little more on the newcomers' faces.

"Glad you asked. He has been injured, nothing serious, from what I could see."

"You went to see him in hospital?"

Wasim smiled. "Unless you're about to die, you're not going to end up in hospital here. No, he is back here, sharing a room with two other men."

"But he is fine?"

Wasim shook his head. "Not sure… he wasn't going to say anything in front of the others. It was all boasting… about the war… the caliphate… Ali didn't say much. The two others did most of the talking."

"I'll go and see him." Henry glanced at his watch. He could spare an hour for the young man.

"Not sure that is a good idea."

"Because?"

"You're still very new at the game here."

"And?"

"They're young guys… they are pumped up and you don't want them to challenge you because they won't trust you. Remember they've been slaughtering people without giving it a second thought… military, civilians… they don't care."

"Fine, fine, I get you. I can't just ignore him though."

"Then do it discreetly. It won't do him any good either if you get into a fight with these nutters."

* * *

The old pick-up truck rumbled along Malahi Avenue and within ten minutes it was parked inside the gates of ISIL's Treasury offices. Henry no longer had to show his credentials for the guards to open the doors. He climbed the steps two at a time, reached the second floor and slowed down. It was never advisable to show too much eagerness in business.

The door of the large office was open. Unusual… The Treasurer had a strict confidentiality policy that would have made a few Western banks blush. Everyone was at their desks but the focus in the room had gone, young men distracted. Hamza didn't stand up as he usually did to greet him. Henry had noticed the Humvee parked in the yard but not given it his full attention. The hair on the back of his neck bristled. Henry moved to the desk he now called his and dropped his rucksack onto it.

Perspiration broke out over his forehead. It was too late to run, time to prove he was still the best at defending the impossible. He took his time moving towards The Treasurer's office, grabbed a cup of water from the water cooler and stood at the door.

The two sandy boots placed negligently onto the desk told him all he needed to know. Al-Haddawi was back from Mosul, victorious, lethal. The Treasurer's round face had lost all its bonhomie. He waved Henry in. Henry nodded, dropped himself into the chair next to al-Haddawi without acknowledging him.

"No money yet?" Al-Haddawi's focus was on The Treasurer.

"That's right."

Henry slowly drank his water.

"You talk a lot but what do you deliver?"

"Plenty, as long as I'm not interfered with." Al-Haddawi threw his head back in a laugh. "It took me and my men no time to conquer Mosul."

"Allah is merciful and bountiful. He rewards the just."

Henry nodded.

The Treasurer's eyes lit up. "But he does not seem to have granted you very much."

"Abu Maeraka thought otherwise." Al-Haddawi's face turned towards Henry in a jerk. His hand had crept to the knife stashed in his boot, but it stopped. Perhaps not just yet...

"You will not get a cent for those hostages and I have a much better use for them."

"Money is only one currency. There are more valuable assets that can be traded."

Al-Haddawi dropped his feet from The Treasurer's desk. "You are too full of horse shit, Englishman."

"I was coming to discuss our next move... with the UK government." Henry turned towards The Treasurer. "A prisoner exchange is one thing the British won't refuse to consider. Helping Abu Maeraka to regain his freedom and join our ranks again is worth much more than the ransom we could get."

The light of victory showed in The Treasurer's eyes.

"What do you think?" Henry had finished his water, crushing the cup in his hand.

Al-Haddawi's hand swept all the papers off the desk, a glass of water broke as it fell to the floor. "These hostages are mine and I will do as I please with them."

The Treasurer stood up, about to call in his men. Henry had already moved towards al-Haddawi. The hatred in Henry's eyes stunned everyone. It had risen in an instant, its intensity almost palpable.

"No... I will choose which hostage to release for Abu Maeraka first, then you can do with the rest of them as you please."

242

The Treasurer pulled back a little. The fight was now between the other two men.

"Our military chief Abu al-Obaidi will decide." Al-Haddawi's face was so close to his, that Henry could see the movement of his dilating pupils.

"No, our leader Abu Bakr al-Baghdadi will decide."

Henry kept an eye on the knife in al-Haddawi's boot.

Al-Haddawi thumped the desk with his balled fists. "You are full of yourself, kafir… but you'll meet your just end."

"No doubt I will. One day, but not today, and not tomorrow either."

"Call the head of our Shura Council, Treasurer, and call our leader too. Let's decide who oversees the operations of our caliphate in Raqqa." Al-Haddawi kicked the chair on which he had been sitting. He opened the door, making it bang against the glass wall, and disappeared.

Henry watched al-Haddawi as he stormed out, displaying his anger for all to see. When he had gone, Henry picked up the chair, went to close the door and returned to his own seat opposite The Treasurer's desk.

"You were rather brave." The Treasurer sat down, ignoring the mess on the floor.

"Or rather foolish."

"Al-Haddawi has become a powerful man." The Treasurer nodded.

"It doesn't mean that he can have whatever takes his fancy."

The Treasurer waved his podgy hand in the air. "No matter. Your idea is a good idea." He picked up his prayer beads from the ground. "How many hostages will it take?"

"Let's try to secure a couple. But hopefully one will do."

"Mattie Colmore?"

"Since her father is a politician that's a good bet." Henry's stomach tightened. Had The Treasurer guessed about Mattie or had they been seen this morning?

"A British MP to be exact. Agreed." A small flash of amusement crossed The Treasurer's eyes.

"Perhaps a man?"

"He would have to be British or American. The Europeans tend to pay ransoms for their people."

Henry nodded.

"I will speak to our leader." The Treasurer picked up the phone. "Is he in Raqqa?"

"I don't know."

Henry looked surprised.

"No one knows where he is at any time... faithful to his other battle name Abu Dua."

"The Phantom."

The Treasurer was still holding the phone receiver in the air, ready to call. A call that he could only make in private.

Henry made to leave. "Two prisoners escaping from HSU Belmarsh: Abu Maeraka and I. That would be a coup that no one has ever managed before." Henry closed the door behind him.

* * *

"That's a very workable idea, sir." Harris and Sir John had moved from his office to the ultra-secure location on Level -2 in the basement of the Vauxhall Cross building.

"I don't share your enthusiasm, Steve. Maeraka was a major catch, one of the most prolific senior members of IS."

"And he is expanding his reach into prisons all around the country without us having much success in stopping him."

"That's true too, but I doubt the Home Office will see it that way."

"At least we need to agree to talk with IS. Give Crowne a bit more time to enhance his credibility and deliver on his mission."

"But what happens if we pull back at the last minute?"

"We'll have to think of a way to make it someone else's fault, not his."

"And if we don't find 'someone else' as you say, what then?"

"I frankly don't know, sir, but at least this solution buys us time and might help put a stop on Colmore's idea of military extraction."

"He won't give up that easily. Any intel from your CIA contact by the way?"

"Nothing yet, but my contact is finding out what he can."

Sir John moved his lower lip over his upper in a gesture Harris had learned to read as doubt. "I won't call my contact at the CIA just yet. Let's find out from yours first whether Colmore is making any progress."

The phone in the room rang, a low pitched buzz that startled both men. Sir John moved over to the desk and picked up. Sir John's eyebrows almost reached his hairline. A flare of the nostrils and he cut the conversation dead, slamming the phone down.

"Colmore is in reception with one of the Home Secretary's closest aides. Does he think he can bully me into taking action?"

Sir John picked up the phone again, calling his PA, and giving clear instructions on where to send the two men.

Harris frowned. "Here, sir?"

"Absolutely. In order to enter this place, they will need to go through more checks. The rooms around this floor have been informed of a visit that requires lockdown for an hour. Let's see who wins the pressure game..."

Harris suppressed a smile. It was good to see his boss being exercised about something or someone.

It took half an hour for Colmore and the accompanying Home Office adviser to reach them.

Colmore entered first. He did not bother to shake hands. Sir John's indicated they should sit around the large table at one side of the room; everyone sat down. Already Colmore was launching into a speech.

"I've spoken to the Home Secretary about our issue." He pronounced the last word with an emphasis on the 's'. Sir John extended a please-go-ahead hand.

"We are all in agreement that the UK cannot be seen to be yielding to these terrorists, whatever their demands turn out to be."

Harris and Sir John waited. Colmore did not need to speak to the Home Office to know this was the UK official policy.

"We equally agree that allowing a third party to pay ransom does not give the right message to terrorists. The government could be accused of facilitating payment through the back door."

"Just the way certain European countries do, in particular the French," the aide piped up. Harris and Sir John kept silent. It was true that Médecins Sans Frontières staff had been released through payments to so-called charitable organisations that had been set up for the purposes of transferring funds to the group that had abducted the medics. And why not? If the government of France wanted to save its citizens… fair play.

"We have therefore come to the conclusion that a military intervention is the only way forward to resolve the current issue." Again the emphasis on the 's'.

"Which means locating with the hostages absolute certainty." Sir John eyed the two men coldly.

"Which is where the immense skills of your operation come in," the aide piped up. Flattery would get him nowhere. Harris pursed his lips.

"And it will take a lot of time before we can gather intelligence reliable enough to mount that type of operation, by which time the hostage might have come to harm."

Colmore stiffened at the words. The aide said nothing.

"But I have an alternative to put to you."

Colmore and the aide looked at each other. What? An alternative they had not thought about.

"A prisoner-for-hostage switch. The UK accepts these from time to time and they have taken place before."

"You would have to find the right IS terrorist to switch and…"

Sir John raised a hand. "We have Kamal Al Qhatani also known as Abu Maeraka serving time at Belmarsh."

"You mean, the mastermind behind the Paddington bombing?" The Home Office aide could hardly articulate the words.

"The very same…"

"You cannot be serious?" Colmore's face had turned crimson.

"I am incredibly serious, unless you'd rather take the risk of seeing your daughter killed before we can intervene."

Chapter Twenty-Five

Hamza had tried to attract his attention, but Henry's mind was elsewhere. The Treasurer was working the ropes, satisfying whomever he needed to, including al-Baghdadi, that they could free Maeraka.

Anger, the old lifelong friend and foe had flared up. Henry needed to go back to his hotel soon and let it pass.

The truck moved along the same road he had taken in the early afternoon. It would soon be prayer time. Henry was looking forward to this moment during the day that might afford him a little peace. Henry parked the truck and moved through the lobby without looking around. He did not know anyone and did not care. Wasim was right – it would take a while for him to be accepted. Infiltration was a slow and painful process of belonging and yet knowing it was a façade. Henry had been good at this in the City. But in the end, he had simply become yet another successful and wealthy banker who played at being a terrorist. What a lot of crap it had been.

"Allo, Abu Shabh, allo…" The young man's voice calling him felt familiar and its sound slowed Henry down. He did not recognise him to start with. Hobbling on crutches towards him, Ali's body looked even slighter than when he last saw him. His left leg was wrapped in heavy bandages that needed changing. Henry stopped and smiled at Ali, waiting for Ali to reach him. Henry threw out an outstretched hand. Despite the smile and the clear happiness at meeting again, Ali's eyes had lost some of their spark. Life had been sapped out of him and what had been stolen would never be returned. Henry walked onto the terrace and found a place where Ali could sit comfortably.

"Wasim told me you were brave." Henry nodded encouragingly.

"We all were. All ready to die so that the word of Muhammad could resound around the world." Ali's voice trembled a little, repeating one of the sentences that had been in turn repeated to him over and over again.

"It does not take away any of your bravery though." Sadness sank into Henry's chest. What were these people doing to this gentle boy who was not meant for the jihad?

"We killed a lot of soldiers, infidels." More of the same rehearsed nonsense. Henry waited for the propaganda to stop and for the real Ali to speak.

"Did you kill a lot of people too?" The question shook him when it came. Ali dropped his head down and nodded.

"The first time... must have been hard."

Ali's eyes swelled with tears and alarm flooded in his eyes.

"That's OK. It's OK to feel sorry, even for your enemy."

"I had to." Ali's voice had become a whisper and the young man's gaze dropped to the ground.

"You did not have any choice and that's what war is all about."

Ali shook his head. That was not what he meant. Henry paused, unsure of what else he could say.

"I had to do it, to prove." Ali had raised his head again. He quickly wiped away a tear that had started rolling down his cheek.

A shiver ran through Henry's body; he no longer wanted to have that conversation, no longer wanted to know what had happened to the soldiers Ali had killed. But here he was, and Ali needed him. Henry nodded slowly, encouraging him to tell his story. It was OK to talk, he would understand.

The word that came out did not make sense and, at first, Henry did not react. What? Ali mimicked a cross and still Henry did not comprehend. Until Ali stretched his arms across. Henry closed his eyes briefly and willed himself to stay where he was... The full force of the revelation would hit him later but now he had to focus on the young man.

"Crucified... And you don't want to do that any longer?"

Ali nodded wiping away the tears that were now rolling uncontrollably down his face, his eyes pleading for an escape. No, he did not want to do this any longer. This was not Islam.

"You can't say that to anybody. You understand?"

Ali nodded and wiped his runny nose with the sleeve of his brand-new shirt.

"You stay here, I'll bring you back something to drink and we'll talk."

Henry found a free drinks dispenser in the hotel lobby. Pressed the button that seemed to dispense lemonade. He was not too bothered about which flavour. Henry needed a moment on his own before he could go back to Ali and make sure the young man did not crumble in front of other people. Henry walked out again through one of the French doors.

Voices and laughter were bouncing off the wall that surrounded terrace. Three young men were talking to Ali; one had started to prod him with his finger and Henry understood in a flash. He dropped the phone into his pocket and ran to the scene.

"Hey, what's so funny?"

The youth turned around. "He's crying." His high pitch voice seeking to imitate a girl's.

"No, he's got sand in his eyes." The smaller one burst into laughter, followed by the other two.

"Three against one, it's you lot who should be crying in shame."

The laughter was cut short like a blade of grass by a sickle.

"He's a coward," the tallest youth shouted, turning toward Henry.

"No, you're the coward." Henry's eyes drilled into his.

The knife came out in a flash of silver. Henry jumped aside, sucking in his stomach just in time to avoid the blade. The blow sent the young men off course. Henry swung his leg high in a back-foot karate kick that got him in the back of the head. The youth fell on his knees and a punch caught him in the solar plexus. His eyes opened wide, so did his mouth, gasping for air. Henry's fist slammed in his face and it was over.

Henry didn't wait – another high back-foot kick into the chest of the second youth who had moved forward; a left punch connected with his lower jaw, sending blood into his mouth and crunching some bones. The third young man had disappeared but Henry was not sure whether he would lie low or come back with others.

"We need to go." Henry helped Ali to stand up.

"What about him?" Ali asked.

"He'll come around soon enough… who were these people anyway?"

"My room-mates."

Henry rolled his eyes. "Your former room-mates. Come on."

* * *

"Did he say that?" Amina's eyes lit up. "Wow. I'm impressed."

"Colmore and the aide… can't remember his name, didn't know what to say in return."

"You mean you don't want to remember his name… and what would you say to having your daughter murdered?"

"Sir John has a meeting with the Home Office Secretary this afternoon." Harris looked at his watch. "Any minute now."

"Is that enough?"

"What would you suggest then?"

"Perhaps placing a call to the Chief of Defence? Wasim gave him some valuable intelligence and both he and The Chief are pursuing the same policy for settling the conflict in Syria. The last thing they need is a cock-up in Raqqa to divert attention away from their plan."

"He did mention a call to the MoD. I guess he had the same idea… a bear of some brain then."

Amina could not help but smile. "Wasim asked that we keep all ears on the chatter coming out of Raqqa. There is a lot of planning going on. He still doesn't know for what."

"If al-Baghdadi confirms his caliphate?"

"More to the point, it depends…" Amina stopped, to check on an incoming email, "How he declares a caliphate."

Someone was knocking at the door. Harris opened it, surprised.

"Ahmed, what on…" He pushed Harris aside. Going straight to Amina's multiple screens, he typed a series of instructions on the keyboard. "You've got to see this. It's happening right now… Live from Mosul. And, yes, I know I shouldn't be here…"

The man speaking was clad in black, a black flowing robe and a black turban. The surroundings in the background looked sumptuous,

250

exquisite pillars carved out of marble. The man was standing at a pulpit, addressing a congregation. The man was confident, working the crowd the way an evangelical preacher would.

"Is this al-Baghdadi?"

"Yes, and this is what he now claims." Ahmed had stopped tapping the keyboard. The man's right hand, index finger pointing towards the sky, kept the rhythm of his speech, slow for maximum effect.

"Where is this happening?" Harris has come closer to the screen.

"Probably the Great Mosque of al-Nuri in Mosul." The voice suddenly changed cadence, its pitch had moved up a tone, the words projected like stones at the crowd.

"The formulation is a little difficult to follow…" Amina frowned.

"He's replicating a follower's address in an ancient style. I can't quite make which one yet, but it's serving a purpose."

"And he has chosen the first day of Ramadan… makes it an even more powerful announcement."

Both Harris and Ahmed nodded in unison.

And then the crescendo came. Abu Bakr al-Baghdadi transformed himself and the future of his group. He announced that ISIL was no longer a jihadi group but that the latest conquest of Mosul and other territories in Iraq and Syria justified its transformation into a caliphate. It was renaming itself Islamic State of Iraq and the Levant, exalting all Muslims around the world to join the only state where true Islam was practised. And leading them in the true fight against the infidels was their caliph, Abu Bakr al-Baghdadi himself.

"Shit, this changes everything." Harris had been fiddling with his packet of gum that was almost empty. Al-Baghdadi had achieved what Bin Laden and Al-Qaeda never could.

Amina passed her hands over her face. "He takes his name after the man who always replaced the prophet Muhammed as prayer leader according to Sunni tradition."

"Well spotted." Ahmed nodded. "And he wears the black turban as those who claim to be descended from Mohammed would."

"Guys." Harris raised his hand. "Guys, we need to give this video a good deal of attention, but my main priority is we engage in understanding how this changes the way al-Baghdadi runs his

251

operation and whether this affects our strategy."

Amina slumped into her chair. The shadows under her eyes had gone darker.

Ahmed left, promising he would keep them informed in real time.

"Steve, this is so not good for RED HAWK."

"I know. Everybody is going to want al-Baghdadi dead."

"And he will know that, too."

"Which means, more protection around him, and more paranoia amongst his people." Harris threw the packet of gum into the bin. "I need a cigarette."

"You should call Jack at Langley now. I'd be surprised if they are not already having talks about launching an attack on Raqqa or Mosul."

"They will need to coordinate so that gives us some time."

Amina took a key from her keyring, opened the drawer at the base of her desk and handed Harris a packet of Camel cigarettes. "It's been in here six months, but I imagine you won't mind."

"You're the best." Harris grabbed the packet, tossed it in the air, deftly caught it and disappeared with his mobile phone. Time for an international call.

* * *

"Have you seen the video?"

"Everybody has seen the video. A whole load of Sunni Muslim theologians and historians are fighting to declare the caliphate void under Sharia law. The Middle Eastern states are doing the same."

"I know but he's not interested in convincing Mid East leaders and he doesn't care about the theologians. He is stirring up the people, especially the young Muslims who want something different. I think IS has become the most dangerous terrorist organisation ever... beyond Al-Qaeda or the Taliban."

"The Taliban were pretty fierce." Jack's experience in Afghanistan had left its marks.

"But they're not asking Muslims of the world to unite behind their flag."

"I'm not saying we shouldn't take them seriously – I've got to admit this is pretty big. With the fall of Mosul, we need to speak with the Iraqis and the coalition nations."

"And that'll take time. I get it." Harris took another drag of his cigarette. He walked to the far end of the glass-protected roof terrace, without paying attention to its spectacular view over the Thames.

"Anything concerning Raqqa, you'll let me know?"

Harris's cigarette was finished. He crushed the butt against the sole of his shoe. Jack kept going on about the Mosul address. Harris opened the packet again, took the lighter out of it and lit a second cigarette. His wife would be furious this evening, or whenever he would go home, but he needed the kick and inhaled the smoke deeply. Harris fired the lighter a few times more in a rhythmic movement, gazing at the flame as it came and went. He let his contact go on for a bit longer, frustrated at the lack of intel coming from the CIA. Jack was not holding back. There was simply not enough transparency between the agencies.

Harris stayed on the terrace to finish his smoke.

There was no denying that Crowne was doing much better than he had expected and that Wasim had done an excellent job of training him.

"You're a hell of an operator Was." Harris released a straight plume of smoke that faded away skywards.

The hostage situation was endangering the mission beyond what might have been deemed reasonable, but reasonable was not a word that made much sense for an operation designed to infiltrate IS heartland. The new caliphate added yet another layer of danger. Despite the offer of an exchange, Harris was certain Colmore would not play ball. And when the politicians and the intelligence community came to an agreement about al-Baghdadi's latest move, there would be hell to pay on the ground in Raqqa. The question for Harris now was how much time he had, or rather how much time Henry and Wasim had before they needed, or even could, leave. Harris doubted Henry and Wasim had had enough time to collect the information they needed but they needed to move soon if their escape had half a chance of succeeding.

Plan B.

Harris inhaled the last of his cigarette. He took the leather-clad mobile out of his pocked and called Brett.

"Henry has scored... He has convinced the ISIL treasurer to let him see their financial report and start working on the legal structure with them."

"Seriously?" Harris fell into his seat. "I don't mind admitting it... I'm almost amazed." Harris shook off his jacket. "A financial report... does he mean a proper presentation of ISIL's finances?"

"Wasim did not give much info on this. I gather he hasn't seen it, but Crowne told him it was exhaustive."

"That's different... good record-keeping... dangerous but clever. So Henry got to see the guts of how they operate."

"Wasim thinks it's genuine as well."

"What do you mean?"

"Henry has committed." Amina pushed her chair back to face her boss. "He has taken THE big step... He has converted."

"It had to be done and he knew it, but still..." Harris nodded. "A bit of positive news is good to hear."

"If he ever gets caught... you know what awaits him, though. Death will be a relief." Amina bit on one of her nails.

"Beg to differ... he knows that, and he is relishing it. There is something of a zealot in Henry. He wants to atone with a vengeance."

Amina's eyes locked with Harris's but he was right. Henry would never shy away from danger.

A life for a life... he had once said.

Amina was expecting a little sparring with Harris, his eyes slightly shut and his right shoulder up... looking how to land his next question.

"Mattie Colmore?" she asked. "What's the plan?"

"What is the plan?"

"Crowne has already moved to Plan B it seems..."

Harris straightened up. By the look on Amina's face it was going to perhaps surprise him. "So he too has a Plan B?"

"Forget about ransom... how about a prisoner exchange?" Amina nodded.

* * *

"Are you absolutely out of your mind?" Wasim held in his anger, fearing it would explode.

"We can't leave him to be bullied or worse."

"I'm not saying we should. I'm saying we need to think how we tackle this rather than your getting into a fight with some of al-Haddawi's men."

Henry shrugged. What else could he have done?

"Have you spoken to MOTHER?"

"Don't change the conversation."

"I'm not trying to. I need to know whether we are good with the Maeraka exchange."

"MOTHER's on board... she just needs to convince the rest of the family and just as well, because al-Haddawi's men would have enjoyed throwing us in one of the stadium's underground cells otherwise."

"Anything else I need to know?"

"No." Wasim cut that conversation short.

"Is MOTHER not concerned about the caliphate declaration?"

"Everybody's concerned about the declaration."

Henry stood up and moved to the stone balustrade. He looked over it, not trying to spot anything in particular, allowing his mind to process the information he had collected so far.

"The operation is not going to last for as long as we had hoped."

Wasim opened his mouth to chastise Henry about the use of the forbidden word 'operation', but why pretend?

"I think you're right. There are too many moving parts and ISIL or rather IS is morphing into something even more radical."

"What's Plan B?"

"I don't know."

Henry nodded. He should have been scared or at least worried. But there was something strangely exciting about not yet having a plan. The buzz he used to feel when finding a solution no one had even thought of before was coming back and he was enjoying the sensation. After all, he had been one of the most successful bankers in London because he could think laterally like no one else could. Granted, a mission in Raqqa was probably a little more dangerous than a complex deal even on the trading floor of a large investment bank, but it hardly felt so to him.

"What's your thinking?" Wasim clicked his fingers.

"Not sure yet. Let me think it through. I've got a couple of questions."

"Go ahead."

"Aleppo is closer to Raqqa than Mosul, yes?"

"Right. Especially on Route 4."

"Mosul is on the border of Iraqi Kurdistan."

"Right again."

Henry came back to sit next to Wasim. "I've noticed that no one ever prays at the same time in The Treasurer's office."

"They don't need to. Muslims have a few hours within the designated times for each prayer to fulfil their commitment to pray five times a day."

"Is there a moment everyone goes at the same time?"

Wasim scratched his head. "That's possible… the evening prayer when everyone goes home might be one. Why?"

"And the last prayer will be lasting what… five minutes for the actual prayer and, with ablutions beforehand, say ten minutes?"

"Stop talking in riddles. What do you have in mind?"

"If we're going to have to bail out sooner rather than later, I'd like to gather as much intel as I can in one go rather than over time as I was supposed to."

Wasim gave Henry a sideways glance. "I don't think I like where you're going with this."

"I'm here to do a job and I wouldn't mind finding a way to complete at least some of it."

"By doing what, downloading data?"

"Yes, onto a USB key. And by taking some pictures of other documents."

"We don't have a USB key."

"Oh yes we do." Henry produced a small black item from one of his army slacks pockets.

"How did you…?"

"One of The Treasurer's boys was a bit absent minded this morning."

Wasim grinned… the rookie was doing good.

"OK, let me see what's on it in the first place."

256

"I don't think you'll find anything. It was left too casually on the desk."

Wasim raised his hand. "Key please."

"I already know the password of two of The Treasurer's boys. All dealing in oil… Hamza is the one who is the most careful… still haven't got his. I need a few more keystrokes for The Treasurer's."

"That's good stuff." Wasim moved the USB key a few times around his fingers. "To be effective you need a few more of these."

"That would enable me to do all the data collection in one go."

"I'll find some more."

"And then… I need people to be out of the office, everyone but me… during prayer time."

"Henry, have you completely lost your marbles? As you said, Prayers last ten minutes, and they'll notice you're not in the room with them."

"Then I need to come up with some reason why I couldn't go, but I need a bit of help from you."

"What? Beg them not to slit your throat when you are caught red handed?" Wasim was not joking.

"That might be helpful… but no. I'd rather you created a diversion so that I have a little more time."

Wasim ran a critical eye over Henry.

"My God. You are completely serious, aren't you?"

"Exceedingly serious. If I can pull data at least from The Treasurer's computer and pick up intel from Hamza's as well as the other two, we'll come away from here with something worth the 18 months of shit we've been through."

"If we save some of the hostages, we will not have come here for nothing either."

"That's true too." Henry avoided Wasim's eyes for a few moments. "But I'm not sure we'll be able to do much for those men who are still in captivity."

"Nor I. But we can try."

"Is it not you who told me to focus on the doable?"

"You're right, but if we get Mattie and perhaps one of the other guys out in exchange for Maeraka, then we may be able to replicate…"

"Was, I know what you're going to say. Find more prisoners to

257

exchange and keep going… But it only really works because it is Maeraka we're talking about and because I know him. Al-Haddawi knows that too."

"That's still not the point."

"Yes, it is, Wasim. It is. If you think it's going to be hard to steal some data from The Treasurer's office, then I can guarantee you it's nothing in comparison with trying to extract those men from al-Haddawi's clutches."

Wasim stood up. It was his turn to walk to the edge of the terrace and look over the drop below. "You can't imagine what he's going to do to them."

"I think I can. I saw it the last time he came to the Treasury. He is a monster. So, what do you want to do? Negotiate the release of all prisoners against Maeraka…? It's impossible."

"Why? The Israelis and the Jihadi do it all the time."

"Except that al-Baghdadi thinks Hamas are a bunch of wusses, who aren't nearly tough enough, and he calls them kafir as well."

"Where do you get that from?"

"From one of the IS magazines… It's in the hotel's foyer."

Wasim turned around to face Henry, his hazel eyes full of sorrow. He had witnessed so much more destruction than Henry had.

"Look, if MOTHER thinks we have a bit of time… Let's see what impact the proposed exchange with Maeraka has. But if she thinks things are going to descend into chaos too fast, then I'll get the information I came here to gather, and off we go."

"OK." Wasim nodded. "Agreed. I'll think about how to give you more time and you concentrate on getting the Maeraka exchange done."

Henry nodded and smiled. "How about Ali then?"

"Do you ever give up?"

Obviously not.

258

Chapter Twenty-Six

"Our leader, Caliph Abu Bakr al-Baghdadi, requires one of you to be sent to Mosul for his entertainment."

The sentence still echoed in the three women's minds.

"You have one hour to decide who it will be."

Gretta pulled a blanket around herself, knees to chest. She had not uttered a word.

"I'll call Abu Shabh." Mattie was about to knock on the door to make her request, but Jean stopped her.

"I know you trust him and I'm not saying he won't do his best to help us, but this is al-Baghdadi, now Caliph al-Baghdadi, asking."

Mattie hesitated, her fist still poised to knock at the door of their bedroom.

"Mattie…" Jean's voice was kind but firm.

Mattie walked back to her bed underneath the window. She had managed to convince Jean to take it in turns to sleep on the least comfortable of the three beds.

"We can't give up… There must be a way."

"We are not giving up, we are resisting within our means."

"Sorry Jean, I didn't mean to imply you both have stopped fighting. I've got to find a way out… for all of us…" Mattie stood up again, pent-up energy almost impossible to control. She sat next to Jean and squeezed her arm. Gretta had buried her face in the blanket. She mumbled something neither Mattie nor Jean could make out. Her body started rocking and it took a long moment for both women to understand the stream of words Gretta kept repeating.

Can't do it, Can't do it, Can't do it.

Jean stumbled out of bed, her feet almost caught in the sheets. She moved to Gretta's side and threw her arms around her. She did not stop the rocking but followed it with her own body, taking in the pain, soothing it. Mattie felt helpless. She had not noticed the despair rising in the other woman, and her inability to help, to find a way out of this desperate situation, was tearing her up inside.

She would speak to Henry and tell him he had to negotiate for all three of them. She rehearsed the conversation in her mind… He might agree. Mattie opened the eyes she had shut a few moments ago without realising.

The silence in the room was heavy with fear and untold violence. Gretta opened her mouth, desperately trying to hold back an uncontrollable shriek that needed to be voiced. Jean placed her hand over her mouth. Mattie joined the two women, holding them in an embrace, tight and desperate.

"Shush, shush, shush, Gretta, you won't be going. Shush," Jean kept repeating.

Mattie squeezed her arm tighter around their shoulders. It was her turn to go to al-Baghdadi.

"I'll go." Jean pulled away from Gretta as soon as she had nodded she had calmed down.

"No, you have both already suffered enough. I will…" Mattie steadied herself. "I can do this."

"Mattie," Jean squeezed Mattie's hand, "You are the only one who has a chance of escaping and taking someone else with you." Her voice was soft but the light in her eyes spoke of her determination.

"Al-Baghdadi can't abuse me as much as he would someone else. He needs me for whatever they are planning to do, to negotiate with the UK…"

"You know that's rubbish." It was a gentle rebuff. "He will do as he pleases and now that he has been made caliph, he won't stop at anything. He needs you alive and that's it. Nothing else."

Mattie looked at Gretta, still holding her blanket so tight her fingers had turned white. She turned her attention to Jean's beautiful face. She had not noticed how striking she was, the soft features of her oval, the large brown eyes and straight eyebrows, but above all her smile, full of generous energy and hope.

"You won't be able to help any of us if you go to Mosul. You need to stay in Raqqa."

Mattie laced her fingers into Jean's hand and tightened them around it. Jean was right.

The door of the bedroom opened again. Jean squeezed Mattie into her arms. She kissed Gretta on top of her head. The dark niqab came over her face. The door closed with an unbearable softness.

* * *

Steve Harris checked his watch again. Brett Allner-Smith was late. Harris relaxed into the comfortable leather chair at Brett's gentlemen's club and waited for his whisky to be brought to him. He did not mind waiting. Brett was on to something and he wanted Harris to know about it. For a toff, Brett was a pretty bright chappie and much more daring than Harris had ever anticipated. He had handled days of meetings with The Sheik so very well, despite the treats and the real danger he was in. He had kept a steady hand on his *business*. Could antiquities plundering and trafficking qualify? Perhaps not in a conventional way, but it gave him rare access to the war zones of the Middle East and its factions, relevant to today's meeting. Brett was willing to visit these countries in order to meet his suppliers and oversee safe transport of cargo of value to them both.

Harris checked the Union Jack mobile; nothing there. James Radlett was still not playing ball. Harris resumed reading the *Telegraph*, the only paper available at the club. Finally, Brett plonked himself in the armchair next to Steve's. Harris took his time to finish the leader article and fold the newspaper.

"How quickly?" He reached for his glass and took a sip of the exceptional Macallan whisky that had been served to him.

"Drinks first." Brett turned to the steward, hardly raising his hand. He did not have to order. The old steward would know what he wanted. His whisky came almost instantly. Brett allowed himself a mouthful. "There is a route I used to use to get my best pieces out of Iraq."

"You mean for the early plundering during the Iraq war."

"I like to refer to it as a salvaging operation; at least my pieces went to appreciating collectors."

"As opposed to international museums where ignorant punters can see them?"

"As opposed to being destroyed by ISIL fighters who can't calibrate their artillery to miss the sites or use them for target practice."

The banter could have carried on a little longer, but Harris wasn't in an indulgent mood.

"Whatever. You have an established route."

"Indeed. It goes through Kurdish territory and then runs into Turkey. It takes time and it is not a route that people tend to use because of that."

"Why do you think it can work then?"

"Because no one else is going to remember it."

Harris took a sip of his drink. "What makes you think I need a route that is so covert?"

"Please grant me some brain. I've now been involved in your goddamn hair-raising operation for years."

"Fine, let's say we go down this route, what are we exactly talking about?"

"It starts in Mosul… you mentioned the city and it's close to Kurdish territory. Rojava is in western Kurdistan stretching between Iraq and Syria. It should still be possible for someone to travel in that territory and cross the border to reach Al-Hasakah in Syria, then make the crossing into Turkey. The terrain is difficult but nothing that can't be managed.

"How long ago did you last use this route?"

"Five, six years ago?"

"That's an eternity in a region like Syria, way before the war started there."

"What do you take me for?" Brett raised an eyebrow. "If I'm talking to you about it now, it's because I have reached out to my former contact."

"Still happy to do business after all this time?"

"Of course, I am professional in all my dealings."

Harris rolled his eyes. Please. "And how much does your preferred contact wish to make out of this transaction?"

"Well, if you are talking something other than antiquities then the price..."

"How much?"

"$250,000 per unit." Brett took another sip of whisky.

Harris did not flinch. "$100,000."

"I would not come up with a price without negotiating in the first place." Brett was miffed. Who did Harris think he was... a petty criminal?

Harris nodded. A crook. A pretty good one but still a crook.

"Perhaps you could try harder?"

"Why don't you go back to base and see what MI6 can afford?"

"I don't need to disturb my boss with this... $250,000 per unit, as you call it, is out of the question."

"You are such a bore. I'll go back to my contact but don't hold out any hopes for a discount."

"I'm always prepared." Harris downed the rest of his whisky and left Brett looking disconsolately into his empty glass.

He placed a call with The Chief... $250,000 per unit it might have to be.

* * *

He would never see him, but the greasy voice of the fixer befitted the man's job. The voice so calm and detached at the start of their conversation had become more engaged as the discussion progressed. Henry translated it as positive results from London. He let the fixer talk up his intervention. Of course, it had been a difficult conversation to have. Of course, there was still a lot of work to do. Of course, he was not charging them as much as he should. Henry didn't care, the idea of spending IS money on a deal that would turn out to be different from the one they were hoping for, gave him untold satisfaction. He doubted Maeraka would be allowed to reach Raqqa, but even if he did, the main thing was that Mattie would be safe and sound. The thought of engineering her release filled him with hope. Perhaps his skills could be put to further use after all.

"Now, for the equally difficult part." The voice of the fixer had changed tone again. "You need to find a place neutral enough for both parties to effect the exchange."

"Near the Turkish border?"

"Perhaps, certain NGOs might facilitate…"

"No NGOs," Henry interrupted. "A direct exchange."

"Have you done one of these before?"

"Why ask… by then you will have been paid."

"But I have a reputation to preserve. I don't do deals if I know there won't be a positive result."

"The UK government won't risk another aid worker being abducted."

"There are plenty of NGOs in the region that are represented by Muslims."

"I don't think IS trust any of them." Henry paused. He was being recorded, or at least listened to, on his phone. Was it a planted question? "It has to be close to IS territory so that we can plan for unwelcome surprises." That would be good enough for whoever was listening, even al-Haddawi's men. The thought lingered as the fixer kept talking. He had always assumed The Treasurer was the man who had ordered his phone to be tapped, but perhaps not.

The voice of the fixer came back in focus. "Will you be there?"

"Certainly. I want to make sure everything goes according to plan."

Henry hung up after agreeing on their next call. Sunset prayer time was approaching. He grabbed his backpack, dropped the phone into it and walked out of his room. It would be the last prayer held at IS Treasury office before everyone went home. An excellent drill for what he had in mind.

* * *

Most men had already retreated to the facilities and started their ablutions. Henry dropped the backpack in the main treasury room. Hamza was still at his desk. He greeted Henry amicably. "Abu Shabh, perhaps we can talk when you have time?"

"Certainly, but first… prayer. It is time."

Hamza looked around the large room. Two other young men were still at their desks. He looked undecided. Henry waited. Hamza called the others. They looked up at the clock on the wall and hurriedly made their way towards the bathrooms. Hamza locked his computer, went through the desks and locked one that had been left unattended. Henry slowly reached the door. Hamza always followed one step behind.

The other men were already done when they reached the cubicles and Henry braced himself. He found one that looked reasonably clean. It took a little less than five minutes. When he came out the booths were empty, apart from one: someone was being very thorough with their routine. Henry reached the prayer room just as the men were bringing their hands towards their bodies. He shook his shoes off, grabbed a prayer mat and joined the congregation. Hamza was nowhere to be seen. When he bent forward for the first move of the ground supplication, Henry lost sight of the entrance door. A moment later, as he stood up again, Hamza appeared at the far end of the room. Asr prayer lasted a little over five minutes. At the end of it, The Treasurer led the believers in a moment of reflection. Everyone was there in attendance to hear the address from one of IS's key leaders.

Henry breathed in deeply as he prostrated himself for the last time. He fastened the laces of his no-longer-white sports shoes. The dirt and grime of the city was already taking its toll. The Treasurer had echoed the words of al-Baghdadi. The caliphate's declaration was the moment of triumph for true Islam... Wasim would have shuddered. Everyone listened in respectful silence. One man, though, was discreetly surveying the others. Hamza's eyes moved methodically around the room. Who are you working for? Henry felt his gaze land on him, and for a short moment their eyes met. If Hamza was not listening to The Treasurer, then neither was Henry. Henry cursed. He left the room after everyone else. Hamza had disappeared promptly after their silent exchange.

"Abu Shabh." Wasim's call surprised Henry. He had appeared in the corridor and seemed keen to speak.

"Trouble?"

Wasim moved closer. "The hostages have been moved and taken

to another place. I don't know where yet. The men who were in Raqqa Stadium and the women in Umm Sayyaf apartment."

"Mattie?"

Wasim nodded.

"How do you know?"

"Not important. Though if you must know, there's nothing a Middle Eastern man likes to do more than gossip... I'm good at it too."

The cold hand that clasped his neck sent a shiver down his spine. Henry walked into the empty Treasury office. Ramadan had started and everyone was keen to reach their home to enjoy freshly cooked food after a day of fasting.

"The hostages have been rounded up and taken to a new location." Henry's jaw clenched as he spoke.

"Abu Kasim al-Haddawi has taken over their guard." The Treasurer did not seem overly concerned.

"There is a small step between guarding the hostages and doing what he wants with them."

"Small but significant one. The Treasury still retains the use of the hostages for the purposes of negotiating the release of Abu Maeraka."

"How are we going to make sure they are kept safe, unharmed?"

"Does it matter?" The answer struck Henry.

"A dead hostage is not going to do us any good."

"Well, as long as no one knows the hostage is dead, does it matter?" Henry was close to protesting. Had he read The Treasurer's intentions' right? "But I agree with you, we need to have them alive for the exchange. Caliph Ibrahim agrees."

Henry's mind went blank. Had al-Baghdadi renamed himself Caliph Ibrahim?

"As long as Kasim al-Haddawi does not scupper my negotiations and the agreement I reached with the fixer this afternoon. The UK government is holding an emergency meeting and we are negotiating a location for the exchange."

The Treasurer stopped his tidying up. The dim rumble of his stomach told him it was time to leave but perhaps he needed to spend a moment more at the office.

"Progress has been made very fast. Why do you think that is?"

266

"Because IS is no longer a terrorist group, it's a state. It has the power to defy the West. An exchange of hostages is the only way to keep Mattie Colmore alive."

"I think you are right." The Treasurer had paused to consider Henry's opinion, his small intelligent eyes scrutinising him for clues. "I am still amazed that the UK should be so keen to save this woman's life, but pleased that they do."

"What matters is that we free Abu Maeraka. I owe him as much."

"You do, and we make sacrifices for someone of such value. Caliph Ibrahim is also making a sacrifice."

The picture The Treasurer had painted made Henry nauseous. But his eyes had grown cold, he detached himself from the thought and focused on the man in front of him. All that mattered now was that he use his anger in the same way he had so many times before, to bring this man down and destroy these people until nothing was left of them. Nothing.

"You look puzzled. Don't you think some of these women may be good in bed?"

"Of course, why not? That is a way of making use of the kafir." The taunt had almost worked, and Henry hoped The Treasurer was convinced enough to let it go.

"The women will not be killed and that is all that matters."

Henry nodded. "If we have to give proof of life, it does."

The Treasurer's belly rumbled a little louder. He took one of the elegant pens on his desk, tore a page from a notepad and wrote an address in large letters.

"They are being kept on the outskirts of Raqqa. If you need proof of life you can go. But I want to know first before you do."

Henry held back from grabbing the note. The Treasurer handed the folded paper to him between his index and middle finger. "I want to know."

By the time Henry was leaving his office, everyone had gone. Hamza seemed to have cleared his desk too. Henry picked up his rucksack and went in search of Wasim.

* * *

He was waiting in the old truck. Wasim sat in the driver's seat. Henry threw his rucksack into the back of the truck; the rumble of the engine and the noise of other cars driving past would nicely cover their conversation. There would be little to glean from his phone. Henry jumped into the passenger seat and indicated with a movement of his hand that Wasim should start the engine.

"I know where they are."

"Raqqa?"

Henry nodded.

"I somehow need to let MOTHER know."

"It's Ramadan now, aren't the tearooms shut?"

"The IS fighters are still using them during the day to access the internet but granted this is more complicated."

"And at night?"

"Some are still open after dusk… not tried any yet."

Henry leaned back in the passenger seat, thinking.

"Are you hungry?"

"That's a strange kind of question."

"Are you hungry?"

"That is usually the outcome of an entire day fasting."

"Great, so are all the other Muslims in this town. Let's go and check out this place when everyone is truly ravenous and thinking about only one thing…"

"Filling up their stomachs."

"Yep… I want to know whether they are safe."

"Don't BS me Henry. You want to check Mattie is safe."

"That too." Henry looked away and waited for Wasim to disagree.

"You can't protect them all from whatever abuse Baghdadi or al-Haddawi have in store for them. You know that."

"I thought you wanted to save the hostages?"

"Don't be an idiot… I do. But I know what we can achieve and what will end up making us share their cells, wherever they now are."

"I ought at least to be able to protect them from the guards… If they touch any of them, I'll come down on them like a ton of bricks."

"It doesn't work like that. You can't dictate to these people. They are al-Haddawi's men, not The Treasurer's."

268

"Got to try. If you don't come with me, I'll go on my own."

Wasim revved the engine and moved into gear.

"You are the greatest pain in the arse I've ever worked with."

"Don't worry, you're not the first person to say that."

"Assuming we get there and they let us approach the area, what are you going to do?"

"I will personally make sure their balls are chopped off."

"Seriously, Henry."

"I am incredibly serious. If the hostages come to any harm, I'll come back for them."

"Fine. Let me do the talking. We perhaps have half a chance then."

Chapter Twenty-Seven

"The Home Office has insisted we need to exchange more than one hostage if they are to agree to the release of Maeraka." Sir John was sitting on the long table that occupied the corner of his office. He had called up digital maps of the region on the large plasma screen that hung on the far wall. Raqqa. Mosul. Aleppo.

"I'm sure it will be just a question of negotiation now. It would be a real coup for IS to gain Maeraka's freedom. If we ask for female hostages, it will be easier. I have a sense from the chatter we picked up that men are not going to be freed that easily."

"Any details I can relay to the Home Office?"

"IS has equipped itself with a large comms machine, magazines, video, tweets, websites... the lot. Al-Baghdadi addresses his followers in very good and well-presented clips."

"You mean they want to use the hostages as... what? Propaganda..."

"I don't know, sir, I just see a pattern which tells me they are ramping up their campaign."

"Poor blokes..." Sir John inhaled deeply and let the air out of his lungs slowly. "Still... we should try."

"Agreed but I don't think we should be overoptimistic."

"Fine, I'll ring the Home Office."

"I have spoken again to the CIA. I don't think there is as much engagement on their side as there is on ours. The FBI is coordinating with the families and leading the US effort to get the hostages back."

"No thoughts of extraction then?"

"My contact sounded vague. He promised he'd come back but then again, he doesn't always get to see everything Langley plans in the Middle East. They must be at least considering extraction as a possible option."

"My thoughts exactly. I made the point that an intervention in Raqqa requires a lot of solid intel and prep. We'll see whether this has registered…" Sir John activated the screens again and the map of Raqqa zoomed in at street level.

A few key sites had been marked with red dots:

Raqqa Stadium, which had become the IS HQ and a centre for interrogation and detention.

Malahi Avenue. The hotel where Henry and Wasim were staying, as well as most of their best fighters.

Fardos Street: address of the IS Treasury building.

A couple of other residences where key members might be living.

The sites were very easy to identify and yet impossible to target, areas well-chosen in providing plenty of human shield protection. It would take more than a surgical strike to eliminate the centre from which IS operated.

Harris's phone buzzed; he took it out, frowning. "Who is this?"

Sir John jumped from the table joining Harris in a few long strides. Harris showed him the screen display. "Amina… take the call."

"What's up?" Harris listened intently and placed the phone on mute. "Intel from the team: the hostages have been moved."

"Put her on speaker."

Harris placed the phone carefully on the table. "You're on speaker, Amina. Sir John is here too."

"Hello, sir, new intel from the team. The hostages have been moved to another location on the outskirts of Raqqa. Both men and women. It's an old disused oil refinery. I have the exact address."

"Give it to me. Raqqa is onscreen at the moment."

"Off Makef Street, coordinates, 35.95940 N, 38.99810 E"

Sir John entered the coordinates into the map database. The screen went black and recalibrated to display an area in which a cluster of old buildings looked isolated from other habitation, flat roofs, ample space for parking road vehicles and to store heavy goods.

"It's a good place to keep people confined in... plenty of space and a very defensible position." There was a small intake of breath by both men. "Anything else?"

"One of the rooms has been fitted with video equipment."

"Did they manage to gain access to it?"

"The site was too well guarded, sir."

"Anything else?" Harris had taken his packet of cigarettes out, fiddling with its flap.

"Something peculiar perhaps. They saw orange suits... similar to those worn by Guantanamo prisoners... lying in the room."

"Thanks, Amina, let me know if anything else comes through."

"Yes, sir."

Harris shook his head. "We are going to have to share this with the Yanks."

"And this isn't going to help our case."

Harris took a cigarette out of its pack.

"Your thoughts?"

"We need to agree on the exchange now. Otherwise, we won't be able to control the flow of events."

"I am doing my utmost..."

"I'm not saying otherwise, sir, but..."

"I know what's at the back of your mind, Steve, but it's not yet the time for an extraction. We need as much intel as we can until the exchange is done."

"But you agree that the situation on the ground has become... precarious?"

"It was always going to be complicated. For the time being we stay put. We need that intel."

Harris nodded. He had always been good at looking convincingly in agreement and doing what he wanted in the meantime.

* * *

The Treasurer's pass granted to Henry allows them through two road checks. Henry could have sworn that the first one had not been there the day before. Wasim parks the old truck in the yard of a factory that had closed for the night. They move to the back of the building and find a strong set of pipes fitted against the back wall. Wasim climbs up first, lifting himself along the frame, placing his foot on the ledge of a large window. A few more careful steps and he is on the roof. Henry follows and he joins Wasim, prone on his belly, binoculars to his eyes.

There is little conversation between the two. They communicate by signs and movements. Wasim hands over the binoculars. Henry can trace the outline of the tallest building in the area. He spots some brand-new trucks and a couple of Humvees parked in its yard. Men are patrolling the perimeter, brand new M249 light machine guns in their hands. Henry recalls the passage in the financial report under the heading ARMAMENT; the sums are large, but some of the weapons have also been reported as seized from the Iraqi and Syrian armies. His brain still thinks finance at the most unexpected of times.

The sun has set an hour ago and food will soon be served to these men and they have not eaten or drunk all day.

"Let's get as close as we can on foot. Then we wait for their meals to arrive." Wasim's low voice has a gravelly tone that makes Henry more alert. They climb down into the wall's shadow. Wasim leads. They duck around vehicles and low walls, then dart away from the buildings towards the old oil refinery. There are a few yards to cover in the open which they won't cross until the guards are no longer paying attention. They haven't got long to wait. The trucks arrive within minutes. They slow down at the factory's gate. The smell of cooking reaches them. Henry's mouth waters. He too has had almost no food all day, although he has broken fast with a packet of nuts and water from a bottle he has kept hidden in his bathroom.

They crawl alongside the wall and it takes them a couple of minutes to scramble over it. The back of the oil refinery is much the same as the one they've just left… pipes running to its top. The guards manning the perimeter have congregated to the front where the trucks have stopped. Henry starts climbing to the roof, followed by Wasim. When he reaches it, he drops on his belly. There is a small door at the bottom of a few steps. They are in luck, no one on the roof is guarding it, or perhaps they have spotted the trucks and disappeared to meet them. Wasim moves to the door. It isn't shut. The gun comes out of his small rucksack. He has managed to find guns for both. Henry doesn't know how but he has. Wasim glances through the small crack in the door and he holds his gun up. Henry stops. They can hear voices. The voices come closer and move away. Wasim risks his head through the doorway. They can resume their search.

The upper part of the building is in darkness. It must have once been offices. They look through the open doors of the empty rooms. At the end of the corridor they reach a larger room. The moonlight helps them to find their way around and spot some equipment. Cameras, sound recording devices, computers... they both advance slowly, mindful not to disturb the items or trip over cables. Henry stops to take in the place: it feels more like a recording studio of a high-end TV station than an old office room in a disused building. Wasim indicates it's time to move on. Henry makes his way back, he stops one more time; there is only one chair in the centre of what looks like a stage. At the back of the chair he recognises the flag, the black IS standard, next to it on the floor something has been dumped. He moves slowly towards it and raises the material. It's a suit. A jumpsuit. Henry slaps his hand against his mouth to muffle a small cry. It is the suit Guantanamo inmates wear. This is no coincidence. These hostages are going to pay. He forces himself to leave the room, his heart racing.

Wasim stands at the end of the corridor. The staircase leads down to an open-plan room on the ground floor. There the light is bright. The floor at the far end has been fitted with iron bars and men are sitting on the floor in this makeshift box prison. Wasim pulls back. The guards have started to arrange food on the main table in the centre of the room. There is another flight of stairs. It leads to the far end of the building. Perhaps the women's quarter. Wasim shakes his head. It's too far to go. Henry is not leaving. Perhaps it's not.

Voices are moving closer once more. And the weight of heavy boots shakes the stairwell. Wasim pulls Henry back the way they came. They won't have time to reach the roof door. They move into one of the empty rooms, guns at the ready. The voices move into the recording studio and the light comes on. The conversation is friendly, even cheerful. They replay a recording. Henry can't make out what it says. More laughter and banter.

274

Henry goes for the roof first, unnoticed. He is waiting for Wasim, five long minutes. He is alert to any noise that comes from below.

Wasim reaches the flat roof too. They climb noiselessly to the ground. Most guards have moved inside and the ones at the door are sitting on the ground cross legged, enjoying some food.

"What is it you saw?" Wasim is back at the wheel of the truck, slowly edging it into the main road.

"The orange jumpsuit that prisoners wear in Guantanamo." A slow rumble goes through Henry's body. The truck picks up speed as they move away from the cluster of buildings.

Wasim changes gear angrily. They can no longer save these people.

"I know how to help you around prayer time, so that you can download the data you have in mind. We'll do it within the next 48 hours."

* * *

The message had been marked urgent. He hoped he had conveyed to James the importance of the meeting. The old Ford Mondeo was full of junk, discarded newspapers, a few sandwich wrappers that had been there for far too long, a half-drunk water bottle that had started to mist over. Harris thought the car perfect for the task at hand. Nothing better than a high-rise estate to put someone in the mood. He had asked James to meet him in the middle of Whitechapel… just to remind him how grim surveillance was for some of the operatives he worked with.

Harris parked the car in front of the Perfect Fried Chicken on Bethnal Green and walked the rest of the way to their meeting point. The weather had turned chilly for the season and rain had already fallen earlier in the day, collecting in pools of dark liquid in which bits of leftover food and plastic bags floated. He crossed the first estate without encountering anyone. He moved to the second group of high rises. A couple of young lads were showing off on their bikes, doing wheelies. Harris zipped up his denim bomber jacket and crossed the road to avoid walking past them. They observed him for a moment, but decided Harris looked uninteresting… cheap jeans, cheap shoes and light brown short-cropped hair that radiated blandness.

He was five minutes late: excellent. James would have been festering in the small alleyway where they had arranged to meet. He hoped.

James Radlett was looking at his watch. He took his mobile out to place a call.

"I wouldn't do that if I were you." Steve's voice carried the distance and James replaced the phone in his jacket pocket.

"You think I'm going to get mugged?" James moved toward Harris slowly. His square jaw face alert yet bemused.

"I don't think so, I know so, if you take out the latest iPhone in the open here."

"This is a strange way to try to convince me to join…"

"Perhaps." Harris had arrived where James was standing. He took a cigarette out of its pack and lit it. "I'm dealing with a situation and I need to know now…" He exhaled and a plume of smoke escaped from the side of his mouth. "… right now, whether you're in or not. Don't care whether you still need to speak to all your SIS ex-contacts to find out what I'm up to or whether you've got a conscience about Henry Crowne."

James's eyebrows shot up.

"If you don't like this place, good… I don't like it either, but that's the sort of cesspit my assets have got to operate in to get results. They don't dither, they don't moan whether they gonna step into shit because they will, but they've got what it takes to do the job."

The two lads must have decided Harris was a new face around and worth a closer look after all. They appeared at the far end of the alleyway. James looked past Harris in their direction. "Fuck off, ya little shits, I'm 'avin a private conversation… Ya 'ear me?" The East End accent at full volume stopped the two dead. There was anger there too. They hesitated. Harris made as if to go after them and they quickly rode off.

"Where was I… Oh yes, you're not so sure anymore. Can you handle Crowne simply because you know how he thinks… maybe, but this isn't going to be cushy investment banking… it will be wherever the op takes you. Think about it. Can't afford to lose any more time."

James's face clouded over. He was not a dilettante but perhaps banking had softened him more than he wanted to admit.

"I'm finishing my cigarette and I'm off."

"Why do you want me to work on the Crowne file?"

"Not on the file... with the man and because he's asked for you. Now don't tell me I'm not levelling with you on that one."

Shock, anger, disbelief... James was taken aback. "This is a joke."

"Couldn't be more serious." Harris took a final drag. He flicked the butt of his cigarette away. The red dot rolled into one of the puddles with a small fizz.

"What's the emergency?" James's eyes had decided on a new stance. Defiance.

"I need to get people out of Syria."

"Aleppo?"

"No."

"Worse than Aleppo?"

"Without a doubt."

James started to walk slowly towards the end of the alleyway. He turned his head to check Harris was still there.

"Let's go back to the Cross and you can tell me what I need to do."

* * *

The fixer had got back to Henry. He listened again to the message he had left over an hour ago. The UK government was asking for a number of hostages to be freed, Mattie Colmore and other British prisoners of their choice. Henry remembered the men he had seen parked like cattle at the same time the fixer was making his call, the recording studio, the jumpsuits... it did not take much imagination to know what was coming next.

Abu Maeraka was worth another hostage to IS, surely. But giving in to the UK would be interpreted as a sign of weakness; not enough men close to Baghdadi trusted him. Al-Haddawi would be the first to exploit the opportunity. Perhaps he could suggest another woman. Mattie had mentioned she was sharing with two others.

Henry closed his eyes. The weight of her forehead on his back felt still fresh and physical. He could not let any of these bastards... Henry stood up abruptly.

Don't go there. He had spoken aloud. He cursed between gritted teeth: the phone in his hand was being recorded. He chucked it in his rucksack, playing and replaying the various scenarios he had been mulling over in his mind.

Henry walked onto the terrace. The trees planted around the hotel were swaying slowly in the breeze. He opened a can of lemonade he had pulled from the fridge and sat down. In a few moments he would call Wasim and tell him what plan he had decided they should follow. It would mean leaving people behind... a lot of people, and it felt like defeat. He would bring back intelligence that would count in the fight against IS. But what was it worth in comparison with abandoning the hostages?

Henry finished his drink in a few gulps. It was time to execute the plan.

Chapter Twenty-Eight

Harris had lost almost two hours going through administrative pain –
necessary, he had been told, even when he pointed out he had filed a
full report on James Radlett a month before. But now that the vetting
process had started, there would be more background checks and a
battery of evaluation tests that would make Harris wish, several times,
he had never started... Still, RED HAWK needed James and Harris
would ask for a special dispensation if he had to. Radlett had contacted
his boss that evening, asking for a leave of absence; resignation would
come later.

Harris took the leather-cased burner phone and dialled the only
number that was saved there. He did not bother to check the time of
day. Brett was on call 24/7 when he was needed. Brett minded, of
course, and that was where the fun was.

"What time does your club close for the evening?"

"Good evening... 11pm."

"Any news on your side?"

"It's late and my contacts don't like being harassed."

"I'm about to ask for one of the largest cash payments ever
attributed to an operation and you're being pissy with me... really?"

"The money's not coming out of your pocket."

"By the time I've asked and it's been agreed, it will feel like my
pound of flesh."

"Shakespeare, *Merchant of Venice*, I'm almost impressed."

"And I'm not even trying, Brett... where are your people?"

"All right... all right, my old contact tells me he can extract goods or… people in the next three days. The longer we wait the more complicated it will become."

"Is he trying to bargain for an increase?"

"No… He is telling me that the region is gradually falling to ISIL and that soon the Kurdish enclave will be so small it will be almost impossible to use for trafficking."

"I can buy that." Harris fingered the cigarette packet he had taken out of his pocket. "How…"

"Reliable?" Brett interrupted. "Let's say I know his business enough to cause him serious trouble if I was minded speaking."

"Bit of blackmail, splendid!"

"No… just a little incentive."

Harris took as much detail as he could from Brett. He liked the route. He knew the terrain. The Kurds and their fighters were the most reliable people he had ever met. Despite Brett's concerns, IS would think twice before making incursions into Kurdish-held territory. The thought of being killed by a female Peshmerga did not sit well with their views on the female condition.

Harris's other mobile rang. Amina had relayed Henry's proposal – ask for a second female hostage rather than a man – to Harris and The Chief. Sir John had pulled back at the thought. He needed to think it through.

"Evening, sir."

"Good evening, Steve. I have spoken with the Home Office. We have been called to an emergency meeting."

Harris held back in hope; meeting with politicians had never been his bag. "Do you need me there, sir?"

"I certainly do."

"Need to change and…"

"No Steve, now… please." The Chief was not looking forward to the meeting either. "My driver will pick you up in ten minutes. I'll see you there."

Harris looked down at his old jeans and his crumpled blue shirt, no tie. He ran a hand over his face; at least he had shaved this morning. He could not do anything about the jeans, but he might be able to do something about the shirt. Harris took the lift to the basement, scrolled down the list of contacts and called the number he was looking for.

"Maureen, are you still around?"

"Who's asking?"

"It's Steve, Steve Harris."

"Little Steve… 'course. The shutters are down but give us a knock when you're down, luv."

The shutters came up and the old lady grinned at Steve. "Little Steve… 'aven't seen you for a time."

"Very kind, Maureen."

"No worries." She tapped the side of her nose and laughed a laugh that spoke of chain smoking for many years. "What can I do you for?"

"I need your help."

She ran an eye over Steve and nodded.

"Not got a proper shirt to wear." She did not wait for an answer. "Let's see." She disappeared at the back of the small dry-cleaning booth.

"Got a nice blue one with a nice white stripe or a plain pink one your size."

"I'll take the blue one, Maureen, you're a star!"

"So you say… I need it back tomorrow."

"Without fail… promise."

Maureen shushed him away with her hand. Harris ran to the gents and changed. He dashed to his office and stuffed the old shirt in his desk. Amina didn't notice the change of shirt… so much for his attempt at looking a little smarter. He grabbed his jeans bomber jacket. It would have to do. Amina's concentration on her screen made Harris stop.

"More news?"

"Not yet." Her face changed colour with the regular flickering of her screens. "I'll send you a text as soon as I have decided on what I am looking at."

* * *

The Home Secretary and Sir John were already in conversation alone when Harris arrived. The glass bowl that served as a meeting room was small but discreet. A couple of the other people were waiting outside. Harris did not recognise him immediately. When he turned around,

Harris identified the aide who had accompanied TRH Colmore MP to Vauxhall Cross. He had opted to stand as close as he could to the room, well positioned to capture how the meeting was going. Harris wondered whether he knew how to lip read. Perhaps an important skill set in his job? Harris moved closer to him and stood facing the office. He didn't care whether the two people in conversation saw him. Harris had decided that he would speak his mind. His assets were on the ground in Raqqa and he was damned if he was going to let a bunch of politicians decide about their safety.

Sir John opened the door and then closed it after him. He nodded to the other men waiting and walked over to greet Harris. "She's coming around to the idea of asking for two women, perhaps three."

"I would rather we stuck to the plan. The fall of Mosul and the declaration of a caliphate changes a lot of things. We are running out of time."

Sir John interrupted by raising his hand. "You don't need to convince me, you need to convince her."

The Home Secretary was in a combative mood. Harris walked in; her aide raised an eyebrow at the casual attire. She didn't seem to mind. "Give me your side of the story." Her firm dry hands clutched a simple biro poised to take her own notes. Harris told her about the progress made with the hostage situation, the intelligence coming from within Raqqa. He would not be drawn on the identity of his sources.

"You're sure the intel can be relied on?" her aide asked.

"Without a doubt," Sir John jumped in. It would be the end of the matter. The Chief of MI6 had validated it, time to move on.

"Why are you keen to make the exchange so quickly?" She was taking fresh notes, not looking at Harris directly.

"Because the situation in Syria and Iraq is deteriorating very rapidly, especially with the fall of Mosul and the proclamation of a caliphate, ma'am. IS is on the up and they will want to show their might to the Muslim world, incentivising others to join... if they are still in negotiation mood, we should seize the opportunity."

"Why would hostages be valuable to IS if not for ransom or an exchange?"

"I can't tell you yet, but their comms team has been very active on social media, and in their online magazine."

"Are you concerned about some form of reprisal?" The Home Secretary had stopped writing, her eyes scrutinising him.

"It's a possibility."

She inhaled deeply, stood up and walked to the window.

"Surely we can try a few more days of negotiations?"

"We don't have a few days, I'm afraid."

"Why not?"

"Because the chatter we are constantly monitoring on social media speaks of a *mighty event*. It is also Ramadan and a good time to mark the Muslim world with deeds that will be perceived as prophetic."

The Home Secretary turned back.

"Do you know the hostages are alive?"

"We do; the men were more recently seen than the women, but nothing indicates the women are not alive as well."

"How many men has your source seen?" Her aide was now tapping on his iPad.

"That's not relevant to this conversation. We know the people we are interested in are alive." Harris avoided looking at the little git, trying instead to decipher his agenda.

"So, your source knows where they are?"

Harris hesitated. This was getting too close for comfort.

"We can't be certain. Hostages are moved around all the time." Sir John's voice had cut into the conversation. A do-not-interfere-with-our-operation tone that seemed to stop the aide in his tracks.

"Do you?"

Sir John stayed silent for a moment, wondering how to reply.

"If the question is whether we could mount a commando intervention," Harris hunched forward, forearms on the table, "I'd advise against it… We do not have enough intelligence to organise an SAS extraction mission, at least not yet. And it will not be an easy ride to land troops in Raqqa."

The Home Secretary came back to sit at the table, silencing her aide with a sideways glance.

"A final question… If we agree the exchange, how soon can we proceed?"

"Once we have a deal, within 24 hours. Everything's in place and we are prepared to offer a location for the exchange that will be acceptable to IS."

"That is settled … do it. Two women." The Home Secretary gathered her papers together and replaced them in a folder marked FOR YOUR EYES ONLY/SIS.

Sir John thanked her. As they stood up to leave the room, her aide took the folder and started a low-voiced conversation with her.

"Harris…" She stood on the threshold of the meeting room, her face turned away from her aide. "Good luck."

Harris nodded and took his time leaving the reception area. The Home Secretary's aide had retraced his steps. Harris dived into an empty meeting room. The aide walked past him without noticing. He was in a hurry. At the end of the corridor a silhouette moved towards him. Harold Colmore MP was coming his way, more determined than a dog with a bone.

* * *

The first call to prayer echoed around Raqqa. Henry rolled out of bed, washed quickly and joined the stream of other fighters moving towards the hotel mosque. A pair of crutches and a smile caught up with him. Ali had made it to the ground floor.

"How's your new room?" Henry smiled back.

"Great." Ali threw his thumbs up, almost losing balance in the process. "I owe you one."

Henry nodded and they entered the prayer room together. Fajr lasted only a few minutes and both men moved slowly to the lounge. There would be nothing consumed now until after dusk, but it was good to sit in this comfortable place. Henry scanned the room quickly… Wasim had not come down for prayer.

"You might be able to help. I'm looking for a new truck, something much better than what I have now. Perhaps one of the trucks that the fighters took to Mosul."

"No problem." Ali's constant use of English sounded out of place, perhaps even provocative, but Henry enjoyed it and replied gratefully.

Henry walked through the large reception area, into the gardens, and found a quiet area underneath a cedar tree. He sat on the ground and took his mobile out.

"Any news?" The fixer had answered almost instantly.

"The UK has agreed to ask for the release of two women."

"Much better…" Henry picked up a stone and threw it at a large fly that had landed on the dry grass near him. "These dogs are running scared."

"They are, Abu Shabh… and they are running very quickly. I thought I would have to negotiate a lot harder."

"Let us be grateful for the might of the caliphate."

"Of course, praise Caliph Ibrahim."

"Go back to them and tell them we're thinking about their offer."

Henry killed the call and smiled. Whoever was listening to his phone could not have faulted the rhetoric of his replies. Perfect as a way of buying him more time.

His next call was to Hamza. The young man was surprised to hear Henry. His voice betrayed irritation and something Henry was not expecting… fear. Henry asked him to check whether The Treasurer was busy. Yes, he was. Could he please leave a message for him to call back? Henry asked about their latest plan regarding the routing of oil through Jordan, the movement in oil prices. Hamza's responses were curt. Henry kept going, determined to find out why this was.

"I have done all we have spoken about." The wobble in Hamza's voice encouraged Henry.

"But we need to start showing results. Let's push to make sure we exceed $1 million a day."

"Why don't you come to the office and I can show you all that I have done." Hamza sounded keen.

"I will, later." Henry pondered. Hamza did not want to be heard speaking to him.

The phone rang again and this time The Treasurer was calling back. "Salaam alaikum."

"Alaikum as salaam."

"The UK government has agreed to drop their requirements for a male hostage. They are trying for a second female hostage instead."

"What do you think?"

"We could probably succeed with only one hostage, the female journalist, but it will take more time. Abu Maeraka is a loss to our cause. His liberation would be one more success for Caliph Ibrahim." Henry squeezed the phone hard. If only he could save just one more person.

"I will think about it. Let us not be too hasty about making our next move."

"A very wise decision."

After he had hung up Henry threw the phone into his rucksack. He wished he could have simply smashed it on the ground.

Fighters had started to drift into the hotel gardens and these would soon be mobbed by a crowd he did not want to mix with. Henry waited for a moment and stood up. He lifted his head towards the rooms that he and Wasim occupied. He had not heard him get up. Henry started walking towards the lounge again, rode the lift to floor 5 and jogged to reach Wasim's room. He knocked... no answer. He entered his own bedroom, vaulted over the small partition wall separating the terraces of their rooms and tried to look through the window. The curtains were still open. Wasim had not been back since they had returned from their evening investigation. Henry knocked at the window. Unsurprisingly, there was no reply.

Henry returned to his room and sat on the bed. A trickle of cold sweat ran along his spine. Something had happened. He had to find out what without sounding alarmed.

Henry went down again, walked around the lobby, hung around the lounge, and surveyed the gardens one more time. No one around he recognised. The truck was still parked where they had left it the previous evening. Wherever he was going Wasim had gone on foot. The obvious place was the tearoom a few blocks from Malahi Avenue. Henry jumped into the truck and drove slowly in that direction. He had no plan, no clear idea as to what to do. The environment felt so much more hostile without someone as experienced as Wasim at his side.

Henry reached the tearoom. He stopped opposite and watched for a short while. It was too early for any sign of activity. No one would be coming to enjoy a tea and a gossip until after dusk and it was way too early for an internet session… the tea rooms now, no longer serving tea, would not be opened for a while. Henry got out of the truck, crossed the street and walked past the shop. The only sign of life was an old man sitting on the terrace. He looked straight ahead, leaning slightly over a stick that looked as old as he was, his fingers going through his prayer beads in a slow yet rhythmic motion. Henry walked past again and realised the old man was almost certainly blind… thick cataracts casting a shadow over his eyes.

Henry sat down a few chairs away. "Salaam alaikum."

The old man nodded. "Alaikum as salaam."

"The tearoom is not open?"

The old man shook his head, not bothering to face Henry.

"Do you sit here every day?"

Again a nod.

"Until late… until it shuts?"

The old man nodded again.

"Something unusual happened last night?"

The old man stayed silent for a long moment. Henry was about to leave; perhaps the old man was not entirely with it. "They took him away."

"Who?" Henry shot back, but the old man did not say more.

Henry ran across the road and climbed into the truck. There was only one place where they would have taken Wasim.

* * *

"Rise and shine. I have some bad news for you." Ahmed's call felt like a cold shower. Amina sat up in bed, glancing at the clock. It was barely 6am.

"What have you found out?" Her mouth felt dry and she drank from the water bottle that she always kept at the side of her bed.

"I'm glad your brain can engage so quickly."

"My brain is fine… What have you found out?" She was out of bed, hopping around the room trying to get dressed as she spoke to him.

"That domain you wanted to trace… It's using a succession of VPNs that bounce around the world and it finishes with a TOR."

"Can you crack the TOR encryption?"

"Possibly, but that's going to take some time and we must be careful not to make whoever is at the other end aware that we're trying to nail him… it will take a few days at least, maybe more."

"Shit… I'll be with you in 15 minutes." Amina hung up, brushed her teeth quickly and forgot about make-up. There was something to be said about living next to Vauxhall Cross, no matter what her ex-husband thought.

Ahmed had brought two strong cups of coffee and presented her with one as she walked through the door of his small office. He had activated the large screen on which a series of boxes had been highlighted over a map of the globe.

"Someone has put in a lot of time and effort to hide this address. It starts with a simple VPN, in case someone becomes too curious and does a check… but then goes no further. You need to dig a lot deeper to find the TOR. Whoever it is knows what they're doing and they're good."

"It's the sort of set-up used for surveillance and analysis." Amina was not asking. She was taking in the enormity of the discovery.

"If you're worried about these people cracking the code embedded into the website used for your assets on the ground, you should be. Although I'm not certain they would have had the time to do it so quickly."

"But they have gone through our messages and realised that we too are using a TOR."

Ahmed nodded. "Definitely."

Harris was on his way when she got hold of him.

"Someone is tracking MOTHER's conversations with Wasim." There was no other way of breaking the news.

"Have they broken our code yet?"

"No, but it's only a question of time."

"Fuck." Harris didn't even feel like having a smoke. "I'll speak to The Chief, we need to accelerate the exchange."

"What about Wasim and Henry?" Amina's face had grown paler.

"I'm aware… And I'm working on a plan. In the meantime, tell Wasim they've been busted. We need to move to the emergency protocol."

"You mean placing a call on Crowne's phone?"

"If that's what it takes…"

Harris left for Sir John's office without calling first. Even in his overflowing diary, his PA would find a slot.

* * *

"How quickly before we know the location?" Harris and Sir John had moved to Level -2 to discuss the latest development.

"I don't know yet." Sir John's tight jaw could hardly let a sound through.

"And the timescale?"

"I've not been told either since it is a US operation. The Home Secretary informed me simply because she's concerned; we have assets on the ground."

Harris moved to the digital map of Syria and Iraq. He highlighted three cities.

Raqqa.

Mosul.

Aleppo.

"Assuming the Yanks go through within the next few days…" Harris moved closer to the map.

"You think they have a SEAL team there already?"

"They have SEALs and Delta Forces in Iraq still… These teams will be operational as soon as they are given the order."

"On the base of what intel though?"

"I don't know, sir, but I'm pretty sure that Colmore would have given them as much as he knew himself. We know the hostages were moved a few days ago. I called Jack at Langley again. A couple of French hostages have been released. Perhaps they were able to help."

Sir John approached the map too. "Whatever the outcome, IS will suspect there's a leak. The hostages have recently been moved… They'll want to find someone to blame."

"This is compounding the issue I highlighted to you earlier... The team on the ground in Raqqa is no longer viable."

"What do you suggest?"

"We are moving to our emergency protocol. This means less communication with the team."

"We have already agreed the hostage exchange."

"But we have not received an answer yet. Whatever happens, we also need to think extraction... soon."

Sir John crossed his arms over his chest. "I think you're right... Options?"

"Two ways... The more obvious, Aleppo... but it means travelling through well-established IS territory. The second way..." Harris had moved closer to the map, looking for the town he had in mind.

"Come on, Steve... I'm not going to get pissed off even if it is unconventional."

"They move inland, reach the Kurdish Territory." Harris was tracing the route with his fingers on the map. "From there they move to Al-Hasakah on the Turkish border and are extracted through there."

"Is that a well-known route?"

"Not for people but for art trafficking."

"That's a very different ball game though." Sir John frowned.

"But if the price is right..."

Sir John looked sceptical. He had not yet been told about a price. Before he could respond, his phone rang. He picked it up and listened to the voice at the other end without saying anything. He chucked the phone on the table where it slid perilously near the edge.

"The window's narrowing... Extraction has to take place in the next 24 hours..."

Harris nodded slowly. He knew what this meant for his assets on the ground.

Chapter Twenty-Nine

It took Henry less than 15 minutes to reach Raqqa Stadium. He stopped the truck and sat in it for a while. He checked his mobile: not yet 8am.

The guards at the only entrance that was still open looked young and yet full of assurance. They were not new recruits. Henry fingered the piece of paper The Treasurer had handed him. It was the only ace he had to play. It would have to do.

Henry parked the truck a few blocks away from the stadium entrance and walked casually along the road, checking the door handles of cars. If he was to play Mr Big he had to present himself at the gates with the right motor. Much to his surprise, a couple of new SUVs had their doors open. Perhaps losing a hand or worse did the trick to dissuade thieves from stealing from ISIL fighters. What about borrowing? He hoped he would not have to find out.

Henry drove to the gates of the stadium. He pulled the dark window down and asked to be let in.

"I am here to interrogate a man that was brought in last night… Wasim Khan." Henry was glad he had chosen to dress in his black shirt and headscarf. The only part missing was a weapon but there was nothing he could do about it. He handed over the letter from The Treasurer. Both men took a look at the piece of paper. It looked official enough. One of the guards grabbed his walkie-talkie and walked away from earshot.

He returned the official paper to Henry. "You have to come back. The prison is closed."

"No, I will not." Henry had spoken without anger. He was a senior member of The Treasurer's team. He would not be made to come back. "I will disturb Abu Hamia if need be, but I will not be made to come back." Henry took his phone out. His fingers scrolled down what looked like a list of names. He was poised to press on one of them.

The guard's close face looked a little less assured. He used the walkie-talkie again without bothering to walk away this time. Henry made a quick move of the hand, wanting the guard to hand over the device. He shook his head and killed the conversation.

"As an exception, you can go in."

Henry eased the SUV through the gates. He parked next to the broad steps that led to the stadium. He walked in and reached another set of guards. He showed his paper again but this time he was escorted towards steps that led into the cool belly of the building. Henry hesitated for an instant. He might never come back up again if he followed the guard. He shook off the sense of dread that had started to creep inside his belly. He needed to find Wasim.

Henry walked down three flights of stairs and stopped at the bottom. The guard kept going along the corridor but he stopped him. "I will wait here." He spotted an empty chair and seated himself on it. "You can fetch him for me."

The guard hesitated but Henry's assurance defeated his resolve. He shrugged and walked towards one of the cells that was close to the entrance. He turned the key and called the man within.

Henry recognised Wasim's tall frame. His walk told him he had been in a fight and the swollen face confirmed it.

"Leave us." The guard moved away a little and Henry jerked his head with impatience. The guard disappeared towards the end of the corridor.

Henry jumped to his feet. "What the fuck happened to you?"

Wasim hobbled closer. "Serves me right for going back to the tearoom next to the hotel... I knew it was a bad place." His speech was a little slurred.

"But what are they saying you did?"

"I wanted to buy a USB key from one of the fighters who seemed to be selling them. It was fine until some nosy bastard asked me whether I had my emir's authorisation to make the purchase."

"Why didn't you call me?"

"I'm not sure it's a good idea for you to try to help me out of this."

"Are you serious? There's no way I'm leaving you behind."

"You may have no choice." Wasim's calm shut Henry up. What was he saying? Henry shook his head. He did not want to consider the outcome.

"Did you pay for the USB keys?"

"Of course…"

"Did they take them back from you?"

Wasim frowned. "They did."

Henry nodded. "It's a con…"

"You think…" Wasim did not finish his sentence. He could see it now. "Bastards."

Henry called the guard. "I want to see the person in charge of this prison. This fighter has been wrongly imprisoned."

The guard's young face went blank. No one had ever made a demand of the sort. He shifted from one foot to another. He called the other guard that was helping to keep the prisoner. The older guard arrived, full of importance.

Henry repeated his demand, adding he was here at The Treasurer's request. The older guard's assurance shifted. Henry could see it now. He had wondered a minute ago how far up the hierarchy the scheme went. Now he knew… just a few guards making money on the sly. At the end of the day, they would free their victim, relieved he did not have to report the unauthorised purchase to his emir.

"Communications are being controlled but not the purchase of items such as USB keys…"

The two guards looked at each other. Their racket was about to be busted. The older guard tried to draw his gun but Wasim sprang into action. He had been put through the mill but was far from incapacitated. His elbow slammed into the guard's throat, blocking his airway. The gun dropped. The young man was not fast enough. Henry punched him in the gut and he collapsed in a heap.

Wasim collected the guns that lay on the ground. He pointed the gun to the face of the older guard. "Give them back to me… slowly."

The man fished three USB keys from his pocket and handed them over with a shaking hand.

"I'm taking him out now. If I hear any of you call out, I'll kill you. If you report this, I'll have you investigated and you'll end up in one of these cells." Henry voice was calm but threatening.

He and Wasim walked backwards. And when they reached the stairs, they ran. They slowed down at the top of the stairwell. Henry pushed Wasim in front of him as if he was wanting to manhandle him himself. The two young guards looked at them, hesitant. But if it was one of The Treasurer's men, why interfere?

Henry pushed Wasim into the back of the SUV. "Lie down when we reach the gates."

Henry drove the car through the gates slowly. He wound down the dark glass window on his side and acknowledged the guard with a short nod. The SUV turned into the street and reached the place where the truck was parked. Henry parked the SUV near to where he had left and hoped the driver was not already looking for it. They jumped into the old truck and were off.

"Shit, Was… that was close."

Wasim nodded. "I didn't see that one coming."

"Did you manage to send a message to MOTHER?"

"Yes, just before I got jumped."

They drove in silence back to the hotel. Wasim was looking through the window, all the way pulling on his lower lip, nervous. They quickly found themselves on Henry's bedroom terrace for a debrief.

"What's worrying you?"

"I think we're now sitting on a ticking bomb…"

"Because I went to pick you up at the stadium?"

"We don't know who's in charge of this nifty little racket but I bet the guards are only a small part of it… Second, I'll be surprised if someone doesn't call The Treasurer and ask why you have a pass… and if he learns you've used it to get me out he's not going to like it… at all."

"Well, I can always say I wanted to find out what the problem was before disturbing him."

"That's not the way it works here… You're not senior enough to make that decision. He's your emir."

"What are you saying? That we need to get out of here asap?" Henry's jaw tightened. He needed another day or so to clinch the exchange between Mattie and Maeraka.

"If we could, I'd say we get the info you need today and leave."

"How about Mattie?" Henry couldn't help it.

"You and I ending up in Raqqa Stadium won't help her a bit."

"You and I on the run won't help her a bit either." Henry had a point.

"Depends on how we disappear... if we make it sound as if we're joining another faction..."

Henry stuck his hands into his thick hair and left them there, pressing on his skull. He had to find a way. "I need to think..." Henry stood up. He needed to be at The Treasurer's office and keep matters as normal as they had been.

* * *

The morning had been painfully slow and unnerving. Henry had been surveying The Treasurer's every phone call, half expecting to be called in. There was no food or drink for distraction. Henry had spent time with Hamza, questioning the results they were having on their new oil strategy. The men The Treasurer had recruited were sharp. They understood fast and could execute with precision. By bombarding him with questions and forcing him to login repeatedly, Henry had managed to crack Hamza's password. The Treasurer had received news about Mosul's central bank. As expected, there was gold, dollars... 400 million of them, and assets saved by the wealthy people of Mosul who had not had time to retrieve them before fleeing, if they could flee at all. No one had seen the fall of the city coming.

No one.

The Treasurer had kept his door shut and Henry's frazzled nerves made him almost lose patience, waiting his turn to speak about the hostages. Henry walked out at midday. The sun was burning his skin and he had become unbearably thirsty. He returned to the hotel, went through the routine check in his room and stuffed his rucksack containing his phone into a wardrobe. Ali was nowhere to be seen and

Wasim had disappeared as well. Henry took out of the fridge a large bottle of water he had kept there to cool, drank half of it and finished a packet of nuts he had bought from a little store next to the hotel.

Henry opened the doors leading to the terrace. The heat almost suffocated him. He sat back on his bed. The assets that Mosul was bringing to the Treasury's purse were making The Treasurer bold. Henry shook his head. He was almost certain he would have to yield to the demands of IS and exchange Maeraka against only one person and that person could only be Mattie. Henry let his upper body collapse on the bed, arms outstretched. He closed his eyes but couldn't find rest. The images of the men trapped behind bars in the old oil factory and the orange suit in the recording studio preyed on his mind.

Wasim was right though. Even if he had not wanted to admit it first. The minute The Treasurer was told he had used the pass he had given him, they were both in deep trouble and he was here to deliver operation RED HAWK.

He stood up again, left his room and walked down four flights of stairs to a place that looked more like a cupboard than a bedroom. Henry knocked at the door but there was no reply. He walked to the deserted lounge. Ramadan made the large welcoming space less vibrant. It was hard not to drink or eat during the day, and the enthusiasm from the capture of Mosul had somehow died down a little.

The young man was reading at the far end of the room.

"Is that the latest IS magazine?"

"Abu Shabh." Ali smiled. He turned a few pages and nodded. "Yes, it is."

"Any good?"

Ali shrugged. "But I have good news for you... I found it."

"A new truck?"

"Better..."

"A large truck... with special ramming bars?"

"Better..."

"A small SUV?"

"Better..."

Henry was enjoying the silly game. "A large SUV?"

"With extra..." Ali was searching for the word.

"Additional feature."

Ali clicked his fingers. "Radio." Ali looked triumphant.

"You're the best." Henry slapped his shoulder and Ali grew a little taller. His face turned serious unexpectedly, perhaps thinking about what Henry would do next with the vehicle.

"When do you need it?" He switched back to Arabic in a low and urgent voice.

"Very soon…" Henry hesitated. If Henry had been a good judge of character when he was in banking, he had been made cautious in IS Raqqa. "Tomorrow." But Ali felt an exception. "How much is it going to cost?"

"It's not for sale…"

Henry pulled back.

"You can have it… you just say you're with The Treasury."

"How do you know that?"

"Everybody knows that here." Ali grinned.

"Is that the way it works?"

"Here… Always… The people who beat me, it's because they are Abu Kasim al-Haddawi's people… They can take whatever they want."

"I get it… But you do not need to get the truck right away. Tomorrow, I'll tell you exactly when."

Ali pondered. He had learned not to ask questions. "I find a way… It won't go anywhere."

Henry left Ali in the lounge. It was almost the end of the day and time to test whether MI6 had been right to trust him.

* * *

"Your boss didn't protest?"

"He did but I have so much holiday, I could take a six-month sabbatical and still have some left."

"How about your team?"

"I have a very good number two…" James smiled at the irony of it. "When can I meet the team?"

"Today, but before that I have a question. I remember reading that you had contacts with SEALs teams when you were in Afghanistan."

297

"I spent some time working alongside their dedicated CIA operative."

"You were with those boys?"

"For a while… I would have stayed but as you know I could no longer follow them on the ground."

Harris nodded. How could he forget about James's injury? "Any chance you could check where they're deployed at the moment?"

"If you tell me why it is you want to know, I can be better prepared."

"There's a hostage situation, with a possible extraction tonight."

"Is Crowne part of that?"

"He is but not in the way you may think…" Harris hesitated but James was committed and part of the team now.

"What then?" James cocked his head.

"He has become one of my assets. He and another operative have infiltrated IS. They're relaying information to us."

James's face dropped for a moment. He walked to the window and leaned forward against the frame. Henry infiltrated in Syria… almost unthinkable, and yet. "What is he looking for… Absolution for all the crap he accumulated over the years?"

"Something like that… But he's not that naïve, he's being practical about his new role. You know him better than most. You have a track record in intelligence. And he trusts you to work with him no matter what."

James stayed silent, his back still turned to Harris. "You can see why I couldn't tell you much when we first met… No one has ever been so deeply infiltrated than my two assets in a terrorist organisation."

"Where are they?"

"Are you still in?"

James came back to the table, pulled out a chair and sat down. Harris could see it on his face… he hated it and yet he wanted to be part of it.

"Where are they? And yes, I'm in."

"Raqqa."

"You mean…" Anger disappeared instantly from James's face.

"Yes… within IS headquarters. To be more precise their treasury operation."

298

"How did they…" James shook his head. "Scrap that question. What do you need from me?"

Harris could have punched the air.

"We need to find an alternative way of communicating with the team in Raqqa. The way we currently exchange information has been compromised. We're cleaning our tracks and moving to the emergency protocol."

James nodded.

"The second thing we're working on is the extraction."

"Did you not have an extraction plan before they left?"

"We did but it relies a lot on the boys telling us how they can best meet at a rendezvous point."

"Very risky."

"They know that."

"Do they know about the hostage intervention?"

"They don't know the timing and they don't know they've been compromised either."

"Let me work on your Plan B… If Henry senses they're at risk, he'll be thinking about this too."

Harris stood up slowly.

"Let's go up. You can meet the rest of the team."

* * *

The UK government had offered a couple of concessions when it came to the location of the exchange. The fixer had again voiced his surprise at the speed at which it had been agreed. Echoed by The Treasurer's opinion.

"Very speedy progress." He looked pleased. "Commander al-Haddawi insists on choosing the final exchange site himself." There was no indication that he considered the request unacceptable.

"As long as I can join the team that will proceed with the exchange." Henry was sitting in The Treasurer's office and the door was shut.

"He will object but, as you brokered the deal… it's reasonable. Caliph Ibrahim will agree with me."

"It will be good to see Abu Maeraka again."

The Treasurer nodded slowly but there was something else. "Our leader Caliph Abu Bakr al-Baghdadi insists... there can only be one hostage in exchange for Abu Maeraka."

There would be no arguing or compromise. Henry tried to replace his anger with a show of mild surprise. "The UK might say no." But they wouldn't and al-Baghdadi seemed to have sensed it.

The Treasurer shrugged. These were the instructions.

Henry looked at his watch. There was little time before prayer, but he still needed to reach the fixer now. Their conversation was short. All Henry had to tell him was that it was al-Baghdadi's decision. He would go back to his UK contact and revert.

The call that might have rumbled Henry had not come. Perhaps it wouldn't...

Allahu Akbar... Ash-hadu alla ilaha illallah... the adhan, the call to prayer, reverberated around Raqqa.

Everyone made themselves ready to leave the Treasury room. It was the call that announced the end of the day for the young men who worked there. Hamza looked around as his colleagues were leaving the room. Henry joined the main crowd and was already kneeling on his rug when Hamza finally joined the congregation.

The Treasurer entered and prayer started. Henry's rug had been placed next to the door. When the foreheads touched the ground, he slid out of the room. Bare footed, he ran out towards the Treasury's office.

The space looked much larger now it was empty. Henry clicked the timer on his watch. He had five minutes.

He took three USB keys out of his pocket. Wasim had delivered on his promise to find more for him. Henry moved first to Hamza's desk, logged in and inserted the key. He moved to the file cluster that dealt with the list of contacts Hamza was using to trade oil as well as details about wells and production levels. The download bar started to move, and Henry switched to another desk. He stopped for an instant, certain he had heard a noise.

Nothing...

He resumed the process, this time harvesting information on the dollar accounts and list of armament suppliers IS was using. The USB key started loading.

The door of The Treasurer's office was locked. Henry knelt in front of it, inserted the long stem of his lock-opening kit into the small hole. He moved another, slenderer stem in, feeling for the catch to grip... the lock was about to give... not quite. Henry steadied himself. His fingers had become moist with perspiration. He pushed a little harder and the door opened silently.

Henry sat at the desk and recalled the moves of The Treasurer's hand on his keyboard. The Treasurer had managed to find a Bloomberg keyboard, proudly though absurdly, fitting it to his computer. Henry had spent too many years on the trading floor to forget the place of each key on the board.

Henry flexed his fingers a few times in the air in preparation and keyed in the password... access denied.

His watch beeped... four minutes to go.

Henry inhaled, focused... he brought back the image of the keystrokes... access denied.

Fuck... it's got to be close.

Henry looked around for a clue. Perhaps The Treasurer did what most of Henry's colleagues did in investment banking: leave their password hidden somewhere on their desk. The large ornamental knife looked heavy and out of place on this otherwise functional desk. Henry lifted it and found what he was looking for. The Post-it gave the beginning of a word and the end with a series of numbers scribbled down and regularly replaced by a new one. Henry smiled – he had guessed right – it seemed The Treasurer had changed his password only yesterday and replaced the final number. The USB key started loading the files Henry had selected... lists of assets, financial statements, corporate structure, more bank accounts...

Another beep... three minutes to go.

Henry rushed back to Hamza's desk. The download was almost complete. The second was doing well too. Henry took out his phone from his rucksack and photographed the room, and the large map on which the oil wells under IS control had been marked.

Beep… two minutes.

Henry swiped from the computers the two USB keys that had completed their loading. He moved to The Treasurer's desk. The transfer bar had slowed down a little… Henry cancelled the timer, eyes on the small hand of his watch… only a minute to go. The bar speeded up as if aware of the pressure. He yanked the key out, locked The Treasurer's computer, closed the door behind him… There was no time to lock it. He darted out and dived into the men's room just as people were arriving in the corridor.

It was time to see whether Wasim's schoolboy idea would work. Henry took a small tub out of his rucksack. The egg that lay in it was still intact. He wrapped it in the tissues he had brought with him and slowly crushed it underneath his foot. The smell of rot spread around him instantly. It made his stomach heave. Henry held his breath, scooped up the wet tissues with toilet paper and flushed the lot down the toilet. He forced himself to stay there for a very long minute and left the cubicle, moving to the wash basin to clean his hands and splash his face.

A voice he recognised was asking for him. His name was mentioned a few times until a shadow appeared in the mirror Henry was facing. He turned around hesitantly, looking embarrassed. "Very sorry… couldn't hold it…" The two other men that were with Hamza nodded, happy to leave the stinking place. Hamza waited for a short moment. Henry splashed his face again and Hamza vanished without a word.

Wasim was at the door. It seemed that today they had decided to wear the same army fatigues and black shirt. The reason perhaps it had been easy for him to replace Henry in the prayer room without anyone noticing until the end. "I told you to stay away from that kebab…" Wasim's face still sore, managed a smile… They had what they had come to get.

Henry grinned back… "I know bro… I should always listen to you."

"Where's The Treasurer?" They were both walking out of the building.

"Gone for the night."

Henry nodded. "We've gained another day."

"Perhaps…"

Time to accelerate to phase 2 of Plan B.

* * *

"We need to get Henry and Wasim to Al-Hasakah." Harris, Amina and James had gathered around the large digital map that was projected onto the wall of RED HAWK's control room.

"Aren't they better off deciding on the best extraction route themselves?" James's eyebrows had formed a straight line, concentrating. "Henry's a good lateral thinker."

"That was the plan, but I would rather have options when we communicate. Wasim will soon see we have activated the emergency protocol. He knows what that means." Amina was zooming in on Al-Hasakah.

"We can have one more comms that passes on info only... so that they know we're closing the website... but I can't give them a location until they can call us from a phone that's not tapped." Harris was playing with his cigarette pack.

James grabbed a chair and sat next to Amina, his mind already working on possible options.

"Kurdish territory is a good idea... but they need to get there..." James was thinking out loud and Amina was about to tell him that stating the obvious was not why he had been recruited. Harris squeezed her shoulder. She kept quiet.

"And in that instance a straight line might not be the best line... I wouldn't go through Syria from Raqqa but through Iraq."

This was indeed lateral thinking.

"But that means..." Harris wavered.

"I know..." James pointed to one city on the map...

Chapter Thirty

The hotel's restaurant had been turned into a vast canteen. Once the sun had set most occupants descended upon it, famished after a day of fasting. It was tough to spend a day without food or water and still go about your business... even more so when your business was war.

Henry's mouth watered as he walked past. The food he had hidden in his room was nothing to compare; still, it did keep him going during the day.

Henry did not bother to return to his bedroom and started queuing with the others. Wasim had disappeared once more. Henry knew what he was after; he hoped it would not once more throw him back into Raqqa Stadium.

The food was plentiful and very good too. A successful army was meant to work well on a full belly. IS was certainly doing that for its fighters. Henry scanned the room for Ali and the three men who had attacked him, but no one was around. He filled his plate to the brim, balanced a large piece of khoubz on top and made his way to the fifth floor. The terrace would have been in the shade for some time and the sunset had brought a pleasant breeze.

He moved to the far side where he had arranged a couple of loungers and a table.

Henry had almost finished his plate when Wasim appeared in the frame of his bedroom's sliding doors. Wasim had gone down to fetch a plate too. He was balancing it over a laptop like a waiter using a tray.

The long-forgotten image of a plastic tray, a plate less well garnished and a mug of tea materialised out of nowhere.

The cell is small, but Henry has learned to see it in another light. Apart from a bed, it has a little bookshelf, a table and a chair. A wash basin and toilet have been squeezed into a corner too. Taking back food to eat in one's cell is allowed at HSU Belmarsh. Henry uses it a lot. He has been told by an ex-con who had become his trusted limo driver that there are three things he needs to do to stay alive in prison… keep a low profile, never trust the screws, keep active.

His plate wobbles a bit on his knees, and he puts it on the table. Memories of past menus seem unreal, veggies cooked so much they're akin to puree, eggs swimming in fat, fruit that only consists of apples or bananas. Henry inhales. He is out now. He has made a choice. Redemption might come if he puts his life in the balance. And what better choice than to have come here to Raqqa… a life for a life.

Wasim put down the plate and laptop on the coffee table at which Henry was eating. He had already started on the khoubz, a half-moon missing from its side. Then he dragged a chair close to Henry's and began tucking in.

"It's taken you time."

"Some idiots started arguing about the last piece of meat on a dish… shouting at the cooks because they weren't bringing food out quickly enough."

Henry was mopping up the last of the meat juices with his bread. "I'm not talking about the food…"

Wasim held the laptop as he would a book, in one hand, fork in the other. "I've had my eyes on this one for a while… it was just a question of opportunity."

"And if you're caught with it?"

"I'm dead…"

Henry shook his head. "That's no longer a good joke, Was."

"We'll be out in less than 24 hours now… I need a laptop to communicate and orient us, otherwise we're leaving Raqqa blind. It's worth the risk."

Henry finished the last of his bread. They would not be leaving until he knew Mattie was safe. That might take longer than 24 hours. Challenging Wasim on this would not bring anything good. He changed the subject.

"Do you think they bought the egg trick?"

"Difficult to say." Wasim took a small mouthful and grunted.

This was so good. "The smell was really convincing though..."

They both chuckled. A schoolboy bad joke that seemed to have paid off.

Wasim opened up the laptop and started to inspect it.

"Didn't you call MOTHER?"

"Not a chance... I can't use the tearoom next to the hotel anymore and I half suspect my name has been circulating in other places."

Henry nodded. "Until your name comes to The Treasurer's ears."

"Almost certainly... a few things are going to start looking odd in any case... The speed at which the UK government is agreeing things. You've pushed, even if subtly, for the exchange of two hostages, your phone spends a lot of time stuffed into your rucksack. I have been asking a few questions, getting people to talk and gossip..."

"And I didn't manage to lock The Treasurer's office before I got out."

Wasim shrugged. "Don't beat yourself up. You did good. I'll download the images you took from your phone as soon as I've cracked that baby. You can then erase them. Whoever is monitoring you won't have noticed you took them."

"I still need a good day to finalise the exchange... and you're right. If Baghdadi has made the decision to ask for one hostage, he has sensed the UK is willing to give in."

Wasim ignored Henry's remark. He too did not want to argue about timing it seemed. "Perhaps Baghdadi is not that keen on seeing Maeraka back in Raqqa now that he has been made caliph." Wasim keyed in a couple of instructions. He nodded, satisfied.

"Perhaps... but at least we know the UK is going to agree." Henry did not wait for Wasim to reply. He did not want to contemplate any other outcome. "Do you think the rest of the building was occupied?"

"What do you mean?"

"I'm not sure the women were transferred with the men."

Wasim frowned. This did not entirely make sense.

"Mattie hasn't called me. I managed to slip the hotel number to her when I saw her last."

Wasim shook his head. What was he thinking of? This could put her in even more danger.

"Or she did not have the time… these people are not going to warn the hostages. They will simply move them as they please."

"Not according to The Treasurer."

"That's a point… Haddawi is not happy with the exchange, but if Baghdadi has decided, he will not interfere."

"Shall we talk about what comes next?" Henry braced himself. "I've been poring over the maps of Syria and Iraq… We need to go against the flow… to reach the Kurdish Territory… in Iraq."

"That means moving inland and away from Turkey."

Henry nodded. "The obvious route is Aleppo… combined with an extraction through to the Turkish border. But if we go that way IS will be looking for us, the minute they realise we have gone. They have too many checkpoints along the way… equipped with RPGs, it makes a helicopter extraction difficult."

"Not if we put enough distance between us…"

"Was, the only way we are going to make it out of Raqqa unnoticed is at night and by going through checkpoints less likely to stop us."

Wasim pushed his plate. "OK, what's your escape route?"

"Mosul." Henry almost held his breath. Wasim shook his head with a grin. "Have you completely lost your mind?"

"Not at all. Think about it. No one will look for us that way. There are very few checkpoints to cross and if we do this with the new vehicle…"

"No… it's not happening."

"What else do you suggest then?" Henry did not argue with Wasim. It was a risky plan, he agreed.

"I contact MOTHER with my new toy, agree a drop zone near the Euphrates river and get out from there… I'm not crossing into Iraq…"

"It takes a long flight over Syria to reach the banks of the river. Even if the helicopters come from the Turkish border. And if we try to get close to that border we also have to go through territory where IS, the Syrian army and anti-Assad rebels all operate. Mosul isn't yet organised… IS is sending a lot of their people there to pick up armament, assets… we could be one of that lot."

"How do you know?"

307

"Everyone at the Treasury is focused on this… looting and stripping Mosul of all its possessions."

"Still not happy… and…"

Henry's mobile buzzed. He lifted it and frowned at the message from a caller he did not recognise. "Who the…" He blinked a few times and handed the phone to Wasim.

"MOTHER has been taken to hospital."

Henry's mind was still a blank. He had forgotten the meaning of the coded sentence.

Wasim sat back in his chair, still staring at Henry's mobile. "They've triggered the emergency protocol."

It took a while for them to gather their thoughts.

"Have we been busted?" Henry finally asked.

"We're getting there fast. If we had been, MOTHER would have called directly. But we need to interrupt comms. They're probably cleaning all sites as we speak to avoid leaving a trace."

"How long have we got?"

Wasim ran a solid hand through his hair. "If we could we'd leave tonight…" Henry was about to interrupt him. "But we can't… We need to think things through. I need to crack this laptop and find some ammo for the guns we picked up from the guards… We leave right after that."

Henry slumped into his chair as well. There would be no communication with MOTHER about a helicopter extraction on time.

"Take me through your Mosul plan again." Wasim picked himself up. Henry cleared his throat and resumed his explanation. It did not feel like a win.

* * *

The rumble of feet along the corridors, voices shooting and knocks on doors still sounded distant. Henry wasn't certain whether this was a dream or reality. He rolled out of bed, put a pair of trousers on and listened. Vehicles were departing, beams of light criss-crossing each other in the darkness of night. Wasim knocked at the sliding doors.

"What's happening?" Henry had stepped out.

"There's an alert... or an attack... I'm not sure."

"Here... in Raqqa?"

"I know... but it's what I've heard. They're all desperate to get themselves shot."

Henry looked at his watch, 1.30am. "Let's ask Ali."

Wasim hesitated.

Henry picked up a shirt. "I'm going." He walked out of his bedroom and ran down the four flights of stairs to the first floor.

Ali was awake, standing at the entrance of his small room. "Not going?"

"Nope..."

The corridor was empty. "Did you say the SUV you've picked up for me is ready?"

Ali nodded. "It's here." He hobbled to his bed, bent awkwardly to reach underneath the frame. "You need this." He handed a set of keys to Henry.

"Well done." Henry was about to turn around.

"And this too." Ali held a spark plug between thumb and index finger.

Henry grinned. "Good lad. Don't go anywhere. I'll be back soon."

Wasim had appeared on the landing. "We have a radio."

They moved to the now empty car park. The SUV had been parked in a remote parking bay, out of the way of daily traffic.

Wasim tuned the radio as soon as they had settled in. Static came on first, but he managed to pick up voices as he tried new frequencies. "They are moving towards Makef Street."

The crackle cut across voices. Wasim strained to listen. "There has been an attack..."

"Where?"

Wasim shushed Henry, eyes fixed on the radio, willing the sound to become clearer.

"Fuck." Wasim slammed the dashboard. "It's happening in the old oil factory."

"What... what's happening?" Henry almost choked.

"The bloody idiots... they sent an extraction team."

"British, US?"

"Don't know..." Wasim kept tuning in and out to lessen the static. "US, I think."

"We didn't send them enough details..."

"They've just stormed the place."

"Casualties?"

"Yes, IS is asking for reinforcements."

The beam of car headlights swept across the car park and Wasim turned the radio's volume down. A person disappeared into the hotel and then the car was gone.

"Let's go back, we won't find out anymore by staying here."

"Surely they'll talk about the hostages."

Wasim shook his head. "It's all about the fight. Let's hope the SEAL team succeeds in its extraction, otherwise..."

They got out of the SUV. Henry removed the spark plug and they made their way back to their rooms. "We need to accelerate the plan." Henry had summoned the lift.

"There weren't that many people who knew where the hostages were."

"And you were one of these people... I know."

* * *

Mattie drifted into sleep. She turned over to find a comfortable position, woke up, memories of the afternoon still lingering. The new location was uncomfortable... hot during the day. Not cool enough at night. The bottled water was just enough to keep her hydrated. Gretta had fallen asleep and there had been no sign of Jean since she had left for Mosul.

Steps that came down the corridor told her several people were coming. Mattie kept her eyes shut. The door opened, two men entered, followed by two women in niqab. The women shook both of them awake, throwing cloths over their faces and pushing them hurriedly down the corridor.

Mattie wanted to ask where they were being taken but there was no point. She slowed down to negotiate the stairs and felt the push in her back, almost tripping on her large robes.

In the old factory yard, cars and trucks were waiting, engines running. Men in orange jumpsuits were being shown into the trucks. Mattie slowed down to check whether she could make out their faces. Another hard push in the back. The door opened. She was being bundled into a car, on her own. She fought back, arching her back to resist. A fist slammed into her kidneys, winding her. Her hands grabbed the metal frame in a final effort. The second blow threw her face first into the back of the car. A woman moved swiftly next to her. Mattie craned her neck to see who was taking Gretta. Her screams unbearable. Mattie muffled a choked cry.

Mattie woke and sat up in a different bed, confused as to where she was. This new room was cool. Water and food had been left for her when she had arrived. She was on her own and the bathroom was almost luxurious. But the upgrade chilled her. She moved to the window and looked at the view... peaceful gardens of a house that seemed so far away from any war zone. She took a small piece of paper from within her bra and unfolded it. She had thought it pointless when Henry had given it to her. How could she ever manage to get to a phone? But she had decided she would find a way.

Tomorrow... tomorrow she would call his number.

* * *

He woke up instantly. The buzz of his phone loud enough to break his sleep. He rolled on his side and picked up.

"Harris."

"The US has dispatched one of its SEAL teams... It's happening now." Sir John sounded fully awake. He had not bothered to go to bed.

"Without prior consultation?"

"Not with MI6, no... it seems Colmore did not think it was necessary." The Chief's voice tightened. "I'll see you at the Cross in an hour."

Harris slid from underneath the bed sheets and moved around the room silently, picking up his clothes with hesitant hands. Sarah was fast asleep, and he wanted to keep it that way.

Harris dressed in the corridor and crept downstairs, welcomed by a waggy tail and low yelp.

"Sorry buddy, we're not going for a walk… a bit too early."

Harris moved to the kitchen, found the dog's favourite dry food and poured some into a bowl marked ARNY – TOP DOG. Corny but it made him laugh. He grabbed his keys and moved to his car. He would be at the Cross in 40 minutes.

Sir John had already arrived. He had called a map of Raqqa onscreen, asking for the redirection of one of Akrotiri's Reaper drones.

"The SEAL team managed to get into the place…"

"Good…"

"Except that the only people left there were the mujahideen…" Sir John interrupted. "There was a good old shoot-out. Several IS hostiles are dead… a couple of scratches on the SEAL side."

Harris remained silent. The hostages would pay the price for the missed attempt. He would rather make sure his own people didn't.

"Don't be shy, Steve… you can say it aloud."

"It's a fucked-up mess."

"Quite." Sir John pushed himself onto the table. "Are you making progress on the Al-Hasakah extraction?"

"The main stumbling block remains…" Harris fumbled a little.

"The price… Do your best and let me know the damage. We no longer have the luxury to delay."

"Thank you, sir." Harris nodded.

"Who is going?"

"Still under discussion…"

"Don't be shy… Hell, if I ran RED HAWK I would go there myself." Sir John grinned.

"We are considering a couple of alternatives…" Harris moved closer to the map. "The issue is that we no longer are in regular comms mode."

"They've been busted?"

"It's only a matter of time, so we killed the website chat and cleaned up… That will give them more time."

Sir John waited for a moment. "I'm not sure I am of any use to you on this… but I can have a conversation with the Home Office to assess damage and with the commander of armed forces."

"Whatever help is appreciated." Harris thought of his request for the very large sum of cash he was about to file with Sir John in a few hours' time and hoped the SAS did not have the appetite for a tour of Raqqa.

* * *

Henry woke up again to the sound of the muezzins' chants from the minarets. He had had little sleep. Despite their efforts they had not been able to find out what had happened to the hostages. He kept wondering what impact the raid would have on them and turning over in his mind the deal he was hoping to secure later on that day. Henry was now certain he had less than 24 hours to save Mattie. How the US military had determined the location of their people preyed on Henry's mind, but he pushed it away. He would not solve this puzzle from within Raqqa. Henry's mind would not be quietened down, so he ran through a scenario that might, just might, save two women.

Henry jogged down the five flights of stairs and was the last to join the prayer room. He shut his mind to the events of the night before and simply followed the flow. He surveyed the room for clues. Some of the fighters looked tired but exhilarated too. They would have stories to tell for the next few days. Ali had arrived early, finding a place where he could sit with his injured leg.

Henry let the crowd of worshippers leave and waited for Ali to join him. They chatted a little until they had reached his room.

"You like it?"

"The SUV?... Grand..." And I need to ask you for one more favour."

Ali nodded. "Sure thing, Abu Shabh."

Henry took three USB keys from his trouser pocket. "You keep these safe."

Ali pocketed them immediately. "No problem... I don't get out." He brandished his crutch as proof.

"What happened last night?" Henry asked as casually as he could.

"You don't know?" Ali's eyes widened. "The Americans... they came." Ali told Henry what he knew already. "They killed fighters... many... but they left empty handed..."

"Empty handed of what?"

Ali shrugged. "I don't know… But maybe they were trying to help people." Ali looked sad and he slowly sat down on his bed.

"Keep safe." Henry turned to leave. "I'll come back to fetch you at the end of today."

Henry walked downstairs again and called the fixer. There was no time to lose.

Chapter Thirty-One

The Treasury room was surprisingly quiet when he arrived. The Treasurer's office door was shut. Unusual. Henry dumped his rucksack on his desk in the separate room that was still his office and moved to the main room, striking up a conversation with a subdued Hamza. Was his reporting on Henry not to the liking of his masters?

"Where are we with the hostage exchange?" The Treasurer had waved Henry in.

"I called the fixer this morning. He's going back and forth… the British are not happy with the single hostage demand…" Henry let it hang but knew no one would dare go against one of al-Baghdadi's orders.

"The English journalist…" The Treasurer moved his hand, indicating Henry should close the door. "The English journalist has become of interest to Caliph Ibrahim."

Henry froze for a moment, stunned. He frowned, hoping his face would convey surprise rather than the feelings bubbling inside him.

"Is that going to create a problem?"

"Possibly."

"I don't think the British government would exchange anyone else against Abu Maeraka."

"Which is also what I said to our caliph, but…"

"Is she still in Raqqa?" Henry held his breath for the response.

"I don't know." The Treasurer didn't lie. The hostages' oversight was not his remit.

"Al-Haddawi will have his way with the hostages now that five of our fighters are dead," The Treasurer said woefully. His eye twitched a little. He might lose a lucrative deal for the sake of revenge. Regrettable.

"I'll call again at midday if I haven't heard from the fixer."

"Good." The Treasurer did not mention the raid on the old oil factory again nor the speed at which the deal with the British had progressed, or even the fact that his office had been left open overnight. Henry's life was valuable until the agreement with the UK was sealed... but after that...

"Al-Haddawi still needs to confirm he is satisfied with one of the proposed locations for the exchange." Henry had stood up.

The Treasurer nodded. He was aware but al-Haddawi would not be rushed.

Henry went back to Hamza, checked the price of oil on the market. IS was gradually approaching $1 million a day... it would almost certainly reach its target in the next few weeks. Henry looked around... he had collated enough intelligence that would make a good read for MI6. The room felt like a squeezed lemon, ready to be discarded.

Henry walked out of the Treasury and back to the hotel. Wasim was nowhere to be seen again. Henry did not want to check on Ali yet. He walked up the stairs to the fifth floor and stopped at the junction between landing and corridor. A slow shiver ran down his spine. He looked around. There was no one to be seen. He walked a few paces toward his bedroom and stopped. A patch of bright light stretched over the corridor floor... his door was wide open. Henry hesitated; he could go back and alert reception, but he decided not to. Instead he moved slowly towards the door looking around for a makeshift weapon. He stopped and listened.

Nothing.

Henry picked up a fire extinguisher and stepped over the threshold. He moved around the room silently, opening the wardrobe and bathroom doors, still nothing. He dropped the fire extinguisher onto the floor and surveyed the scene. The room had been thoroughly searched. No doubt about it this time. It was an in-your-face intrusion. It was meant to scare him. The few bits of food Henry had left on the small table had been scattered around. His few clothes had been searched, the pockets turned out. The mattress had been pushed off the bed and a pillow cut open with a knife, its innards strewn over the carpet. Henry did not bother to clear up the mess. He ran to the first floor.

Where was Ali?

He knocked at the door, tried the handle. It was locked. Henry reached the foyer. There was no sign of him. At reception he asked to use the phone. "My battery is flat." The man did not argue. He was there to facilitate, not question. Still, he might be keeping an eye on the guests' movements. Henry picked up the phone and gave the same scruffy man one of his best crushing looks. The man made himself scarce. Henry dialled Ali's mobile. It went to voicemail. Henry turned around and went to the hotel's gardens. He had to find Ali.

* * *

"The Crypto team confirms that the origin of the intrusion messages comes from a server in the Middle East."

"Raqqa?!"

"They're not sure yet."

"Shit."

"We must go dark for a few days until we know for sure."

"Wasim knows there's a problem?"

"I've used the emergency protocol and directed it to Henry's phone."

"What was the latest before we stopped?"

"Crowne was attempting to lift as much data as possible from The Treasurer's office. It was our last comms at 15.17 Raqqa time."

"And then nothing?"

"That's right."

"We don't know how they are faring now that the rescue mission has tanked."

"We can't communicate, Steve." Harris took note. Amina was calling him by his name. "We haven't even had time to speak about the extraction plan. I have zero visibility on their thinking when it comes to that."

"Radlett is on board and Brett is doing well. Something is coming together."

"Thanks for sounding reassuring but I need to see the nitty gritties of the plan before I am overjoyed." Amina moved her hands over her tired face. "Are you intending to send Radlett on the ground?"

"I haven't asked yet."

Amina shook her head. They needed someone on the ground.

Harris changed the subject. "Did Wasim comment on Henry?"

"He seemed pleased, but I did not concentrate on asking for an HR review of Crowne's performance."

"I'm not criticising." Harris moved to the window, its green glass today giving the office a moody glow. "We need that intel. It might be a game-changer in the fight against terrorism."

"We need to bring them back so that we can get that intel," Amina corrected.

Harris turned back to face Amina. "I'm not going to let our guys die out there."

Amina did not reply. Her face, still drawn, told Harris she knew that the outcome was not entirely up to him.

* * *

Henry returned to his room, opened the terrace door and stepped outside. Despite the shade, the temperature had reached an uncomfortable 30°C. He had not seen Wasim since last night. Where was he? He moved to the balustrade and leaned forward. He could see a large part of the gardens and the car park from there. He was hoping he might perhaps spot Ali. Henry craned his neck and methodically surveyed the ground below. There was no one he could recognise.

He sat on one of the deckchairs, elbows on knees. He had not had much time to reflect since he had started this journey from the UK to Raqqa. It had been all about learning to infiltrate and then becoming a convincing convert in the jihadi camps of Turkey. Had he been too ambitious… again? Too ambitious to think he would make it as a top MI6 operative. His involvement with the IRA had been in the field of finance, a subject at which he excelled. But now, in the middle of a war zone, where people around him were demonised for thinking differently and punished in a manner he had never imagined existed, Henry Crowne might have reached the limit of his endurance.

The film of sweat that rose at the back of his neck was not the result of the searing heat. Henry checked his watch again. He had not seen Wasim for almost 12 hours.

Henry stood up. Back at the terrace balustrade, he leaned forward again. No one had moved. If he could not spot Ali soon, he would have to break into his room and check where the USB keys were. He waited a few minutes and decided to go downstairs first to report the intrusion. Not doing so would be a tell-tale sign that he had perhaps something to hide. He ran down the four flights of stairs to Ali's room once more and then he would have to go to reception and speak to them.

Henry knocked at Ali's door; still no reply. He tried the door – this time it was open. "Ali," he called softly as he opened it. Henry stepped inside and stopped dead. Ali's room too had been ransacked. There was very little to damage in this diminutive space, but the bed had been overturned. Someone had also taken a knife to an old armchair. The little clock Ali seemed to carry everywhere he went had been crushed by a heavy boot. Henry forgot about swearing. His stomach churned.

He retreated slowly, made sure no one was around when he left. He forced himself to walk slowly to the ground floor. He stopped for a few seconds as he reached the bottom of the stairs. Someone was trying to push him to make a mistake. The scruffy porter was speaking to another man. He started stabbing his fingers on the counter. The receptionist turned towards Henry with a smile.

"I need to…"

"Hey…" Someone was calling for him. He turned around. Wasim was walking through the hotel foyer in a slow yet purposeful manner.

"Never mind, I'll speak to you later." Henry's natural cool assurance had been dented.

"What's up?"

Henry did not reply until he opened the door of his room.

"This…" He moved away from the entrance to let Wasim in. Wasim moved his head towards the terrace. They both walked through the sliding doors, closed them and settled on the deckchairs.

"When did it happen?"

"I don't know but I discovered it one hour ago."

"I only left my own room a couple of hours ago. I would have heard."

"And there is more. Ali's room has been searched too. I can't find him either."

"The word circulating around amongst the fighters is that someone tipped off the Americans."

"Shit." Henry slumped in his chair. "I'm so very close with the hostage exchange. Although…"

"If we get caught it's going to make things worse for Mattie," Wasim interrupted.

"And if we leave it's going to make things worse for her too." Henry dropped his forehead on his clasped raised hands. "Baghdadi is interested…" He didn't know how else to put it.

Wasim's phone rang. He looked at it with annoyance but checked the caller. "Salaam, where are you?" His face a mixture of hope and concern.

Henry mouthed, "Who is it? Ali?"

Wasim nodded. "You need to come back as soon as you can."

Wasim frowned. "I can't explain but call me when you're back in your room."

"Ali is fine. He has heard rumours about betrayal…"

"Is he on his way back?"

"So he says…"

Henry inhaled deeply. Some good news.

"If you report the mess, the IS police will be called."

"Really?"

"Without a doubt."

"They will need to speak to you. Possibly take you away to a police station somewhere in Raqqa."

Henry had picked up on Wasim's train of thought. "Which means that I won't be able to call the fixer and push for an exchange to take place."

"Exactly so."

"OK, change of plan. I'm not reporting this, and neither should Ali."

"If they had found the USB key, they would have come barging in for you already."

"For Ali first and then for me…"

"I'm calling the fixer again. You go and check that Ali's still got the USB keys."

"And then?"

"We need to find out where Mattie is."

Wasim was about to ask why. He pulled back. He needed to speak to Ali first.

* * *

The apartment looked different when she arrived. Yet another place, ruled by women for women. The door opened quietly and someone came in, surprising her with the soft touch of her hand. Mattie sat up in bed, sheets clutched against her body. The face looked familiar. She recognised the young woman who had looked after her when she first arrived in Raqqa.

"Where are we?"

"The same place as before." Gulan went to the window and drew the curtains open.

"Is it early?"

"It's almost 6am." She came back to the bed on which Mattie still lay. "Are you hungry?"

"Yes please."

"I'll bring you something."

Mattie rubbed her eyes. She had not heard the muezzins' calls to prayer and wondered whether the water that had been left on the bedside table had been spiked. She swung her legs onto the floor, walked to the bathroom. It was well furnished and supplied… shower gel, soap, body cream, shampoo… and scented oils. She was being prepared and these preparations were not meant for a hostage exchange. Perhaps al-Baghdadi wanted to have his fun before he released her, if he released her. She pushed the thought out of her mind. She would shower, make herself look decent and find a way to call Henry.

Breakfast arrived, tea, dates and an egg cooked over tomatoes in a small oven dish. Mattie started eating and had to exercise restraint not to wolf it down in one go.

Gulan looked towards the door she had left open. Anyone could check on them at any minute. There was silence in the apartment. Her hand moved into the folds of her abaya and took a large piece of khoubz out of one of the pockets. Mattie smiled and placed it underneath her pillow. No words had been spoken, but their eyes met, showing gratitude on one side and kindness on the other. Gulan took Mattie's now empty plate away. The key turned in the lock.

Mattie sat back on her bed. It was only a matter of time before they came to pick her up the way they had done Jean. She closed her eyes and tried to remember the layout of the apartment from when she had first arrived. She tried to recall her movements. Was there a phone, a good old-fashioned phone with a landline? She squeezed her eyes shut as if the answer could be summoned easier. She couldn't remember. Frustrated, she stood up and walked to the window. From there she could see the street, leafy, large... a few cars on the road on the street beyond the front garden. She had not seen any women at all walking in the street, even in groups. Still, women would have been expected to tend to the food and cook for the men they were looking after.

Two men had parked their truck in the semi-circular drive that led to the front door. Mattie held her breath. Could this be it? Men taking women to the local shops for food.

Mattie walked to her bedroom door now that the men had disappeared into the building. She stuck her ear to the door. Faint noises came from the end of the corridor. Then voices that made her jump. Could she have been right? People were talking in what she thought was the lounge, but then the voices stopped. She went back to the window. Out they came, the two men she had seen and a woman carrying baskets. She could not quite make out who the woman was. No, the men were taking women to the local shops to buy food. It was by now almost 7am. The market would be open already. She recalled the market she had visited when she had come to Raqqa previously, the shack-like structures, supported by wooden or metal poles, raffia and thick tarpaulins stretched overhead to protect the fruit and vegetables from the sun. There was no door and no walls, just a long stretch of stalls, full of colour and delicious smells.

Relieved, she realised this might be her only chance. She waited for the car to leave, waited five more minutes and went back to the door. Her knock sounded more like a rattle at first and then became more forceful. "Please can someone open the door?" The key turned in the lock and she stepped away. Gulan looked surprised. Mattie stayed put. Gulan would not cross the threshold of the room unless she was invited to. "Please, please, I must call... a friend... Abu Shabh."

There was no reaction. Mattie, the foreign prisoner and the battle name of an IS fighter did not seem to make sense.

"Please... Gulan, I need to speak to Abu Shabh."

Gulan now looked scared. She did not know what to do. She had not been told that Mattie might ask for such a call and what her response should be.

"He is waiting for my call."

A deep softness rose into her brown eyes. But more than this, the understanding that what she was about to do might transgress the rules she had been asked to follow and that there would be a price to pay. Gulan nodded and let Mattie go to the lounge. She pointed towards an object Mattie could not remember seeing. A good old-fashioned telephone.

Chapter Thirty-Two

Harris had moved to the spare room, despite Sarah's protest that she did not mind the nightly calls. Amina, James and he had switched their working hours to fit Raqqa's time zone, two hours ahead of GMT. His alarm rang at 4.30am. The dog had made his way onto the bed and did not budge when Harris got up. Harris was out of the door within 30 minutes and even the rattle of dog food being shaken in the box did not persuade Arny the top dog to come down. Harris got into his battered old Ford Mondeo. No one noticed him on the road, and he liked it that way.

Amina had already arrived, screens populated with data and maps.

"Any news?" Harris stood over her and handed over a coffee from the coffee machine.

"Nothing, but there's a lot of activity from the IP address we've now identified and confirmed is located in Raqqa."

"Which means?"

"That they are trying to get Wasim to reply to their product offers to check whether his past conversation trail matches this new one."

"But he could justifiably ignore them."

"Not a good idea… we've taken control of his account anyway so for a while we'll be talking to them and give Wasim a bit of extra time."

"I thought he was connecting from various tearooms in Raqqa?"

"He does but he will still have to leave his name to have access to the PCs… the beardos are obsessed with data control."

The door opened and James came in. He looked alert and prepared for a long day at the office. Working in investment banking had some advantages; waking up at 4am for a day's work was one of them.

"Henry's good at knowing when to cut his losses." James had been listening to the update.

"Even if he and Wasim are preparing to leave, we need to give them the extraction timetable and rendezvous point."

"Which needs to be in Kurdish territory, hence Al-Hasakah. I get it." James rolled his shoulders. "I'd like to join the extraction team."

"I hoped you might say that." Harris's eyes moved briefly to James's legs.

"My old injuries are fine. So long as I'm not asked to do a parachute jump or hike with a 60-pound pack on my back on difficult terrain, I'm good."

"The Chief is speaking to SAS command. We'll know this morning who the extraction team is going to be."

"Do we have men in position close by?"

"Not sure, there may be SAS positioned with the US military. Basra is too far away to fly an op over enemy territory, extract, then come back."

"Then it'll have to be Cyprus, and they'll need to agree a refuel in Turkey. Maximum range of the Apache is 450 km."

James moved closer to the map open on one of Amina's screens. "I make it 700 km between Cyprus and Al-Hasakah. With the men and army equipment, an Apache can't go much faster than 250 km/h, so that'll take about three hours."

"That complicates matters." Harris rubbed the back of his neck.

"Agreed, if you need to tell Turkey about the extraction it will take a day or two to get the OK."

"I have a Plan B..." Harris said almost to himself.

"Which is?"

"Back in a moment... keep me posted on the phone if anything happens." Harris grabbed the burner phone with the black leather casing and was about to walk out.

* * *

Wasim and Henry had decided to divide the task. "Let's split the search?" Wasim replaced the stolen laptop in his rucksack.

"I'll go to some of the cafés in Raqqa where the young fighters hang around. You do another tour of the hotel." Wasim stuffed the hard drive into a pocket of his army slacks.

Henry was not listening. "The phone... The phone's ringing in my room." They both hesitated, then Henry remembered. He ran through the sliding doors onto the terrace, vaulted over the low wall and skidded into the bedroom, lunging at the phone to pick it up. The line went dead.

"No... wait... wait." Henry dropped onto the displaced mattress, still holding the receiver in his hand. He slowly put it back into its cradle and put his head in his hands. Wasim had appeared on the terrace threshold.

"I thought it might have been..."

The phone rang again and this time it had not finished its first ring when Henry picked up. "Mattie..." His croaky voice filled with hope. He grabbed the pen and paper that lay on the bedside table. Henry was nodding as he wrote "Go back to your room, stay there, wait for me. I'm coming."

Wasim had disappeared on his search and Henry walked along the corridor to Ali's room. He opened the door after knocking softly. It was still in the same state of disarray he had found a couple of hours ago. Either Ali had not been back or he had gone downstairs to report the disturbance.

Henry again investigated the lounge and visited the garden. Young men were gossiping, dozing off, reading IS propaganda magazines and watching videos on their tablets. No one was paying attention to him, clad as he was in the standard army fatigues, black shirt and black scarf around his head. There was no sign of Ali anywhere. All the loungers and chairs were taken up. Henry finished his round. Where else could he look?

He climbed the few steps that led up to the lounge, about to return to his room, then stopped. Why not? Henry walked out of the hotel entrance and round to the car park. The SUV had been moved into the shade and its windows wound down. Ali was sitting in the driver's seat, listening to music on the radio, eyes shut, drumming the rhythm of what he was hearing on the wheel.

326

Henry could not suppress a smile. "Enjoying the ride?"

Ali jumped, his face dropped, and he looked scared for a moment.

"Been here a long time?"

Ali stammered some inaudible apologies, a little red in the cheeks.

"Relax, I'm not annoyed. I've just been looking for you everywhere." Henry's face grew serious. "Do you still have the USB keys I gave you?"

Ali smiled, happy he could do right to repay his use of the car. "Yes, always with me." He fumbled around and fished the items from his trouser pockets one after the other.

Henry could have hugged him. "Great stuff." Henry walked around the bonnet of the SUV and climbed into the passenger seat. "Have you been back to your room?"

Ali looked puzzled, his eyes a little wider. He shook his head.

"OK. Your room has been ransacked."

Ali frowned. He could not understand the word…

"Someone has gone into your room and turned it upside down."

The frown deepened on his brow. "Why?"

"I don't know but we need to go back."

Ali nodded. They both got out of the car. Before they left, Henry removed the spark plug from the engine and handed it to Ali. They walked in silence until they were about to enter the hotel. "You go in first. I'll see you back at your room."

Henry waited, then entered the lounge from the gardens. He took his time to walk through the comfortable armchairs and low tables and saw what he was after. When he reached the table, he bent to redo one of his shoelaces and lay a magazine he had found in the gardens on top of it. He picked up the basic mobile phone together with the magazine. Sometimes it felt good to be a thief.

Ali had replaced the mattress on his bed, stood up the chair that was lying on the floor and folded his clothes into a neat pile. He had collected the pieces of the old alarm clock and gathered them into an old scarf. Henry knocked and entered. Ali's eyes looked moist. His smooth features lined with distress and fear. Henry moved to the chair, turned it around and straddled it.

"Have they taken anything?"

"The Qur'an my mother gave me." This was spiteful and Henry wondered whether the three men who he had handled yesterday were to blame.

"I'm really sorry about this. Are you thinking about reporting it?"

Ali shook his head.

"That's a wise decision, nothing good will come of it." Henry glanced at his watch. "It's almost noon. I am going out for a short while. Stay in your room. When you pray at Zuhr time, stay in your room too. I'll come back to fetch you, OK?"

Ali nodded again.

"I want to hear you say OK, that you'll do as I say."

"OK. I will do as you say, Abu Shabh."

"Good."

Henry stood up, put the chair back where it belonged and opened the door.

"And lock the door as well."

* * *

Harris had ignored a call from Sir John. He knew what it was about and needed time to finalise his own plan.

The Club was busy yet quiet. Harris always felt he was entering a timewarp he enjoyed disturbing. His insistence on saying *please* and *thank you* to butlers and stewards when Brett had instructed him this was not the *done thing* gave Harris the deepest satisfaction.

Brett was seated in the corner he favoured, already armed with a glass of the excellent Macallan. Harris joined him and sank into a large armchair.

"Progress?"

"Some. I've convinced my Kurdish contact to have a conversation with some 'people' in Al-Hasakah. After that it's proving trickier."

"How much time will that take?"

"Twelve to twenty-four hours, no longer."

"The time frame may tighten up so keep trying."

328

A waiter discreetly appeared at Harris's side. "Would you like to order, sir?"

"Sparkling water, please."

Brett had lifted his glass from the small table on which it sat and stopped mid-air.

"Are you on one of those ridiculous detox diets?"

"Nope, not my style."

"Right." Brett's glass continued its journey. He sipped the amber drink with contentment. His face grew serious, tight mouthed, his brow slightly furrowed. "Are you that concerned?"

Harris exhaled briefly. "At the moment I need all my wits to see this through." He had never shown doubts to Brett but perhaps today was the day.

Brett pushed his back into the leather armchair. "Is Crowne one of them?"

Harris shook his head. "Brett, you know…"

"You can't give me that info otherwise you'd have to kill me. I know. But still I take it as a yes."

Harris waited.

"I rather like the thought that the Irish peasant is going to have to owe me one." Brett extended his hand to replace the crystal tumbler on the table precisely where he had picked it up from. It was almost empty. Brett considered having another one but then thought better of it. He sipped the last of his drink and stood up. "No time to lose, I've got to firm up with my Kurdish contact. I presume the cash transfer is in hand?"

Harris nodded.

"I'll call you when the final details are set."

Brett left Harris behind. Harris leaned back in the leather chair. He now needed to let his team in Raqqa know their rendezvous point.

* * *

The old truck rumbled along Fardos Street. He had to go back to the Treasury office one last time. The sun was at its zenith and the temperature in the vehicle almost unbearable. His stomach fluttered as he approached the entrance of the building. He slowed down. The guards did not ask for his pass. Was it a good sign? Perhaps not.

Henry climbed the two flights of stairs to the second floor and entered the main Treasury room. No one noticed him. All the young men were on the phone making deals that would ensure IS had a sustained revenue stream.

Hamza had disappeared. Whoever he had been working for had not received the results they were expecting.

How frustrating. Henry imagined it was al-Haddawi and if it were his frustration must have boiled over after this morning's failed trap.

Henry sat at his desk and checked his watch. It was almost 11am in London. Time for MOTHER to come through. The fixer could be calling at any moment. They had agreed an update, whatever the result. Henry searched on the computer. He had received an encrypted email through Mail2tor. Henry used the encryption code on his machine, entered his password. The fixer had decided to send the exchange terms for Abu Maeraka in writing. Clever guy… covering his arse was probably good, although Henry doubted IS would unilaterally rescind the contract if the results were not to their liking.

Henry read through the terms, and he smiled. The Treasurer's office door was shut once more. He was on the phone, having an angry exchange with someone. He slammed his hand on his desk, and his raised voice reached Henry. None of the other men noticed, or perhaps they did not want to notice. Henry waited. He was buying time until tonight, and a deal with the British government provided a little breathing space until then.

The Treasurer stood up and banged the phone down. Henry went back to his screen. His mobile rang. The Treasurer wanted to see him. Henry walked into the office and waited to hear what the man had to say.

"Leave your phone outside the room." He gave The Treasurer an amazed look but obeyed.

"What is happening? Where is Hamza?"

"Hamza no longer works at the Treasury." The answer was curt. Henry nodded. He could think of one reason. Al-Haddawi had had a mole at the Treasury, Hamza had been it and The Treasurer had realised.

"The British government has agreed to our terms."

The frown on The Treasurer's forehead eased off. He had reached his prayer beads and started rolling them around his fat fingers. "Tell me."

Henry went through the terms.

One female hostage in exchange for Abu Maeraka. The exchange would take place in the old city centre of Aleppo. Both parties to take position 1 km away from one another. The hostage and Maeraka would be accompanied by one person. Any attack would incur immediate retaliation. The life of one of the hostages still held by IS in Raqqa would be cut short. The exchange would take place in two days' time.

The Treasurer looked satisfied. "Only Al-Haddawi's men will be involved in the exchange."

"Why can't we send some of our people?" Henry asked.

"My thoughts exactly… Al-Haddawi is riding high on his Mosul success, but he forgets who finances the war effort."

"What does Caliph Ibrahim say?"

Some intake of breath. The Treasurer was not going to tell on what basis senior men were judged in the Caliphate. Those who offered themselves as martyrs had the upper hand. The only hope The Treasurer had was for al-Haddawi to join the land of milk and honey sooner rather than later.

"He is eager to see Abu Maeraka again."

Good reply. Henry nodded approvingly. The clock on the wall was indicating 2pm. He had a few hours to go before he could retreat to his hotel.

"How about sending someone from the Treasury to do the exchange? Perhaps al-Haddawi can provide the fighters but the Treasury provides the man who helps free Abu Maeraka."

The Treasurer's finger stopped on one bead and seemed to squeeze it tight. "How about you?"

Henry did his best to look eager and pleased. He had bought himself a two-day respite, after which his future was less than certain. Henry settled back in his chair.

Henry had spent more than two hours with The Treasurer. It was all about alternatives, planning the exchange, talking risk through, applying mitigation. The Treasurer's round face had become flushed with content. The plan looked well thought through. He could with confidence discuss it with al-Baghdadi and his war council.

Henry stood up and The Treasurer's face suddenly dropped. Henry was about to sit down but he realised that The Treasurer was looking past him into the room that spread in front of his office. A small chill ran down Henry's spine. Only one person could cause The Treasurer to be concerned.

Al-Haddawi entered the office without knocking. He ignored Henry, sat on one of the chairs in front of The Treasurer's desk, swung his legs up and set his dirty boots onto it.

"So, Treasurer, you have a deal?"

"We have a way of releasing our brother Abu Maeraka from the infidels' clutches, yes."

"And you think your 'fighters'" – Al-Haddawi smirked – "will be able to withstand an ambush?"

"My fighters are at least as good as yours." The Treasurer's cheeks had gone a little redder than usual.

"Shame I did not see any of them when I took Mosul."

"Shame you did not offer to test them when you took Mosul."

Al-Haddawi cast an eye on Henry. "And what is he going to do?"

"Make the exchange," Henry answered.

Al-Haddawi's light brown eyes ran over Henry with scorn and yet for a fleeting moment he showed surprise. Henry was not only a pen-pusher, he had the guts for the front line.

Henry leaned on the back of the chair he had occupied, now half facing Haddawi. Something in Henry squirmed, a bubble of anger rising in his stomach. Memories of Belfast flooded his mind and he closed these gates promptly. He would not allow al-Haddawi to get under his skin.

Haddawi's eye ran from Henry to The Treasurer, from The Treasurer to Henry. The slight flare of his nostrils, the crease at the corner of his eyes, it was more than contempt.

It was hatred.

Al-Haddawi stood up and turned to face the door. Before Henry could move, Haddawi's foot caught the leg of the chair on which Henry was leaning, throwing both to the ground. The fall was farcical, and Henry hit the floor like a puppet that had lost its strings. A hand of steel stopped him from getting up and lunging into his opponent. Henry started to laugh. It was a low rumble that shook his body in a small spasm until it became an outburst of derision and scorn.

Was it the best Haddawi could do?

Henry sat up to see Haddawi's back disappear between the rows of the computer screens.

"See you in two days' time. Big man." Henry stood up and straightened up the chair.

The Treasurer grinned. He was backing the right horse.

Chapter Thirty-Three

Henry had waited at the Treasury until after prayer time. It was hard to stay calm when he was still wondering whether a call about Raqqa Stadium and Wasim would be placed with The Treasurer, and even harder to stay put when he had told Mattie he would be coming for her. But he could not afford to break the routine. He left as soon as he could and walked to the small shop he had once bought coffee from. It had just opened, and men were purchasing foods that would be consumed after sunset. Henry made his selection and bundled the lot at the back of the truck. He drove back to the hotel, dumped the truck close to the entrance, took the food he had bought and stepped in. Henry climbed the steps to the first floor two at a time and walked to Ali's room. The young man asked who it was through the door when Henry knocked. Good… he was learning.

"Make a bundle with your clothes and be ready when I come again. And keep these with you."

Ali nodded. He did not ask why. He did not care. All that mattered was that there was perhaps a way to escape this living hell.

Henry climbed the stairs to the fifth floor. He found Wasim in his room. "I've cracked the laptop finally but I'm not taking the risk. Any contact by phone?"

Henry shook his head. "No contact by phone… They're waiting for us to make the first move."

Perhaps we can?

Henry produced a basic pre-paid flip phone out of one of his trouser pockets. "I lifted this from some young guy who was not paying enough attention to his stuff."

Wasim nodded. "That's good."

"I spoke to Ali. He's ready." Henry handed the device to Wasim.

"For what?" Wasim turned the phone over in his hand and opened the battery case to check for tracking devices. He was taking no chances. His brown eyes grew darker as he asked the question. "What have you said to Ali?"

"Nothing, except to be ready for anything."

"Do I have to play the bad guy every time you make your next move?" Wasim was not shouting but his voice had lost its usual calm. "Are you telling me you want to take Ali with us?"

"I am." Henry held both hands up in an attempt to pacify Wasim. "Hear me out..."

"No. Haven't you learned anything?" Wasim slammed the desk with his fist.

"Hear me out, please..." Henry's face froze. Wasim was not the shouting type, so perhaps he had to listen to his objections. "Ali has helped us, the new car, the USB keys..."

Wasim had stood up, pacing his room, hands at his waist. "And he can identify the car... I get that."

"He also knows Mosul, much better than us. He has just come back from it." Henry waited for Wasim to stop.

Wasim ran his sturdy hand through his hair, creating a wave of black curls.

"He will know where the checkpoints are." Henry carried on. "And..." he hesitated.

"You don't want to leave him behind, do you?" Wasim shot a dark eye to Henry. "We need to deliver the information back to London and by the looks of it, deliver Mattie as well... We're stretching ourselves very thin."

"Granted, difficult but not impossible. Ali does not want to be here. He is not going to be a problem."

Wasim stopped pacing the room. "Fine, but if there is an issue with Ali, you will have to deal with him, you understand me?"

Henry held his breath for a moment. His chest hurt and he released the inhalation. Henry gave a slow nod.

"I want to hear it from you Henry. You will deal with him."

335

Henry closed his eyes. He heard himself say the words.

"Yes, I will deal with him."

* * *

Sunset at 7.45pm.

Henry went back to his room and changed into fresh clothes. He might have to live in these for a while. The same khaki combat trousers, black shirt, a pair of special ops boots in a camouflage pattern. He spread the contents of the rucksack on the bed. His bugged phone had been left in the bathroom after he had taken his shower and would now stay there for the foreseeable future. He stuffed a couple of T-shirts at the bottom of the bag, matches, compass, small torchlight, multipurpose knife, his small notebook and pen, a bottle of water and the Glock they had taken from the guard at Raqqa Stadium. Henry unclipped the magazine. He had taken the gun apart yesterday, cleaning it meticulously, pulling each piece away and reassembling the gun methodically. He actioned the slide once more, pressed the trigger a few times. The grip felt solid in his hand. He slotted a magazine into the catch and slid the gun into the side pocket of the rucksack. It was now 7.30pm. The fighters who lived in the hotel would soon start to congregate towards the canteen again.

Wasim walked through the open window that led to the terrace. He too was ready. Henry rolled his camouflage jacket in a ball and stuffed it in the bag. "Done."

"Phone?" Wasim's face had grown serious: time to focus on the task that lay in front of them… Escape from Raqqa.

"In the bathroom."

People started to fill up the corridor. The men were leaving their rooms to go to the ground floor. Henry and Wasim waited until the noise had died down. Henry opened the door.

"Let's go." His voice was low and did not betray his heart pumping in his chest.

Both men slid into the fire escape, silently descending the concrete steps that led to the ground floor. They waited another five minutes in semi-darkness. The sound of voices kept coming – the entire hotel seemed to be on the move. Henry used his small torch to check whether the door that opened onto the garden was alarmed. Wasim took a multipurpose knife out of one of his pockets, directed Henry's torch to create enough light and cut the wire. Henry opened the door a fraction.

No one around.

The garden was now empty. They walked round the building stopping from time to time to listen to the sound coming from the hotel. The smell of cooking made Henry's mouth water. Dinner would be the main attraction of the evening for a while.

Wasim grabbed Henry's rucksack and disappeared towards the SUV. Henry started walking towards the hotel lobby along the path that led from the secluded gardens to the hotel entrance when two cars drove through the main entrance and round the driveway. Four men dressed in the requisite black uniform and equipped with sub-machine guns jumped out and walked through reception. They knew where they were going. Wasim had noticed too. He kept going without hurrying. Henry froze. He retraced his steps and climbed the few stairs to reach the terrace. Men were queuing to pile food on their plates. Laughing, shouting. No doubt exchanging stories of their combat exploits. He mixed with the men and merged into the mass of people. The men that had just walked in were now surrounding the receptionist, dwarfing the man. He ran in front of them to lead the way. They were walking up the stairs. One man positioning in front of the lifts. Henry retreated to the far end of the lounge, slid towards the toilets and the fire exit. He climbed the stairs two at a time and reached the first floor.

As he turned into the corridor he came face to face with an older man. He stopped to see where Henry was going. Henry kept walking towards the end of the corridor, choosing a door at random. It seemed to satisfy the old man who turned into the landing and started walking downstairs. Henry retraced his steps and knocked at Ali's door. There was no response.

"It's Abu Shabh, open up."

Henry heard the lock turn. He pushed the door to get in. Ali's small bundle was ready, time to go. Ali hesitated for an instant. Henry grabbed the food he had bought earlier. "We must go now." Ali nodded. He too was ready.

They walked to the fire exit, reached the gardens. Henry stopped. There was still no one in the gardens, but he could hear voices on the terrace. He turned around and walked in the opposite direction. A small wall separated the gardens and the car park. Henry and Ali scaled it and reached the secluded parking lot. The SUV was waiting for them. Henry jumped in the front, Ali at the back. Wasim slid the car steadily out of the hotel's driveway as men were walking out of the hotel front door. Their car turned left into Malahi Avenue and deserted streets. Ali was clutching his little bundle of belongings. They looked at him in the rear-view mirror. There was nothing else showing on his face but fear.

"The Treasurer is looking for us." Wasim took some of the back streets.

Henry turned his head as Wasim drove past a street he thought he should have turned into. "What are you doing?"

"We've got to get out of here right now... Within a few minutes the streets are going to be crawling with The Treasurer's men looking for us."

"No way..." Henry's face jerked to face Wasim. "I'm not leaving her behind."

"We have no option. We must get out of Raqqa immediately." Wasim clenched the wheel so hard that the veins of his hands bulged. He was focused on navigating the SUV through the maze of Raqqa's small streets.

"Stop the bloody car..." Henry slammed the dashboard.

"No." Wasim kept going, moving steadily towards the outskirts.

"They'll kill her if we don't get her out."

"You don't know that."

"I gave her my word..." Henry's rucksack was in the back. He turned around, met Ali's panicked face for an instant but still yanked the bag across and stuffed it in the small well in front of his feet. He fished the USB keys out. "These are in the inner pocket rucksack." Henry fetched the Glock from the rucksack, shoved it in his waistband in the small of his back. "Stop the car or I'll jump as you're driving along."

Wasim glanced at him. Henry's hand was resting on the door handle. He meant what he said. Wasim parked the car at the back of an old building. "Every minute we delay could cost us our escape. This is the mission."

"Saving the hostages has become part of the mission."

They turned to face each other awkwardly in the car.

"You take the USB keys and go ahead. I'm getting Mattie out." Henry had become resolutely calm.

"You won't make it out of Raqqa alive."

"I'll take my chance."

"Henry, the exchange deal with the hostages is agreed... Mattie has a good chance to come out of it unharmed."

"She won't and you know it."

Wasim slammed the wheel, reversed in an angry semicircle spin and drove back towards the centre of Raqqa. "You have five minutes... If you're not out by then, I'm driving off."

"Understood."

They reached the block of apartments that was their new destination ten minutes later. Wasim parked the SUV a few streets away.

"Five minutes."

Henry nodded. He donned his camouflage jacket and left the car. Two guards were at the door, eating from a plate that was overflowing. Henry did not acknowledge them and just walked in. He stopped from time to time on his way to the second floor, listening for movements in the building. He walked to the door of apartment 2 and knocked loudly.

There was nothing for a moment. He knocked again as the locks were unbolted one by one and the door opened on an old woman in full niqab.

Henry pushed his way in. "I have come to take the British journalist away. Fetch her for me."

The woman had closed the door and did not move.

"Shall I fetch her myself?" The anger in his voice did not need to be faked. He was taking Mattie away whether the old woman liked it or not.

"I have not been told." The woman hesitated, the eyes underneath the niqab unsure.

"I am telling you now…"

The woman turned around towards the lounge and entered the kitchen. Henry did not wait for her to come back. He ran down to the last door in the corridor and tried to open it. "Mattie."

He heard footsteps. "I'm here. The door's locked."

Henry assessed the wood panel, good quality but nothing his army boots could not handle.

"Step away from the door."

Henry gave it a vicious kick. The sound of splintering wood echoed around the walls. Henry gave the door the foot again. This time the hinges caved in and it flew open in a crash of metal and wood. Mattie had dressed in a black abaya and niqab. He crossed the threshold and she threw herself in his arms. He held her tight for a few seconds.

"We must go."

The old woman was running towards them. Henry couldn't draw his gun, as the shots would surely alert the guards. He let her come towards him. The swing of the knife she was holding missed him, just. A back-foot kick came down with a vengeance against her back and the woman collapsed on the floor. His fist did the rest and the woman stayed still. Mattie hesitated and stepped over the limp body.

They walked out of the apartments. The guards stopped eating for a moment. They saw a man with a woman in his footsteps and smiled, a man about to have a good time.

The SUV was waiting a few yards away from the entrance. The door opened and Mattie stepped in, next to Ali. Henry looked around. The car slowly glided forward. Mattie took the face scarf down and Ali's eyes widened. His face broke into a joyful smile. It was good to see Mattie again.

"Ali, do you have the clothes I asked you to bring?"

"Yes, Abu Shabh."

"Give them to Mattie."

340

Wasim shook his head despite himself... brilliant idea.

"Change into these. They will be looking for two men with a woman in a truck, not four guys in an SUV."

"Short hair was a good idea after all." Mattie took the bundle of clothes. Mattie started taking off the abaya and Ali turned away from her. Even in the darkness of the car, his cheeks glowed.

"Close your eyes. I'll tell you when I'm finished."

Mattie wriggled out of the heavy dress. She had very little on underneath and Henry caught himself looking at her in the rear-view mirror. She smiled back at him with a side look that was humorous rather than offended. It was Henry's turn to feel his cheeks warming a little.

* * *

Wasim again avoided the main avenues of Raqqa. He turned into small streets and down little lanes as if he had lived all his life in the city. They had lost 20 minutes and Henry gave him a sideways look. He could have sworn that, despite the strain to make up the time, Wasim had had a weight lifted from his shoulders. He too did not want Mattie harmed.

"Did a good recce of possible exits when you were at the Treasury," Wasim answered Henry's puzzled look. His grip on the wheel was firm and yet fluid. It was gone 8.30pm when they reached the outskirts of the city. Wasim slowed down, found a slot and parked the car.

"We are about to drive into Fardos Gate Street, getting out of the city. There is a checkpoint that we can't avoid. We are on a mission for the Treasury, destination undisclosed." Everyone nodded.

"OK." Wasim moved into gear. "Let's do this."

The checkpoint came into view at the next bend in the road: four men, armed with sub-machine guns. Two of them were surveying the street and two leaning against the bonnet of the car that helped close the road. The light had not completely faded away, but Wasim had switched on the headlights as they had resumed their journey. His window was the only one down. He greeted the soldiers that slowly came his way. They looked around the inside of the car briefly as

Wasim produced the letter embossed with The Treasurer's seal.

"It's late to be leaving Raqqa."

"We need to reach our destination by morning, no other choice if we are to fulfil The Treasurer's orders."

One of the guards had moved to the other side of the car. Henry felt the Glock against the small of his back. He returned the soldier's stare with irritation and impatience. The guard finished his inspection and chatted to the other man in a low voice. Wasim's hands had turned white on the steering wheel. Henry could take the two men standing next to the car easily. It would be more difficult to deal with the two men at the gate.

The first guard leaned against the window and handed over the pass. He jerked his towards the gate that stood in their way. "Safe journey, may Allah protect you."

"May Allah protect you too, brother." Wasim eased the SUV toward the gate. One of the guards opened it. He drove away as quickly as he could without arousing suspicion. A long exhalation came out of everyone in the car. It seemed they had all forgotten to breathe for a short moment.

* * *

They had been driving in silence for about three hours, each lost in their own thoughts, when Wasim turned off Route 3 into a side road that looked badly maintained. "We all ought to eat something, and I need to get the map out to decide on our best course across the rough terrain."

Mattie and Henry had moved to the boot where food had been packed for the journey. Ali got out last. He did not know where he was and looked around for clues. Henry called him and his grumbling stomach told him he needed food. They ate quickly what had been brought out and spread on the car's bonnet. No one spoke, focused on the food and the journey ahead.

The landscape was almost lunar. They had left behind the lush greens of Raqqa's suburbs, and the fields that grew along the Euphrates river. Mattie walked a few paces away from the car towards a desert of flat stones and dust. She watched the other men and wondered who had decided to take Ali with them. She had not asked where they were going but her sense was that they were heading towards Iraq.

She understood.

Scrambling an SAS force to drop in the middle of Syria or Iraq required planning and a knowledge of the location they were targeting for the operation. They had to get nearer a base the UK or perhaps the Peshmerga operated from.

Basra was at least 1,000 miles away. Their best bet was with the Kurdish fighters. Mattie had written about the new women fighters of Kurdistan, fearless and hard as nails. She had been amazed by their determination and their ability to put their lives on the line. Each carried a hand grenade and when asked why they had said they would never be captured alive by IS.

Henry and Ali were speaking. The young man froze, stunned. He started shaking his head and Mattie could hear raised voices. She ran back towards the group. Wasim had joined Henry in trying to pacify Ali. The young man dropped to the ground and started sobbing.

"What on earth is going on?" Mattie had knelt next to Ali.

"We're going to Mosul." Henry's voice was flat. He did not dare look Mattie in the eye.

Mattie's throat tightened. She had been made to watch the scenes of the IS victory on TV and had been forced to close her eyes at some of the scenes. She had seen her fair share in her years as war correspondent but never so much gratuitous violence of that magnitude. "Why?"

"Because everyone is going to look for us going towards Aleppo."

"But Aleppo is, what, five hours from Raqqa."

"Then we have to make contact there and be extracted. Aleppo will be swarming with IS fighters and cells, factions fighting for and against Assad." Henry's face had regained its determination. That was not the right route.

"Mosul, no one will be looking for us there, and from there we make contact with the Kurds."

Mattie tried to put a hand on Ali's shoulder, but he edged away. He took the bottom of his black shirt and wiped his face with it.

343

Henry crouched down too. "It's OK. You've seen some terrible things out there, but we have to contact people who can help us." Henry had switched to Arabic.

Ali shook his head. "You know nothing..." he replied in English.

Wasim had taken his laptop out of his rucksack and laid it on top of the car bonnet. He tried to pick up a signal but there was nothing there, unsurprisingly. "We wish there could be an easier way," he added.

Ali half turned his face towards him. He turned back around, Henry still crouching in front of him. He nodded slowly and stood up to meet Wasim's eyes.

"Then," Ali's voice was still trembling and broken, "you need to know what to prepare for."

Wasim walked back to the SUV and jumped into the driver's seat. Henry and Mattie joined him. Ali looked around before getting in. In a few moments he would tell them all that he knew, and that effort would be heart wrenching.

Wasim had decided on a route... They would be avoiding main roads, concentrating on dirt tracks and rough terrain crossing. They had been driving over flat terrain for over an hour when the track started to steepen. Mattie recognised the typical bulk that formed part of the Iraqi landscape. Rocks carved into hills and crevices, dried by the unforgiving sun and eroded by the winds that blew all year round. The SUV started to shake one way, then the other, and the bumpy ride quickly became an odd rhythm. Wasim had slowed down almost to a walking pace. The vehicle kept sliding on the flat pebbles that the rock had broken into before they themselves turned into the grey dirt that pervaded everything. Everybody was silent, in an effort of concentration, willing the vehicle forward.

Mattie checked the clock on the dashboard. It was almost midnight. The sun would be rising again in five hours' time. This did not leave them much time to ensure they reached Mosul by the morning. She was trying to remember the layout of Mosul when Wasim pulled hard on the brake and the car stopped abruptly.

The track ahead had turned into rubble. Wasim wound down the window and put his head out. They were close to a ridge. There was little room for him to open the door and he could not quite see where the drop was on the other side.

"I'll go and take a look." Henry pulled his rucksack onto his knees. "I can lead you with the torch until we've reached safer ground."

Wasim nodded. Henry opened the door and moved a foot out to leave the car. He could not find solid ground and his body started to tilt sideways. He could feel the sucking effect of the void below. Two hands grabbed him and pulled him back in. The car slid sideways a little. "Move to the left." Wasim shouted. Henry threw his weight towards him. The car stopped rocking and remained still.

Henry slid cautiously back into the seat and directed the beam of his torch onto the side of the vehicle. There was hardly any space between the wheel of the car and the sheer drop to the ravine below.

"I need to get to the other side." Henry squeezed over Wasim and pushed his body out through the open window. The SUV started rocking again. Henry stopped when he was halfway out. When the rocking stopped, he moved out as slowly as he could. The road had narrowed dangerously. He directed the light towards the roadside. There would be just enough space for the car to move across the rubble. Henry walked up the slope and reached the top. The entire road was a mess of collapsed rocks and earth. He directed the light behind the car. They couldn't turn back. This was going to take time. Time they did not have.

Chapter Thirty-Four

Henry's mobile phone had not moved from the hotel. Amina checked the GPS location again. She did not yet want to think the worst. OMA had not reported any chat on the platforms IS used, nothing on WhatsApp or Facebook. James had been a real sport. He had brought back some Nando's chicken from the restaurant underneath the Vauxhall arches and managed to find Caffe Italia after Amina had mentioned it was the best. It was about to close but he had begged for two large cups of the strong Italian brew.

James was reviewing all the data they had collected. There was nothing he could contribute... yet. "You say they are still going ahead with the exchange?" He had moved his chair away from his desk to come and sit next to Amina. "If Henry and Wasim have been compromised, it may be that we need to use Abu Maeraka as a bargaining chip," James wondered.

"I made the point to Steve. Steve has made the point to Sir John. Sir John's reluctant to speak to the Home Office. He'd rather not disclose MI6 has two operatives in Raqqa until absolutely necessary."

James shook his head. "He worries about leaks."

"And the Home Office wants the deal done, it seems."

"Colmore MP is pushing?"

"Not so sure. There must be something else. Releasing Maeraka against a single hostage is not a good deal."

Amina fell silent. Her forehead now bore a permanent crease that never softened.

"Henry is resourceful... the damned man conned everyone in the City, me included."

"Yes, but you're not IS are you?"

"Still, my feeling is that they have left Raqqa. Henry knows when to cut his losses. He went to get the data he was after back to London. If anybody can pull it off, he will."

"And Wasim won't be in touch until they are way out of that city… agreed."

"Is there any other device they might have used that can give us their whereabouts?"

"Wasim had removed the hard drive from his laptop as he reached Raqqa. In case his laptop was investigated."

"That was wise." James nodded. "Has it got GPS?"

"Yes, but…" Amina thought things through. "You've got a point… Wasim would not have left it in his room. He would have carried it around with him at all times."

Amina brought up the map of Raqqa. Wasim's hard drive had roamed around an area of Raqqa that was suburbia, towards the north of the city. The tracking was showing the device coming and going over the same ground in loops and then moving to the edge of the city where one of the main exit roads lay.

James took over the mouse and clicked on the map again. He zoomed on the furthest point the hard drive had reached.

"They've left the city going north-east."

Amina moved closer to her desk, eyes retracing the tracking lines of Wasim's hard drive. How could she have missed it? The pattern became clear. Wasim was on reconnaissance, trying to establish the optimal way to leave Raqqa. He had started yesterday late and resumed his driving around in the morning.

"They've left already." James's eye glimmered with excitement. "Wasim's left his phone behind as a decoy. They are on their way."

Amina walked to the large digital map that stayed permanently projected on the office wall. "If they have left, they will seek to make contact asap. But they need to put some real distance between Raqqa and their contact location… also the cover can be patchy."

"Agreed… or perhaps they are seeking contact not only with London but with other friendlies."

"Two options. The Syrian rebels or the Kurds." Amina traced the patches of territories that belonged to both groups.

"The Syrian rebels means Aleppo," James's voice trailed.

"That makes sense. They could reach Aleppo in four or five hours."

"But they'll encounter roadblocks, patrols and the entrance into Aleppo will be risky coming from the east." James shook his head. "Why leave the city through the north-east in that case... it adds travelling time."

"Another decoy?" Amina suggested. "Still it's the obvious route and exactly where everyone is going to look for them."

"Correct."

"OK." Amina ran her fingers along the digital map again. "If they want to reach the Kurdish army, they'll go towards Iraq."

"Which is what the tracking map of Wasim's hard drive tells me."

"Al-Hakasah is a possibility. Steve is working on this..."

James surveyed the map for a moment. "But a direct route between Raqqa and Al-Hasakah takes them through a large expanse of IS territory, and then territory that's being fought over by Assad's army and the rebels."

"And they don't know about Steve's plan because he couldn't connect with them in time," Amina agreed.

"I'd go to Mosul." James had stood up and moved over to the map as well.

"That's crazy... you worry about IS territory and yet you think Mosul is safe for them."

"It's not about safety... It's about improbability and doing what no one will expect them to do whilst achieving their goal."

Amina looked puzzled. "OK. It's improbable they may want to cross the desert and go to Mosul of all cities, granted."

"And because the territory between Mosul and Raqqa has not been consolidated within IS territories yet. There is a large Kurdish community in Mosul. They're more likely to find the right contact there."

Amina made a face. "And the Kurdish territories extend right to the outskirts of Mosul."

"Exactly."

348

"We need to speak to Steve."

James looked at the clock. It was gone 10pm.

Amina dialled Harris's mobile. He picked up after the second ring. She placed the phone on loudspeaker and took him through what had been discussed.

Harris did not interrupt.

"We've just received information about the exchange." Harris's voice sounded tired.

"Still between Aleppo and Raqqa?" James moved closer to the phone to place his question.

"That's right."

"What's your thinking?" Harris perked up at the thought that James might have a way to delay the exchange.

"Not sure. They can't do this in the open. They know there will be a drone strike the minute Maeraka is released."

"I've asked myself that." Harris muffled a yawn.

"Then we don't have the final location yet… They'll change it at the last minute."

James changed tack. "Does Maeraka know he's coming out?"

"No way. No one wants him beating the jungle drum about his release at least until it's done."

"Perhaps, but if Maeraka knows he's coming out and other people do too, then al-Baghdadi and his war council will find out that he knows. They will want the exchange to be a success."

The phone went silent for a while.

"I doubt the Home Office is going to be willing." Amina bent towards the phone.

"Who said he would go through the official channels?"

"We force their hand on Aleppo, this helps with our exchange too and it focuses them on the wrong city." Harris loved it.

"Got to make some calls…" Harris killed the line.

"Now what?" Amina finished her coffee.

"We wait."

* * *

The SUV was crawling along the track. Wasim had insisted Mattie and Ali leave the vehicle. Henry kept shining the torch to the right of it to help Wasim navigate the path. It was well past midnight and the sun would rise in four hours. Mattie and Ali had gone ahead equipped with their own torch. The worst was yet to come. A part of the track had crumbled away to such an extent that a couple of planks had been used to lay over the ravine. Henry stopped Wasim from continuing. He went to check the makeshift bridge and tested the planks with the heel of his boot. The wood beneath stood firm. Still they looked perhaps strong enough for a small truck but may not withstand a large SUV.

"You'll have to get over them as fast as you can…"

Wasim nodded and brought the SUV to the edge of the rubble. Part of the right hand wheel would hang over the side of the wooden structure. Henry moved a few yards ahead, giving Wasim enough room to accelerate. Wasim revved the engine. The SUV leapt forward with a sharp crunching noise. The planks started giving way under the weight of the vehicle and as the back wheels moved over them, they collapsed into the void. The wheels spun, sending rocks flying around and the SUV jumped over the large gash in the track. The sounds of falling debris reverberated from the ravine.

Henry ran to the bonnet and banged it with the flat of his hand. "Bloody well done!"

Wasim fell out of the car. He sat down on the track for a moment. Mattie and Ali shouted in relief.

Henry gave his shoulder a gentle squeeze. "Shall I take over?"

Wasim nodded. "I'm done for the night."

* * *

The track improved and it soon led them to a dual carriageway. They had reached Route 47, a direct line to Mosul. It was now gone 1am. Henry pushed the car's speed to over 60 mph. They needed to make up time.

By 2am a few lights had materialised in the distance. They were approaching the border between Syria and Iraq. A checkpoint had been erected there.

350

IS or Iraqi forces?

Wasim took a Sig Sauer out of his backpack. Another gun had been left beneath his seat. Henry cast an eye towards the back of the vehicle, sliding the gun in his trousers' waistband. Mattie's face was hidden in the shadows of the dark windows. Ali moved forward, head between the seats.

"Is it IS?" Henry looked at him in the rear-view mirror.

"Yes." Ali looked back at Henry. "Two days ago, when I came back, it was."

"Let's switch."

Wasim nodded. It would be more credible to have a fluent Arabic speaker at the wheel. The switch happened in a flash and the SUV started moving forward at a good pace again. Ali had spoken little about Mosul. After his warning it seemed he did not want to recall what he had seen there.

"Do you know any of these people?"

"No."

"Good."

The man saw the light of the car approach and they moved forward towards it. The Kalashnikovs were prepped, ready to be used in a flash. Two men in the front, two men at the back, looking alert despite a 2am check. Wasim opened the window. He greeted the young men as they approached the vehicle. He presented The Treasurer's letter. One of the men shone a torch into the vehicle. The second guard moved forward and took the paper, inspecting it with his own light.

"It's dangerous to be on your own at night with a single vehicle."

"But we have to take the risk for the good of the caliphate… Inshallah…"

The young man was still fingering the pass, unconvinced.

"We need to reach Mosul by early morning."

The pass was handed over to the other guard. They were in no hurry to let them through. Two other vehicles had been parked at the side of the road. If they had more fighters waiting in them, there was no hope of escape.

Ali bent forward. Henry's jaw tightened. You'll have to deal with him. If Ali wanted out this was the time. Henry was reluctant to reach for his gun he could feel in the small of his back. He heard the young man murmur a few words to Wasim he did not understand.

Wasim slapped the wheel and quoted the Al-Ahzab, one of the Qur'an's sura that spoke about believers' courage, those who remained steadfast against the hypocrites who ran for safety, abandoning the Muslim army and doubting Allah and the Prophet. A slap in the face couldn't have shamed the young man more. He waved at the other guards, handing over the pass to Wasim. The gate opened and the SUV sped through.

"Well done. Al-Ahzab sura... brilliant idea." Wasim smiled, shaking his head.

Ali poked his head through the headrests. He was smiling at last. His face turned serious again. "There are another three roadblocks before we reach Mosul."

The glow of sunrise had appeared on the horizon. They had gone through two roadblocks already; one last one before they reached Mosul.

Henry was back at the wheel. They would switch again before the last checkpoint. He had squeezed a bottle of water in the door's pocket and took a few slugs. Everyone in the car was asleep. Ali had proven helpful once more. Henry was glad of it.

Henry opened the window to let in some fresh air. He cast an eye at his crew. Mattie was asleep, her eyes quivering slightly. The dark scarf that she had wrapped around her head jihadi-style suited her. Henry's stomach fluttered. He was glad she had left Raqqa with them. Wasim's head had rolled slightly towards the side of the vehicle, his arms crossed over his chest, napping.

Henry yawned, took another sip of water. The colours in the sky changed gradually, a range of purples, pinks and soft yellows that spread over the landscape, giving it form and life. Wasim moved around in his seat, finding a more comfortable position for his broad back. Gratitude was too weak a word; Wasim had been a teacher and someone he would call a friend. Never judging, simply accepting the man he had to train for who he was.

The sun finally poked over the horizon. Henry slowed down a

352

little. Despite the rising sun a cluster of lights appeared in the distance. The lights of Mosul had not been extinguished yet. Henry glanced at his watch. Almost 4.30am. They would be entering the city's suburbs in half an hour. Henry nudged Wasim a little. He grunted quietly and opened his eyes with difficulty. He rubbed them with his curled fingers in a child-like manner.

"Are we there?"

"Almost."

"OK. Need to change driver."

"As agreed, I'll wake the others when we are back on the road."

Both men got out of the car, stretched, yawned. Henry finished his bottle. Wasim splashed some of his water on his face and drank the rest. The SUV was now covered in dust and a dent had appeared on the driver's side, no doubt inflicted when crossing the hill on the dirt track. Wasim jumped into the driver's seat. Henry joined him in the front seat. The journey continued. Henry stretched his arm between the front seats and shook Ali's arm gently. The young man woke up with a jolt.

"We're nearly there."

Ali rubbed his eyes, and for a moment his face looked puzzled. Where was he? The memories of the journey and those of its destination made him focus, with only one feeling showing. Dread.

Henry woke up Mattie last. He took the hand that was resting next to her leg on the seat and squeezed it gently. She smiled and opened one eye.

"I was dozing." She stretched a little, rolled her head around slowly. There was something boyish about her that Henry found attractive. She reached for the water bottle in the side pocket of her seat and drank the lot.

"What do you remember about the approach to Mosul?" Wasim's words reminded everyone that they were approaching the city.

"The crosses, and..." Ali hesitated. "The executions... lots of them."

The silence that followed was only interrupted by the faint sound of the car rolling on the road.

"What about the city itself?" Henry's throat felt dry and strangled.

353

Navigating his people safely in and out of Mosul was certainly going to test his resourcefulness as well as his mettle.

Something changed in the atmosphere of the car. Mattie was the first one to react. She stuck her head between the two seats, unable to ignore it any longer.

"Do you smell that?"

"We're approaching," was all Ali could say. The young man retreated into his seat and brought his knees to his chest, burying his head into them. The smell grew stronger and both Henry and Wasim noticed. Wasim wound up the window. His shoulders rose a fraction, his hands grasped the wheel more tightly. Henry was still puzzled. The smell was a mix of acetone and rotting meat, so pungent it made his stomach heave.

There was still no one on the road and Wasim slowed down the vehicle. In the distance they could see it. A sea of crosses. A vision of what Calvary on Mount Golgotha might have looked like 2,000 years earlier. There were perhaps 20, 30 crosses, maybe more. Henry's stomach lurched and he had to use all his will not to vomit. Most crosses had a body nailed on them, in various states of decomposition, the birds having already started their work in the early morning sun. They drove slowly, unable to say another word.

Mattie was the first to break the silence. "Who are they?"

"Iraqi army fighters." Ali's voice was muffled, his head against his knees, eyes shut. The smell intensified and the other three brought their scarves over their noses and mouths. Henry could see in the distance a mound of freshly dug-up earth alongside a long trench. He no longer had to ask Ali what it might be. They were passing mass graves, ready to receive the victims of IS summary executions. Henry counted four of them and a bulldozer had started creating another. The engine bulk, the teeth of its digger hanging in the air, felt ominous.

Was Mosul such a great idea after all?

The last checkpoint before entering the city was deserted. One guard was standing alongside the makeshift gate. He looked tired and grumpy, ready for the changeover. He cast an indifferent eye over the vehicle, focused briefly on The Treasurer's pass and opened the gate.

Everyone remained silent for a moment, still stunned by what they had just witnessed.

"Much easier than I thought." Henry felt he had to say something.

"We need to find the Kurdish quarter of Mosul." Wasim had picked up speed.

"Kurds like the Chahalis live on the left bank of the city. Al-Jaza'r or Al-Noor." Mattie had poked her head between the two seats. "I can get you there."

Henry turned his face away from the road. Mattie's profile was close to his shoulder, the delicate line of her nose, the slight curve of her cheekbone.

"How do you know?" Wasim sounded doubtful.

"I covered the 2003 invasion of Mosul by the American army. Two sons of Saddam Hussein were killed there. I hung around a bit longer once it became safer to move around the city. It's very beautiful and ancient... a place where many religious people have coexisted for centuries."

"People who left or tried." Ali had unfolded his legs.

Wasim and Mattie directed their attention to negotiating the streets of Mosul. It was almost 6am and the city should have been waking up. People would start going about their business before the blazing summer heat of the midday sun. But Mosul had become a ghost town.

Mattie craned her neck, moved from between the two headrests to her side of the window. "I know where we are. We are arriving on the eastern side of the city." She closed her eye in an effort to remember. "There is a roundabout of some sort... and then... turn left and you're very close to one of the bridges, crossing the Tigris."

Wasim accelerated and the car came quickly to a complex set of converging roads. He took a sharp left again.

"We're in the Muhamadeen district where the vaults of the Trade Bank are... the ones we're supposed to be investigating," Henry reminded everyone. He bent forward to check the gun underneath his seat was ready for use and lowered his window, ready to take a shot. To his surprise another vehicle had stopped at the bridge checkpoint. The truck looked well used and dirty. The man who owned it was standing on the road, the door still open, hands over his head. One of the guards was looking into the truck. A few boxes containing supplies were gathered together under a tarpaulin sheet. He took a couple of apples out of one of the crates, rubbed one a few times against his jacket. He handed the second apple to the other guard.

Wasim moved closer, almost level with the truck. The smaller guard turned his attention away from the driver.

"We need to cross the bridge as soon as possible." His voice was blunt, giving orders that would not be challenged. He presented The Treasurer's pass. The man's angry face relaxed.

"We are going to Al Muhamadeen, to inspect the vaults of the Trade Bank on behalf of The Treasurer."

The SUV looked dirty, but it also looked brand new and expensive. They had travelled from Raqqa overnight. It must be important.

The smaller man moved his head towards the bridge. The second guards swung the gate open and Wasim rushed through.

A few vehicles had now appeared on the streets. Most of them bearing either the flag or the seal of IS painted on their bonnet. Wasim followed the main road for a short while and turned right towards the older part of Mosul. The building looked ancient, a rich architecture, ornate, with mosaics, carved woods and delicate decorations. Mosul would have been a beautiful city to visit.

"Where now?" he asked.

Mattie squinted. "Turn left at the next big intersection, then keep going straight on. We should drive past the Mosque of Prophet Yunus. We enter Al-Jaza'r after that."

The buildings became more modern. Trees had been planted in the small gardens that lay at their entrances. The area felt wealthy and inviting. The large dome of the mosque appeared on their right as Mattie had predicted. They had reached Al-Jaza'r.

Wasim drove on and found a smaller street in which he parked the car. Henry walked towards one of the apartment blocks. He mechanically checked the Glock that he had stuck again into the small of his back. The main entrance of one of the buildings looked deserted. He rang the doorbells… no reply. Henry pushed the wooden door expecting resistance. It gave way and he entered quietly. He closed his hand over the grip of his gun. One of the doors was ajar. He waited outside, listening for anything that could indicate a presence. He opened the door with the tip of his boot. Henry drew his Glock and

356

stepped in. The property had been ransacked, debris of crockery and ornaments lay on the floor. He walked across the ground floor slowly, encountering the same disaster landscape, scraps creaking underneath his feet. He stopped to listen again. Nothing. He reached the first floor. Bedroom doors were open. Henry hoped that whoever had lived here had left in a hurry and that the ransacking had happened afterwards. He came down, walked out and signalled that they could come in.

"Let's set up camp here." Wasim dumped his rucksack and handed Henry his. Mattie and Ali followed carrying their meagre belongings.

"And let's decide what we need and how we're going to get it." Henry closed the door and joined them inside.

Chapter Thirty-Five

Steve Harris killed the alarm before it started ringing. Sarah was asleep and he gingerly swung his legs out of bed. For a short moment he sat hunched forward, thinking about the previous evening's meeting at the Home Office. There had been recriminations and finger-pointing. Still, the exchange of one hostage had been agreed. His team on the ground had gone dark. They had almost certainly left Raqqa, but he was not sure for where. Mosul was an option. James and Amina had put forward a good case for it. Brett's contact had been tough when it came to the money... he had presented his begging bowl to The Chief... $200,000 per person was a rather large donation... but he hadn't received an are-you-insane reply. There had to be hope.

A warm hand landed on his back and its contact reminded him he was halfway out of bed. "Sorry." Harris murmured "Did I wake you?"

"No." She squeezed his shoulder and nudged closer to him. "Are you working a real time zone?"

"Yep." Harris turned back and leaned on his elbow to get closer to his wife.

"How many time zones are you working then? You came back late last night."

"I'm... It's complicated at the moment." Harris took her hand and gave it a warm squeeze.

"Don't worry. Me and the dog are doing fine... I'm just making sure you have enough rest."

"Thank you. You're a star." Harris landed a kiss on her neck and Sarah giggled.

He sighed. "Got to go."

Sarah disappeared underneath her covers and Harris stood up. He so wished he could have stayed.

Amina was already in. Three cups of piping hot coffee were waiting in the Caffe Italia holder. She too had had little sleep. James had arrived last, grumbling about the journey. He had brought up a map of Mosul on his computer, looking at the details of the city's neighbourhoods.

"If the Kurdish connection is the link to follow, they've got two options, Al-Jaza'r or Al-Noor."

"Not many people have had time to flee, according to OMA." Amina was sipping her coffee, one of many that would keep her awake during another gruelling day.

"And the traffickers will know that. The immediate problem is how they can make contact without looking suspicious." Harris's hoarse voice made him sound crankier than he was.

"Perhaps we could make contact with the Kurdish cells in the Dubok area? They might be able to help."

"Why not... I'll see what contacts the Iraqi desk have there..." Harris finished his coffee. "But I bet they tell us all their efforts are focused on pushing back IS."

* * *

"You don't trust me?" Ali was sitting in the passenger seat. Henry, at the wheel, was following his instructions towards a shopping centre a few blocks away.

"Why do you say that?"

"I could take the car... do the shopping alone."

"I haven't known you for long, that is true... I won't lie to you, but it's not the reason."

Ali gave him a doubtful look.

"It is safer if we go in pairs in Mosul and I have to learn the layout of the area."

The explanation seemed to do the trick. Ali's forehead lost a few of its creases.

The shopping mall appeared at the corner of a small street. Henry parked the SUV at the end of it and they both made their way to the store. It was surprisingly busy: men who were unmistakably IS were out doing their shopping. Henry spotted the electrical shop he was looking for. He hesitated before entering, surveying the goods available from the shop window. The shopkeeper looked worried behind his counter, men in black shirts were browsing through the items on display, asking him questions. Henry could not dither any longer. He walked in and picked up a few items, a couple of chargers, batteries. Already phones had been confiscated and there were none on display. Ali had moved further inside the shop. He came back and nudged Henry. He had spotted a small portable TV. Henry nodded... a good idea. The two men had stopped their browsing, watching with interest the few items that Henry had laid on the counter. They seemed interested to find out what banknotes Henry would be producing to pay. Henry deliberately lined up his Syrian pounds. They retreated at the size of the denomination and the wedge he held in his hand. Henry and Ali took their time to walk out of the mall, then round the corner, rushed to reach the SUV. Henry glanced back towards the shops. No one had followed them.

They repeated the process for food and petrol in two different stores. So far so unexpectedly good.

"The Wi-Fi is weak." Wasim was helping to offload the car.

"We may not need it." Henry took the charger out of the bag he had brought in.

"If I were a Christian, I'd sing Hallelujah." Wasim took the charger, plugged in the phone and sat on the ground next to it, still working his laptop.

Henry looked around. The debris had been swept away and the furniture left behind, rearranged at the back end of the room, away from the windows.

"Outside?" Ali had come in with a brush and pan.

"Leave the crap that's still outside the door... we'll use it as an alarm if someone comes close." Henry moved to where Wasim had sat down. He checked the phone. The little battery was pumping in energy like a slow-beating heart. In a short while they would be able to communicate.

Ali set up the TV. He moved the antenna around to get an image... but only grey static materialised on the screen. He tried again the position of the aerial and the sound of a news programme reverberated around the room. He turned the volume down. He started searching for the right channel to watch.

Wasim ignored the TV and called up a map of Iraq he had saved in a file on his laptop.

"If we go north, we enter Kurdish territory." Henry nodded. He sat down next to Wasim. Mattie and Ali were still focusing on the TV.

"But we need a contact. The Kurds are not going to listen to four people dressed in the IS uniform and they certainly are not going to believe two of them are MI6 operatives."

"That's true..." The phone beeped. The battery was full. Wasim picked it up... time to let MOTHER know they had reached Mosul.

* * *

The DATA OPS team that covered Iraq and Kurdistan was working an emergency 24/7 schedule. The shock of the Mosul battle and the unstoppable IS advance had put the department on high alert and shocked everyone. Except perhaps their Kurdish contacts who had thought the Iraqi army was grossly underestimating IS.

"Do you have a moment?" Harris approached the desk of one of the analysts. He made time for Dan whenever he needed it and Dan was happy to reciprocate. They went to one of the small secure meeting rooms.

"What's up?"

"I need to know whether any of our Kurdish contacts can extract people from Mosul?"

Dan whistled. "That's a big ask. IS is trying to push past Mosul at the moment."

"I'm sure they are, but still. There's a large Kurdish community in Mosul or perhaps was. I'm sure people are desperate to leave."

"And the Kurds are likely to help..." Dan looked up to find the clock on the wall. "I'm due to have a catch-up call in ten minutes with

361

one of my contacts. You can join in if you'd like. He'll give you a realistic update on the Kurdish army resources near Mosul."

A few people he knew had gathered for the call. It was all about IS's new caliphate. The Kurdish forces were as ever keen to tackle them, but they needed help and their relationship with the Iraqi government was always strained.

The Kurdish agent who came on the line was late. He had been assembling the latest data for the call and it was not good. "IS is pushing and succeeding on several points. We have no support from the Iraqi army. IS knows the terrain well. Some of them are either ex-Iraqi army who have deserted or former members of Saddam Hussein's Ba'ath party."

"How well connected are they locally?" Dan asked.

"Very well… and they can exploit the weaknesses of the Iraqis. We need better weapons and more equipment. IS has seized a whole arsenal of guns, RPGs… helicopters and armoured vehicles in Mosul."

Harris introduced himself. "What is the situation in Mosul? Are you able to extract people?"

"Very difficult. We are trying to help those who are now stuck there but IS is closing its fist over the city. In a couple of days, it will be almost impossible, and our commander won't take a chance. He needs his men on other fronts."

"What about today or tomorrow?" Harris persevered.

"We can attempt to extract people tonight, just after nightfall."

Harris nodded. "As people prepare to eat after the day's fasting?"

"Correct. It's usually a good time. If your people can be at the rendezvous point, I'll speak to Commander Sanjabi and come back to you in an hour."

"Much appreciated." Harris had moved close to the loudspeaker to make himself heard. He withdrew and sat down. He might as well listen to the rest of the conversation – important information might come his way.

His mobile vibrated, a little buzz that usually irritated him. But today Harris could not take the phone out of his pocket quickly enough.

"Made contact, need you back in Control Room asap."

*　*　*

Amina and James stood in front of the large map of the Middle East. They had meticulously reviewed the latest intel from OMA on the progress of all the protagonists in Syria and Iraq. A phone rang and it seemed unimportant against mapping the terrain and the area around Mosul. James turned around. "It's your phone, right?"

Amina nodded, froze for a second: MOTHER's phone was ringing.

She almost tripped over to reach it and lunged to press the answer button.

"Hello," was all she managed to say. The aged voice using a voice transformation program sounded comforting.

"Mother. Your son Wasim is here." She could hear the strain mixed with relief in his voice.

Amina forced her voice to remain calm. "It is good to talk to you, Wasim. It has been a long time, my son."

"I have been busy. We are no longer in Raqqa."

Amina exhaled. The line was secure and Wasim was free to speak openly.

"We're in Mosul."

"You are?" Amina was not sure whether she was relieved or worried.

"We are, in the Al-Jaza'r district, the Kurdish quarter. We have found a place that has been raided and is empty."

"Is Henry with you?"

"Yes, and we also have Mattie Colmore with us."

Amina blinked a couple of times. "But the hostage negotiation is still going ahead... it's been agreed."

"If it is, Mattie is no longer the hostage."

"Harris is getting in touch with the Kurdish army to seek an extraction." This was a more pressing issue and they needed to know. The door opened, and a startled Harris dashed into the Control Room.

"Speak of the devil." Amina pressed the loudspeaker button and Wasim's voice filled the room.

"We're in Mosul."

"Don't repeat what you said to Amina, she'll brief me. I've had the Kurds on the phone. There will be an extraction tonight. They're giving us the rendezvous point in a couple of hours' time."

"I think we're safe till nightfall… But IS is all over Mosul. Al-Baghdadi has moved there after his caliphate address…"

"No longer your problem. Is Crowne OK?"

"He is. When you speak to the Kurds tell them we have four people to extract." Harris frowned. Amina mouthed *Mattie Colmore* and Harris broke into a grin.

"Mattie Colmore is with us and also a young fighter who has helped us escape."

Harris's grin disappeared. "An IS fighter?"

"That's right."

"I don't know whether the Kurds are going to allow that."

Wasim remained silent for a short moment. They could hear a muffled conversation at the other end of the phone.

"It's four or nothing." Henry had just come on the line.

"I'm not sure you're in a position to make that decision."

"I'm not sure you can afford to lose the intel I'm bringing back." Henry's bargaining voice had the right edge to make Harris think before he replied.

"Look, he's a young guy who is not a threat. We couldn't have made it here without him. Besides, he might become a good asset." Wasim had taken over from Henry.

"I'll see what I can do," Harris grumbled, but everybody knew he would do more than that and do all he could to get everyone out of Mosul.

* * *

The TV was working well enough and Ali had tuned into Bein HD4, the IS channel… video after video of propaganda, punishments for those who did not comply with IS rules followed by short lectures on its interpretation of Islam. Then came professionally slick short films of fighters, guns at the ready, throwing themselves into combat against the infidels and always defeating them. The news bulletin topped the hour, broadcasting reports of IS advances into new territory and more propaganda.

364

Henry and Wasim had decided to take it in turns to rest. Ali and Mattie had already disappeared and got much needed shut-eye too.

"I'm not surprised that some of the kids buy into all that crap." Henry could not help but comment.

"I know, it's well presented, polished. Not the amateurish rubbish everyone thought they would produce." Wasim yawned. Henry stood up from his cross-legged position, stretched. "You go first. I'll make some coffee and wait for the call, unless you'd rather talk to Harris?"

"Nah. I rather like the way you handled him. He sometimes needs to be told it the way it is." Wasim disappeared as well.

Henry didn't switch off the TV for fear he may lose the connection; still, the drivel annoyed him and he turned down the volume to a minimum. He walked to the kitchen, found an old dallah. He spooned coffee into it, poured some water and waited for the coffee to come to the boil. The blub blub of the pot and the aroma of the fresh brew somehow relaxed him.

He poured some into a thick glass cup, added some sugar and drank it slowly, in small sips. The liquid was burning hot. He had always liked drinking his tea as soon as it was made, a small habit he had taken from his mother.

It was now about 11am. He glanced again at the TV. More of the same. A woman was being punished by applying a jaw-like instrument that dug into her flesh. She had forgotten her gloves and shown her hand in public. Henry turned away from the screen. He had seen enough horrors in Raqqa and Mosul in only six days to know he had to deliver the USB keys to MI6.

* * *

We know where Mattie Colmore is had been Harris's message to Sir John. The first phase of the hostage-for-prisoner switch was only a few hours away, with Maeraka leaving HSU Belmarsh for one of the military air bases in the UK. He would be flown to Cyprus and then dropped by helicopter into Aleppo for the exchange.

"She's in Mosul with your team?" Sir John also seemed to be living off coffee judging by the impressive stack of empty cups piled on his desk.

"That's right, sir. I'm in touch with the Kurdish army. One of their commanders is ready to help with a possible extraction as early as today."

"Then what?"

"It depends whether the Kurds can deliver them close enough to the final rendezvous point we discussed near the border with Turkey."

"Why not pick them up from Iraq?"

"Because IS now has command of the helicopters left in Mosul by the Iraqi army and their weaponry has become much more sophisticated."

"You're telling me that flying an SAS team into the area is too risky?"

"Al-Hasakah is in Syrian Kurdistan and only five hours away from Mosul even if they take the side roads or dirt tracks. If the Kurds can escort them to the border with Syria... It will work."

"You've got a contact there, I presume?"

"I do."

Sir John drank some coffee; his eyes were focusing on something Harris could not see.

"IS is still talking exchange. I presume they have decided on a switch of hostage and not told us."

Harris nodded. "They can't afford to admit they've lost Mattie Colmore."

"Who knows about this?"

"My team and yourself."

"No one at the Home Office?"

"No..." Harris bit his lip a few times. "And if we leave it that way a second woman can be freed."

Sir John tapped his fingers on his desk a few times. "So, we say nothing. Get the exchange done, then what? If the Home Office realise we have not said anything it will be your head and mine on the block."

"And we will have freed Maeraka." Harris couldn't quite argue against that. "Unless we can guarantee a hit on him after his release."

"IS are not stupid. That's what they will expect. This is being done in Aleppo for a good reason."

"We could try to renegotiate, now that Mattie is not in Raqqa," Harris suggested. "But she's not out of IS territory, yet."

Sir John shook his head. "If we tell them we know they've lost her before they are safe, IS will send everyone looking for them."

"Colmore will do anything to avoid having his daughter's name linked to the exchange though," Harris fretted.

"I presume so too. His daughter for a much-wanted terrorist. Not good for someone who is so much against negotiating with terrorists."

Harris followed his idea through. "If we don't disclose what we know about Mattie to the Home Office, this would save him the embarrassment. He won't have any reason to complain."

"I know where you are going with this." Sir John kept stirring his coffee without drinking any of it. "You've got until the end of today. Then we disclose Mattie's situation."

* * *

Henry had nearly succumbed to sleep when Wasim appeared in the main room to take his turn.

"No update." Henry rubbed his eyes. "Not sure what to make of it."

"Probably a good thing." Wasim stretched. "You've turned the TV sound down?"

"May not be a good idea for sounds to come out of an empty apartment."

Wasim nodded. There was nothing wrong with being a little paranoid.

Henry walked to one of the bedrooms and lay down on the mattress that had been stripped of its bedding. He went straight to sleep.

A knife is at his throat. He does not want to open his eyes. He feels the sharpness of the blade that is about to cut his skin.

"Don't say a word." Someone is whispering and yet the words are spoken with such hatred. "You betrayed us." The voice's sharpness drills into him. "You've betrayed all of us."

Henry cannot move. He cannot defend himself for it is time. He betrayed the people whom he had called friends in London. He betrayed The Treasurer but of that he is glad. And yet there is Ireland, the O'Connors, for whom he has sacrificed his career and who have sold him to the British. Henry's chest burns. He wants to

367

cry out that he had believed and that he can be redeemed. The knife moves slowly. The pain is immeasurable. He opens his eyes wide. He yells a silent scream that will never be heard.

Henry sat up on the bed, his hand around his throat, panting, his body covered in sweat. He looked for the water bottle he had brought with him into the bedroom and finished it off in a few long pulls. He looked at his watch; he had slept for an hour. Henry shuddered and ran a hand over his face. He had not had one of those nightmares since he had left Belmarsh.

Why now?

Henry rolled onto his side and stood up. He made his way downstairs to join his team and stopped before entering the room. Mattie had also moved back to the main room. She looked peaceful, settled close to the TV and chatting with Wasim. Strong Mattie. Irresistible Mattie.

Ali was still asleep.

Henry walked into the room and joined the other two crouching in front of a tray on which someone had laid food and more coffee. Mattie smiled and asked whether he wanted anything. Henry nodded and she stood up to refresh the coffee. Henry cast an eye towards the TV set to avoid following Mattie's silhouette out of the room. Henry and Wasim talked once more about their next move. The TV had again become a feature in the background.

The noise of a broken cup startled them both. Mattie had dropped the cups she was bringing back. She stifled a cry with her hand. A programme was showing three faces. People whom IS had branded betrayers and infidels... most wanted amongst all. Henry, Wasim and Mattie's faces flashed on the TV screen with a one million dollar reward attached to their names and the praises of Commander Kasim al-Haddawi for being on the chase.

Chapter Thirty-Six

Harris was pacing up and down in the small meeting room. The call with Commander Sanjabi of the Kurdish Peshmerga had been delayed once more. It was already 1pm in Mosul.

Could the team make their way to Al-Hasakah from Mosul alone? It was a ridiculous idea. But so far Henry's plan had worked. Who would have thought they would go to a town already captured by IS?

No one... including IS itself.

Still the caliphate was well organised, and their use of good media cover was surprisingly savvy. They would soon put this to good use to track them down. Dan finally entered the room, already wearing an apologetic look.

"Heard some intel from the Kurds, the IS insurgents are marching towards Erbil. With their latest Iraqi recruits, they've got momentum."

"You mean Sanjabi can't extract my team until later? Is that it?"

"He said tomorrow at the earliest, perhaps even the day after that."

"That's not going to cut it." Harris paused, distracted, biting his lip a few times. "How about you tell them there is a journalist involved... If they get it right, she will do an interview of them?"

Dan raised an eyebrow. "Should you even be telling me that?"

"Almost certainly not, and most definitely not them, but I've got to get those guys out today."

"OK, it's your call, but..."

"Yes, yes, if it goes tits up I'll be in the firing line. I've been told that once today already."

"I'll speak to them again and call you back as soon as I have."

Harris walked out in a huff. This was a bloody war zone in which various factions were trying to kill each other in the most gruelling of ways and IS was the worst of the lot. What did Dan expect? A form filled in triplicate? Harris stopped in his tracks. He had not heard from Brett since yesterday. Time to remind the British aristocracy it had a deadline to meet. Harris's phone chimed: a text had been delivered.

Urgent, need you asap. "Shit, what now?" Harris broke into a jog to reach RED HAWK Control Room. Both Amina and James were on their respective computers, searching through data frantically.

"I've got it," James shouted. Amina rushed around to his side of his desk. Harris found them still not knowing what he was looking for. The short TV package was now playing on YouTube in a loop. It showed three mugshots of Henry, Wasim and Mattie, and confirmed a reward of one million dollars for their capture.

"When did it start showing?"

"A couple of hours ago. Wasim called as soon as they saw it."

"It's a lot of money too." James had moved to another screen to check the rate of exchange.

"If they don't leave Mosul today, they're fucked." Amina's clenched fist against her mouth distorted the words. But Harris got the gist.

"I've asked Dan to push the Kurds again."

"Otherwise they are going to have to chance it on their own." James's voice had the authority of a reliable risk assessor.

"They need the Peshmerga cover, otherwise they'll run into some of the other factions – Syrian army, Syrian rebels or even the Kurds if they don't know they're infiltrated agents – who'll shoot them first and ask questions after." Harris's phone chimed again. A text from Dan. *Commander Sanjabi on the phone now.*

Harris rushed out of the door, ran along the corridor, barely missing a couple of colleagues round the corner.

Dan was ready for him, holding the office door open. The call was on hold. Dan unmuted the phone. "Commander Sanjabi, my colleague is here."

"Good afternoon, Commander."

"Good afternoon. You speak of a journalist that is in Mosul?"

"That's right."

Words became muffled. Another conversation was taking place in the background which Harris could not make out. "…a woman with the name of Mattie Colmore?"

Dan frowned. Harris did not care. "Yes."

The line was muffled again, and another voice came on the line. "Good afternoon. This is Colonel Nahida Ahmed Rashid. If Mattie Colmore needs us we will help. Commander Sanjabi tells me you need to extract her today."

"Yes. There is a bounty on her head and that of the other people with her of a million US dollars."

There was a silence at the end of the line that lasted a long moment. Should he have told them that? "Then we will extract them tonight. I will give you a rendezvous point and the name of the team leader in one hour."

"Thank you." Harris closed his eyes and inhaled deeply. The phone went dead. Only one hour to go.

* * *

Wasim had moved the TV to the far end of the room where its glow could not be seen through the window. The mobile phone had been plugged in to keep it charged and everyone had huddled around the TV on the sofas left behind.

Henry checked his watch yet again and Mattie put a hand on his wrist. Her touch was warm and confident. He managed a smile. Had he made a mistake in choosing Mosul as the contact point for the Kurdish army? He let his head drop softly against the back of the couch and closed his eyes. It was already 3pm and the phone had not rung yet. "What are our chances of reaching Al-Hasakah unaided?"

"Next to zero." Wasim let his back slump into his seat.

"We could move property tonight… we can keep changing."

Wasim nodded. "If we're going to do that, we need a recce now. Curfew starts at nightfall. We'd have to move to the new place before then."

Henry leaned forward. "OK. I'll go with…"

371

The burner phone ring interrupted him. Wasim picked it up. He did not speak, simply nodding, looking for a pen and paper. Henry found a pen in his rucksack. Wasim wrote a few words on the back of his hand and hung up.

"We have a rendezvous point with a Peshmerga unit, in the grounds of Hasib Zkria mosque. 19.45. Code name: MOTHER."

"We need a map. How about your laptop?"

"IS monitor signals… not a good idea."

"We need to find a good old-fashioned paper map then…"

"I go." Ali had stood up slowly. "They don't know my face. Back to the shopping centre… I find map."

"I'll come with you." Mattie's confidence amazed everyone. "It's a woman they're looking for, not one dressed as a man. Besides, Ali can't drive with his wounded leg. I'll be fine." Henry was about to protest but he met Mattie's eyes. She would not change her mind.

"I've been in more war zones than you have, gentlemen… mark my words." She took the keys of the SUV and disappeared through the back door.

* * *

They came back much later than anticipated. Henry had started to check his watch every five minutes. The gate into the back yard opened softly. Wasim had been waiting in the kitchen manning the back door. Ali hobbled in first, holding a sheaf of thickly folded paper in his hand. He had bought two maps. One of the cities, one of the region stretching beyond the Iraqi border. Mattie came in last, secured the door and walked back into the kitchen.

"There were more cars on the streets than I had expected. They looked more like patrols than locals, but I can't be sure."

It was already 5pm. In two and a half hours' time, once the sun had set, they would make their way to Hasib Zkria.

Henry spread the map of the city on the floor. They all sat around it. Ali spotted the place, despite looking at the map upside down. The mosque was not far, only three blocks away.

"Perhaps we could walk it?" Wasim's voice sounded dry and gritty.

"So that we don't attract attention with the SUV." Henry nodded. "That could work."

"How about Ali?" Mattie frowned.

"I can do it, even with a…" Ali was looking for the word, "… stick, no crutch." His finger moving in the air to summon the right word.

"It's only a quarter of a mile and we can go through the smaller back streets." Wasim measured on the map.

"Compromise," Henry offered. "Let's drive the SUV through the back streets up to the first main road we have to cross. Then we finish on foot."

Everyone nodded. Wasim folded the map and retreated to one of the bedrooms. Henry had kept his rucksack with him. He sat back in the corner of the room where it lay and went through it methodically. He went through the ammunition he had left. Two spare clips for his Glock, three spares for the smaller weapon he kept hidden under the seat of the car.

The call to prayer resounded around Mosul. Ali disappeared for a short moment. Henry and Mattie prepared some of the food that was left in silence. Mattie uncapped a bottle of water, took a few long pulls and passed it to Henry to finish.

* * *

Dusk had settled over the city. The heat of the sun no longer made the air tremble over the road and pavement. They had not switched on the lights in the apartment and the semi darkness gave the room a gloomy look. Henry had spent some time at the window that looked onto the front garden. One vehicle had driven past and it had attracted his attention. But it had not returned, and he had started to feel a little more at ease.

"Ready?" Wasim had slung his rucksack over his shoulders, the Sig Sauer stuck into his belt and the spare clips in the pockets of his army khakis.

"Let's do this." Henry threw his own rucksack over his left shoulder. He pushed his Glock into the small of his back. Ali and

373

Mattie were already in the backyard. Henry closed the kitchen door behind him and Wasim half opened the door into the back alley. There was no light in most of the houses or flats around the small back streets. The area was almost deserted.

They climbed quickly into the SUV and Wasim started the engine. It came to life with a low rumble that echoed around the empty lanes. He drove slowly towards the end of the alleyway and eased the front of the car into the intersection. He turned left immediately into another back alley and made a few more of these turns avoiding the main streets. Wasim took a final left and came to an abrupt stop. Three vehicles had been burned down and left stranded in the middle of the lane.

"Shit." Wasim slammed his hand on the wheel.

Henry had turned back. "I saw a couple of cars pass the top of the lane as we were turning into this alleyway. We can't go back."

Henry opened the door. "Let's go. We're not that far from the main road."

Wasim went first, walking close to the walls of the buildings they passed along the way and crossing small gardens that looked well-tended.

In the darkness of night, Henry stopped and listened. The sound had gone away but was back again, much louder this time. Henry caught up with the other three and stopped Wasim. "There's a car in the area going up and down the streets." Henry's voice was low and urgent.

"OK." Wasim and the other two had stopped in the shadow of a building's doorway. "We're nearly there. The next road is the largest one before we reach Hasib Zkria. We'll go one at a time. There are trees in the central reservation. We'll make use of those."

"Understood." Henry fell back and waited for Mattie and Ali to reach the top of the lane. He found a couple of abandoned cars and crouched behind them. Wasim disappeared in the distance, running across the main road to reach the central reservation. No traffic came; he was in the clear. Mattie went second and she too was in luck. As the young man stood up to cross, the beams of a car lit up the alleyway in which they had stopped. Henry rolled into shrubs to take cover, but

Ali was in full view. He launched into a desperate sprint, half running, half hobbling to escape. Ali did not cross; instead he turned into the main road, in the middle of the tarmac. Henry was too stunned to tell him to stop. The car accelerated and took a sharp right turn to catch up the runner. Henry ran to the end of the lane, drawing his gun. The sound of a car hitting a body, the impact of flesh against metal, told him all he needed to know. Henry turned into the road. Wasim had appeared on the other side of the large avenue, urging him to cross now. Four men had left the car, rushing to check whether the runner was still alive.

Henry shook his head. He crouched behind a large SUV, risking his head to one side. A few yards away one of fighters was standing over Ali, prodding him with his boot. The young man yelped and tried to hold back a scream. In the beam of the car's headlight, Henry recognised one of the men who had served him at the shopping centre. Rage twisted his gut. He trained the gun on the driver who had just left the car when another SUV turned into the road. The news had already spread, and soon more men would be arriving and tell al-Haddawi they had found what he wanted. Henry retreated behind the vehicle that was shielding him, hesitant. There were now nine men surrounding Ali, too many to take on.

Henry bent forward, running across to the central reservation and in a second dash reached Wasim. "We can't leave him."

Wasim looked around for an angle from which to take the men down. The men had their weapons with them and the rifles they carried were more than a match for the guns Wasim and Henry had. He shook his head. Ali shrieked in pain. One of the men laughed. The next cry sounded inhuman, a voice speaking of torture and terror. "Kill me."

Henry and Wasim froze. It could not be Ali... But the scream came again. A plea, by someone who knew what would happen if he was interrogated by these men.

Wasim shook his head again and retreated slowly into the darkness of the building hiding them. He dragged Henry with him. "We need to go..."

Henry let himself be led away, almost stumbling. They reached the back of the building. In a few yards they would enter the next set of alleyways. Henry's body straightened, he shook Wasim off and retraced his steps running. He reached the street and drew his gun.

Three gunshots.

Ali stopped screaming.

* * *

They ran without stopping, turning into a maze of small lanes. Wasim was in front, Mattie following. They kept running through the gates of Hasib Zkria mosque, left open for early prayer. They turned into the grounds of the mosque and followed the wall of the garden surrounding it. Out of breath, they finally collapsed in the shadow of some of the bushes that had been planted there years earlier. No one spoke. They listened.

The shots that Henry had fired had surprised everyone and it would take time before they found the empty shells of Henry's gun. The area would soon be teeming with IS fighters and cars.

At the foot of the minaret, a light flashed several times.

Mattie nudged Wasim. "Yes, I saw it."

It came back again. Wasim fished a torch out of his rucksack and responded. Three flashes, stop, three flashes.

Two silhouettes moved out of the shadows towards them. Wasim waited to stand up until they were closer. When he did Mattie followed him. "MOTHER sent me." The voice behind the dark scarf said.

Wasim hesitated. Had he heard right? The scarf came down and Mattie suppressed a cry. "Sliman Vechivan…"

"Mattie Colmore…" The two women hugged tightly. "I could not leave you behind."

Henry had finally risen too. "We don't have much time. The cars are at the back of the mosque. We must go."

Sliman led the way along the garden walls and through another gate. Two Jeeps were waiting. She indicated to the three of them to join her in the second Jeep. She had not asked where the fourth man was. There could only be one explanation.

The Jeeps moved around the back streets swiftly. The vehicle leading the way slowed down regularly and then picked up speed as the roads were clear. The head lights were turned off, no need to attract the attention of other cars coming along some of the streets they crossed. The Jeeps abruptly came into the open and lurched forward through local fields. They slowed down as they reached an odd-looking dirt track. Sliman turned around towards them. "The River Koshr is almost dry at this time of the year. No one will try to find us driving inside the riverbed."

It took less than half an hour to leave the outskirts of Mosul and when the Jeeps crossed the bank of the Koshr into flat land, the terror of Mosul had been left behind in darkness.

* * *

Amina put the phone down and took a moment to compose herself. "They're out of Mosul."

Harris punched the air.

James had wrapped his arms around his body as the call came in. He let go and shook his head. Incredible.

Harris looked at the clock on the wall. It was just after 9pm in Iraq and 7pm in London. Sir John had said until the end of the day.

Abu Maeraka had been moved to an isolation cell at Belmarsh. In a few hours he would be moved outside London to RAF Northolt base, then flown to Cyprus. By early morning tomorrow he would be prepared for the exchange.

IS had chosen a different female hostage without disclosing it to the British. Was IS so confident they could fool everyone? Or perhaps they believed that at the time of the exchange the Westerners would not leave a white female in distress in the clutches of IS. And they would be right. Still, keeping Maeraka until they had reached Al-Hasakah was still an option. No rush to let The Chief know…

"Need to discuss options." James had gone back to his desk, observing from behind his screen.

"Not yet." Harris stretched and yawned. "I need a coffee. Anyone else want one?"

There was a unanimous *yes* and Harris took a walk to Caffe Italia. The night was still young. He would call Sir John shortly before midnight to update him.

***

They were driving across the countryside. The Jeep shook and bounced on the dirt tracks. The driver was good, negotiating difficult terrain without slowing down or losing control. "Kathoon is one of our best drivers," Sliman had said. Mattie had introduced Sliman, the commander of an all-female Peshmerga unit, who had finally been called to play a decisive role in the fight against IS.

The Jeep slowed down and soon came to a halt at the bottom of a small hill that announced a change of landscape and formed the ridge of a low mountain. Sliman got out and raised her binoculars to her eyes. She surveyed the hill, did a 360-degree check of the landscape around and came back in.

"There's activity towards the south-east, but they are far behind. It could be nothing but better be careful. We'll drive you to the border with Syria. From there it is only 50 km to Al-Hasakah."

"How about the YPG?" Wasim's voice sounded unsure.

"They are around but we couldn't find anyone at such short notice."

"And the rendezvous point in Al-Hasakah?" Wasim craned his neck to take in the terrain.

"I was coming to it. When we reach the border. I'll show you on the map the best route to get there. I've got navigation tools and equipment."

"You mean?"

"Guns of course – without proper guns you are not going to get very far in this country and…"

A faint noise stopped Sliman. She killed the headlights of the Jeep. The second vehicle followed suit and the three vehicles crawled against a couple of boulders. The noise intensified and everyone recognised the chopping sound of rotary blades. A couple of helicopters were coming their way.

"Out of the car." The Peshmerga came out, rifles at the ready, and took position. Kathoon opened the boot and found a place next to Sliman, leaning against the bonnet of the car for balance, an RPG lodged over her shoulder. The searchlight moved around like a slender beam drawing an abstract design. It searched the cluster of rocks that only lay a few yards from the two cars and moved on. No one shifted even after the sound of the rotor blades had faded into the distance.

Sliman got up from behind the Jeep and stood her fighters down. "We are not very far from the Syrian border. They won't come back this way, but we need to hurry."

The two Jeeps started their tortuous voyage up the steepening slopes. It only took 20 minutes to reach a dual carriageway. Kathoon stopped the car and got out. She walked to the back of the Jeep and took out a map and compass. Sliman stretched the map over the bonnet of the car and took Wasim through the details of their next journey. More dirt tracks that cut through difficult terrain would enable them to join a main road to Al-Hasakah. Sliman assured them the Syrian Kurds had been alerted and she handed over a letter from Colonel Nahida Ahmed Rashid. In the boot there was plenty of equipment: three assault rifles, 12 extra clips, more clips for the Glock and Sig Sauer.

"This is all we could afford, but I hope this might be of help." Sliman nodded. She shook hands with Wasim and Henry. "I hope to see you soon, Mattie Colmore… In Erbil."

Mattie hugged her friend again. "I promise, I will come back and write about your fight."

Sliman squeezed her shoulder. She turned back and climbed into the other Jeep. "May safety accompany you."

"May safety accompany you." Mattie answered back.

The Jeep turned around and started its trip towards Iraq's war zone. Wasim folded the map so that the route they were taking was left visible. He opened the driver's door and pushed it on top of the dashboard.

Mattie hesitated. She turned toward Henry, who had not said a word since they had encountered the Peshmerga unit. She knew it was about Ali and there was nothing she could say that would make the loss of the young man bearable. Silence and patience were sometimes more healing than words.

She climbed back into the Jeep. Wasim was ready to drive away but he too understood, allowing Henry a little more time to make himself ready.

"He has never lost anyone before, has he?" Mattie asked.

Wasim looked at her in the rear-view mirror. There was little light, but she felt the intense scrutiny of his glance. "I understand what it feels like."

Mattie too was looking straight into the mirror. "No, you don't understand… he pulled the trigger."

Chapter Thirty-Seven

RED HAWK Control Room smelled of pizza and strong coffee. It was gone 9.30pm. Harris had been on the phone to Brett several times during the day and he had finally communicated the details of the rendezvous point in Al-Hasakah to Harris. The Peshmerga had contacted the Syrian Kurds, allowing safe passage. Now was the most difficult part.

Wait.

Amina had delayed going to the bathroom until she was ready to burst, and Harris was going that way too... They just needed a call from Henry and Wasim. Harris took some comfort from the fact that Commander Sanjabi had not called him. If the journey to the Syrian border had gone awry, he would have known by now. There had been no chatter or traffic on social media apart from the frenzied search for the three most wanted infidels. Harris was certain that IS would have advertised their success and paraded their prisoners on the media if they had succeeded in finding them. According to his calculation Henry, Wasim and Mattie should now be crossing into Syria.

Harris's phone rang. He cast an eye to the display screen... Sir John was calling. Shit. He was not expecting this. He had still a few hours to go... Harris stood up. "I need the bathroom."

Amina reached for her phone and picked up Harris's line. "Good evening, sir. ...Yes..." She nodded. "But he is not around."

"... I don't know where but will tell him you called... Certainly." She put the phone down.

James smiled. "Did he buy it?"

"Not a bit of it."

Harris came back. "Did he buy it?"

James smiled. "Not a bit of it." He was checking the contents of his overnight bag. He would make his way to RAF Northolt in a short while. At 10pm Abu Maeraka was sitting there already, waiting to be transferred to Cyprus.

"Did he say it was urgent?"

"He did." Amina shrugged. "But I'm sure he'd say that anyway."

Harris mechanically picked up a piece of cold pizza and started to chew on it. It was greasy and rubbery but somehow it helped his deliberations. He wiped his greasy fingers on an old paper napkin. "Call me if anything happens." Harris picked up his mobile and left.

Harris stepped into Sir John's office without ceremony.

"I don't want to know what you know," was not the welcome Harris had expected.

He stood in front of The Chief's desk, taken aback. "OK."

"Colmore has been on my back through the Home Office. He wants to know who will be sent alongside the negotiator team to effect the exchange from our end."

"Do we have to tell him?"

"He's insisting. And I can't say we haven't decided. So… I need a name."

Harris nodded. "James Radlett."

Sir John blinked. "How long has he been with us?"

"He joined yesterday." Harris felt the beginning of a smile spread across his cheeks.

"Ah well, an eternity."

"But he was an intelligence officer before he decided to join the City."

"How long ago was that?"

"Fifteen years ago."

"Another eternity." Sir John tapped his fingers on the desk. "Clearly you trust him."

"He has already been invaluable."

"Fine."

Harris nodded. Another idea had been germinating in his mind and it had popped out perhaps at a decisive moment.

"Could I be hypothetical?"

Sir John eyed Harris. "Go ahead." He sat back in his chair.

"We know the team which now includes Mattie Colmore is being hunted by IS."

Sir John waved at him to carry on.

"Perhaps she could be part of the deal after all... with a conversation along these lines... We know you don't have Mattie Colmore and the two other men who took her anymore. We know where they are and if you keep trying to find them, we won't release Maeraka. We will let the jihadi community know you failed him."

"In short, IS is losing face."

"IS can always tell its followers they've killed the two men for all we care. With Mattie they can say it was part of the exchange after all, Mattie and the other woman they have selected without telling us."

"That's bold." Sir John had dropped his head to one side.

Harris waited... it was bold indeed.

Sir John's hands spread over his desk.

"Do it."

* * *

The Jeep had crossed the main road and turned into yet another dirt track. Wasim was at the wheel, hands clenched at 10 and 2 o'clock. Henry was silent when he settled in the front passenger seat and he still had not spoken a word. Wasim occasionally glanced at him and Mattie wondered whether there was anything she could say that would unlock his numbness. Anything was better than this slow descent into hell.

Wasim slowed down to check his bearings were right. He grabbed the compass and orientated it. Soon they would start driving up another of those steep elevations to reach a small mountain top.

"We're almost at Al-Hawl. From there I should be able to contact London."

Henry's face was still turned toward the window, looking into darkness and seeing only one image, that of Ali's death.

"What you did was courageous." There was a tremor in Wasim's low voice. "It was."

Henry's body jerked forward. "Stop the car." His voice almost inaudible.

Wasim looked at him.

"Stop the bloody car."

Wasim slammed the brakes. Henry opened the door before the car had stopped. He swayed and almost tumbled when stepping outside, then moved a few more steps.

Collapsing onto his knees, he was sick, retching, his hands barely supporting him. Mattie got out of the car and walked slowly towards him, the way she might have approached a wounded animal. She reached for his shoulder. He shrugged but she kept her hand there, a light touch. "It was courageous." She waited.

Henry sat back on his heels. Mattie handed him a bottle of water. He took a sip. He squeezed Mattie's hand and stood up. "One day I will kill al-Haddawi."

* * *

They had reached the small village of Al-Hawl. It had taken a steep drive along a ridge, on a track carved into the rock that could barely accommodate two cars passing. Henry kept checking for mobile reception, but the little bars had proved elusive. They suddenly jumped and wobbled on the screen when they reached the top of the hill. Wasim parked the car as soon as he could. He took the mobile from Henry and got out to make the call.

Henry seemed to have returned to his bubble of silence after stepping back into the car, only commenting once on the strength of the mobile signal. Mattie poked her face between the two seats and reached out for his hand. "I meant what I said to you."

Henry let his head fall back against the headrest. He was trying to say something and yet it seemed beyond him.

"You know what they would have done." Mattie squeezed his hand tight.

Henry squeezed her hand back. "I never thought." His voice was broken. "I never imagined... I could take the life of someone..." He let go of Mattie's hand and moved his hand over his eyes. "...of someone who..."

"Who was a good man?" Mattie completed his sentence. Henry opened the door and walked out again. He needed air.

Wasim was still talking to London. Henry breathed in deeply. The anger had been replaced by pain beyond what he had ever experienced. Yesterday had changed his life forever. And he was no longer certain that the change he had so wanted was worth the price.

Henry walked around the car and reached Wasim in a few steps. "I need to speak to Harris." Wasim looked surprised but the steel in Henry's eyes made him nod. He handed over the phone.

"Harris, Crowne here." Henry's voice was measured yet determined. "I presume the exchange is still happening?"

"Good. I'm going to be part of that." Henry fingered the USB keys in his pocket. Harris was not happy with the idea. "You want the data I collected... you get me there. It's early morning here and I have a few hours to reach Aleppo. I'll expect James to meet me there."

Henry killed the call, handed over the phone to Wasim and walked back to the car. Wasim started the engine. "What did Harris say?"

"It doesn't matter. He'll deliver."

* * *

With Henry's demand, Maeraka now had to be exchanged. Harris should have been furious at Crowne's new-found assurance but he rather liked having to deliver Maeraka in return for another hostage. Time to let the fixer know. Harris savoured the idea. There would be no intermediary for this conversation...

"I know IS no longer has Mattie Colmore. I know IS has a bounty over three people of interest to the British, including Mattie Colmore. I know IS means to exchange another hostage for Maeraka."

The fixer's silence made Harris smile. The fixer had not been told.

"That is what will happen. IS calls off the hunt. I don't care what crap they publish on their shit media about the two men. We exchange the other hostage for Maeraka. The official story is that Maeraka has been exchanged for Mattie Colmore. This is not negotiable. I will call you back in one hour." The call ended. Harris was grinning. He was back in control.

* * *

There would be no escape on the next portion of the road, a sheer cliff on one side, a deep ravine on the other. As soon as they had left Al-Hawl, Henry had switched places with Wasim. The rendezvous point with Harris's contact was on the outskirts of Al-Hasakah, an old petrol station, the first they would encounter. Wasim had been sent a picture of the place on the mobile. It was hard to miss. They made good progress and the map showed they would be over the Al-Hawl ridge and out in the open in a few minutes' time. If there were any checkpoints, the end of the ridge would be an ideal place to stop vehicles. The beam of the headlights showed the stone face slowly losing its elevation. They drove past a strangely high walled construction partly carved into the rock that looked dark and asleep.

"We're only 10 km away." Wasim had folded the road map on his knees and from time to time checked progress with his torch.

"Six miles to the centre of Al-Hasakah or the rendezvous point?"

"The centre of Al-Hasakah…"

Henry nodded. The full moon and clear sky were helping them make out the terrain. A few constructions appeared along the road. Square, squat, flat-roofed houses that so characterised the Middle East. There wasn't any light in any of the dwellings and for a moment this small part of Syria looked like any other country, fast asleep, making itself ready for another war-free day.

"Shit." Wasim pointed out to a movement on his right. In the distance a beam of light was moving fast. Another car.

Henry killed the lights of the Jeep and reversed to the bunch of houses he had spotted a few moments ago. The Jeep wobbled when it entered the rough track that led to them. He stopped the car as close as he could to the first house. They all lowered themselves into their seats. The beam of light kept running along the road, towards them. It had slowed down gradually.

The car was now crawling along the road. The occupants must have spotted movement and were looking for its origin. The car stopped 200 yards from the small hamlet. Henry had drawn his gun. Wasim was slowly loading the rifle Kathoon had left for them.

"Any activity?" He had lodged a clip into the magazine holder.

"Nothing." Henry's head poked out a little, sheltered by the wheel. Wasim wound down his window slowly and placed the rifle in position, the long barrel resting on the window seal and the side mirror. He adjusted the rifle's scope. "Two passengers and one driver."

"What are they doing?"

"No movement."

The car started moving slowly again. It crawled past the group of houses. Wasim moved the rifle around, training it on the car until it was out of his line of vision. Suddenly the vehicle sped away. Henry waited until the beams of its headlights had disappeared to put his Glock away. He started the engine again. Only five miles to survive.

* * *

Harris was speeding along the M40. He was only a mile from RAF Northolt station. He was joining the flight after all. The fixer had reported back and it seemed IS wanted Maeraka freed more than MI6 had anticipated. The flight was due to take off in 15 minutes. It could no longer be stopped. Harris would place the official call with Sir John, informing him that Mattie Colmore was with his team, only once airborne.

Harris arrived at the gate and presented his ID. The guards radioed in. "Better hurry, sir, the aircraft is about to depart."

Harris drove into the complex at speed, parked the car near the hangar where he knew the aircraft would be leaving from… A young man in uniform greeted him and they both ran across the tarmac. The steps were about to be pulled up. "Wait… Wait." Harris sprinted towards them. The cargo Airbus A400M back door dropped down again. Harris rushed in and the door closed right behind him.

387

Harris took the first seat available and strapped himself in. The push of take-off moved him backwards into his seat. He loved that moment... diving into the thick of a mission...

Live.

* * *

The petrol station looked as old and worn out as it did on the picture. Henry stopped before going on the approach. It was 2.07am and all around stood still.

"I'll go and check it out." Wasim grabbed his gun.

Henry killed the headlights of the car and moved the Jeep slowly forward. He stopped 100 yards from the station. Wasim opened the door quietly and crouched until he reached the end of the bonnet. The walk to the main building was exposed. Wasim was about to dash towards the pumps when his mobile beeped. A text had just come in.

You have arrived. Flash your lights 3 times.

Wasim read the text back to Henry.

"I guess we're going to find out quickly whether Harris's plan has worked."

Henry flashed the car's lights as instructed. A car pulled out from behind the building and flashed its lights too. Two men stepped out of the car and waited. Henry moved the Jeep slowly towards them. They looked inconspicuous and ordinary. The man who advanced first towards the car was in jeans and wearing a leather jacket against the morning's fresh breeze. Henry stopped the car and Wasim stepped out in turn.

"Salaam alaikum." He walked towards Wasim. "I am Malek. MOTHER tells me you need help."

"Alaikum as salaam. I'm glad MOTHER has sent you." They shook hands.

"This is Rami. We'll take you to your next rendezvous point near the Turkish border." Rami waved from inside the car and Malek walked back to it. He turned around. "After Al-Hasakah you are in deep Kurdish territory. IS will never dare venture there." Malek grinned.

Wasim exchanged a few more words and came back to the Jeep.

Rami led the way onto the main road and they were off. He chose the ring road around Al-Hasakah, avoiding the city altogether, and both cars sped along Route 716, towards the border.

Mattie had said very little since she had spoken to Henry last. She looked at the two men in the front seats. They were so different. Wasim, calm, solid, respectful and yet uncompromising when the time came. Henry, a quicksilver mind, emotions raging inside and yet absolutely focused when he needed to be. She sat back and took a deep breath. She had never been on her guard and under threat for so long. And although she did not want to cry freedom too soon, she could feel that both men had relaxed somewhat.

"How did you meet Sliman?" Wasim glanced at Mattie in the rear-view mirror.

"I wanted to write an article on the Peshmerga after they were involved in some of the most important battles during the Iraq war. I discovered they had a unit of female fighters. At the time they were only used for support rather than on the battlefield, but these women were ready to fight. I spoke about that in my article. I knew that if given an opportunity they would fight as hard as the men did."

"Did you stay a long time?"

"Almost six months, it was incredible." Mattie had stuck her head between the two seats. "I arrived in November 2003 in Iraqi Kurdistan, in Erbil. In December 2003 the US forces with the help of the Peshmerga captured Saddam Hussein and in January 2004 they captured Hassan Guhl. At the time no one knew how important he was, but he turned out to be the Al-Qaeda source who helped track Bin Laden."

"What about Sliman?" Henry had caught Mattie's eye in the mirror. He looked tired but was enjoying her story, a way of discovering who she was beyond the articles she wrote.

"She had just joined the Peshmerga. She was my contact, made sure I could go wherever I wanted. We shared the same digs." Mattie's tales about her time with the Kurdish fighters made the drive go quickly. Henry almost missed that Malek's car indicated a turn.

The colours of dawn had started to illuminate the sky, in a few moments the sun would appear, and they would have crossed the Turkish border by then. Malek's car turned into a small lane surrounded by fields and agricultural land. In the distance, Mattie thought she could distinguish a couple of helicopters' silhouettes. Her stomach somersaulted...

Rami stopped 500 yards from the makeshift airfield. Henry stopped the car and was about to step out.

"Don't worry, you need to go now." Rami had driven the car alongside Henry's.

Henry extended a hand. "We can't thank you enough."

Malek smiled and banged the roof of the Jeep. No time to lose. Wasim wished him well and the Jeep sped along the lane.

The SAS team had been deployed around the aircraft. They had spotted the Jeep and moved into formation. Henry slowed down. Wasim made the call and was put through to the squadron leader. "We are on the approach, 100 yards away from you."

Henry kept advancing at a slow pace. Two soldiers came forward, guns at the ready. Henry, Wasim and Mattie left the car slowly. Another man was approaching. Mattie removed the man's scarf from around her head. Henry and Wasim did the same, hands lifted over their heads.

"It's fine. Let them through."

The helicopters were waiting; the handshake from the squadron leader and the ring of soldiers that closed around them almost overwhelmed them. Mattie hugged Henry, she hugged Wasim and Wasim slapped Henry's shoulder. They had made it.

"We need to go." The squadron leader jerked his head towards the helicopters. "The sun will be up any minute now."

The doors of the two Apaches were open and the SAS team retreated gradually from its position in smaller concentric circles. Four men jumped into one of the helicopters. Henry helped Mattie to strap herself into one of the central seats in the other. He squeezed her hands, looking deep into her eyes. "You're free." Mattie squeezed back, hovering between laughter and tears. The rotors started to turn, gaining momentum and throwing dust into the air. Henry squeezed tighter. His hand let go in one swift move. Mattie's eyes hidden. She moved forward, hands outstretched. "Henry..." She struggled against the safety belt but already she was airborne. "Henry..." Her cry disappeared, drowned by the deafening noise of the blades beating the air.

Chapter Thirty-Eight

Henry stood for a few moments until the Apache had flown over the Turkish border. "Time to go." The second SAS team was about to board.

"I'm not going." Wasim looked at Henry and smiled the attractive smile that made the dimples in his cheeks go deeper.

"But why? What? Where?" Henry shook his head.

"I'm going back to Iraq. The Peshmerga need me more than MI6 and I'm fed up with fighting IS from afar. I need to be part of a people who are not frightened of fighting this war."

Henry felt lost for a moment. Wasim had been more than a patient and capable teacher, he had been a friend. "I think…" Henry ended up nodding. "I think I understand." He managed to continue. "How will you get back there?"

"Malek is waiting for me at the end of the dirt track. He'll smuggle me back into Iraq and I have Sliman's number." He moved the mobile in the air.

"Guys, it's now or never." The squadron leader had one foot inside the cabin of the helicopter. They had to go.

Henry and Wasim hugged, a brothers' hug. Wasim slapped Henry's back. "You're ready." He stepped back from the Apache and returned to the Jeep.

Henry boarded as the rotors started beating the air again. The craft hovered slowly over the ground and soared suddenly. The Jeep had already turned back and was speeding down the lane. The Apache banked left and crossed the border.

Henry sat back in his seat. His weariness had suddenly caught up with him. The squadron leader indicated that they would be in the air for a couple of hours before they reached Aleppo. Henry did not want to think about what had just occurred, focusing on what needed to happen next. He closed his eyes, knowing there was nothing more for him to do but rest and be ready.

* * *

Amina had just managed to go to sleep. The dream was strange, as many dreams can be… she was back at the office. Dozens of identical phones had been installed in RED HAWK Control Room… old-fashioned phones too, big black heavy pyramids, with equally heavy receivers. The cords that linked the receivers to the boxes kept twisting in on themselves, making it difficult to pick up the phone and answer. One of the phones was ringing and she couldn't find which one. Every time she picked one handset there was no one at the other end. She started running around, desperate to answer, to no avail… until Amina opened her eyes and leaned on one elbow… her mobile was ringing. Her hand moved swiftly towards it and almost pushed it off the bedside table. She sat up. "Hello."

"Ms Brown?" She recognised Sir John's voice, sounding harassed and weary.

"Yes, sir." Amina was wide awake.

"Have you heard from Steve?"

"Not recently, sir."

"I've had Colmore on the phone…"

"Is he trying to stop the exchange?" Amina had switched the light on, scrambling around the room to find her clothes.

"He hasn't wasted any time in calling the Home Secretary even in the early hours of the morning." Sir John's tone sounded less drained.

Amina would not relent. "Has the Home Secretary decided or still hearing arguments?"

"I'm having a call with her, her aide and Colmore in 20 minutes' time."

"Do they know the exact time of the exchange?"

"They know it's this morning."

"It's almost 7.00am in Aleppo, sir. In an hour's time agent Harris will be making his way to the rendezvous point. He will switch off his mobile to concentrate on comms between agents…"

"Understood, I need to keep the discussion going for half an hour…" Sir John mused.

"Why don't you try to patch me in… That might gain a few minutes."

"That's a plan."

Amina rushed out of the door and just made it into her office as her mobile was ringing again. She checked the clock on the wall. It was gone 7.40am in Aleppo. Another 20 minutes and Harris would be in the clear.

Colmore was on the attack the instant Sir John finished his introduction of who Amina was.

"It is inconceivable a terrorist caught in the UK, for atrocities carried out in the UK, could be released when the hostage was no longer a hostage." Colmore's well-trained orator's voice was in full flow.

"We have no visibility on who the other hostage is?" Amina butted in.

"All the more… all the more to reconsider this exchange." The pitch of Colmore's voice had risen once more.

"There are Europeans and American female hostages in Raqqa." Amina kept going.

"It is not our concern. The UK government is not an NGO or the Salvation Army."

"I'm not sure the UK government should turn a blind eye to the plight of these women in captivity… sexual abuse and torture." Sir John was on the attack too.

"The US would never agree to such an exchange for one of their citizens, whereas the Europeans, if they are happy to pay, as it seems they are… allow them." Colmore did not care…

"Unless you are concerned that your daughter's fate has not been confirmed yet?" Amina had just had an idea…

Colmore stopped for an instant. Amina held her breath. Had she read the man right? "Of course not." Colmore burst out at the implication. "I will not put my family interests over the national interest."

There was a clear intake of breath at the other end the phone. Amina nodded to herself. If Colmore would not put his family interest over the national interest, it was certain he was prepared to sacrifice both to his political career.

The conversation was almost over. The Home Secretary asked for additional information which neither Sir John nor Amina had. She made her decision.

* * *

Henry woke up with a jerk and for a minute did not know where he was. The noise of the helicopter reminded him he was on his way to Aleppo's suburbs. The squadron leader smiled and handed over a set of headphones with mic. "We are ten minutes from the landing point."

Henry nodded. "Are we still in Turkey?"

"No, but we've been following the border until a couple of minutes ago. We're now in Syria. Twenty clicks from Aleppo."

Henry bent sideways to get a better view of the land. The Apache banked right. A Chinook helicopter and a couple of Apaches were already on the ground with four vehicles arranged in a convoy line. Henry's chopper touched down. He shook hands with the squadron leader, and jumped out before the blades had stopped throwing dust into the air. Henry hunched forward and moved towards the convoy. A familiar face stepped out of one of the cars. Steve Harris was walking in his direction. He was pleased to see Harris looking the way he felt, red eyed, dishevelled... looking like shit.

Harris stopped, surprised. He jogged towards Henry. "Where is Wasim?"

"He's not coming back."

"What do you mean?" Harris looked lost.

"I'll tell you when we are on our way to Aleppo."

Harris frowned and shook his head to dispel the news. "The USB keys?"

"When we are on the way to Aleppo."

Harris rolled his eyes. "Fine, let's go."

They joined the last car.

"What's the plan?" Henry asked.

"We've got a few hours before the exchange. I'll tell you when we're in Aleppo." It was not a tit for tat. The driver was a local man, vetted no doubt, but why take unnecessary risks? "Tell me about Wasim."

* * *

They reached the centre of Aleppo for Fajr, the first call to prayer. Maeraka had been placed in the third vehicle in the convoy. They entered Aleppo though the newly developed part of town, large avenues and well organised streets, far from ideal for an ambush. The car left new Aleppo and moved into the old city. They turned into a couple of smaller streets and stopped in front of a house, ancient and elegant, a construction of grey stones and carved wood. Two men in the front car stepped out first. They surveyed their surroundings and one of them gave instructions via his earpiece. The door opened and Henry recognised the silhouette; a hooded Maeraka was being led into the safe house.

"Let's go." Harris and Henry followed. Henry could not quite shake the unease at seeing James again, but he needed him for his plan. He had to make it work.

The house was dark and cool. Henry followed Harris along a corridor and up a couple of flights of stairs. "Where is the exchange taking place?"

"Al-Madina Souq."

"Kilometres of corridors and alleyways."

"And they will have planned their escape." Harris opened the door of a small room. "Gentlemen, I don't need to introduce you to one another... Don't kill each other just yet." Harris closed the door behind him.

Henry saw it on his face. James had not expected the transformation. There was no Savile Row suit, no Hermès tie. The clean shaven, impeccable Henry had become a bearded, unkempt man, dressed in old army fatigues. James was looking for something he needed to recognise and found it. Henry's steel blue eyes had not changed, intelligent, quick witted and focused.

"There are a lot of things I'd like to say to you, James." Henry's voice had changed. "But we haven't got much time, so if you're going to deck me one for all the things I did, you'd better do it quickly."

James took a step forward and Henry braced himself for the impact; if James wanted to throw a punch, he wouldn't resist. "So, what's the plan?" James moved to the table at the centre of the room. He unfolded a map of Al-Madina Souq. From the smallest of boxes, he took out what looked like a beetle. "I've come prepared."

Henry walked to the table still expecting some reprisal, but James's calm felt convincing. "What's this?" Henry pointed to a small command console. James handed it to Henry. "I won't be able to use a Reaper drone, so I got the next best thing. I'll be able to follow you and the others. This little bug has a 2 km range… not bad."

Henry delicately picked up the miniature drone. Clever. "I have a score to settle with someone who will almost certainly be there to pick up Maeraka."

James nodded. He did not need an explanation, just direction. "You want to be at the exchange and follow?"

"That's right."

"If you look at the map of Aleppo, you can see that the quickest route out of the city lies to the east."

"Why east? Has IS advanced that far?"

"They are very close to Aleppo and have almost certainly infiltrated the suburbs around the M4 and Route 4."

Henry leaned over the map, arms supporting his muscled body.

"They'll need to take the quickest way out of the souq towards…" His fingers traced a route out of Aleppo. "…the M4."

"Correct… it gets them to Raqqa in four hours, a little more perhaps, but it will also be the fastest."

James pulled up a chair and sat down. He took a pen out of his jacket pocket and drew a small cross on the map. "This is the exchange point." Henry sat opposite to James. They were doing, after six years, what they used to do best. Plan their attack.

* * *

He had changed his clothes to mix better with the crowd. Jeans and a checked blue shirt that he did not tuck into his trousers so that it concealed his Glock. He had trimmed his beard into a full square crop, a sign he did not belong to any radical type of Islam. Henry had managed to snatch a couple of hours' rest before the exchange. He came back to the room that James had not left.

"We're good to go." James handed him a cup of coffee.

Henry took it gratefully. He reviewed the map once more. "I'm good…" Henry took a sip. "I've memorised the map."

James handed over a small Bluetooth earpiece that would keep them in communication.

"Where's Harris?" Henry pushed the small device into his ear.

"He's having a final debrief with the exchange team."

"Do they know I'm going?"

"They don't know what you're planning, and Harris won't tell them."

"Good." Henry checked his watch. "08.35."

James checked his watch and synchronised it with Henry's '08.35'. He slung a small rucksack over his shoulder. Henry did the same. "Let's go."

* * *

Harris checked his watch. They were only 30 minutes away from exchanging Maeraka. The two agents who were taking him to the rendezvous point had clear instructions. Anything going awry and it was a shoot-to-kill situation. Harris donned his bulletproof jacket. His mobile buzzed. The Chief was calling him. Harris pondered. He let it go to voicemail.

The cars were ready. Four cars had been gathered as back-up. Maeraka came out into the light and blinked. His small frame dwarfed by the two men on each side of him. He was walking slowly, a strong cocktail of drugs swimming around in his bloodstream. The cars left the safe house and drove for 20 minutes. They stopped in front of one of the entrances to Al-Jumrok Caravanserai, one of the oldest parts of the Al-Madina Souq. The covered alleyway was quiet, vendors organising their shops for the day. Two of the men that were part of the escort went ahead and came back after a few minutes.

All clear.

Harris gave the OK. The men took up position at various key locations in the little covered lane. Maeraka was taken out of the car and made to sit in a café. There was now five minutes to go. He played the message from Sir John. Colmore was trying to convince the Home Office to stop the exchange. Harris shook his head in anger... *No fucking way.* He dropped the mobile back in his pocket.

Henry had taken up position a few streets away. The souq was a maze of lanes, corridors and shops with exits leading into different alleyways. It would be impossible to follow the footsteps of the people who picked up Maeraka exactly. But they had to exit eventually. Henry and James had decided on two possible exit routes. Al-Haddawi would not be at the exchange, but he would be somewhere in Aleppo, ready to reap the glory of yet another remarkable deed. Mosul... Maeraka's freedom... There would be no stopping him.

"M is in position." There was good reception and James's voice was clear.

"Received." Henry browsed through the shops, ignoring the hustle of the merchants.

"Three people are approaching, two men and one woman in niqab." The bug was in the air, transmitting images to James.

"They have stopped."

"M is standing up."

"The woman has removed her face mask. Only one man is walking with her now... T-shirt and jeans, no visible weapon."

"M has started to walk towards the woman... Harris is walking with him."

"They've all stopped, five metres away. M and the woman are walking alone."

"IS has got M... We've got the exchange. They're walking towards you."

Henry started walking at a fast pace along the corridors, following

Maeraka's group two lanes apart.

"Which direction?" Henry pressed the earpiece deeper inside his ear.

"East, straight line to the Red Gate."

Henry increased his pace. He was in front of the men. Maeraka's drowsy walking was no doubt slowing them down. Perfect.

James had found two taxi drivers. They were waiting for Henry at separate locations near the exit. "Your taxi is ready at the Red Gate."

Henry walked out of Al-Madina Souq. The driver was waiting in an unremarkable black Citroen. "Salaam alaikum." Henry got in and sat down.

Maeraka stumbled out and was pushed into a black SUV.

"Follow that car." The driver obeyed. He had been paid handsomely for his service.

The SUV immediately turned right and left into the back streets and small lanes of central Aleppo. The taxi driver was doing well, not driving too close and yet never losing them. The SUV turned into a large avenue. Road signs indicated the exit to the M4.

"They are going straight to the M4." Henry relayed to James. The SUV turned again into a side street and dived into an area that started to look different. The old architecture and elegant constructions were gradually replaced by older, cheaper houses. The people looked different too. More men dressed in long white robes, women in full niqab.

The SUV slowed down and prepared to cross yet another road. The driver gave Henry a worried look. "Too dangerous?" Henry asked in Arabic. The driver nodded. "I'll drive. Let me have the car." The driver opened his door and Henry took his place. He sped across the road and delved into a maze of smaller streets. The SUV had slowed down. Its occupants must have now felt in more secure territory.

"Where are we?" Henry asked James. "We've just stopped."

"You're in the middle of an area that does not seem to have any particular name, but you are 15 minutes' drive from the M4."

Henry drove past the stopped SUV, turned right into the next street and parked the taxi. His jeans and shirt had been a good idea in Al-Madina; he did not look very convincing in this Salafist neighbourhood, but it would have to do. He left the car, retraced his steps and risked a glance at the corner of the street where the SUV had stopped. The doors of the SUV were open. Maeraka had already been moved inside one of the houses. Henry pulled back and checked the back of the properties; a small passageway, long and narrow, meandered there. Two men came out of a house and stared at him. He returned their stare without flinching and they carried on.

"I'm moving into a small lane at the back of the property in which they have taken Maeraka."

"We're getting close to the max range of the beetle." James was on the move. "I'm walking onto the street to increase the range."

Henry heard a dull hum. The little bug had just flown into the lane. It landed onto one of the houses' window sills. Henry had pushed his body into a doorway, listening for clues. He stopped. James flew the beetle higher into the passageway. "One further house to your left."

The bug landed on another window sill, sending images of a light coming on in a room and a man entering. He undressed and changed into the clothes that had been prepared for him.

"You're there."

Henry looked at the wall that shielded an inner courtyard from the lane. He found a few rough and displaced bricks and pushed himself alongside the wall. He softly rolled over onto the other side and crouched, looking out for any activity. The smell of cooking and coffee told him the place was lived in. Henry took his gun and held it low. He reached into his rucksack and fitted the silencer James had brought with this new piece. He took out two extra magazines and placed one in each pocket. He checked the door. It was not locked. Henry nudged the door open and heard voices. He let the door close softly. They were walking upstairs. He waited.

The voice he wanted to hear finally came from the top of the stairwell. Al-Haddawi was claiming victory for the release of Maeraka. The tall shadow of the man moved down the stairs until he appeared in the hallway. He greeted Maeraka with a brotherly embrace that was too effusive to be real. Henry squeezed his body against the wall and took aim through the crack of the door, but the angle was not right. He could hear that another car was arriving in a short while to take them away from Aleppo. Al-Haddawi moved into the ground floor room. Henry followed the wall to a window. The glass was old and cloudy. It was hard to get a clear picture of what was happening inside the room. The two men had sat down where a couple of low sofas had been arranged. Maeraka was facing the window. He looked so different to what Henry remembered. Older, frailer; HSU Belmarsh had taken its toll.

Al-Haddawi had asked for some tea; a young man brought two cups and left. Henry returned to the door. Someone else had come down the stairs. The car had arrived to take Maeraka away. In a moment al-Haddawi would disappear too. Henry looked around, grabbed an old bench that looked sturdy enough and placed it at an angle against the door. It would not hold for long, but it would be enough.

Al-Haddawi stood up and Maeraka followed, then left the room first. Henry would have happily gunned them both down, but he had to choose. He also wanted to savour the moment when al-Haddawi would recognise him and for that he needed him alone.

That moment is now. The window is slim enough to succumb to a well-placed kick. Henry clings to the upper ledge and his boot crashes through the centre of the frame. Splinters of wood and shards of glass fly into the room. Henry effortlessly slides into it, with a feline and lethal agility. He trains his gun on al-Haddawi. The man drops his tea. He looks for where his gun should have been, but it is not there. Careless or too confident.

The surprise in his eyes gives way to fury when he recognises Henry.

He lunges forward. Allahu akbar he forgets to cry.

The first salvo hits him in the chest, stopping his advance. The second is a clear head shot.

Already people are coming downstairs. Henry jumps out of the window, runs through the yard and climbs over the wall. Men run into the room, on his tail. He doesn't look back but hears the discharge of a gun. He comes to the end of the alleyway, dives into the taxi he has parked. Someone bursts out of the small passageway. Henry floors the accelerator and turns right. The shots that he hears miss their target.

He doesn't stop at any major junction, creating a flurry of car horns. The car

keeps going until it reaches the Red Gate. A black SUV is waiting. James opens the door. Henry abandons the car in the middle of road and jumps in.
It is done.

* * *

The hot water was running on his back, loosening the muscles knotted by two days without sleep. Henry lathered his body, shampooed his hair, but before that he had shaved his beard. His face looked a little odd, tanned and weatherbeaten on the upper part, pale and angry on the lower. Henry finally turned the taps off, grabbed the large towel on the rail and dried himself methodically. The bedroom had been simply furnished but it was comfortable. He would leave Akrotiri base shortly for an undisclosed destination. Henry found a pile of fresh clothes on his bed, a pair of jeans, a white T-shirt and comfortable boating shoes. He had just put on his jeans when he heard a knock at the door. He downed his T-shirt quickly and opened. He took a moment to recognise her. Mattie had transformed herself too. Pair of tight jeans, fitted T-shirt, sports shoes… still, the same tomboyish look.

She stepped into Henry's room and let her face fall against his chest. "You made it."

Henry pushed the door shut. He loosely wrapped one arm around her waist, breathing in her scent. "I thought… you would have gone by now," he whispered.

"I needed to speak to Harris… about the story in the press and also…" She closed her arms around his body, pressing hers against him.

Henry pulled back a little, just enough so he could see her face. He traced the line of her cheek and smiled. Mattie let her cheek rest gently in his palm. "…and also I wanted to see you."

"What are you going to do?" Henry drew her closer again.

"My plane leaves in three hours' time." Mattie moved her hands gently underneath his T-shirt and ran her fingers over his back.

Henry brought his lips to her neck. "Let's not lose one more second then."

* * *

Henry had expected a plane ride to one of the debriefing sites he had been told about but instead he took a short helicopter ride across the ocean from Akrotiri. He guessed the recuperating site was in Crete, but he had not been told and he didn't care. He had been given time to adjust and time to debrief MI6 about what he had seen, the contents of the USB keys he had brought back and the photos Wasim had sent to MOTHER. He still could not speak about what he had seen in Raqqa and Mosul without anger and dread. But the weeks of rest had started to have an effect. Harris had discussed with him a new operation, codename SHADER, a systematic bombing campaign against IS positions and oil production sites in Syria and Iraq. It had started bearing fruit and IS was losing territory.

Henry's minders did not have a name, but he rather liked calling the two men by their codenames... Tom and Jerry sounded perfectly fine. A couple of months ago Jerry had brought back from the UK a thick file that Harris had sent him. Henry had now read it several times. He liked its contents. His new legend was turning his past into a distant memory. Henry stretched. He poured a little more coffee into both cups and grabbed the file again.

"Tom tells me you've memorised all the details." Harris had picked up his fresh cup and waited.

"Another couple of weeks and I'll be ready."

"Good." Harris sat back and took a sip. "We've worked on your legend in the country you're travelling to. We'll set up a four-week inception phase... then you engage."

Dear Reader,

I hope you have enjoyed IMPOSTOR IN CHIEF as much as I have enjoyed writing it!

So, perhaps you would like to know more about Henry Crowne. What are the ghosts that haunt him? What is it in his past that made him who he is?

Delve into HENRY CROWNE PAYING THE PRICE series with

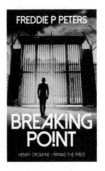

COLLAPSE:
mybook.to/COLLAPSE

BREAKING POINT:
mybook.to/BREAKINGPOINT

NO TURNING BACK:
mybook.to/NOTURNINGBACK

HENRY CROWNE PAYING THE PRICE, BOOKS 1-3:
mybook.to/HCPTPBKS1-3

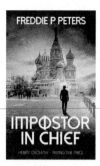 

IMPOSTOR IN CHIEF
mybook.to/
IMPOSTORINCHIEF

RED RENEGADE
mybook.to/Env1F

Or check out my new series

A NANCY WU CRIME THRILLER:

BLOOD DRAGON:
mybook.to/BLOODDRAGON

Acknowledgements

Yet again another team effort to bring this book about... Thank you to the friends and professionals who have so kindly supported me.

Cressida Downing, my editor, for her no-nonsense approach and relentless enthusiasm for books... mine in particular, Jessica Bell for designing a super new cover and my production team with new names and old friends Sarah Woodcock, Andrew Chapman, Aimee Dewar and Helen Kavanagh. Helena Halme, an author in her own right, for giving me expert advice in marketing my books.

To the friends who have patiently read, re-read and advised: Helen Janecek, Susan Rosenberg, Kate Burton, Bernard McGuigan, Alison Thorne, Elisabeth Gaunt, Anthea Tinker, Geraldine Kelly, Malcolm Fortune, Tim Watts, Gaye Murdock, Kathy Vanderhook, Kat Clarke.

It's also time for me to ask you for a small favour...

Please take a few minutes to leave a review either on Amazon, Goodreads or Bookbub.

Reviews are incredibly important to authors like me. They increase the book's visibility and help with promotions. So, if you'd like to spread the word, get writing, or leave a star review.

Thank you so very much.

Finally, don't forget. You can gain FREE access to the backstories that underpin the HENRY CROWNE PAYING THE PRICE series and get to know the author's creative process and how the books are conceived.

Read FREE chapters and the exclusive Prequel to the HENRY CROWNE PAYING THE PRICE series: INSURGENT

Go to https://freddieppeters.com and join Freddie's Book Club now...

Looking forward to connecting with you!

Freddie

Printed in Great Britain
by Amazon

32284424R00235